The
Catalyst

Bradley Walker

First published 2017
Published by GB Publishing.org

Copyright © 2017 Bradley Walker
All rights reserved
ISBN: 978-1-912031-97-9 (paperback)
978-1-912031-96-2 (eBook)
978-1-912031-95-5 (Kindle)

Cover Art © Sean Hynes

GBP
GB Publishing.org
www.gbpublishing.co.uk

I dedicate my debut novel to my parents; Anthony and Audrey Walker. My dad's memory lives on in everything I do; my mother's endless overtime has never gone unappreciated.

Acknowledgement

I must say a huge - but painfully brief - thank you to:

Ryan and Ali, the most supportive housemates I could have ever hoped for. Jess, Mellisa, Liam, Shaunna, Melanie, Rachael, Matthew - who made my Liverpool life the most wonderful experience. To Karl who showed me that following passion transcends age, but maintaining a balance is difficult. To Christopher and Jake P. whose geekiness served as welcome escapism through some difficult years. To Scott, whose mutual insomnia allowed us to traverse Azeroth together - I would have lost my mind if not for you. To my friends from GAME, namely PJ and Alex. To Leah and Marc, who took me serious when I said I was writing a book, though, made sure I'll never be as good as JK. Rowling. To Chermaine, whose dedication and companionship on those post-work writing sessions were what I needed to spur me on. To Sean Sweeney, whose advice, friendship and blunt professionalism laid the foundations for my self-belief as a writer. To the ever changing Cambridge team - you put up with me at my most stressed and I adore you all dearly. To Derek, George and Wills; this book is product of their expertise, patience and encouragement. To my siblings, Paige, Ryan, Michael and Tony - they allowed me to trade footballs for fireballs without judgement. Especially Tony who fronted the money for a laptop I couldn't afford. To my grandparents, Les and Cathy - the most wonderful and gentle human beings. To Jake, who has such a wonderful soul and geniality, he's been an angel and hasn't once doubted that I could complete this. And finally, to you, the reader. Without your mind, this story has no home. I owe you so much.

Chapter 1

Estate agents are villainous – evil incarnate. In fact, when the Devil himself wishes to move from one depth of hell to another, he shudders at the thought of having to approach an estate agent. I just can't stand their artificially bright teeth, their slicked hair, chemical tans and of course, sickeningly dapper suits. They are the absolute personification of terror.

Unfortunately, this is how I, Kurt, spent my day. Jo, George and I had been going from company to company, filling in details, discussing prices, enduring patronising phrases such as, "that area usually doesn't accommodate for a budget so modest," or, "the property is perfect for you, but as you're just out of university, the landlord would need trustworthy guarantors which not all of you can provide…"

'Not all of us' meant me and we all knew it. George was from a super-rich family. We met each other at Freshers three years ago and he kept buying people drinks – I, of course wanted to get drunk as quickly and cheaply as possible so I naturally gravitated towards him. I'm not an alcoholic, I am just so socially inept that the prospect of speaking to people at the best of times fills my whole soul with anxiety. He was my cash cow at the start but now one of my (two) best friends.

Jo, she was not from a wealthy family, but they were comfy enough to live cosily and help her out here and there. That is until she decided that was not the university experience she wanted. By the second year she had declined any help from them. She got her own job to earn her own money, buy her own clothes and pay for her own leisure time. She revelled in telling her parents, "It's my money, it's my body – I can get a tattoo if I like, thank you very much." She didn't get a tattoo, she never wanted one, but she would be damned if they told her otherwise.

I, on the other hand, could barely afford microwave meals. I managed to get a part-time job with zero prior experience - probably due to my lying about having experience. I worked before lectures, I worked after lectures, I popped in to work during the two-hour long class breaks to make up extra time. I was constantly tired and still my bank account wept tears due to never serving its purpose and always being stuck in my overdraft – poor thing. I pitied it.

This was our financial situation for the three years. So when the estate agent tutted, mm'd and aah'd, chewing her lips as her pencil-drawn eyebrows artificially represented a furrow before finally admitting "The guarantor fell through so we have had to put the house back on the market." I felt incredibly worthless.

Jo and George didn't take it so bad – they never did. George once offered for his mother to be my guarantor, as his father was his own but after realising that made me feel awful, he apologised but made it clear the offer stood if I should ever need it.

We left the estate agent's feeling slightly defeated. We still had two months left in our current student house so we were not too worried but we would have liked it sorted as soon as possible.

"Ah well," Jo said as soon as the door closed behind us. "If I'm honest, I wasn't really a big a fan of that one anyway – awkward location."

"Are you serious?" George asked with pure shock in his voice. "It was right next to the station!" In my peripheral vision, I saw Jo shoot him one of her stern glances and he added with haste, "So imagine having to listen to those trains constantly."

Jo nodded her head slightly and smiled.

"Sorry..." I mumbled. Jo scoffed at my apology.

"It's alright Kurt, mate." George muttered back, probably begrudgingly but he knew better than to anger Jo.

We were walking for a while in silence as the sun beat down on us. My mouth was so dry I couldn't even moisten it with my tongue – it just felt like sandpaper on coarse stone. My brain was conflicted with being incredibly annoyed that yet another flat was taken away from us because of my family and the need to just sleep and be done with the day.

"Jesus. It's roasting, isn't it?" George said to neither of us in particular.

"Summer, George. It happens." Jo replied, her tone as dry as my mouth.

"Blummer, Beorge. Blit blappens." His response was lazy in thought and delivery.

In Jo and George I found two incredible friends. Jo and I were usually on the same mental wavelength even though we didn't have a lot in common when we first met. We were on the same course and ended up bonding over multiple instances of people asking something stupid and our mirrored looks of annoyance, disbelief, anger or boredom catching one another from across the room.

She came up to me one day after a year-long lecture (dramatised for effect) and started to complain about the majority of the class – I appreciated that. She was cynical. I was cynical, it was pleasant. That's something people don't understand a lot: cynicism may not be a wonderful trait, but mutual cynicism is a bond stronger than nearly anything else, even my hate for ignorance... and I *really* hate ignorance.

After that we sat together for lectures and just connected. She was beautiful and extroverted – most of the people I spoke to over the three years were either introduced to me by her or spoke to me hoping I was a gateway in to her good books. I didn't mind, I made a good friend and that was difficult for me.

"Shall we go for a quick drink or something by the fountain?" George asked. "My treat!" He quickly added knowing that I'd turn down any needless spending where possible.

George was unlike Jo, but still wonderful company. He could remain relaxed in the face of the Grim Reaper, he ate as if trying to break a world record, he could sleep through torture but he entertained two of my favourite things: cooking and gaming. I was never adept at this kitchen wizardry, but George could walk in to a kitchen with a sack of flour, a tin of beans and some seasoning, then an hour later emerge with a delicious three-course meal. He was skilful and always made too much. I enjoyed being the one to share the large portions with him as we played games.

We got on so well in the first year, seeing each other almost every day that we decided that we should leave the student halls we all lived in and find somewhere together.

We moved in to a student house in second year. We drank, we argued, we partied, we ate, we gamed, we slept, we stressed, we survived. The same thing happened for third year and it got to a point where the three of us came as a packaged deal. *Buy one Kurt; get George and Jo free.*

Feeling dejected, Jo and I chivalrously agreed to let George spend his money on us. We went to a corner shop to get our drinks, plastic cups and ice. Yeah, George was one of those people who bought ice. The corner shop wasn't too far from the fountain. A sweet blonde girl seemed to be the only one who worked there. She was nice enough, but always looked really tired and on the brink of tears.

I always felt sorry for her, so naturally, I avoided going in if I could; not in a rude way, I just don't want people to be sad but could never muster the courage to ask if they were okay. It was easier for me to avoid things that made me uncomfortable in life than face them. That was my general mantra. I hid behind George, who had spoken to her at length once when we went to a house party close by. Since then, he always thought they had a customer-shopkeeper friendship, but he was too oblivious to see she didn't enjoy the questions.

3

"Just these please, love." He said as he rested the clearly necessary student supplies on her counter. Jo rolled her eyes as she always did when George called someone 'love'. The shopkeeper nodded and let out a little smile. I wondered if she would pop George's stuff in a plastic carrier bag or the bags under her eyes. Then I apologised in my head for being unnecessarily rude. "How's the brother?" George asked. She looked up at him, with wide eyes.

"Still the same, but that's good." She said in her Polish accent, avoiding eye contact.

"I'm sure he'll be fine." George said and handed her a twenty. "Keep the change." She nodded and smiled her thanks as she bagged his purchase. She opted for the plastic bags. We walked out. "Bless her." He added under his breath and then just like that she was forgotten about.

We trawled to the centre of town where the tiniest little fountain bravely spurted water out all year round. Upon arrival, we realised we were not the only people who had the brilliant idea of occupying the single water feature in the area. There were groups of friends sitting on the brim of the fountain, parents sitting on cardigans and towels whilst their children licked what remained of their short-lived ice creams, couples laying side by side as they were slowly being cooked alive and old people sitting on the benches dotted around the outskirts of the fountain square probably cursing the youth for their energy and general existence. The elderly and I had that in common.

George, Jo and I waded through the sea of sweat-drenched animals at this watering hole before we found a path of clear pavement that was far enough away from the fountain that we may as well have sat at home and ran the bath. There was a wooden stick with a gooey red puddle around it, a recent murder scene for an ice lolly. We sat down. George began to pour the drinks whilst Jo was enjoying a rant on how a guarantor shouldn't have that much of a sway in your accommodation when you're no longer a student anyway. The conversation rambled on, but I just felt awful.

"I think I'm just going to go home to have a little nap," I announced after remaining silent for too long. Jo gave a lingering look of suspicion, but I left with haste before she could question it. "I'll see you back at the house."

I trekked home in a foul mood, cursing the estate agents under my breath. Once home, I made my way to my room, threw my jacket to the floordrobe and slumped heavily on the bed. It wasn't long before I could feel sleep's tendrils pulling me to its embrace.

As soon as sleep came, I could hear a faint voice trying to call for me as if from a different room. There was something it required of me, information it

4

needed to give to me, but I couldn't quite make out what it was saying. It was as if it was speaking in English and a different language at the same time; it was both distorted and concise. It stopped suddenly, then an overwhelming feeling of abject horror washed over me. As quickly as it all came, it stopped. There was a moment of calm, then my eyes opened.

I found myself floating in a black, insubstantial void. There were tiny bright dots in the distance, speckled around like stars, a stark contrast to the blackness. I looked around this strange place, my body completely weightless, in my dream state accepting it as just the way it is. I felt quite relaxed. That is, until I could see something darting toward me at a startling speed.

This strange object was surrounded by a silver nimbus which left a trail behind like a comet. If it weren't about to collide with me, I would consider it a beautiful sight, akin to a shooting star. As it approached, I tried to call for it to stop but my voice trapped in my throat. I winced as it collided and wrapped around me, *hugging* me.

"You're real! You're here." An excited, silken voice came from it as I felt two hands feeling around my back as if to check I was indeed actually there. "I knew you'd come. I knew you'd find a way to visit! Melanie, please let me explain-"

"What?" Is all I could muster in my confusion.

At the sound of my voice, it unwrapped and travelled a few metres backward. Floating before me was a beautiful girl. Silver hair fell to her shoulders; it danced around, swaying and undulating as if underwater. Her piercing blue eyes narrowed with scrutiny.

"You're not Melanie." She panted in a tone that seemed to indicate disappointment and frustration.

"No, I'm- Uh. Sorry, I'm not Melanie." I answered. Her eyes closed slowly as a single tear rolled down her cheek. She shook her head and I began to feel guilty for being Kurt, rather than the Melanie she sought.

"Who are you?" She demanded, slowly closing the distance between us until she was inches away. Her skin was flawless, her eyes penetrating. Her silver hair shimmered even though there was no light nearby. She was the epitome of natural beauty.

"Uh... I'm- My name's Kurt." I answered tentatively. "I'm nobody. I think." My stomach began to flutter. There was something about this dream that was making me feel uneasy. My cognitive thought was as potent as if I was awake, I could *feel* the physical impact when she collided with me, her breath on my face. This couldn't be a lucid dream – this was something deeper, something more.

"I was so sure. After all this time, she finally found..." She whispered, her eyes flicking between each of mine. She wiped the tear from her cheek. "I felt her." She muttered. "I heard her. I sensed her. She *was* here." It sounded as if she was trying to convince herself. She placed her head in her hands, then suddenly, she removed them causing me to jump. She was on the cusp of tears but she asked hopefully. "Do you know Melanie, child?" Which was strange considering she looked to be my age.

"Uh." I tried to recall every person I had ever met. "No, sorry. I have no idea who you mean."

She grunted and began to look around, darting in different directions with impressive agility like a dragonfly. "No, no. Please. I need to see her." She shot off in the distance, leaving me floating helplessly for a while. My mind was racing, I felt like I needed to throw up. Something was wrong. So very, very wrong. After a few minutes, she returned to me. "How did you get here?!" Her voice was rife with accusation.

"I- I don't know, I fell asleep and... here I am." I was feeling anxious now, my stomach was churning violently. I was trying with all my mental might to wake myself up.

"Don't be ridiculous." She spat, suddenly vicious. "An average child can't just appear here."

"I don't know where *here* is!" I insisted. "I don't know who Melanie is. I want to wake up."

"You're not asleep! This is all wrong. This doesn't make sense." She flew around me gracefully whereas my entire body was shaking involuntarily. "I've never seen you in any of these windows."

"Windows?" I repeated, completely lost. "Please, I have no idea what's going on. I read an article that said if you're stressed or scared you should be forthright about it, so here is me respectively requesting you please leave me alone and allow me to end this dream."

That seemed to be the wrong thing to say. "No!" She roared. She held her hand out and my body began to move with her. I was travelling at incredible speed, but there was no wind, no resistance. She indicated the sporadic bright dots that were shining all around the void and began to talk quickly. "These are people – the minds of people! All of them incredibly gifted, most of them unaware." She said. "I have spent years here since I fell sick. Years! I thought I had died. I thought this was the afterlife, until I realised I was one of these people. Gifted. My body's inactivity let my mind's potency develop

6

exponentially, allowing it to truly wake up – that must be what happened. I have tried in vain to make contact, but they're unaware – they cannot see me, they cannot hear me.

"I was certain my Melanie would be here, she always had a fantastic mind. She had to be counted among the brilliant, but no. I searched and searched; new windows appeared, new minds, but never my daughter's. Never the only one I wanted." We were heading to a small cluster of the bright dots as I wondered how someone so young could have a daughter.

In this proximity, they looked completely different. As if etched in the void, it was a tangible vision – emanating a strange warmth. We stopped at one, I could see images inside from someone else's perspective, as if I was playing a first-person game. It was misty and glazed, but I could clearly see two hands making a bed. I had never witnessed something so mundane looking so incredible. The girl let out a frustrated sigh and we shot off in the direction of another. It was clear this was tedious to her.

"So, tell me - with all these people - how someone like *you* has managed to bypass these windows and enter straight here. What do you know of this place?" The anger in her voice kindled my fear.

I began crying as I often did when scared. "I swear, I have no idea what's happening. I don't know where I am. I don't know who you are. I don't know any Melanies. I'm asleep, I'm dreaming, this is-" My speech was stopped as she halted suddenly, slapped her hand to my mouth and let out a gasp.

All around, these strange windows began appearing. Some sparked in to existence like a faint candle in the dusk, whereas others bloomed, blazing impossibly bright. Silver hair was mumbling to herself, her voice now adopting the same fear I was feeling. "Impossible." She uttered to herself.

"What's happening?" I asked through her hand, my words were lost but my terror was clear. Though I was clueless, her fear was infectious. My throat tightened, my tears renewed. "What's going on?"

"How are you doing this?" She screamed, letting go of me and turning until we were face-to-face. It was clear to see she was terrified, these windows continued their invasion in their multitudes. There were millions of them, and still, more continued to appear. An impossible amount. It looked as if the two of us were trapped in the midst of a galaxy; floating helplessly as the stars themselves were brought in to existence. She was soaring around, witnessing the creation of these with her hands over her mouth.

"I haven't done anything. I promise." I responded, as tears fell freely. "I'm scared. This isn't real!"

7

"Stop lying!" She slapped me across the cheek and the pain, contrary to my protestation, was very real. "I've spent so long trying to understand this place – trying to find Melanie, then I sense her, I race to her and find you! Now this is happening?" She shouted, looking back out with a mix of awe and helplessness at the expanse. "How?! What are you doing?!"

"I'm crying!" I whined, then flinched as she went to hit me again. "Please don't." I didn't care how pathetic I sounded. This was so very far from my comfort zone. I needed to leave, I didn't care what was happening, I just needed to escape, to remove myself from this situation.

"How is this possible? Only those whose minds are truly awake show up here. Only those with-" Her voice trailed off and her tone changed, it seemed realisation had set in. An echo of a gasp escaped her. She understood. "Oh no. This can only mean…" She looked to me, her fear and anger transformed to pity. "Stay safe, Kurt." She said and then pushed against my chest with incredible force.

I woke up. My body was drenched in sweat, my clothes clinging to my skin. I sat bolt upright, breathing heavily. The dream had truly terrified me, I was shaking. I rubbed my eyes to rid my vision of blurriness. The morning sun spilled in through my little window casting the room in a gentle orange glow. My eyes widened in horror.

All my belongings, the contents of my room - my books, my clothes, my games, my ornaments… were suspended in mid-air.

Chapter 2

I gasped in fright and everything fell to the floor. A hot flush of fear washed over me, I was about to throw the blanket off my body when, without moving a muscle, it lifted up and threw itself on to the floor.

"Oh my god. Oh my god, oh my god, oh my god," I said to myself. I got out of bed and felt my heart beating as fast as the clip-clopping of a racehorse's hooves. My legs were weak, I stumbled in to the wall and threw my arm up to stop myself from falling over completely. My hand landed on one of my photographs and slipped, ripping it off the wall. Instantly, it rose from the floor and floated into my hand. The sudden realisation that *I* was doing this hit me like a truck. It felt incredibly natural.

I began to feel dizzy, my vision blurred before clearing again. My stomach was spinning like a washing machine. I keeled over and threw up on the floor. "What's hap-" I tried to talk but I threw up once more. My body let out a violent shudder in revolt.

"Telekinesis," a voice echoed. I screamed. It was a woman's voice, deep and concise. "You have developed telekinesis," it said again. "Do not be scared - you always had this ability in a way, it lay dormant in your mind but now it has shown itself. You are not the only one." I looked around for the source of the voice, terror dictating my fight, freeze or flight response. I wanted to flee, but I didn't know what I was fleeing from. "Do not be anxious, I am going to help you. Your friend, downstairs - she needs your help. She has developed an ability too. Go to her." It sounded strangely familiar.

Jo was in trouble! I stood up slowly and made my way to my bedroom door. It opened before I got to it, my mind gripping the handle and twisting it, unlocking it. I walked with effort down the stairs; I could still feel the door. I closed it behind me without looking.

Outside Jo's door, I took a deep breath and then opened it. When the door swung open, the deep calm began to wane as terror attempted to reestablish itself. Her room was heaving with myriads of spiders. The walls were a tumultuous mass of dark spindly legs crawling over one another. There were thousands of them adorning Jo's belongings, writhing and scuttling to and fro, making it look as if the room itself was alive.

From Jo's bed, thick webs draped down the sides. More spiders clung to these webs, patiently waiting for prey to devour. They moved slowly, predatorily. The floor was a fluid puddle of tarantulas, there was a faint scuttling backdrop as each one of them tried to stay on top of the others. Their pincers were opening and closing hungrily.

I noticed two large humps laying on the floor, spider's blanketing most of them but leaving two clear images. I froze in horror. My parents lay below this ocean of furry limbs and bulbous carapaces. Their eyes hollowed out, their mouths lolling open. A smaller tarantula slowly climbed down from my mother's forehead until it found something interesting in her mouth. I watched as its last leg disappeared inside. I began to tremble as I felt my mind starting to black out.

"That is a projection. An image. They are not real. Try to focus." The voice echoed in my mind once more, it was distant and faint. My whole body was shaking, my parents lay dead before me and I couldn't rush to their bodies without wading through thousands of spiders, my worst fear. "Exactly," the voice said. "It is your fear, this is your friend's ability. She is the source, but your own mind is creating the image. Look on the bed, focus on your friend."

I tore my eyes from my parents under the blanket of tarantulas to see Jo sitting on her bed. She was holding her knees up to her chin and staring blankly ahead. "Fantastic, Kurt." The woman's voice said. "Focus on your friend. *Focus* on her." My heart rate began to slow, my eyes locked on Jo. The spiders all around the room began to fade, they lost their colour and they grew translucent until after a few seconds, Jo's room was back to what it always was. Everything organised, spotless, clean and of course, devoid of arachnids and dead parents.

"Oh my god," I gasped, almost fainting when it was over. My body was no longer frozen, I was still shaking, but I was in control. I walked over to Jo on legs that felt like jelly. "Jo?" I said, my voice weak. "Jo, are you okay?"

"Get him out!" She shrieked suddenly. "Get him out of my room. Get out." I started to panic with her. I looked around to see who she was talking about when her wayward fist caught my chin with a force that knocked me off-balance.

I stood up and as the voice advised earlier, I focused on Jo. This time was not to escape a vision, but to help. I could feel her body flailing around in my consciousness. I wrapped my thought around her and gently lifted her up from her bed. She was still lashing out, suspended in front of me. I gently tightened the grip holding her arms in place, then her legs until she was rigid. I rotated her and sat her upright. Her eyes were wide with terror. She didn't even seem to realise she was momentarily levitating.

10

"Jo, look at me. It's me. Kurt. You're fine. You're safe! There's no one here." Tears were streaming down her cheeks which is when I noticed I was also crying. "I'm going to hug you and let you go, don't lash out." I could feel her trying to break free of my hold, she still wasn't paying attention.

I hovered her toward me and embraced her tightly. I let go of her with my mind and she threw her arms around me, pulling me in to a vice-like grip of a hug. Her head rested on my shoulder as she sobbed. "It's okay. It's okay. You're fine." I said, happy that she was no longer terrified and that my chin was safe from dislocation.

"Fantastic." The woman's voice said and then my mind fell silent. Jo's sobs were the only sound in the room. I had only seen Jo cry a handful of times and even then it was usually fleetingly before she decided it was not worth the pain and switched her emotions off - I had never seen her this vulnerable, this scared, this upset.

"I had a horrible dream." She whimpered through post-crying spasmodic breaths.

"It's okay, Jo. You're fine. You're fine." I said, mustering as much paternal instinct as I could but I think I was trying to convince myself as much as her. The image of the tarantula's leg disappearing in to my mother's mouth replayed in my mind's eye and I hugged her tighter. After hugging for what felt like some millennia, her grip loosened and she grabbed my hand and pulled me to her bed.

"Kurt, I'm so sorry. I haven't had a dream that bad since- I can't remember. I don't even know." She mumbled, her eyes were focused on the carpet.

"Was the dream like, uh, was there a girl with silver hair?" I asked, curious to see if she had the same dream.

"No? I had a headache and it felt like I woke up, then at the bottom of my bed, I saw him standing. Kurt, it didn't feel like a dream. I was terrified." Her voice was faintly hoarse.

"Jo, I don't think you were dreaming," I said. "Something's happened. I dunno what exactly, but look." I stood up from her bed and her hand shot to my arm and pulled me down. "Don't worry, I'm not leaving. Look. I need to show you something."

I began to tell her about the dream I had of the silvery-haired girl and how it ended. "Then when I woke up, my stuff was, like…" Saying the words felt ridiculous. I grabbed her diary. "Jo, this is going to sound stupid but my stuff was floating, that's what I was doing to you a second ago." She looked at me

11

and even in her vulnerable state she managed to give me a look of annoyance.

"Kurt, don't take the-" She started, but then I let go of her diary and allowed my mind to keep it floating. She gasped and scrambled backward, pushing herself up against the headboard. "What are you playing at?" She spat at me as if this was deeply offensive to her.

"I don't know, Jo! I don't know. Something's happened to us, I'm telling you." I floated the diary over to her as easily as if I was handing it to her physically. "Whatever you saw, that was something you can do. There was a voice in my head." I edited myself quickly. "Let me reword that. You've got something as well, I don't know what it is but when I came in to your room, it was covered in-"

"Guys?" George called out to us from his room. "Guys, are you awake?" There was urgency in his tone. "Jo, Kurt?" His voice grew from calling to shouting, I heard his door slam open in the hall.

Jo stood up, the shock and confusion in her face morphed in to desperate determination. She threw the diary aside, grabbed my upper arm as if I was being placed under arrest and pulled me out of her room.

George was standing at his door, one foot in his room and the other in the hallway. He looked at Jo and me, as we opened the door. "Come here!" He winded his arm round gesturing us to come and hurry up simultaneously.

George's room was half sport fanatic, half geek haven. Posters of his favourite football team were placed next to anime posters. He had weights on the floor, above which hung a blank screen for his projector that he used as his PC monitor. When we usually entered George's room, he would be sprawled on the bed as the monitor displayed his games, but now he had his favourite news site up which was run by an independent group of reporters. There was a giant flashing 'Breaking News' across the top of the webpage; underneath was a looped video caught on CCTV depicting someone placing their hand on a large brick wall, his hand began to glow a midnight blue and the wall crumbled revealing a domestic interior in which a mother was holding her child to her chest. There was no sound, but I could see her scream in utter horror, crying and shouting something to the man. The man walked up to her until she was blocked from view, then the next thing I saw was the man being thrown backward and the lady looking at her hands as if they were a brand new invention.

"Look, there's stories like this everywhere. All over the world. The internet's full of them." He dived to his desk on which his keyboard and mouse usually sat. "I thought it was some joke thing at first, but look," he began to scroll down the page and there were news articles, images, and more videos showing all manners of incredible and impossible things.

Jo gasped and threw her hand toward her mouth. She looked at me, her eyebrows furrowed with worry. "Is that what's happening to you? To us?" She asked. George's eyes darted between us both.

"What? What do you mean? Can you both- what's happened to you?" He asked, anxiously.

I opened my mouth and closed it again, looking back at the screen. My mind was blank, words failed me. "I- I-I can." My hands slowly rose to my mouth, mimicking Jo. "I think I'm going to faint." I felt light headed, everything seemed light and ethereal. I took a deep breath to steady myself.

I was brought to my senses when outside there was a deafening explosion which shook the house itself. George swore - which was almost as loud as the explosion - Jo screamed and my heart skipped a beat. My legs, seeming to operate of their own accord took me out of George's room, down the stairs, past the kitchen, and finally to the front door. Jo called for me to stop and I heard their feet pounding down in my wake.

I swung open the front door, my curiosity was being fuelled by adrenaline. I took a step outside, there were shouts and screams in the distance. A few people were scuttling around at the end of the street. Someone ran right past our garden and I tried to run after them so I could ask what was going on, ignoring Jo's protestation, when I heard another explosion, this one closer. I jumped in fright and almost fell to the ground, but instead, my body continued to rise.

In my mind, I could feel my awkward gangly limbs, my weedy frame, my unimpressive chest all encased and steadied. I looked down to see George with both hands placed on the back of his head, his face exasperated and shouting something that was unintelligible. Jo running toward me with her hand out as if she was a child that just lost her balloon. I looked down at them, whilst I was still in the air. I looked down at them, as I realised I was controlling this.

I looked down at them and gasped in amazement as it dawned on me that I was actually *flying*.

Chapter 3

I felt elated. I was flying! My stomach was fluttering as if I was just about to lurch in to a drop on a rollercoaster, but I knew I wouldn't drop. Without exerting any effort, I lifted my body higher. I heard Jo gasp but it didn't matter, nothing mattered except for the fact that I was *flying*.

Just like I did with the items in my room and Jo's diary, I *thought* about locomotion and I began to move. It was slow at first, but I knew how to work it, my telekinesis holding me was as dexterous as when I used to make my toys fly as a child. It was simple. *Think* about moving forward and forward I moved. *Think* about ascending or descending, up and down I went. *Think* about the speed, faster and slower I went. I zoomed up and down the street, with sheer unadulterated thrill.

The screams I heard when I first left were still sounding in the distance, but they were irrelevant - I was in my own little world. I felt better than I ever had. I could feel my clothes billowing as I shot through the air. I reached the end of the street when there was another explosion. Though this too was far away, the scale of what was happening took root. I hastily turned round and headed back to my house where Jo and George were standing at the door.

"Isn't this incredible?" I shouted, not being able to hide my smile. George looked terrified whereas Jo just looked livid.

"Kurt, get in here," she barked. "Right now!" I descended to the ground. There was a gentle tap as I withdrew my ability and my feet made contact.

"What's up?" I asked trying my hardest to sound innocent.

"Kurt, we have literally no idea what's going on and you go, well, *flying* down the street. Are you stupid?" She said then followed with, "George, move out the way. Close the door behind us." But before we got to the door, there was yet another scream, this one was closer. I jumped and my body drifted upward once more. It seemed that even though I could control this, there were times it acted instinctively. There was a shout from the same direction of the scream, when just a few houses down, a door flung open with a slam.

Out of the door poured a multiplicity of translucent pink and purple spheres. The world reflected from their surface. Most of them were tiny, but a few were much larger. Jo's grip on my arm loosened. I watched as they scattered across the garden, before they stopped, suspended in mid-air as if they had every right to be there.

"What's going on? Jesus, Mary and Joseph-" George's limited knowledge of biblical characters was cut short as a final bubble flew out of the door, this one was larger than any of the previous which still hung in the garden like bizarre baubles. The difference was this had something in it. A young girl.

She was sitting within as if it was her own private pod, her legs crossed and hands outstretched across the diameter touching either side. She looked to be around twelve years old and she was howling with laughter. A scream preceded the appearance of her distraught mother who burst out of the house as if it was a gun and she was the bullet.

"Honey, please!" She screamed through tears. "Please come down. How are you doing this?" She shouted as she began trying to hit the bubbles within her reach. As she made contact with one, the surface absorbed her impact and her hand shot backward with such force that she displayed a magnificently terrible pirouette and was thrown to the ground. "David, will you *please* get her down!"

A man emerged from the house, he had a house robe and thick glasses on. "What makes you think she'll listen to me?" He slurred. "She's never listened to me before. She takes after her dad in the stubborn department. Why don't you give him a call?"

"Oh, David. Don't start that now." She shouted as she bent over. She stood upright with a rock in her hand. She threw it at a larger bubble. George's, Jo's and my head followed the trajectory as it left her hand. It hit the top of a pink bubble and rested on it for a moment. With a quiet *pop,* the bubble opened up, letting the rock fall in and closed up again like a very unimaginative snow globe. She let out a grunt of anger. "Honey, stop it. Get here right now!" She mustered as much authority as possible, before pleading again. "Please?"

"I think they're drunk again." Jo said. I looked at her. She looked incredulously at the couple, momentarily more shocked that they were drunk at this time in the morning rather than the daughter floating in mid-air. Incredulity gave way to frowning as her eyes focused on the young girl in her personal orb, then back to the adults. "Look at the parents," she added. It looked as if she was right, the man was swaying on the spot and the mother almost fell over as she stepped forward.

"Shall I go help?" I asked, unsure of if I really wanted to. It was a 'do you want my seat?' kind of help where you feel obligated, but you don't really want to give up your seat, or are worried you will offend the helpee.

"Leave it, mate. They're mental, just get in where it's safe." George said. He wasn't being completely heartless. The mother had threatened to get us evicted once because she thought we stole her dog. Don't get me wrong, I would happily invite a strange dog in to our house and treat it as royalty, but I would never steal one. She also drunkenly knocked on our door one night claiming Jo stole her make-up, regardless of the fact she was white and Jo wasn't.

The mother dropped to her knees. The man, seemingly bored of these incredibly beautiful bubbles and his partner, sighed in exasperation. "Here we go." He grumbled, as if the issue here was his partner's dramatics.

The bubble containing the girl popped and she began to fall. Jo let out another gasp, whereas George took a helpless step forward. I threw my hand up to try and hold her steady, but I couldn't mentally grasp just her.

My mind was thrown in to midst of the orbs like a child in a ball pit, but it was too much to concentrate on one thing. It didn't matter, the young girl had it under control. She clapped her hand and a bubble formed out of nowhere just feet from the ground. The top of the bubble opened to allow her inside, then closed above her with a rippling effect. All around her, the other bubbles began to pop and dissipate. The one holding the rock seemed to have surreptitiously moved closer to the man but it just missed him as it fell. He took a step back with fright, pushed against the door which swung open leaving him to fall on his back.

Her mother stood up as the last bubble which was her daughter's sphere, popped, leaving the garden devoid of pink and purple. She hugged her daughter, then held her at arm's length to shout at her. She was hugging and reprimanding her in turn before the man grunted and stormed in to the house. They both followed in behind him, the girl apologising but still smiling.

"It's impossible." Jo stated with complete conviction, even though she had just bore witness to the whole thing.

"It's not right, that's what it is, or isn't. Whatever," George grunted. "Get inside." But his order was ignored, as they usually were, this time because there was another distant explosion.

I allowed them to walk ahead and as soon as they were inside, I slammed the door shut with my ability, plucked myself from the ground and fuelled by adrenaline, soared down the street. I made a swift turn around a corner, then another before freezing in my tracks.

There was a column of thick, black smoke rising from a blazing car. The frame of the vehicle was charred, the tires had melted in to the floor. The stench was overwhelming. I looked around to see if there was anything I could do, when a man ran outside a house facing. He approached the car as if the flames were of no danger, splayed his palms and began to grunt with effort.

The fire began to act in a way it had no right to act. As if obeying some silent command, the flames began to behave themselves. They rolled up the side of the car and gathered above it in an enormous sphere. The man began to move his arms as if pulling an invisible rope; the fire decreased in size before it completely dissolved, leaving only the black skeleton of the car.

The man wiped the sweat from his forehead, then noticed me. He shook his head to convey utter disbelief, then after spotting something behind me, he hastily retreated in to his house.

I spun round to see a ball of crackling plasma travelling like a juggernaut toward me. It left destruction in its wake, the concrete road cracked as the ball traversed it. I tried to ascend, but in my panic, I lost focus and dropped to the floor. I began to scramble backward to put more distance between it and myself but it was too fast. It was seconds away, giving off an intense heat. Then it stopped, suddenly.

I guarded my eyes as it began to spin on the spot, faster and faster until like the ball of flame it, too, began to decrease in size. Moments later it started to take the form of a human. I was dumbstruck to see before me, a frail old lady who was hunched over a Zimmer frame.

"Hello." She chirped in a sweet old voice as if she was just passing me in the street.

"Hi." I replied, my voice cracked with the fear. I'm not ashamed to say I was crying once more.

"Lovely day, isn't it?" She said in a sing-song voice. In fairness, it was a nice day, so I nodded, still in utter disbelief of what was happening. "You be careful now." She advised. Her dark skin began to glow a yellowish hue, before the very substance changed back in to that of the plasma sphere. The lady began to spin and grow, until once again the crackling ball was before me. It waited until I moved out of the way, then shot off leaving an echo of laughter behind. I watched as it hit the burnt-out car which not only failed to inhibit its momentum, but went flying aside if it was a pin hit by a bowling ball.

I continued down the street feeling nonplussed and a little numb. I sincerely couldn't tell if I was feeling excited or anxious anymore – it was as if my emotions were being filtered before my brain could decide exactly what I was feeling but regardless, on I floated. I wanted to turn back, but I couldn't. It was quiet for a while until just ahead of me, a black disc formed out of nothingness. I stopped to study it. It was just a thin disc suspended in mid-air, but there was something else about it - it seemed to have a deceptive depth. I gingerly approached it until I heard a commotion coming from *within*. I flew higher, to get a look from a different perspective but there was no point, it remained stubbornly inanimate.

"Watch out!" It shouted at me. I panicked and didn't quite manage to move in time. A body shot out of the centre of the disc and collided with me. I lost concentration and began to fall, but again, my ability worked by itself and grabbed me before I collided with the ground. The other person wasn't as lucky. "What's your problem?" A girl shouted with disdain before another black disc formed on the floor below her. The girl shook her head at me and was about to step in to it.

"Wait!" I pleaded.

"No?" She replied with an inflection and jumped in to it. When she entered, it closed behind her.

I ventured onward, slightly perplexed but the need to understand what was happening still guided me. I was travelling at a steady pace down street after street. The closer I got to the centre of town which was more densely populated, the more my heart sank. There were broken walls with rubble laying in front of them, destroyed lamp posts emitting sparks, trees snapped clean in two, windows shattered, scorched slabs of pavement, bus stops crumpled, roaring fires where they simply ought not to be, cars smashed, pools of red that I actively avoided and all manners of inexplicable phenomena.

I stared in surprise and slight fear at a house encased in a giant dome of blue, which I could only guess was some force field. The house itself was perfectly untouched, but next to that house, was another with a large hole in the wall; the rim of the hole was glowing bright orange as if someone had decided to scorch the wall out with a blowtorch. My brain started to race and the anxious-excitement amplified.

This was clearly happening everywhere. People had woken up this day with strange new powers, incredible abilities. This changed everything! What would this mean for religion? For science? How could people research and find answers for something of this scale? What could have caused something like this? And if people had unbelievable powers at their disposal what would happen with authority, the government, society-

My train of thought was delayed when I was lazily hovering above a tiled roof. There was something strange leaning against a chimney. It was human in form but completely lacking in substance. I floated toward it. It pushed off the chimney with surprising vigour to greet me.

18

"Brilliant, isn't it?" It had a man's voice but could only be described as a three-dimensional shadow. There were no distinguishable features anywhere on it. I could see the chimney through him, but it was like looking through a dusty window. "This whole thing, it's brilliant." He repeated. I could only grimace in reply. "We," he added ominously, "are the new age." Before flitting across the roof in silence. Just as he slid down the side of the building and out of sight, a lot of things happened at once.

There was a deafening, churning brontide. Though it was far away I could feel my body vibrate from it. I lost my footing and slid down the roof, banging my head against the slate as I fell. Just as I rolled off, my telekinesis steadied me. I turned around to locate the source of the noise but couldn't see anything. Then from the clouds, there was a fulmination and a resounding crack, as a gargantuan black pillar, wreathed in a purple energy, shot down. The churning sound followed as the pillar made contact with the ground. Interwoven in this deafening noise was a chaotic cacophony of voices; shouting, screeching, yelling, begging and raging.

The pillar faded in to nothingness and the churning sound trailed into an echo, but the caterwauling of cries continued. I was still floating and rubbing my head when I noticed there was a pattern forming in the sky. I blinked to try and focus, but it didn't help. There was something visually odd about it. The pattern was being created by a dark swirl, blurry yet focused at the same time. It was a swarm. A swarm of dark dots.

They were difficult to look at, there was a quality to them my eyes couldn't quite make sense of. They continued their campaign across the sky creating this pattern – two vertical lines joined in the middle by a shorter horizontal one – which is when I could finally understand why they hurt. They weren't dark dots; they were incredibly bright. So bright in fact that it made the light of the morning sun look dim in comparison. The first shape remained there as these bizarre fireflies created a second. That's when I realised they were *letters*. My mouth had dropped open by the time the third letter was completed. I didn't need to wait for the last one, but I hovered there aghast as it was finished.

The word that was emblazoned in the sky: **HELP**

Chapter 4

My eyes followed each shining letter and I pulsed with terror. I was hoping on some level that I could just ignore it and wake up in my bed again without my belongings floating but no, as stubborn as Jo in an argument, they hung there.

I mustered up all the courage I could... and began to fly in the opposite direction. I wanted to help. I so wanted to help but I was too scared. Sometimes there had to be an objection to the *Catch-22* of needing to help people. This had to be one of those times.

The man on the rooftop saying 'We are the new age' didn't sit right with me. This wasn't exciting anymore. I was travelling over ruined houses, smashed windows, overturned cars - the remnants of people's homes and lives. Looking down from the height I was travelling at, I could see fires sporadically dotted about the long streets and winding alleys as well as in the midst of the bright green fields and parks, blazing over this town that I had grown to love like fallen stars. I began to descend, suddenly flying made me feel anxious. I felt vulnerable, like a target.

I let go of myself when I was close enough to the ground and dropped down, I began to jog down the street. I didn't know exactly where I was, but I wanted to stay out of sight. My anxiety was at boiling point now, then again, my anxiety is usually at boiling point.

I had only been awake for a couple of hours and the world was already going to hell, everything around us crumbling before my very eyes. I felt empty as I was jogging down the street quietly as possible. I would halt in my tracks every time I saw someone else, even if they hadn't seen me or were too far away. I stood still with my hands up, preparing myself to flee or fly if I had to, or wait for them to pass. I got a fright every time I heard a distant shout or scream. I almost fell over three times from losing my footing. So, when her voice sounded in my head once more, you can understand why I almost died of sheer panic.

"Where are you going?" She asked. I yelped and swore loudly before deciding I should do what I usually did when I was confronted. I pretended not to hear it. "If my thoughts can be transferred to you, it does not take a genius to glean the opposite is true. Where," she repeated, "are you going?"

"I'm going home. I think people are dying. My friends might be in trouble, I want-" I said trying to make an excuse up for myself. I knew they would be at home, I knew they would be fine, but I wasn't. I wanted to be with them. I wanted to hide from this.

"They are safe. Trust in me." And I wanted to. My whole body trusted her, but my fear was overriding it. "Someone needs your help." The voice stated, calm as a still lake.

"Who? Who needs my help? I don't even know anyone else. They're all Jo's and George's friends here, how can they need my help?" I said, again aloud.

"A boy is being sought by dangerous people. You must get there first." She insisted. "Kurt, do not run away from a life you can save." I stopped jogging and doubled-over, hands on knees trying to catch my breath. I shut my eyes tight. The word 'HELP' shone behind my eyelids, taunting me. My conscience battled - but quivered in the face of - my morality.

"I really want to. But I can't. I'm sorry, I can't. I'm scared. I've got no idea what's going on. I need to get home. I need to contact my parents, I need to reach somebody-"

"You need to help someone who needs you." She finished for me.

"Who are you, why are you asking *me* of all people?" I shouted. I wasn't certain if my words echoed in my head or in the deserted street.

"I am only trying to help. I have asked others, but you have a control over your ability; you are close to the boy." She continued, "I am trying to save thousands, but I need you to get this child. Go!"

I took two steps in the direction I thought would bring me home before stopping. My throat grew tight with guilt. I let out an aggravated grunt before ignoring my instincts and lifting my body up once more. I ascended above the buildings surrounding me until I could see the giant 'HELP'. What if it was a trap? What if I would reach it only to find out it was to a human what a zapper is to a fly? What if... I knew I was making excuses.

The closer I got to the bright foreboding word, the louder the din rose. It wasn't long before I could hear the whole thing. It sounded fake, all the different voices, all the grunts and roars, the blasting sounds, the crunching, the smashing and the thuds. It was as if I was back in George's room with his surround sound. That's all this was. A game.

A figure shot up into the sky. I jolted backwards when I realised there was an eerie quality to it. It wasn't flying like I first thought; it's limbs were limp and lacking strength. They dangled beneath it as it rose, it reached its peak before beginning to fall. The limbs bent backward in a way limbs had no right to bend and I realised the ragdoll in front of me, this person, was no longer a person - it was a corpse. Something had launched it in to the air. I

21

watched it as it fell behind a tall building which the HELP shone proudly above. *It's a bit late now.*

Though my courage was no longer with me, I allowed my adrenaline to push me forward. I hovered, slowly and shakily to the building that blocked the ragdoll from my sight. I landed on the roof rather harder than I intended and my leg gave way.

I looked up. Though the shining word above was a monolith of strange energy, consisting of thousand miniature motes of light, it was silent. I tore my eyes away from it and carried on toward the metal railing which surrounded the perimeter of the roof. I grabbed it tightly, my knuckles white with pressure. Just for good measure, I let my ability envelop the metal to anchor me. With an almost cartoon-like gulp, I looked over the edge of the building. It was chaos!

The fountain area I was at yesterday with George and Jo was now a moving image of brutality. The fountain itself had been uprooted, laying on the ground a few feet away. The view was so vivid, so active and colourful that it almost looked like a choreographed dance. I scanned the scene below me, before my vision finally managed to settle on a fist fight, but this was not the usual scrap.

One of the brawler's paws left a trail behind it, a strange void that looked as if it ripped the space-time continuum as his punch was thrown. The woman the punch was intended for dodged it just about, then with startling speed, she caught the man's wrist. He tried to kick her but it was too late, he was thrown clean over her head and slammed in to the concrete. The woman swung the man by his arm again, revealing cracked ground from where he crashed in to it. She let go as if he was shotput and off he flew, scrambling in the air before the trajectory allowed the sea of fighting to swallow him whole.

Just as he was lost from sight, a shock of purple whizzed around a small group of people. It looked to be the same substance as the giant pillar. It slalomed through the group as if they were traffic cones. Most were too preoccupied to even notice it. The purple ribbon suddenly grew taut, those who were trapped in its embrace instantly vomited.

The colour of this ribbon changed to a blood red and they all fell to the ground as one; coughing whilst some of the frailer and daintier victims fell in to seizures. I followed the length of the ribbon to its source to see a tall man wearing pyjamas and a fedora. He yanked the red ribbon and the people were pulled toward him, a spider collecting its flies. He seemed to be enjoying himself. There was a charged energy in the way he was moving.

22

Just above him something began to form. A circle. A black disc! It was identical to the one I came across earlier. The man still manipulating the ribbon had no idea this was happening. Another formed below him. He fell through it and exited the one above, slamming in to the floor. The ribbons faded away to tatters. The man disorientated, got to his feet only to fall in to another portal. I did not see him reemerge this time.

I sighed in relief. Someone whooshed past the top of the building in front of me and then dexterously changed direction, making a bee line to the centre of the chaos. The 'HELP' still shone brazenly, but with so much going on, there was little I could do to discern for whom it was intended. Which one of these were the boy the voice wanted me to save? I wanted to fly over, but it would be tantamount to suicide – I didn't have the courage. I couldn't even try low-cut shirts; how could I possibly brave this?

My attention was drawn to the left of the opening. I saw a ball of ice shoot out of an individual's hands; it shone with a bright blue quality and a trail of faint fog followed in its wake. It hit a rather brutish looking woman who was holding half a lamp post in each hand as if they were light as chopsticks. Though she was small, the lamp posts were swinging around with ease until the ice hit her. I expected her to freeze up as I've always seen ice powers work in cartoons and games before, but that was not the case. The ball hit her in the small of the back, her spine bending backward on impact. She fell to the ground near enough snapping in half, her head smashing in to the cobbles where she squirmed in pain. The lamp posts dropped with a thud and a clang.

Upon seeing this female fall, something darted toward her as quick as a flash. It ran on all fours - like a quadruped but the anatomy was all wrong. It got close to her, where it stood upright like a human. The colour of this creature rippled like oil caught in sunlight, a rainbow in a dark backdrop. It circled the fallen girl and crouched at her feet. Just as she struggled to stand, the creature pounced at her. She fell backward once more, a pink liquid spewed forth from the attacker's mouth and hit the girl in the face before it began to claw violently, primally at her body in an attempt to maul her.

Its hands were human, but the ferocity was not - it was a scene fit for nightmares. Her legs began to flail as she tried to free herself, but it was no use. She managed to catch one of the creature's arms mid-swipe, the pink liquid now mixing with the red blood from her lacerations. The creature was clearly startled, it looked at its arm locked in her grip, then jumped off her whimpering and crying as it tried to escape. Her free arm lunged in its direction, scrambling for purchase until she gripped its throat. With a yank, the creature's arm was pulled clean off.

The creature's howl pierced the hum of aggression, managing to draw the attention of the fighters nearby. Those who turned around saw this woman, covered in pink and red goo, holding a severed arm. The creature was still howling, it placed its remaining arm underneath the gaping wound as blood, bright and red spurted out, creating a pool on the floor below.

As if all those around had practiced, as if this was part of this horrific dance, they stopped their fighting and focused their attention on this couple. The woman dropped the arm whilst her other hand tried to wipe her face clean. She need not have bothered. A surge of colours in the form of various beams, bolts, spirals and energies shot toward their direction. As they all joined, there was an explosion so impressively colourful, that different circumstances would have deemed this inspiration enough for any painter. The people responsible for the projectiles were thrown backward and as the explosion fizzled, there was no woman or creature. Just two ominous vapours crudely outlining their last moments.

There was a roaring from below and the ground itself began to crack open, creating a fissure which travelled down the centre. The ground tore apart, no matter whether it was paving, cobbled or grass. It tore as if it was paper, the crunching sound was deafening and knocked many of the fighters off balance. A river of fire began to fill the crevice. I watched a man who was leaning out of a window halfway up another building. This liquid fire, that was not quite lava poured from his open arms.

The people that fell in to the fissure burned up, those who were alert began to flee, avoiding being caught in the orange death that poured toward them. The man closed his arms then opened them, just like a bird trying to take flight. Out of nowhere, a large van crashed into him. It crushed the wall, bricks scattered from the impact as if they were trying to escape it too. There was no way the man could have survived that. The van hung there for a moment, teetering half in the crushed wall and half out, then as if in slow-motion, it lurched backward and fell to the floor with another crash.

The giant 'HELP' above had apparently served its purpose, whoever had made it had now finished because all the particles that composed it fell down, dancing in the sky like rain, slowly cascading, making a breathtaking display. Ignoring this were two people engaged in an airborne fight.

A woman wearing a bicycle suit and another wearing a onesie were floating with no visual aid and seemed to be completely comfortable with this. The particles of light were bouncing off their bodies, but apparently were inflicting no damage. That was until something like a shining pink hula-hoop shot from Onesie toward Bicycle Suit. It travelled through her stomach, until the she was in the centre. She tried to fly upward out of the circumference, but the ring reduced in size and caught her ankles. Another ring shot out of Onesie, whose feet and hands were glowing pink. She pushed out her chest and a third ring emerged, shooting toward Bicycle Suit. She was trapped in the sky, no way of escaping now that the other hoop wrapped around her chest pulling her arms tight together. As if she suddenly realised humans can't fly, Bicycle Suit began to fall in time with the remaining particles of light. I called out in horror and Onesie looked at me. Her chest began to glow pink.

"No! Please, I just came to help," I shouted, fear clear in my voice. "Please don't."

Her chest dimmed, but the limbs remained bright pink. "Go home, kid." She shouted, as if she was some hardened military veteran.

"I want to, but…" Her chest began to glow, I let go of the railings and used my telekinesis to surge me backward. A pink ring crashed in to the spot where I just stood. I looked up to see if she was firing another. She was not. Her attention was drawn to the opening.

There was a whirlwind of darkness forming in the middle of the fighting, it looked slick and wet like sludge or oil but it was fluid as water, yet it flicked and curled as if fire and smoke had mated to create this tumultuous darkness. The whirlwind grew larger, spanning out, gaining more ground. Everyone stopped fighting and began to flee. Whoever was close to the whirlwind was snatched in to it. Shadowy tendrils, shot out, wrapping around their limbs and pulling them in to the centre. Onesie and I watched in horror. Two people landed next to me and held up their hands in a sign of ceasefire. They watched as the velocity of the whirlwind slowed until it was just a giant dark cone of a strange shadowy substance.

This gargantuan structure began to peel at the top, folding over like some hellish flower. Soon it was completely open, creating a thick layer that spread out to the whole opening below. The people that were sucked in to this maelstrom were standing rooted, bound by the thin curling stems. At the centre of this, a large black podium erupted creating a level platform. Standing on this stood a tall, thin woman surrounded by a small group. I couldn't make them out properly, but the woman's body seemed to shift and sway, wrapped in this bizarre physical darkness.

A few people who were trapped could still use their abilities, but as all manner of projectiles shot toward this woman, large black tendrils or thick walls shot up to take the impact before falling back to the sea of shadow in a lava lamp style. It was terrifying and fascinating. Ability after ability soared toward her, and she stood without even flinching as her coal-black ocean did the work for her. They soon gave up after they realised their onslaught was futile - she could not be touched.

Her arms began to move, she was gesturing, she was *talking*. One of the people beside me gasped as some of the slender threads began to unfurl freeing people one by one. My jaw hung open at the sheer power of this individual. She had quelled that entire fight, every single person was bound by her ability and she was now standing in the centre, as confident as anything giving a speech that I could not hear. She turned her head, uttered a few words and those on the platform with her ran off in different directions.

There was a raw shriek behind me, on the other side of the building. I snapped out of my stupor and flew to the other side of the roof. I looked over the edge. A group of people were travelling down the street, there was a girl behind trying to stop them, holding on to their arms, pulling with all her might.

One of the group turned to face her and with brutal force punched her square in the cheek. Beads of light emitted from the place of impact and she dropped to the floor, holding her face. They were the same beads that the giant HELP consisted of. I climbed the railing and was about to jump off.

"Leave them!" The voice in my head said urgently. "It is too late, go home." I froze as my conscience battled with her order and my guilt. I had only come here to save this person, and now I was here I was being told to leave? It heard my inner conflict. "That is correct. Go home."

Two of the group members were carrying someone, the girl stood back up slowly and rushed over to them. One of the individuals turned to her, two ropes shot out from his shoulders, wrapped around her arms and slammed her in to a wall. How could I leave her? I had to go down, I had to fight. I jumped over the building and allowed myself to freefall until I was beside her which is when I caught myself, then tapped down gently. "Are you okay?" I asked, helping her up as the group rushed on.

"Please. My brother..." She cried. "They have Patrick. Please, get him!" I knew her. It was the shopkeeper George always spoke to. The one who always looked sad. I looked down the street after the group. Though there was something telling me to leave them alone, though my very instincts were urging me to go home, my morality won over and I ran after them.

"Wait!" I shouted. The boy who slammed the shopkeeper in to the wall turned around, seemingly more annoyed than angry. He looked me up and down, raising an eyebrow. I lost my breath. His whole body was a brown-green colour. He seemed to be covered in a murky sodden bark rather than flesh. His eyes were a forest green, his hair black straw. He smiled revealing brown chunky teeth.

"There's a group of us," the Treeboy said in a deep grumble. The ropes grew out of his shoulders again, on closer inspection I could see they were vines. They began to approach me slowly, before he stopped with a look of confusion. It looked as if he was trying to solve a math problem in his mind, then he shook his head and the vines retreated. "I wouldn't bother if I was you."

He turned and I felt fury rising in me. The voice in my head told me to leave again, that I was outnumbered, outmatched and out skilled but I ignored it. Too many times in my life I had been overlooked by others who assumed they were better. I picked him up with my ability and slammed him in to the wall with a ferocity that made me wince.

I began to run toward the group when something caught my ankle and I fell. My ability caught me just before my chin crashed to the floor and lifted me back to my feet. "Guys?!" The Treeboy shouted. I lifted my foot up quickly, but his vine was still wrapped around it. My hands and telekinesis began to fumble with it. I managed to free myself, but by now, the rest of the group were there.

There was a girl, her skin was a pale green; she looked at me through yellow eyes – the pupils were slits, she was smiling, revealing razor sharp teeth; a small girl, about half my height but clearly mid-twenties, her hands were clamped to her ears whilst her eyes were squinting as if in pain; a tall boy, wearing a long trench coat, sporting a slick black goatee and shoulder length hair – he was holding a silver blade in his hand, resting its point on his own arm; two boys - one with hands the size of pavement slabs and the other who looked (in comparison to the rest) rather average were dressed in beige jumpsuits with numbers printed on the breast pockets which I could only assume meant they were convicted criminals. It was these two that were carrying the shopkeeper's brother.

He was a feeble looking boy; small, thin and pasty-white, dressed in a flimsy gown. He had no hair, no strength. Were it not for his eyes lolling around, I would easily have mistaken him for a corpse. He did not struggle to free himself from their grip, he didn't seem to even notice he was there.

"Leave them *alone*." The woman's voice demanded inside me. "They will kill you!" It was no longer asking or guiding me, it was angry and desperate. Every fibre of my being was screaming for me to obey, but I heard the footsteps from the shopkeeper as she tried to catch up, only for her to slump back down, exhausted and defeated. I ignored the voice, my bravery bolstered by the unfair treatment of the poor girl. I threw my hand out, throwing the girl half my size in to the air and knocking the blade from Goatee's hand simultaneously.

The pale green girl lunged at me, her mouth opening unnaturally wide. I threw my hand forward in panic and she slammed in to a wall of thought. Her yellow eyes narrowed with confusion and pain, before I pushed my thought and slammed her down. The boy with the big hands and the average looking boy did not move, they continued to hold the sick boy as if he was a delicate antique.

"You two, run." Treeboy shouted to them. "If anything happens to him, she'll give us to the shadow herself." They obeyed his command and began to run off. So, they were with *her*? The woman from the opening. He turned on me then, two sharp wooden stakes covered in a green gelatinous substance protruded from each of his wrists. He pointed them at me and they shot out at a startling speed. They were too fast; I held up my hands helplessly, but once again my gift instinctively saved me. I could feel the needle-like point of the stake, severely sharp, in my thought.

I dared to look from behind my hands. They were both floating inches away from my head – he had tried to *kill* me! My body shuddered as I was subjected to a fusillade of solid, razor-edged leaves. They too, were caught in my field of thought. Treeboy grunted in fury. Goatee had retrieved his blade, the small girl had recovered from my launching her, the pale green girl was back up, rubbing the back of her head. They all stood facing me, only my ability stood between us. I began to quiver.

I scrambled backward as I heared voices approaching from behind. The group before me looked toward them, then as if Satan had just risen, the colour drained from their faces. They were clearly horrorstricken. "She'll kill us if anything's happened to the kid." Treeboy shouted, beginning to retreat. "Come on." I watched in awe as his body dispersed in to thousands of leaves, which scattered away down the street, all following one another. The rest opted for the more natural method and ran.

Thinking I was safe, I stood up and turned. The colour then drained from my face, too. I fell back down with weak legs. At the opposite end of the street was a tidal wave of pure shadow travelling slowly. Ahead of it was the woman from the opening and two others. She nodded and they ran down the street whereas she, in contrast, walked calm and steadily.

I was trembling. I couldn't focus, I couldn't fly; the two were almost upon me now. I curled up and enveloped myself in a ball of my power – it was my last defense. Then, their footsteps reached me but continued. They *ignored* me. I braved a look to see them running down the street, the same direction the group ran with the shopkeeper's sick brother, probably ensuring he was safe with the others.

I glanced back down the other end, the shadow lady was closer now. The shopkeeper was mere feet away from her and unaware of what was about to befall her. A second wind of energy coursed through my body, I jumped up aided by my physical thought, pushed myself to the shopkeeper, plucked her off the ground and threw her in to one of the shops close by. I followed in after her, then turned to the door and threw my hands out, reinforcing the whole wall with telekinesis.

It felt like years passed, but soon enough, sunlight was blotted out and I saw the shadow lady walk past the window. She stopped outside the door, then slowly, as if purposely trying to spark my anxiety, turned to face me. I was sobbing, the shopkeeper behind me whimpering. I re-focused the wall of thought so there was no way she could get in.

There was a gentle knocking on the glass window, I looked up and her lip curled as she made eye contact with me. "Hello." She said, the calm in her voice juxtaposing the entire world outside. "My colleagues insisted the boy was here?"

"Leave us alone." I begged. "They went down there, your gang of convicts. They took the boy and ran." She frowned. "Please! Please leave us alone!" She rolled her eyes and continued walking down the street, the shadow following behind her cast the entire store in darkness. After a few moments, sunlight filled the store once more. The shopkeeper and I were safe. She spared us.

"Patrick." She cried, hunched in the foetal position. "Where is Patrick? Where is my brother?"

Chapter 5

The shopkeeper and I made our way to my home quickly. She didn't say much, just followed behind me weeping and sniffling as she went. I tried to hold her hand once to help lead her but as I reached out for it, those dazzling particles emitted from it and spun round her. She snatched her hand to her chest as if shocked it happened, her eyes looking at mine red raw, her bottom lip curled out in misery.

It was rare to find a structure that was not damaged in some way, even if that damage be some strange remnant of an ability lingering on. We walked past a garden in which the grass was scorched, yet above it hung a slowly undulating aurora. The smoke calmly rose and as it reached the chatoyant aurora, it mingled, both waving in a hypnotic motion.

Often there were people alone, sometimes in pairs or small groups we would hide when we saw them, or flee. We were startled at one point when hiding in a garden as the door behind us swung open. Her beads of light were once more involuntarily spilling to the floor. A woman stood with a man while two children peered from behind them. The woman threw her hand up, a large sheet of a rippling translucent quality formed in front of them.

"Get out." The man said. It was not angry or forced, it was calm. He was suggesting it. His wife looked at him, then back to us. She raised her other arm and with her index finger, tapped the bizarre wall in front of her, it rippled at her touch as if liquid before settling once more back in to its solid state. "You won't get past her, so get out." He repeated, this time his voice hoarse and high. I hastily checked if the street was clear. It was.

I turned back and nodded at the couple then smiled at the kids. When I caught their eye, each one of them retreated behind the safety of their parents. "Stay safe. Good luck." I said.

We picked up the pace. The shopkeeper sobbed quetly, leaving me feeling more than out of my depth. Jo would know what to do in this situation. People tended to flock to her with their problems, trials, errors and mistakes, sobbing in to her shoulder and she would sit, listening to every last one of them offering no judgement and copious amounts of support, yet try asking Jo something about her own feelings and the answer was usually a swift dismissal with a roll of her eyes.

We had made it to the house unscathed. Jo must have been watching because as soon as we walked up to the doorway, the door swung open. She was standing there with a look on her face that scared me more than everything else I had saw this day. I walked in trying to avoid her gaze. The shopkeeper followed behind me, Jo held her hand out for a moment to stop us before her face softened as she realised she knew her. Jo moved her hand letting us enter with a confused look at me. I gave her a shrug between *I'm sorry* and *please don't shout at me.*

I walked in to the kitchen where George sat, normal as anything, with a cup of tea in his hands. Another cup left untouched must have been Jo's. George looked at me. "Mate, what are you playing at?" He stopped when he saw the shopkeeper behind me, jumping out of his chair and offering it to her. She was hugging herself and looking at the ground but accepted the chair gratefully.

Jo remained in the hallway for a moment before gently closing the door and joining the rest of us in the kitchen, her eyes quickly flitting to my hands. I had picked up her cup of tea without even noticing, I never knew what to do with my hands. I offered it out to her but she shook her head. "What happened out there? Are you okay?" She said. Her voice wasn't the same angry disappointed teacher tone it usually would have been.

"I flew over there-" I began but she shot me down with a look.

"I wasn't talking to you," She spat.

"Of course you weren't, why would you be talking to-" I mumbled but when I noticed the fires of hell blazing behind her eyes, the rest of my sentence trailed in to petulant nothingness.

"Don't push it, mate. We've been worried sick," George advised, probably for the best. There was something buried in his voice, a bitterness.

"Are you okay?" Jo said again to the shopkeeper. "What's happened? Are you hurt? Do you want a drink? George make her a drink. What do you want?" With a swoop, Jo's housecoat was off leaving her in pyjamas and it was over the poor girl's shoulders. She gripped each lapel with her fingers and idly caressed the fabric still looking at the floor. Jo ripped off some kitchen roll as George started filling the kettle with more water.

I chewed my lip as I watched Jo's eyes rest on the girl waiting for her to start talking. She didn't. She sat there as new tears began to roll down her face. She opened her mouth, then closed it again. The silence was killing me. "I was flying down the street when I saw a car on fire just around the corner," I began. Then I told them of what I saw during my impromptu expedition. Jo's stubborn frustration with me dissipated as I told her of the things I witnessed. When I got to the part about the word in the sky, the girl let out another whimper. "Then the woman with all the shadow turned the corner of the street we were on," I said. Jo covered her mouth with her hands whereas

George just stood there, with a teabag in his hand staring at me blankly. "When the people with - I'm sorry, what's your name?"

She looked up and with a meek voice answered, "Lana."

"Thank you, Lana. When the people with Lana's brother saw this woman - this shadow woman, they panicked. Apparently they were supposed to bring him to her and she wouldn't have been happy if something happened to him. She sent two people to regroup with the others and I just pushed Lana into the shop and waited for it to be over. I've honestly never been so scared in my life."

"That doesn't make sense, though," George said. He seemed surprised to say this out loud. Jo, Lana and I stared at him which spurred him on. "Why would these people be after some random sick kid - I'm so sorry!" Lana looked up as if George had just ripped her heart in two. It was strange seeing someone else make the social faux pas for once. Jo gave her shoulder a reassuring squeeze. "But why would they go after someone like that? Why would this woman be after him and, if they *were* getting him for her, why would they run when they saw her? Especially if they all had these *stupid* powers as well?" George contorted the word 'stupid' as if it was disgusting in his mouth.

"Honestly, George, if you saw it, you would have run too. Even if you were her best friend, you'd have ran. She stopped a battle without even trying, for Christ's sake!" George gave a simple, unconvinced shrug.

The kitchen was silent once more as Jo mulled over the story. George finished making the cup of tea for Lana. Every so often we would hear someone outside, either running past or in the distance but it was mostly quiet. My insides were squirming as my mind replayed the morning. My insides squirmed as no one spoke. My insides squirmed as George put the cup of tea in front of Lana and she didn't even acknowledge it. My insides squirmed a lot and there was usually one way I would fix awkwardness...

"Lana's a lovely name." Unnecessary conversation to fill the silence. I began to ramble about Lana Del Rey and even hummed one of her songs.

"Kurt! What're you doing?" Jo said and I couldn't be more thankful that I had a reason to stop talking. I shook my head and turned away, opening my cupboard to get some food out even though I wasn't hungry. I just needed to occupy myself. "Lana?" Jo said softly. "Do you have any idea why they would have wanted your brother? Any idea at all?"

"No," she said, "he is sick." There was an intake of breath accompanied by a shudder. "We know no one around here. Nobody knew him. We only came here to get his sickness looked at," a deep breath and a lengthy sigh.

"My parents gave up on him. It is expensive to look after someone so ill. I knew I could help. They say I was young and lived in false hope. I tell them I prefer to live in false hope than let Patrick die because we had none." She gently wiped a tear away, reached out and grabbed the cup of tea. She slowly brought it to her mouth and sipped at it. Jo sat in the chair next to her. "The people came in asking for... for... I don't remember the word." Her lip trembled and Jo placed her hand on Lana's thigh to lend support. "I said I don't know what that is. I said I don't know what they want." Tears began to stream down but she fought them, she continued with the story. "They destroyed my store."

"That's horrible," Jo shook her head bewildered. "Why?"

She thought for a moment. "I don't have the reason. They shouted and began to destroy everything. Then I screamed as two with different skin came in. I thought they had costumes on. They were green and brown. When I screamed," she held her hands up. "Lights came out of me. They burst out of me. Everywhere." She studied her hands. "The people ducked and I tried to run to my brother but I was stopped. One of the people, the green and brown boy had ropes."

"That's the Treeboy I was talking about." I said but Jo erratically waved her hand to silence me.

"They wrapped around me and he threw me to the side." She rubbed her elbow as if the pain was back for the story. "I try to run to the back door where Patrick is, but he punch me and throw me outside my store. My own store. I screamed and banged on the door trying to get back inside, but he pushed the door closed to stop me. I tried to smash windows but I was too weak.

"I was crying and scared for Patrick. Scared for myself. I wanted more than anything to get my brother and go. The lights began to- to-" she searched for the word, "whirr around my hand. That is when I noticed they were mine, a part of me. They listened to me. I throw my hand up in the air and *whoosh* they go up and I make them spell 'help'."

Jo looked at me, piecing together that the word from my story was the one Lana had created. I spoke to confirm, "Yeah, that's when I-"

"Shut up, Kurt!" Jo snapped. I opened my mouth to argue, but her eyebrows rose so instead I slumped on to the counter defeated. She turned back to Lana. "Go on, sweetheart." Lana gave a weak smile as thanks. Jo had done it again, managed to get someone to confide in her.

"The boy noticed the word and made his friends hurry. I still could not get back inside. I kept on hitting the door and looked for something to smash the windows with, but it was no use. Four of them had went to the back door that goes up to the flats. I hear my neighbours scream, I see their windows smash. I knew they would soon get to Patrick. I was crying, and- and-" The sobs renewed, she tried to speak through them but it was almost inaudible. "They come down carrying him. He is sick. He didn't know. He needed my help. He had a bad night, he had one of his seizures but they didn't care. They just took him." The sobbing turned in to wails and Jo hugged in to her.

"Don't worry, Lana." Jo said. "I think we can piece the story together from what Kurt told us before. Come to my room, we need to get you cleaned up." She grabbed Lana's hand who rose instantly without question, as her body shook with the heaving cries. Jo led her out the kitchen.

I waited to hear Jo's door close before I sighed, dropping in to the chair that Lana just occupied. "This is mental, isn't it?" I said to George who looked at me as if he just noticed I was there.

"Yeah, you could say that." He said, the same strange quality in his voice as before.

"Bless her. She was an absolute mess, she couldn't stop crying when I saved her." I told him, leaving my potential breakdown out of the story. He nodded his head slowly and rolled his eyes. "What's up with you?"

He snarled at me, then sighed sadly. "Sorry, mate. It's just all a bit much." He went to say something else, but decided against it and left for the living room. I sat alone for a minute feeling awkward, but relieved to be alone. Then I remembered the weird shadowy man on the roof. *We are the new age.* The words swam around my mind. I felt as if someone was watching me, as if someone was there in the room with me and for all I knew, they could have been. I rose, forcing an air of calmness until I left the kitchen and then sped up to the living room. George was standing over the couch, looking under the cushion. "Where's the remote?" He asked without looking up at me.

"I don't know. Who used it last?" I asked, knowing full well it was him.

"I don't know, Kurt. That's why I'm asking where it is." He answered, his reply salty enough to provide for every fast food restaurant.

"George, what's up?!" I said, letting the annoyance in my voice show. "I said what's up?"

"I just want to get some news, see what's happening everywhere else." I stared at him blankly, then as if to help me understand he added, "last time I checked there had been over two hundred deaths in this country alone, mate, and that number was constantly rising."

"What?" I was genuinely shocked. How come so many? Surely not everywhere could have been as bad as this was. "Shall we call the police?"

34

"Are you stupid? First of all, Jo already tried that but even she knew there was no point to it. They're engaged or it wasn't working or something. Mate, this is global. I want to check what's happening. So, I'll ask again, where is the remote?"

"I don't know." I shrugged as I began to look around the room with him. I lifted the couch cushions, George had stopped to watch me. There was a pair of underwear underneath one of the cushions. They definitely weren't mine but his gaze made me feel uncomfortable, I picked them up and shook them as if the remote could drop out, then continued searching mumbling 'Nope' and 'Not here either' to myself every time I picked something else up.

"Can't you just use your thingy?" He asked. "Like, just pick it all up?" I let my ability fill the room, I felt it fill the gaps in between the cushions, under the table, around the lamp as well as all the little bits and bobs like water flooding in to a container. I picked all the contents of the room up at once. Then I felt it. I let everything fall except for that and hovered it toward him. He snatched it from my hands. "Was that necessary?" He asked.

"You told me to do it." I replied, my voice indignantly high-pitched. He clicked at the remote two or three times before realising it wasn't working, he checked the battery compartment to find it was empty. Suddenly, he launched the remote across the room as hard as he could. Just before it hit the wall, I plucked it out of the air and let it drop gently. "What the hell is up with you?" He ignored me as he went over to the TV to do the unimaginable: Turn it on manually. "George? What's happened?"

This wasn't like him. He was usually always so relaxed. The TV switched on, the black and white static fuzziness danced on the screen. Quietly he said, "Jo said you walked in to her room today. That she saw something and you came in and helped her or whatever. She wasn't clear."

"Yeah. She was kinda reticent when I asked her about it, too. She had like a vision or something." I said. A tingle ran down my spine when I thought of the carpet of spiders over the projection of my parents, all wriggling and writhing in her room. "I think that's her power, some weird mind thing, but she was doing it to herself."

"Well, there you go." He sounded as if he had just won an argument that clearly should never have been in question. "Whatever this is, it's dangerous. It's unpredictable, isn't it? You guys shouldn't be using it willy-nilly." I couldn't help it. I could tell he was about to get in to whatever had been annoying him, but he'd never said 'willy-nilly' in his life and you can't just bring stuff like that out when you're having a serious conversation. I tried to suppress my giggle when he saw my mouth twitch. "Oh grow up, Kurt."

"I'm sorry. Honestly, I just…"

"Look, by the sounds of it, everything out there is going to crap. We can't get in touch with the police, people are *dying* and here we are stuck in this house. We can't really leave because we don't know what is gonna happen. So don't you think we should try and find out what's going on? Just before you both go ahead and get yourselves killed or something?" He finished staring at the TV.

It dawned on me then. The way he was speaking. *You guys. You both.* "George?" I asked, thinking I already knew the answer. "What, er… What can you do?" My voice lowered, quiet and serious.

He tore his eyes away from the screen and looked at me. "Nothing, Kurt. I can't do anything." As soon as he said this, my brain reacted in a way that I never thought it would. George, the rich, attractive guy. George, the talkative, easy-going, friendly guy. George, the one people noticed before me couldn't do anything. I had woken up with telekinesis and George, 'the alpha male', couldn't do anything. For the first time since I met him, I was better, I was superior. *We are the new age.* My stomach churned and my throat swelled up. I felt terrible for even thinking this

"Maybe it's a- I dunno, a passive thing?" I began with a shrug but he held his hand up to silence me.

"Save it, mate. I can tell. Nothing's changed. I don't have anything." He slumped in to the chair and rested his head in his hands. I sat on the couch feeling bad for what just went through my mind. I vowed there and then that I would never think like that again. That wasn't me, it was some pathetic echo of the invisible wimpy Kurt from my youth - I was better than that. I will never think I'm superior to anyone else. I didn't have the right.

We were sitting in silence for a while before we heard the soft footfall of Jo and Lana coming down the stairs. Jo walked in first. George did not budge an inch but I watched as they came in. Jo led Lana to the couch where I was sitting, then tapped me on the shoulder. That meant I had to sit on the arm so she could have the cushion. I did it without even thinking.

"Why are you watching the fuzzy screen?" Jo asked.

"Remote isn't working." I said.

"Yeah, but, you stood up and turned it on. Why turn it on if you don't want to watch it?" She asked.

"I wanted to see if there's any news, Jo." George said as if that was the final word.

"Oh, are you in a sulk again?" Jo sighed clearly having had enough. "Look, for all we know you might have developed something as well. You could - I don't know... breathe underwater? Talk to animals. Have unbreakable bones or something, but if not, it's not our fault. So get a grip and turn the news on if you want to check what's going on." The tension in the room crushed my body until my bones were ground in to dust, or, at least I wished.

George got out the chair and for a moment I thought he was about to launch in to an attack, but he dropped to all fours in front of the TV and began to click the buttons of the *Freeview* Box. Each one was blank. Jo told him to check the internet which was pre-installed on the TV. He typed in the name of the indie news site he preferred, which slowly loaded up and was brimming with information.

The headline 'Acts of Terror' boldly topped the page. The screen switched from a still image of rubble to a recording. The camera panned up and down some motorway showing a pile-up of cars.

George scrolled down and clicked on to a video. At first the camera was shaking, all that could be seen was a crowd running in every direction, a cacophony of screams and cries blurring out the TV's speakers. When it steadied, it focused on a structure and followed it up to the top. It was the Eiffel Tower. There were strange black objects hovering up at the top.

The camera rose in the air. Correction: whoever was holding the camera rose into the air. As they ascended, there were people scaling the tower in all manners of ways, some swinging up as deftly as a monkey in a jungle, whilst one person's body slithered around the structure like a snake. The weird black objects that could be seen hovering from the ground now became clear as they were almost on level. It was a group of people aloft next to each other.

They were set out in a 'V' formation, the man spearheading the group had a faint cloud around his body. It pulsed, swirled and swayed as if it had a mind of its own. The camera blurred for a moment as it tried to focus. When it achieved this, the characteristics of the cloud became unmistakably clear. Bugs. The cloud consisted of hundreds of different species of bugs.

Behind him, two of the others looked as if they needed no assistance to defy gravity at all. A woman at the back left of the V had large wings spanning out to about six feet each. They were black and furry, but there was a strange glisten to them when they reflected the sunlight, an almost ethereal glow. The last guy on the right side of the V was holding on to a disc, he seemed less confident to be flying up there, but menacing all the same.

The man with the swarm of insects was watching whoever was recording. When they were on level, he let out a wide smile. He began to shout, his voice had a strange tremor to it but there was no doubt he was angry.

Jo urged everyone to hush even though no one was speaking. I stole a quick glance at Lana who no longer looked as if she had been crying, but as if life itself was exhausting. I turned away quickly looking back to the screen. Jo had stood up so she could hear it better. She prided herself on speaking French fluently even though she only ever took it for three years in secondary school and never brushed up on it.

"Okay. Wait. He's going too fast. Okay. He's trying to form a team? Yeah, a team. Okay. French. French French. Oppression? Does that mean oppression?" She asked herself and then flapped her hands at George to stop him before he opened his mouth. "French. French. French. Okay, that was definitely something about the police. Okay, now he's pointing at the cameraman," she told us as if that was a gesture that needed translation. "Decision. Ally. That was friends or an alliance or something. *Slow down.* The cameraman has to choose! He's talking too fast! Why do they speak so fast? Something about family. Oh my god."

She stopped short and clapped her hands over her mouth. The camera swung down and there was a struggle as whoever was holding it tried to escape, the streets of Paris swinging sickeningly in its view. A woman's laugh boomed making the camera shake. The screen was blacked out by the swarm of insects and the video ended. George silently clicked for the next one to play.

We were watching a soundless video that looked out on a house. The windows were smashed and the walls were charred. A fire was raging inside of it. People were running frantically back and forth around the garden. They were soon joined by a young black-haired boy who stopped in the middle of the crowd. Water began to spout from his hands in incredible volumes and unbelievable speed. As the crowd parted to give him space, we could see a bright figure blazing in the middle of the garden, rocking to and fro, the grass around it was burnt black. A man was bent over trying to *speak* to it.

It moved suddenly, which is when I realised it was a *woman*. She threw her head backward in despair, smoke issued from her mouth. Her whole body consisted of embers glowing red, orange and yellow. From her eyes were two blood-orange streams of what looked to be molten lava. She was clutching something black to her chest. She looked at the man speaking to her, shook her head vigorously then wailed again. She was distraught, inconsolable and uncontrollable. A ring of fire formed around her body and shot out in every direction.

The person talking to her was hit by it, and screamed. He patted at the area of his flesh the fire made contact with, then continued to speak to the woman ignoring the pain. He was pointing at the black thing she was holding, and was apparently asking her to give it to him. The black haired boy continued to battle with the blaze consuming the house.

The man, seemingly having had enough, tried to yank the black thing from her, but the woman held it tighter and pulled back. She stood slowly, shaking her head and pushed her arm out, telling the man to get away. An orange swirl danced around her hand before a wiry five-pointed star shot out at him. Even without sound, I could hear the shriek of grief she gave. She went to run toward the man, before stopping suddenly, retreating, shouting to the large crowd. She clearly had no control over her actions.

White hot fire began to encircle her, licking at her fiery frame. Embers and sparks grew wildly until she was fully encased. The black-haired boy turned around upon hearing the commotion. He threw one hand out toward the woman, then brought his other hand round in a whipping motion. The shell of flame that encased her was now cocooned with dark blue water. Even through this, she still shone inside like a stunning mythical creature's egg. The water itself began to crystallise until she was encased in a layer of thick ice. There was a moment of stillness before the ice that encased her absorbed the impact of her supernova.

However, that moment ended when the TV itself exploded in front of us. Jo's startled scream didn't help to settle any of us as a chain of explosions followed suit. The lights blew, the lamps shattered, all the electrical items we owned that were plugged in were victim to some surge. There were bangs and pops all around the house and outside of it. I didn't realise I did it at first, but I had filled the room with my ability once more. A reaction to the fear; a defence mechanism. I turned to see a shard of glass inches away from George's arm.

Lana began to sob again, Jo was stood shaking and George's eyes focused on the shard of glass that almost cut him. It probably couldn't have done that much damage to him but he looked as if he had just had a near-death experience. My voiced faltered. I coughed. "Is everyone okay?" I daren't move a muscle. I ensured nothing else could move either. This bizarre tableau held for a while until Jo gave a weak hum of agreement.

Then the voice entered my head once more. "You and your friends are not safe." It said. "Do not tell them I am guiding you, but make them leave as soon as possible. I am already on my way. Find somewhere safe, then I will come to rescue you. You have to trust me." She said, then added. "Be sure to follow my orders to the letter this time – I do not want you to risk your life as you did earlier."

I looked from George and Jo to Lana. "We aren't safe here. There's too many people about." I said trying to muster as much authority as possible. I was never a leader, but they were too shaken up to question me or argue. They nodded. "Let's get ready and leave."

Chapter 6

After half an hour, we were ready. We opened the door and stared out at the street, checking up and down before leaving. Considering yesterday, when the sun was doing its best to melt everything its rays hit, the temperature today was strangely cold. George, Jo and Lana stood behind me. It took me a while to realise they were waiting on me to leave first. I swallowed my fear and stepped out the house.

Each step I took made me nervous, each turn made me question if this was the right way to go, if this was the right thing to do. It made sense, being around too many people could only cause complications. I knew the general direction in which the town faded in to fields and forests, but it wasn't a short walk - in fact, it'd take a good few hours. I remembered it from when I first arrived in the town, but my sense of direction was questionable at the best of times, never mind with a three-year gap.

We travelled mostly in silence. I didn't want to draw attention to the destruction wrought on the places we knew. Piles of rubble ubiquitous, pothole-strewn roads, fires of varying magnitudes were commonplace. Vehicles were crushed, their tyres slashed, burst or melted. Windows, like the lamp posts were smashed or cracked, walls lay flat on the ground with broken fences.

The general consensus between us seemed to be as long as we didn't mention the things we saw, they could not affect us. If anything seemed too dangerous, I would walk in a different direction. Whenever we saw people, like when I was with Lana before, they would flee or if it appeared they were not going to, we would. The last thing we needed was another fight, our goal was to get out. Following that goal was the only thing stopping me from breaking down. Once we were in this woman's safety, she would take control and I could break down then.

Everything began to blur. Fantasy seemed to have wormed its way in to - or rather - crashed head-on with reality. Strange substances splattered across the floor emitting curious fumes or sounds. We gave those a wide berth. We walked on and on trying our hardest to keep the pace, to stay out of sight, to avoid any further confrontation.

"Wait." Jo said from behind me. I stopped and turned to see her holding Lana's hand. George was behind them, his gaze now focused on Jo. "Look." Jo whispered. She was frowning as she pointed. I followed the direction of her finger and my eyes found what hers already had.

The wall of a house had been destroyed, the bricks scattered around the floor. White dust blanketed large planks of wood. It looked as if a bomb had gone off. My eyes scanned the scene. A leg jutted out of the detritus, causing my stomach to lurch suddenly.

I pushed the wooden gate open and the whole fence fell to the ground with a soft thud. Jo and I approached the scene whilst George and Lana stayed at the bottom of the garden. I held both my hands up and gently caused everything in my ability to float. Underneath lay two bodies, side by side. There was a strange pool of water surrounding them. It was lighter than water, like a solid mist. Jo bent down to check if they were breathing but I stopped her. My ability had already enveloped their bodies, I could sense no breathing, no heartbeat. I shuddered.

I hovered the two gently off the ground, levitating them over to the centre of the living room and placed them delicately on the middle of the carpet. We both stepped over the rubble. A picture stood on the mantelpiece of the dead couple and a young boy of around five years old. Jo mumbled something, I could feel tears trying to fall from my eyes, but if I started, I knew I wouldn't stop. We covered the couple with each end of the carpet. Jo grabbed the picture of the family and placed it on top of them. For a moment, we stared at each other and silently agreed there was nothing more we could do. We had to leave.

It felt like we had been walking for days. The clear blue sky started to fade in to a purple dusk, clouds had crawled above the town and the cold I felt earlier had intensified. I was not entirely sure if the chill was coming from inside myself or not, but still, I felt it in my bones.

The surge of electricity that destroyed all our appliances in the house must have spread throughout the town, or maybe whatever plant that provided this area power had been attacked, I wasn't certain, but it was eerily quiet.

"Where are we going, mate?" George groaned. For someone who was in to his sports, he did not like unnecessary exercise.

I thought of how to answer at first. Whether to tell him there and then that I was following a bodiless voice. "Uh, if we keep heading in, uh, this direction we should get there."

"You haven't got a clue, have you?" He accused, not even trying to hide the annoyance. "Why are we following him, Jo? You know he's got no sense of direction."

"No, I do, I just can't remember exactly how to get there." I defended.

"Where's *there*, mate?"

"Just out of town, anywhere. It makes sense to get away from too many people, doesn't it?" He just stared at me. "Doesn't it, Jo?" I asked and she chewed her lip in reply.

The last time I had been this far out was when my parents drove me down... my stomach lurched. I forgot about my *parents*. I hadn't thought about them much at all since I woke up. A sudden panicked fervor possessed me. I needed to try and get in contact. I had to go back and find a way-

The voice resonated in my head. "You have been nothing but brave and incredible since I contacted you, Kurt. Keep it up. I shall see you soon." *See me soon*? My temporary fervor sated and on we trod – whatever thought was just occupying my mind had been ousted.

*

We must have walked a good few miles, darkness had invaded the sky, painting the world in a shroud of shadow. The destruction was not as severe this far out and George kept pointing at houses that looked abandoned or undamaged in the hopes that we would agree to stay there for the night. There was still no electricity, so the streets were completely dark. My hometown up north had as much light pollution as this city, but now all we had was the moon and even that was being dimmed by clouds. Still, a pale-white glow limned the world below. It was beautifully terrifying.

After we walked in silence for a long time, Lana began to talking about her brother again. The love in her voice was clear. It seemed that their family had almost left him for dead, but she refused to do it. He was diagnosed with cancer and his health declined rapidly. Treatment worked for a while, but it was expensive and the doctors said they could not guarantee it. She left the country with her brother, their grandmother lived here so Lana stayed with her for a while before gaining citizenship. Since then, every penny she earned went on new treatment and Patrick's comfort.

"I will never forget how he looked before he got on the plane," she said, wistfully. My mind had worked around her accent now, she was much easier to understand - maybe that was because she was no longer sobbing. It seemed she needed this. "He had not left the house in days. The doctors said he may not be well enough to fly. It could make him worse. But I asked if he would try for me. He nodded and he came. His eyes lit up." As she said this she conjured thousands of little lights which joined to make one large ball. "Brighter than this!" She held the light above her and pulled her hand away. The ball stayed atop of her, allowing us all to see ahead of us easily. "Then he coughed and coughed. I told him we could leave it, but he was very brave.

He knew I put so much in to this and he wanted to try for me." She smiled sadly. "I need to get him back."

We were all quiet for a while. Jo walked adjacent with Lana and they linked arms. "We'll find somewhere to sleep, then we can plan something. Okay?" She said, her voice strong and convincing. Lana rested her head on Jo's shoulder. It was as if they had been best friends for years: the Jo effect.

"Lana?" George piped up after not speaking for her whole story. "I don't mean to be rude, but… If you could have used your little lights, then why didn't you use them before? We've been struggling to see for a while now."

"George," Jo called in shock, but under her personal illumination, Lana smiled.

"I cannot before," she said simply, "but I can now."

"What do you mean?" George asked, genuinely curious.

"Before I was sad, I was crying. When I made the word in the sky, it was because I needed to. I was angry. I was desperate. I needed to ask for help and I did it but I don't know how." The ball zoomed ahead, illuminating the path ahead. "Now when I speak about my brother. I feel calm. I feel happy. When I speak of him, I know I can control it. I cannot explain properly in English but it feels now as if I am just moving it with my hand."

"That's like me as well," I said. "It just feels really simple to use. It's like, yeah, like Lana said as if I'm moving things with my hands. As if I've always been able to do it but just never tried it before."

"That's mental." George said, but it wasn't a nasty comment this time. He sounded genuinely intrigued by our control over these new additions to our lives. "What about you, Jo? Can you just *do* it?"

Lana's orb had retreated to her head and hovered above her. "No. I can't." Jo admitted quietly. It sounded like that was all she had to say. No one said anything for a few seconds, then Jo continued. "When Kurt came in my room this morning it was like I was stuck in this dual-consciousness. I thought it was a night terror at first. One part of me knew Kurt was there and that I was safe, but the other part of me was focusing on something else. It was like I couldn't tell which one was real." She paused. "And at the same time, I could sort of feel something else, like thousands of tiny creatures and I realised this was something to do with Kurt. It felt like I was dreaming but I knew I wasn't. It's really frustrating that I can't explain it properly. This weird duality. I don't think I can just activate it like these two. I think whatever I can do will only affect people, not the way Lana can conjure her lights or Kurt can lift anything up, know what I mean? I think I need a mind."

"What do you think has happened?" George asked quickly. "As in, where do you think all this has come from?" I thought for a moment and was about to answer when a scream pierced the silence. Instantly, Lana's light dimmed and darkness washed over us once more.

"What was that?" I asked, my voice urgent and hushed.

"A scream, mate." George replied matching my tone.

"No, I know but..." Another howl, this one coming from a different direction.

"Someone's being attacked. Someone's in trouble. Something's happening." Jo listed the unhelpful ambiguities, joining in the urgent hushes.

"What do we do?" I asked, my muscles though tired, tensed up.

"We go help them." Jo said as if there was clearly no other option.

"I don't know, it seems a bit dodgy to me." George said and I nodded.

"Yeah, George has a point. It's a bit of a risk, isn't it?" I said to Jo hoping she would take the bait. Not that I didn't want to help people if they were in trouble, but I was tired. I was scared. I was hoping the next plan of action would come from the woman in my head, not another fight, another confrontation. "I think we should stay put, or just go in a different direction."

"No!" Lana's voice was loud. "We help. If you did not come to save me I could be dead or kidnapped too. If you did not save me I do not want to think what could have happened. We go and help them. Yes?"

Before I had a chance to argue this, Jo agreed. She looked at George and me whilst still nodding meaning she agreed on our behalf as well. "It's the right thing to do, Kurt. You know it."

"What?" George said. "So we're just going to run willy-nilly in to danger?"

"Why do you keep saying willy-nilly all of a sudden?" I asked trying to play for time but as if to spite me, there was another scream.

"No," Jo said, ignoring me and answering George. "Kurt, your ability is useful enough for you to go and check one out alone. Just have a look at what is going on and if it's too risky, come back here. George and Lana can come with me, we'll do the same. Check what's going on and if it's too dangerous, come back here."

"Wait, that's hardly fair," I argued.

"You stopped a group from beating me up. You run if it's scary, yes?" Lana said and Jo nodded her approval. She grabbed Lana and George by the hands and began to run toward where the second scream sounded. As Lana ran, a few miniature molecules of light emerged from her feet. She said something aloud that I couldn't hear and then the lights stopped.

I felt absolutely terrified. I was alone. I couldn't even remember where the noise came from so how could I go and offer assistance? It pierced the night once more. I swore under my breath and began to jog in that direction before lifting myself off the ground, flying at speed. I soon arrived at a row of houses. My chest began to tighten in fear, paranoia taking over when in the distance, a strange orange glow appeared.

Mustering my courage, I let myself touch down at the opposite end of the street from where this spark was. I crouched in a garden and peered over the wall. After staying there for about a minute trying to locate the source of the glowing ball, I decided that the street was safe. Just as I was about to fly, I heard footsteps. I snatched my breath trying not to make a sound.

I watched as a woman approached the orb. She placed her hand in the centre of it and it disappeared. I heard her say something in a loud whisper, but it wasn't clear. It was rushed and concise. There was a *pat, pat, pat.* More footsteps.

I stuck to the shadows but decided to slowly advance toward her. My eyes had readjusted to the darkness and I could see her hand locked with a young boy. The boy was standing slightly behind her. I jumped in to the garden a few feet away from them, I could hear sniffling. That was when I realised just how quiet it was here. The woman's heavy breathing and the young boy's patterned sniffles were the only sounds that broke the silence.

The whole street was abandoned, but the boy had clearly been crying. The woman stopped suddenly. Another orange ball manifested. It darted over in my direction. I crouched further down to hide away and, of course, I kicked a bin over. I caught it in my mind, but it was too late; the clatter I had already made was so loud that it was possibly echoing around entire globe.

The orange glow grew brighter, darted in a zigzag and was now hovering just above me. There was a faint humming sound issuing from it. I was clearly visible now crouching by the fence - which was just a second ago bathed in darkness. She glared at me and the reddish-yellow glow descended. I jumped to the left to dodge it, but my right hand naturally swung up and collided with it. I winced waiting for some burning or instant pain, but instead I felt a rather pleasant level of pressure. I couldn't move my hand at all, the rest of my body could move but that hand was frozen in place. I stood upright. My head was inches away from the orb. I pulled away as much as possible with the rest of my body, careful not let it touch more of me.

"Let me go." I wasn't sure if I was trying to sound intimidating or pleading but I couldn't find another way out. I had to ask.

"Who are you?" She asked me.

"Let me go and I'll talk." The hum grew louder and the pressure on my hand increased from relaxing to intense. I bared my teeth trying not to show her the pain I was in.

"Are you with him?" She said as she let go of the child. With one hand she made a motion, like lifting up an invisible box, and the glow started travelling toward her – my hand firmly stuck in the middle pulled the rest of my body with it. With her other hand, she summoned a second orb which she shot at lightning speed and it caught my right foot.

"Who? Let me go!" I tried to yank my arm and my foot away but it was no use. They were stuck in place. I started to grow agitated. This is why I shouldn't try to help people. "I heard some screams and I came to investigate. I came to help."

"If you came to help, why would you be sneaking around?" She roared.

"I was being cautious. Was it you screaming?" My eyes began to water from the sensation.

"No. It wasn't. It was my sister and she's just been *taken*." She slashed both of her hands in front of her and the two orbs split separate ways, pulling my hand and foot in opposite directions. I let out a yelp when she said again, with venom in her mouth. "Where is he?"

"Where is *who*?" I asked. She summoned a third orb, this one was purple. The orbs around my foot and hand turned purple too and I could feel the grip intensify. The pressure evolved in to a crushing and burning sensation, the hum changed pitch and grew louder – either that or my bones were now literally screaming in agony.

"If you don't tell me, I'll crush you." She said as the third purple orb shot out and halted just in front of my face. I could see her through it cast in a purple hue, but the glow burned my retinas. Using the pain as motivation, I closed my eyes and let my ability reach out in front of me. I focused on the child with her, letting my thought encase his whole body. As I plucked him off the ground, he let out a gasp. She turned to him as quick as a flash, his protector. I brought him over to me and hovered him above the purple glow.

"You hurt me and you'll regret it," I warned through clenched teeth. Threats didn't suit me in the slightest, but there was nothing else I could do. I felt terrible. A cheap move by me, but, it worked. The glow around me disappeared, my ears ringing in the absence of the hum.

"Please don't," her eyes focused on the boy, "let us go." She started to cry. My guilt constricted my throat. I don't know why I jumped to threatening her rather than trying to talk it over. If I was ever faced with the possibility of a fight before all of this, I would usually try and talk my way

47

out of it, or run away. Not fight fire with fire (usually because it would be a case of my foe bringing the fire and me the tinder) but here I was.

"There's a man, a boy. I don't know how to explain him. He didn't look right," she explained. I stood there rubbing my hand to massage the muscles inside. I placed the boy back down beside her and he hugged in to her. "He just… attacked my sister and ran off." She said. She was kneeling down now, hugging the kid tightly. "He pulled her to him, turned the corner and was gone." She wiped the tears from her eyes and composed herself. Taking the boys hand and holding the other one aloft, another orange glow formed.

"What did he look like?" I asked but her face contorted and she pointed.

"There!" She shouted. She pushed the boy to the ground, then in an arc above her, rose five balls: yellow, orange, blue, purple and red. They shone bright like a rainbow and the sounds created a beautiful harmony with one another.

I spun round and in the light of her orbs could see a barrage of dark objects. My mind created a wall in front of me. I felt these objects as they hit the wall. They felt *familiar.*

The orange orb shot from behind my head in the direction of the lamp post revealing a figure. He was quickly bathed in light before he expanded into hundreds of leaves. My heart skipped a beat. Out here? Treeboy!

"Him?" I shouted in shock.

"Him!" She shouted back. "James, stay down." She barked at the kid. I chanced a look to see a green, golden and brown ball circling above him. Each with their own hum, adding to the solemn lament that filled the empty street.

Treeboy rematerialised on the floor. A sickening smile spread across his face. The colourful lights danced across his body, but the green colour of his strange flesh was still prominent. He shot a vine out of his shoulder towards the woman, as it approached thorns grew out of it. His eyes met mine and grew wide before they narrowed with a beady smile. Another vine made its way toward me, but I curved it with my thought, deflecting it. As if created for efficiency, the vine that I deflected started its new assault on her. It whipped in to a yellow orb, froze like my hand did, then burst in to flame. He roared in pain, detaching the vine from his body and letting it fall.

The three of us then began a dance of abilities. The woman was creating orbs, hurling them at Treeboy, whilst trying to ensure the kid was safe. Treeboy, in return, was shooting out sharp wooden stakes and hundreds of razor sharp leaves; I was deflecting where I could, allowing currents of thought to change the trajectory of his projectiles, producing walls to protect us from particularly overwhelming onslaughts. Every so often, something Treeboy threw at us would hit one of her orbs and explode, fizzle away, freeze in place or burst in to flame – each time, a different note emitted.

Over the grunts of effort, the chorus of orbs and the child's terrified cries, I could hear Treeboy *laughing.* He was enjoying himself. When an orb skimmed past his flesh, he cheered and whooped with adrenaline. I tried countless times to encase his body in a mental shell, but the number of vines snaking out of him made it difficult to contain. Whenever he faltered, whenever it seemed like we had him, he would disperse, sweep further down the street and reform.

Suddenly, a plethora of his vines made their advance as one. I threw my hand up and twisted it, concentrating my ability. A few of the vines tangled, but there was a yelp. The kid had been snared by some of the others that I couldn't grasp. He fell to the ground and was being pulled toward Treeboy, like an angler reeling in a fish.

I focused my telekinesis around the kid, when Treeboy started jeering. He was expecting me to do that. Before I knew it, a vine wrapped around my arm. I gasped with shock and tried to pull it off. The woman grabbed at the kid, pulling him back, not daring to use her orbs in case she hit him. Another vine wrapped around me, and another. Without her helping me, I was overpowered. He swung me with force in to a garden wall and the wind was knocked out of me.

He began to approach her, the vines wriggling and writhing. I lifted my body up, scrambling to break free, to get close to her, when from his mouth a faint dust exuded which was illuminated by her glowing orbs. This dust cloud spread around her and she started coughing, the lights started to dim until they disappeared. I was night-blind, having relied on her orbs to see. There were whipping and slapping sounds from his army of vines as he continued his attack.

Now my eyes were adjusting I could make out his silhouette standing over them before he turned, his terrifying form approaching me. Once more, I was trying to encase him but it was too strenuous a task for my panicking mind. I encased myself hoping I could hold off anything he threw at me when he stopped suddenly. "Why, he'll just-" He panted. It hurt to breathe, each intake of air burned my lungs. He grunted in frustration then, burst in to balls and travelled down the street.

I took a moment for myself allowing the confusion and disorientation to wear off. I was out of danger, I squirmed free of his vines and stumbled over to the woman and the boy.

Gashes and lacerations covered most of them, blood was oozing out of the wounds but that was the least of it. She had been disfigured. Large nasty boils and welts covered her body, her cheeks were incredibly swollen. The skin was bubbling as if she had bathed in acid, her tongue was hanging out but, even with my eyes still adjusting I see could it was blacker than the night. I tried to help her up, but her body was limp.

I checked the child and shuddered as I saw he was just as cut, just as disfigured. It struck me then, that the dust that came from his mouth, must have been some noxious toxin, some spore cloud - something poisonous, deadly and acidic. I knew then that I couldn't let him get away. I knew then that I had to *hurt* him.

I was driven by anger. The injustice to what I had just witnessed fuelled me, the motivation to find him focused my mind tenfold on mobility and I began to soar through the streets at an incredible speed. Wind was whipping at my face at such a force that I could barely keep my eyes open.

I zoomed high over houses, lights and beams were being thrown far in the distance – that must have been back toward the town. I was not deluding myself any more. I knew that each spark, each beam or glow, each and every projectile was someone shooting their new found powers at someone else. I knew that all these people were fighting, dying, desperate to survive below me. Now, I could truly see the hell this new world was.

Silhouetted against the moon in the distance, someone was floating with a *van* held above their head as another figure tried to speed toward them. Just before the second figure reached the first, the van was spun in an arc smashing clean in to them. Even with the distance between us I imagined the crunch of the bones under the impact. Another death. Another life lost. Another figure on the rising toll.

I faltered in the air for a moment, wanting nothing more than to be back with George and Jo. With Lana. *No.* This Treeboy had just murdered a woman and child in cold blood, right in front of my eyes. I couldn't let him get away with it. If I let him go, he could kill many more. I had to - I had to kill. I was soaring once more. I flew low enough through the streets so that I wouldn't be an easy target to anyone else above street level, but high enough that anyone actually on street level couldn't attack me on a whim.

I stopped over a park where I heard a panting and rustling sound. I lowered myself down to the ground and there he was, keeled over, panting, apparently unaware that I was right behind him. I crouched down like a lion ready to pounce. With my ability behind me, I launched myself forward, shoulder first and caught him right in the small of his back. He slammed to the hard grass with a gasp. He jumped up and turned round and I took a step backward, cautious of vines or the spore cloud. "Why?" I asked. My body heaving with anger rather than exhaustion.

"Because they tried to stop me," he replied as casually as if he was talking to his old friend.

"So you killed them? A woman and a child!" I tried to shout, but it came out as a squeak.

"No, no, no," he said, mockingly offended, "*two* women and a child… that time." He threw both his hands up and stakes began to protrude from the wrists once more. I held my hands up letting my ability create a bubble around his. I could feel the wooden stakes trying to shoot out, so I focused on them, pushing them back in. He screamed in agony. That made me feel good.

My ability was somehow stronger with my rage. *Pop.* His body scattered, the ball of leaves violently spinning and swirling in a vortex before me. I tried again to grab at the leaves but it was futile. My ability was not dexterous enough, before I even had a chance to try and create an area of telekinesis to trap them all in at once, he was already on the move. I followed behind, even in this darkness I would not let the leaves lose my sight.

He flew out of the park and the leaves scraped the cement as he headed toward a robust building ahead. For a moment, I thought he disappeared instantly until I got closer and realised there was a ramp heading underneath. A sub-level carpark.

I knew following down would lead me straight in to a trap. Instead, I launched myself in to the air, scaling over the building with ease. There was a group of teenagers hugging in to themselves on the top, they cried out when they saw me but I ignored them. I scanned the floor as I reached the other side, I spotted the exit to the car park and lowered myself. This was the perfect chance to get a sneak attack.

I felt something slice into my arm, I looked to where it cut me and blood was pouring down. He was already out, standing facing me. He launched a stake, but I strafed away easily. I propelled my body like a torpedo toward him, keeping a barrier in front of me should he try and shoot at me again. I was absolutely exhausted by this point, my body aching all over, but the anger I was feeling was still fuelling me. His vines withdrew, he turned and ran after he noticed what I was doing. Everything I flew past was completely destroyed. I felt sick. This was an *apocalypse.*

He was at the end of the street, turning every so often to shoot stake after stake but they would meet the barrier and ricochet off. I could see he was just as tired as I was. An army of wriggling vines made their advance but I barrel-rolled, avoiding them. I led with my shoulder, in preparation of impact, this time I was aiming for his face directly. I wanted to crush the cartilage in his nose. I wanted to make him scream in pain again. Just before I hit him, he winked and I felt razor-sharp leaves slice all around my body as I slammed in to the wall behind him. He had expanded just before impact.

As I turned around, disorientated, I could feel my arms once again constricted by his vines. I focused on them, a hundred snakes, and tried to tear them off but that only motivated the constriction to intensify. It seemed he could *feel* each vine. He was standing a few feet from me. We made eye contact. My eyes wide with panic, his narrowed in confidence; the vines undulated with my power but his grip was holding me firm. It was his ability against mine, I managed to conjure a ball of thought around us, and with a great struggle, began to unfurl his constriction from within.

Once free, I let my ability focus on him. He was tightly enveloped, like a hand in a glove. I picked him up and slammed him in to the wall that moments ago, I crashed in to. He grunted in pain. I pulled him out and then *smack* into the wall once more. I could hear faint noises behind me, but I was not going to be distracted. I finally had him. I slammed him in to the wall three more times, each time trying to hit him harder than the last. Now it was *my turn* to enjoy this. My turn to hurt him. I spun him round, amber tears were streaming down his face, green and red oozing from his nose.

"Why did you kill them?" I roared but before he was given the chance to answer, I slammed him into the wall. "Why did you hurt Lana?" *Slam.* "Where is her brother?" *Slam! Slam! Slam!*

"Please," he shouted, ooze dribbled from his mouth, "please. Stop." He coughed. I felt something loosen in his mouth - I yanked and he whimpered as I tore three teeth out. "Please help me!"

"Help you?" I repeated incredulously. Again there was a sound behind me, but I was too focused. I would not let go. I would not be caught off guard, that was how he got me before. We promised Lana we would look for her brother. This was the only chance. "Where is Lana's brother? Why did the shadow lady want the sick kid?" There was a groan from behind, but Treeboy didn't answer. "Where is he?!" I screamed once again, my voice screeched slightly.

I slammed him in to the wall again. This time, when I pulled him away, his body was limp. I gasped sharply, the intake of fresh air stung my lungs. Panicking, I let him go and he fell to the ground. I walked over to him, hesitantly, anxiously. "Are you okay?" I said, hearing the irony of it. I wanted nothing more than to hurt him, but as soon as his body grew limp, fear gripped me. Did I really want to kill him? I did before, but now…

I turned him over with my ability so he was laying with his back on the ground. I laid my thought over him like a blanket and my heart skipped with relief because his was still beating. He was alive.

"I think that is quite enough," said the woman's voice in my head. As soon as I heard her, I dropped to my knees and began to sob and shake. She was back. She promised she would save me.

"Please," I begged. "Please, you said you'll save us. Please, I don't know what to do."

"Kurt, I'm sorry." *Jo's voice*? She was crying and I felt delirious. "I tried to use my ability to stop him but, I couldn't. I couldn't. It wouldn't grip his mind. I'm sorry." My mind was giving up, I was about to pass out and my whole body welcomed it.

Then the first voice sounded again. I noticed the quality differed slightly. "Turn around," she said. My body was in the throes of involuntary shakes when I forced myself to turn. Standing before me was Jo, George and Lana. George was holding the hand of a young boy. In front of them stood a woman, thin and tall. Her hair was tied back in a sensible style, next to her stood a young girl who was staring at me blankly - expressionless. George walked over to me, the young boy following him.

"Do the thing, Anthony. Please." George begged. The boy looked at him and nodded. This boy, Anthony, a child of about five-years-old, laid me down and sat on top of me. His skin was rough, wet and cold. I looked at him, he too, seemed to be of a greenish hue but I was too confused, too worn out to question it. He held his hands up and a flush of water flowed all over me. It felt wet and dry at the same time. Lana created a ball of light above me so the boy could see what he was doing. The consistency of the fluid was wrong, it was thin, half-wisp half-liquid. It reminded me of something, but I couldn't focus now.

As the strange, ghostly water spread over my body I began to feel… *wonderful*. The pain I was experiencing left as if it decided it had something better to do; I could feel my wounds closing over and fusing together, fixing themselves. After a few seconds, there were no injuries at all. I was simply absolutely exhausted, my body begged for rest and I willingly succumbed.

Chapter 7

I found myself once more hovering in the midst of the strange galaxy. The star-like windows shone and burned in the distance; I could see colour and images flashing in some of the nearer ones. Silver Hair was floating in front of me facing in the opposite direction. My body was frozen, I couldn't move or speak.

"Hello," she said without looking and a shock that felt like electricity coursed through me, freeing me. I flexed my hand and legs, enjoying the sensation of controlling them once more. "I believe I owe you an apology for my behavior in our last meeting. I was confused and angry, so on, so forth. No harm done." She said as if she had been forced to.

"Uh… Don't worry about it." I replied unsure of how I got back here.

"Come and look at this." She said quickly. "I need your opinion." She was hunched over studying something. I floated there for a moment realising she wasn't going to guide me. I stretched my limbs out, then began to move them in tandem with one another. I achieved locomotion – it was different than flying with my telekinesis but not too dissimilar. As if I was swimming on currents of air. I made my way over to her. "What do these look like to you?"

She indicated two windows floating next to each other. One - though the perimeter was shining with an illuminous white - was blocked out; the centre sported a stubborn, unshifting darkness which covered the vision inside unlike the rest of the windows. The other was smaller, the perimeter was not as bright as the first and though the body was still blocked, there were hints of movement and flashes within.

"Uh, they look like windows?" I offered not exactly sure what I was supposed to say.

"Yes!" She agreed gleefully. "So, you agree they are similar to the other windows – they have the same properties, do they not?" I nodded at her slowly. Her hair was ruffled at the front, she was clearly flustered. "Good. Good. But, do they seem different at the same time?"

"Uh…" I studied them again. I was unsure of what she was trying to get at, this was not what I needed right now. I pointed at the first one. "That's all black so you can't see what's inside," then pointed at the second, "and that one is basically the same."

"Exactly. Good, Kurt. Good." She beamed at me, and nodded. "Now, do you think it's possible that whoever these windows belong to are somehow blocking us from seeing what they see?"

"I guess that's possible." I replied. "Anything is possible right now." Then memories of what happened whilst I was awake began to flood in. "You need to see it out there. It's chaos. If you'd have seen what I have…"

"I have seen it," she stated dryly. "Through these windows. I can see the whole world from any of them. Except these two!" She hunched back over, stroking the side of her face and pouting her lip out in thought as if these two dark windows were more interesting than the plethora of vibrant ones.

"So, all these windows, they're from the people outside. The people in my world?" I asked.

"Your world was my world before I got sick, Kurt." She stared at me. "For me, it took years of my body remaining inactive for my mind to explore and unlock itself. Not only has something out there kick started the same process in billions of people, but it has simultaneously acted as a catalyst. Sped it up to a point where people are mastering their gifts already.

"You know," she continued, "for a long time I missed it. I've tried every way imaginable to wake myself up, but watching from this perspective – what people are doing to one another." She shook her head, bewildered and disgusted. "Cowards now have the power of an army at their fingertips and are capitalising on fear. It's despicable."

"I've seen it." I pictured Shadow Lady walking toward Lana and me. "Some people seem to have a weird control of their abilities. Even I do, it just feels like an extension of myself."

"I suppose it is." She mused. "Which brings me back to these two. Do you think it is possible that they are actively blocking others from seeing their thoughts? Or if not," she swiftly moved toward me, grabbed me by the shoulders and stared straight in to my eyes with her beautiful blue ones which were beginning to tear up. "Do you think that there is something else stopping me? Perhaps they are in trouble, unconscious, somehow trapped in their own abilities or someone else's?"

I threw my hands up. "I don't know how it all works out there. I have no idea." I freed myself from her grip. "I suppose it's possible. Why?"

"I have a reason to believe that this here," she pointed at the larger of the two, "is my daughter's window." I looked at it, then back to Silver Hair not exactly sure what to say. She continued to study the two for a few minutes, drifting slowly around them to get a look from every angle.

"What makes you say that?" I finally asked with hesitation when I realised she wasn't going to say anything else. "Out of all of them, why these?"

She hummed to herself, then began to explain. "I can't say for sure – it's a sense more than anything else. Dogs can identify one another with smell; cats use pheromones to mark territories with scent." She nodded slowly to herself as if convincing the both of us. "Something on a deeper level has drawn me to these."

"So, if one is your daughter's, who's is the other one?" I asked, unwittingly playing the Devil's advocate.

"Therein lays the problem," she grunted in frustration. "That's what doesn't make sense. I've noticed that they appear in proximity to others for a reason. Since all the others bloomed here, I have managed to deduce that your window will appear within close range of someone else within your family."

Instantly, I grew excited. "So, you can find my parents?"

"If they have abilities," she said and elation washed over my body, "and if I knew where your personal window was. Possibly. But," she waved her arm as if washing my hopes away. "I can't be sure if my deduction is correct." She turned from the windows then, her eyes glistened and she blinked a few times to hold back the tears. "Kurt, I'm ashamed to say one of the things I have longed to apologise for is," she took a deep breath, "my vehement refusal to respect her life choices."

"I… don't understand." I admitted, but she read it wrong.

"I know. I know, I'm ashamed to admit it. I don't understand it either. Even before all these new windows opened, I had seen people like Melanie – why anyone would welcome the unwarranted abuse is beyond me." She was shaking her head in shame. "You have to understand, it was a different time. Things like that weren't taken kindly to in my days. But I've had more time than I can say to ponder on it now." That's when I noticed it. The eyes that were staring back in to mine, they held years that betrayed the youthful skin. There was wisdom in them that had matured over decades.

"Which is why I'm so confused." She spun back round to look at them. "If my guess is correct and windows appear in accordance to biological connections, it *can't* be Melanie. She wouldn't have a child." She couldn't fight any longer. She began to cry, the tears journeyed slowly down her cheeks, twinkling and reflecting in the memories. "But it *has* to be. I've never been so sure of anything."

My insides began to squirm. People crying is always difficult to cope with, never mind coming from someone whose age I couldn't discern whilst floating in the control centre of the world. I reached my hand out and patted her shoulder with a quiet 'Awww' and 'There, there'. She didn't slap my hand away so it must have been welcome – apparently, all it takes for someone to welcome my touch is years of grief ridden solitude. Then out of obligation, "If there's anything I can do-"

At that, her head shot up, her mouth slightly open. She began wiping away her tears. "Actually, there is." She croaked. "Kurt, you are linked to her somehow. I don't know how, but when I found you here, I still stand by the fact that I did sense *her*. You have to find her out there. She may be trapped in her ability somehow, or someone else's. I'm not sure how long I've been in here so cannot guess how old she will be." She raised her eyebrow after thinking of more things she could use as identification. "It doesn't make sense for her to have a child, but times change, she may have. If so, it seems the child too, is trapped in a similar fashion. Kurt, find them. Free them! I need to apologise to her."

I don't think she was aware that she had just given the most ambiguous description possible, but I nodded supportively. Anything to keep her from crying. "Look, I can only say I'll try. I can't promise anything – please understand I have no idea what's going on out there." Her face contorted in to a frown. "But," I added quickly. "I'll try! And if I do find her - or them - will you help me look for my parents-"

*

There was a sharp pain in the side of my ribs. "Oww!" I cried and jumped up. My head hit something and I fell back down. I was in a seat. I looked around to see we were on a bus. Almost every seat was full. A lot of people were asleep, some were awake and hugging in to one another. I could hear someone crying a few rows behind me. Next to me Jo was looking down.

"Sorry, you were snoring. I didn't mean to hit you that hard." She said.

"Where are we?" I croaked in reply.

"A bus. That lady - she's kind've a bitch - but she's saved everyone here. Loads were already on here when we got on." Jo said quietly as she surreptitiously looked round at others on the bus. "She found us, as in George, Lana, Anthony – the little green kid - and myself before we went to get you. After she saved us from the attackers she made us come with her. Said she knew who you were and where you were." Jo placed her arm on the seat in front of her and pulled her body forward looking down the aisle of seats. She came back to me and whispered. "It was weird Kurt, all these people were attacking us, full on hatred in their eyes, then they stopped when she showed up. They just stopped. Even though I was terrified, as soon as she came I just felt safe. I can't really explain it."

"What?" I managed again, still half asleep. The image of Silver Hair was still floating in my mind.

"Okay, well…" Jo then went on at length, explaining what had happened to them whilst I was away complete with different voices and accents. Apparently, the area they went to scout was clear and they became suddenly aware of how stupid it was letting me go alone.

Just as they went to make their way back to me, they heard rapid footsteps and distant crying. They froze, waiting to see what was happening, when the boy, Anthony, came in to view.

As soon as he saw them, he ran and was begging for help, but they couldn't make sense out of him as his sobbing marred his speech. Not long after, a group of adults - that she believed didn't have abilities because they were carrying weapons - came running around the corner.

When they saw Anthony with them, they demanded he be handed over as he killed one of their nephews, but when Anthony vehemently denied it, Jo said she 'just knew' he didn't do it. "He's only about six, you could tell he was telling the truth."

When they refused to hand him over, the group made to attack them. She said Lana was furious, clearly drawing from the anger of her brother being taken in similar circumstances, and her beads of light took on a different property, somehow having the ability to physically hurt them. Jo herself had managed to use her own ability. "It was weird," she explained, "I could *feel* their minds, and when I willed it, I made them think they were seeing something else. Simple as turning on a light switch." She shook her head gravely. "I don't know what I can do, exactly, but again, I could feel that duality. I could see in one of their minds that they were trapped in a coffin – he started clawing at thin air screaming to be let out. The other sped of thinking he was being chased by a rabid dog with glowing eyes and, like, mottled, rotting flesh." She shuddered.

"Anyway, as I turned around I saw George had threw Anthony to the floor and dove over him, making sure the others couldn't hurt the kid." She shook her head and exhaled to indicate her rage. "But, just as I was about to get the others to stop hitting George," she looked behind cautiously and dropped her voice, "they stopped of their own accord. They just stopped fighting. I turned around to look at Lana and the people attacking her had stopped as well. Then it was weird, I felt *super* calm. Like everything was happening the way it was meant to. Like there was nothing wrong with what had happened in the first place. This was all how it was meant to unfold. I wasn't scared, I wasn't angry, I wasn't worried. I was at peace.

"Then the woman was there." Jo looked down the aisle once more with her 'is-it-safe-to-gossip' eyes before giving me her 'yeah-it-is-safe-to-gossip' nod. "She just stood there with that little girl, as casually as if they were just taking a stroll walking a dog. She told the attackers 'These are innocent. I suggest you all go and find safety before sunrise.' And Kurt, when she said it, it was as if it was the best idea in the world. The attackers all ran away and she looked at me. I said 'Thank you' to her and went to help George up. Lana came over to help as well, a ball of light above her now. I could see all the cuts and marks on her face.

"We helped them up. Anthony, he kept saying 'Thank you, thank you, thank you' like over and over. Then this weird water stuff came out of his hand, which he used on us. It covered George first and I tensed up for a second, but all George's cuts started to *close up* in front of us. The skin *literally* fused together with no marks. Then he did Lana, then me. All my pain was gone, well, you know, he did it to you before you fainted.

"Then we found you fighting." She shook her head with a contemplative grimace. "Kurt, it was horrible. I started crying straight away. You were literally *dripping* with blood and you were screaming at this guy. You were asking about Lana's brother and kept slamming him in to the wall. I tried to run and help you, but the woman held her hand out to stop me. Lana started crying saying 'That is the boy. He knows where...' But the woman held another hand out cutting Lana off mid-speech. She was watching you, her eyes narrowed as if she was taking in a piece of art. When her hands were out in front of us, it dawned on me that the best idea was to stay put and not attempt to physically intervene. I'm not too sure why. The boy you were hitting, I didn't see him properly, but he was all weird-coloured too, but different to Anthony, he wasn't doing too well and I'd never seen you that angry. I kept shouting but I think you were too blinded, well, deafened by rage. Who was he? What did he do?"

Jo was looking at me expectantly and I realised it was my turn to tell the story. George snored loudly behind us. I told Jo about what happened to me when I left to try and help the first scream. I told her of the woman, her glowing orbs, her thinking I was an attacker, then Treeboy appearing. I told her he was the one with the group that attacked Lana, that he killed the woman and the kid. Her eyes opened wide with terror as I continued my story. I told her about chasing him, about his powers and how in control of it he seemed. Tears filled her eyes. Jo did not suit tears and I felt uneasy. "I'm sorry," I said quickly, trying to stop it. "I didn't mean to scare you, I was just so angry. He killed that orb woman and the kid and I just saw red. Please don't cry." I added.

"I'm not crying because of that. I let you go off on your own, you could've died, Kurt. I would've been to blame for that." She said and grabbed my hand, squeezing it. I'm sure she meant it in a friendly and compassionate way, but it felt as if she was trying to dislocate my bones.

"Don't be silly, Jo. You had no way of knowing what was gonna happen and I do have a weird amount of control of my ability already so you were just calling the shots as you saw them. Honestly, don't stress."

We sat in silence for a while. I looked through the gap between the back of Jo's and my chair to see George sleeping with his mouth wide open, drool glistening down his chin and nostrils flaring with his snores. This boy, this Anthony who had healed my wounds was curled up and leaning against his shoulder. George's arm was around him. Now I could see him properly, his skin was more like scales, rigid and forest green. His hair was black, his nose slightly less pronounced than a human nose normally would be. Yet, there in his sleep, this creature who looked almost half-reptilian was still clearly a young boy. His chest shuddered with a heavy breath. Poor guy had been through a lot and here he was, with the rest of us. All in the same boat, or, I guess in this case, bus.

I looked around the bus at those awake. There was a milky pale girl. She had long hair that could not quite decide if it wanted to be frizzy or straight. It fell in front of her face and bushed around her shoulders. She held one hand flat open in front of her, then with the other hand on top, she held a finger out and began to twirl it as if it was a spoon stirring sugar in to a tea. Something began to form in her hand. She became transfixed with a small, strange grey disc that rose in to a twister of smoke. She stopped twirling it with her finger and delicately pulled her hair back, fixing it behind her ears.

Ahead of her sat a boy. He wore a pair of thick glasses that looked almost too heavy for his body to support. He had a flat and greasy mop of hair which flopped lazily on top of his head, whereas his body was weedy and spindly and when *I* can say that about someone else, you know it's bad. He was just looking at his lap and shaking his head. Next to him, a boy was talking. This boy was muscular, his hair short and his face strong and chiselled as if carved by a sculptor.

I looked over at Jo, whose eyes were closed but eyelids were flickering. She was still awake, but just letting herself think. I jumped when I looked ahead. There was a Japanese guy looking right back at me. He noticed my fright and grinned, flashing a set of perfectly straight and white teeth. His hair fit perfectly on his head, amongst all the ruin I had seen today, his hair was a wonderful contrast. Each strand seemed to fall exactly how it should, the style a perfect complement to his bone structure. I felt hideous in comparison. My eyes could not leave his hair, it was perfect. I guessed my face would be greener - with envy - than Anthony's scales behind me.

"Hello there," he said, his accent, crisp and well-spoken. "My name is Shinji." He reached his hand over for me to shake. He sounded too cheerful considering the circumstances.

"Hi, uh. My name's-"

"Kurt, I know," he said. My mouth opened wide for a moment.

"Are you a telepath?" I guessed.

"Eavesdropper." He replied. "The woman who saved all of us is the telepath, I just heard your friend telling you the story. She said your name a lot." His eyes flicked to Jo. I looked at her. Her eyes, in turn were now opened and she was looking at him with furrowed eyebrows. "Hi Jo, I hope you don't mind my listening, but I couldn't help it, really. I mean, you are one row behind me."

"Not at all." Jo said. Shinji reached his hand out for her to shake. She took it without hesitation but her face remained suspicious. "Why are you so happy?" She asked, not to keep herself in the dark.

"Oh, I'm sorry. I must look heartless." He said, but the smile remained. The perfect teeth still on show. The flawless hair, mocking me. "It took me a while to decide to introduce myself, but, you both seem like wonderful people. I'm just happy to be alive. We all have our stories from this, but you two were not actually in danger."

"Then you didn't hear the story." Jo said, stubbornly.

"Sorry, I worded that incorrectly." He chewed his soft lip for a moment. "You two *put* yourself in danger to save others - that's incredible." There was no sarcasm in his voice. He meant what he was saying. The praise made me feel uncomfortable but I smiled at him regardless.

"This is Aaron," Shinji said as he looked down at the chair beside him. "He's really nice," he added. "Aaron, say hello to Jo and Kurt." There was a sigh, then a fumbling in front of us until another face popped up. He looked very innocent, around our age; black hair sat flatly on his head and his brown eyes constantly flicked between Jo and me.

"Hi, how're you doing?" Aaron said. His accent a strong and rhythmical Northern Irish.

"How're you doing." Shinji mimicked. "Isn't his accent incredible?" I looked at Aaron, who did not seem as jovial as Shinji.

61

"Nice to meet you, Aaron." Jo said and held her hand out. He shook it, then I held mine out. His handshake was weak compared to Shinji's, but he smiled all the same.

"How long have you two known each other?" Shinji asked, opening the question for either of us.

"Just under three years now." Jo replied. "We met at Uni."

Shinji beamed at that. "That's really sweet."

"How about you two?" Jo asked indicating Aaron and Shinji.

"About four or five," Shinji's eyes looked up as if he was counting in his head. "Yeah, four or five hours."

"Hours?!" I said louder than intended. "Hours?" I whispered to compensate.

"Aye," Aaron said.

"Aye." Shinji copied. "Sorry, I really don't mean to do it." He added quietly, genuinely apologetic.

"M found me earlier-" Aaron began.

"Who?" I asked, confused.

"The mindreader," Jo answered. "The one who came to us. She just told us to call her M."

"M found me earlier," Aaron continued, "and brought me to this bus and then we parked up for a while. I saw you were passed out when you came on, but the bus outside has this weird black liquid covering it," Aaron said. Jo and Shinji nodded at the description. "When she makes the driver park it, she turns the lights on in here and the liquid covers all of the outside. Not quite sure what it does, but must keep people away or something."

"Yeah, it does," Shinji confirmed. "When she found me, I was alone. She explained it acts as a repellant in a way. I couldn't see it at first, it wasn't until she pointed it out that I could make out a vague shape. I was in awe when I realised it was a bus." He looked at Aaron who had decidedly now given the story over to Shinji. "When I got on, most people were asleep or paired up, or crying. But Aaron here, he was inspecting the most beautiful ice rose."

"A what?" Jo asked incredulously.

"Yup," Shinji said, brimming with pride. "Turns out he can conjure water, ice and steam." He said and Aaron's face reddened as he blushed. "Show them!"

Aaron looked at Shinji as if to argue, but his shoulders deflated, giving up the fight before he even started. He held his hands and contorted them in a way that looked as if he was holding the strings of a marionette. From his fingers and thumbs, ten small streams of water trickled downward. I pushed my back further in to the chair before it could land on my lap. Shinji chuckled as the water began to collect as if there was an invisible basin. This floating puddle split in to two, one over my lap and one over Jo's. Aaron's tongue was trapped between his lips and wriggling with concentration. Both puddles of water began to ripple, obeying Aaron's silent commands, folding and weaving within itself. Before long, pure water replicas of Jo and myself were floating in front of us.

"Hold your hand out." Aaron said and we did, both of us in awe at the detail. They began to freeze in front of us, giving off a slight crunching sound as if a layer of fresh, crisp frost was being trod on. The two replicas were now solid ice figurines.

"That is incredible." I said without even realising the words were leaving my lips. Jo was turning the figure in her hands, scrutinising the entire thing. She was clearly impressed, Aaron wouldn't appreciate this but if you did something that made Jo react in the way she did now, you were going to go far.

"Isn't it fantastic?" Shinji said as if he had made them himself. "He liked to paint beforehand, or construct models," Shinji started as if he was reciting a well-learned speech. "So, his attention to detail is second nature. It seems this reflects in the control of his ability." Aaron smiled at Shinji then looked back toward us. The two figures burst into steam, which hung in the air like a weak fog before disappearing completely.

"What about you?" Jo asked, staring at Shinji. "What can you do?"

"I can kill people with eye contact alone." Shinji said, void of friendliness. His eyes rolled backward in to his head, the pale white left within them focused on me. I grabbed Jo's hand in panic and she gasped from the pain of it. Then Shinji's eyes were back and he was laughing. Aaron shook his head but was smiling. "I'm joking!" He managed to say through laughter.

He apologised then paused before speaking again. "I'm not too sure entirely what to say, because I haven't experienced it, but, I guess, well... I can put people to sleep - as easy as that." He snapped his fingers together. It went quiet for a moment. I looked at Jo to see if she was asleep but she looked back at me with a 'Why-are-you-looking-at-me?' face. I turned back round to Shinji. "I didn't do it then," He said simply. "I can put people to sleep but I don't know how to wake them back up. They do it themselves, just like normal sleep, I suppose."

Shinji began to regale us with the story of how he discovered his power. Somehow, he found this necessary to start with his birth in Japan. The rest of his family still lived there but he lived here with a friend of his mother's. Not long after Shinji was born, his father died. His mother had not wanted to stay in Japan because it was too painful so she moved here as her best friend owned a small company. He grew up here and his mother's friend's small company turned in to a big company. He was happy and rarely wanted for anything, but appreciated everything.

His mother passed away a few years ago and his family offered for him to come live with them in Japan, but he had his own PR job at the company and had grown fond of the frail old lady from whom he rented. Apparently, she loved baking and that was ideal because Shinji loved cakes, though you couldn't tell by looking at him - the pangs of envy gonged in my stomach.

It was his frail landlady he inadvertently used his ability on. He woke up feeling different, like there was a physical itch on his mind. "It felt like I had a slinky travelling around inside of me. I went downstairs to ask Mrs. Wallace if she could advise any medication - she always had some pills in her purse or a traditional remedy that I was skeptical would not work, but always did, or, if I should just take the day off work but she was standing at the window clutching the curtains tight." He sighed. "She was always quite reclusive, but I'd never seen her act like this. I asked her what was up and she kept telling me it was 'The rapture, the rapture, Shin, the rapture is here!'" He paused as he looked from Jo to me. Aaron was watching Shinji unblinking. He had clearly heard the story because he was not reacting the way Jo and I were through the whole thing, but still, he listened intently.

"I asked her what she was talking about, but she grew hysterical. Then I felt this, uh, this slinky - as it were - bounce from my mind. It was like I could feel a tangible thought flit out of my mind and land in hers. She dropped to the floor."

He went on to say how he began to panic wondering what had just happened, he picked her up and could feel she was still breathing, propped her on the couch and put a blanket over her. "Emergency services were engaged at first, then there was no ring-out tone later. Then after a while, she woke up.

"It wasn't long before her grandchildren barged in with weapons. One of them had met me before, I think if she didn't, they would have attacked me. They just picked her up and brought her outside. That was it. She was gone and I was left alone." He looked at my face, full of pity, then grinned. "It's okay. I'm just happy she's safe. But when I went outside…"

His story then was similar to ours. Fighting, looting, wondrous abilities and at the end, this woman, the voice in my head, she came with the young girl and picked him up. He said they walked through the streets and no one paid them any attention, as if they were invisible. Until he got on the bus. "And you know the story from here."

Aaron's story was simpler. He had actually been on the phone to his parents during the early morning. They were asking if he could get home, they were scared and panicking. It was quiet back home. Safe. They went on to tell him he should be out of the city at least. His mother had developed powers of their own. He hadn't been given the chance to find out what exactly the ability was because as he began to panic, he conjured water from the palms of his hand and destroyed the phone.

"They'll be safe," Aaron said already having placated his fears and convinced himself. "They're tough, especially my mammy, and we live right in the middle of nowhere. Our nearest neighbour is about a twenty-minute drive. I'm not worried about them at all." After he left his house, he realised he had quite a potent control over his abilities. He travelled from fire to fire trying to extinguish it. "I didn't know what else to do, at least that made me feel like I was helping somehow."

I could tell already that both Shinji and Aaron were nice people. They opened up instantly, but not in an attention-seeking way. That sounds awful, but I meant I could tell they were telling their stories to tell it, not to get sympathy or attention from us. Plus, both their stories involved helping people. On top of that, they had only known each other for a while and they were already comfortable in each other's company.

The four of us began to talk about what we think could have happened to bring this on. During our talking, the bus would stop. The strange black liquid would cover the windows and the lights inside would come on. We would wait for a while then M would come back with more injured or crying people, but safe people, at least.

The conversation between the four of us began to fizzle. George woke up at one point, mumbled incoherencies then went back to sleep. The bus droned on and on, conversations between the other passengers cropped up here and there but it was mostly quiet. The atmosphere was tangibly tense as people mulled over what had happened to them, praying their families and friends were safe, trying to comprehend the scale. It wasn't long before Aaron and Shinji had turned around and fell asleep naturally, no need for Shinji's ability it seemed. Jo was leaning on my shoulder and I just stared out the window as the miles disappeared under our wheels.

65

The sky, as if showing me that there is hope (or adhering to nature as it has done for eons) began to brighten. The black night turned in to a cloudy dawn which was soon, as we travelled further, a cloudless morning. We were clearly far away from any sizeable city or town. Every so often we would pass by a field in which a few houses were stranded in the middle like an uncharted island in a sea of green, but mostly there was nothing. I wondered if this M woman had intended this, avoiding any heavily populated area in the hopes of not risking confrontation and, of course, our lives.

I was fascinated by this woman. She was the reason Lana was still alive, or at least, not as beaten as she could have been. Whilst everyone else turned in to brutes and criminals, she remained level-headed. She had personally travelled to collect all these people on this bus, she was the reason we weren't fighting for our lives back out there. As if reading my mind, she stood up and looked at me. A curt smile of acknowledgment spread across her face, then she looked around at a few other individuals, giving a slight nod every so often. She sat back down again and a wave of appreciation washed over me. She saved not only my life, but the lives of my friends. I owed her everything.

My cheek was planted against the window. My eyes were lazily taking in field after field after vast field. I was fighting to stay awake, mostly because I was scared of facing Silver Hair in my sleep but also because I would only be dropping off out of boredom. The bus soon began to decelerate. A giant forest that looked like it spread for miles surrounded us. A few small buildings came in to sight as we pulled in to a cute rural village. Most structures here were at their highest two levels, the houses were small and lacked any extravagance, the stores were simple – no high street in sight. We navigated the village for a few minutes.

One building stood out. It was larger than the rest, the architecture carefully crafted as if from a different era. It looked like I was staring at a heritage site that had been untouched for historic accuracy, the words *Town Hall* were emblazoned in gold atop the entrance. There was a small school next to this building, it looked as if it could barely hold two hundred people but with the simplicity of this town, I reckoned that would be more than enough to satisfy demand.

We pulled into a large opening that the town hall and the school looked out on. I smiled thinking about the history they contained. I looked out the opposite side of the bus and was surprised to find a rundown building; the signs were barely readable, the windows were either cracked, smashed or boarded up. The stairs leading up to it had not been painted over for a long time. It seemed so out of place with the other buildings. I shuddered when I thought about that building's history.

Most the people on the bus were still sleeping. Those awake, like me, were looking out of the windows at our surroundings. M stood up once more and travelled down the aisle of seats, gently waking people up. The small girl travelled behind her, staring dead ahead, not paying attention to any of the passengers.

As they approached where I was sitting, M smiled at me again and I smiled back feeling as if a celebrity I adored had just made eye contact with me. I nudged Jo sharply to wake her up, showing M my willingness to help.

"Ow, Kurt. What the hell do you think-" Jo moaned but her voice trailed when she saw M nearby. M nodded her appreciation at me and I smiled a goofy smile. She woke up Shinji and Aaron, then walked behind us waking up George and Anthony, then Lana and the strangers behind her.

"We're here," I told Jo.

"Where's here?" She scowled, rubbing her ribs vigorously.

"I'm not sure. There's literally nothing around here but a forest and fields a few miles back. It's beautiful, though," I admitted, genuinely appreciating the town. I was so used to city life, moving from a small city to the big city, that small places like this fascinated me. Beautifully picturesque. This is the sort of town I pictured the famous romantic poets to live in, surrounded by nature, friends and family as endless muses. Once everyone was awake, M stood at the head of the bus.

"Thank you all for your bravery and admirable behaviour during our journey. I know it was long and I am more than aware it was tiring, yet, all of you have showed wonderful levels of co-operation which is a virtue that will help us through these dark times." Everyone was silent, staring ahead at M unblinkingly. "This town was once a small thriving community, but has long been emptied of civilians. Therefore, it is absolutely the safest place to reside until the chaos and bloodshed dies down. As you are all aware, the world out there has drastically changed overnight. With any tragedy, the imminent response is often as catastrophic as the initial cause." She shook her head slowly, frowning. "That is why I left this town, to save as many innocent souls as I could. You truly deserve to be here and I am only sorry that I could not bring more." She paused for a moment, her gaze fell to the floor with sadness. It was as if I could feel what she was feeling. "Once I have you settled in, I will attempt to head back out there in the hopes of rescuing more people." I adored her. She was altruism personified. I was in awe of her... and the fact she could stand in front of a bus full of strangers and speak?

Wow. "Before we get to the ins and outs of what has happened - and rest assured I have my theories - we must first consider creating a comfortable environment for those present. I believe that is our priority. Now let us get off this stuffy bus."

As soon those words left her mouth I realised just how stuffy the bus was. It hadn't bothered me before, but now it was as if the moisture in the air was drowning me. Everyone stood up. I turned around catching George's eyes. He shrugged at me and I shrugged back.

Once off the bus, people were stretching and yawning. My bum was almost dead and standing upright was more of an effort than usual. Anthony was standing next to George holding his hand. In the light of the day, Anthony was magnificent. This change had genetically altered him. George looked down at him and said something, Anthony smiled. He was a short boy, his skin had transformed to forest green scales, whereas certain points pervaded with a lighter green. It glistened in the light, though, his hair was a slick black. He furrowed his brows, and narrowed his amber eyes - his face struck something in me. He reminded me of someone, but I couldn't place it.

Lana joined us, her eyes were red raw. She had definitely cried recently, but she let out a wan smile as we made eye contact. Shinji and Aaron gravitated toward us. Aaron was still rubbing his eyes and yawning as if waking up from a thousand year slumber, whilst Shinji looked wide awake, his hair still exuding perfection - the antithesis to this whole disaster.

Once everyone was off the bus, M addressed the group again. I felt a strange sense of belonging then; these poor people were saved by M just like me, these were in trouble and she went out of her way to protect them. I shuddered thinking about what each person possibly could have witnessed before entering her bus. What horrors out there were happening that I hadn't even imagined? I felt queasy so tried to empty my brain and just listen to her words.

"Please do not feel obliged to stay here. If you wish to leave, you may do so, but we are a self-sustaining facility and have vast amounts of supplies here. I insist you let us feed you, tend to your wounds and allow you to rest."

"Excuse me?" Jo called out. My whole body tensed up.

"What're you doing, Jo?" I whispered.

"Excuse me?!" Jo called out louder. M stopped talking and looked in our direction. Her eyes flickered at me for a moment - and I wanted to sink in to the ground - before resting on Jo. M smiled curtly at her and Jo continued. "A lot of the people here are hurt." She said, stating the obvious.

"I am happy to see your new ability has not affected your previously existing talent of observation. I am very aware that people have been harmed. We have the facilities in my la-" M was saying, but Jo cut her off again.

"This boy. Anthony. He can heal people. You saw him with Kurt," She glanced at me and I looked away. "It took him a few seconds. Shouldn't we heal the people who need it before we continue?"

M stared at Jo for a few seconds with no emotion betraying her face. "But of course, considering your friend Anthony is comfortable with someone deciding what he should do in his stead?" She smiled.

"Anthony won't mind, will you?" Jo said looking at Anthony who seemed as if he had just been thrown on to stage without knowing his lines. "George?" George looked at Jo then to Anthony.

"Don't worry, mate." He said. His voice gentle, big-brotherly. "They need your help. Will you do it?"

Anthony looked at all the people staring at him. A few were gawping at how he looked, whilst others did not seem at all bothered by his scaly skin. Hesitantly he nodded and held his hands out. The strange ghostly water began to trickle around his hands. Aaron, upon seeing the strange substance stepped toward Anthony and knelt. Anthony's hands began to ripple as more ghostly water spouted to heal Aaron, but Aaron shook his head and lifted his own hands up.

The water travelled over to Aaron and he began to manipulate it with his own ability. "Hello," Aaron smiled at Anthony, his face soft and caring. "I'm Kurt and Jo's friend." He said, looking in our direction. We nodded at Anthony. "Can I help you heal all these people?" Anthony looked at George who smiled his approval. Shinji beamed at Aaron.

"Okay," he said gingerly, his large amber eyes staring at the ground. Anthony stood with his hands above his head, spewing water out like a fountain whilst Aaron stood behind him, making intricate movements with his hands. The ghostly water followed his orders and paused in front of the two ready to heal those who needed it.

The first person to step forward was a guy with short hair, a thick almost muscular build and light brown skin. He knelt down in front of the two and put his neck to his chest. I gasped as I saw a fresh slash running down the back of his neck framed in a dark red splotch. As the ghostly water made contact with it, the broken skin fused together and the boy looked up at the two healing him. He hugged Anthony excitedly then moved on to Aaron before walking back in to the crowd; there was an impressed muttering that spread between them all. Then the rest came, their wounds closed up, bruises disappeared, burns faded and everyone muttered their thanks.

M watched them at work, seemingly impressed with their display of kindness and, of course, I assume their abilities. Once everyone was healed, George congratulated Anthony on helping and picked him up giving him a piggyback. Shinji praised Aaron for helping and doing it with style at that.

"Well, that makes things easier in a sense," M continued as if the interruption never happened. She looked to Anthony, then to Aaron. "I thank you both for your thoughtful actions," then she looked to Jo. "I appreciate your reasoning, but please do not interrupt me again. I wished to study the wounds caused by abilities out there in order to combat future cases. Maybe Anthony will not always be where he is needed, did that cross your mind?" Jo opened her mouth then closed it again. "I suppose all that matters is people are healthy. However, henceforth, should you wish to question my methods, you will speak to me in private." I couldn't tell if it was an order or a suggestion but my whole body seized up, terrified of the possibility Jo would argue, but miraculously, Jo just stared back in silence. "I have protocols for a reason, not for you to render null.

"If anyone feels they would still need to come in to the lab to be checked out, stay behind. We have medical facilities due to the nature of our research." There was a shuffling in the crowd and as if she sensed that these words made people uncomfortable, she added. "I am an evolutionary scientist. We have a hands-on approach in our research and are often here for months at a time - accidents happen so we required such facilities, until we could arrange transport to the nearest hospital or medical facility." This seemed to work fine. Everyone relaxed, including me.

She indicated the run down looking building - a crude motel facing the town hall and the small school. "This will be your new home until everything has calmed down and order has been regained." She stated. I stood staring at the motel. Surely it would make more sense to stay in the beautiful town hall which could clearly house more people. However, I did not dare challenge M and I could only hope Jo wouldn't either.

For a moment, it looked as if her eyes darted to George, but I couldn't be sure. "Please take your time to check this village for anything you think could add comfort. We have dormitories in our laboratory, but they are not the homeliest of places. They are blank and clinical - you have permission to take whatever you wish to add personality to your assigned rooms." She gazed out at the town then addressed the crowd again. "Do not worry, this

70

place is completely abandoned and has been for some time. It is now maintained mostly as a masquerade for our research facility, so feel no guilt.

"This town is small, you cannot get lost. You can see the town hall from almost any point and we have plenty of daylight ahead of us. Please collect what you want and bring it back to this opening. I will be waiting here. My staff," as she said this, a group of people came out of the motel behind us. They were dressed in black trousers and white shirts, each carrying a large tray and a jug. "Will help you carry your stuff to the dorms. May I please ask you not to speak to them? They have a lot to do, least important of those jobs is to care for you, so they should not be side-tracked at all. Just to forewarn you, I have given them strict orders to refuse to even acknowledge others. If you need anything specific, you can write a letter and pass it to a staff member - they will bring it to me and we will work from there. The system works - obey and trust it."

One of the staff members came up to our little group and held a tray out. There were sandwiches, sausage rolls, sweets and other morsels that can only be considered as 'party food' on it. I realised just how hungry I was when I saw these. Everyone around began helping themselves to their own trays. I muttered a word of thanks to the black haired, blue eyed staff member carrying our food and drinks, but he did not reply.

"Feel free to eat until you are full. If you do not feel up to travelling through this village, that is understandable. You may sleep first, then search later," she said. I fought a strong urge to run up and hug her. How could someone so important, so intelligent and busy be so wonderful a person?

"Well, I think that is all for now," She said simply. "As I have said, I will remain here if you need me." Then, her tone of voice changed quickly. "Do not leave the boundaries of the town. Be back before sunset."

Chapter 8

A number of people lingered behind picking away at their trays. The staff members stayed stock still like bizarre statues only moving once the tray was empty. M stood for a while watching people walk off, she made a quick scribble on a notepad that seemed to have come from nowhere, then she quickly turned around to head into the motel. Some people followed behind her gently sobbing, few were whimpering whilst others wailed.

Aaron and Shinji stayed with Jo, George, Lana, Anthony and myself. We began to walk in the direction of a cluster of houses thinking that would be the best place to get homely items. I mean, it makes sense.

"So, whaddya think?" George asked. "She's a bit, a bit…"

"Rude?" Jo offered.

"You're only saying that because she made you look stupid," George said.

"Look stupid?!" Jo was incredulous. "How did I look stupid?"

"Because there you are with your 'I am Jo and I have a better idea' and she already thought of that!" George parried. He wasn't being nasty or hateful, he was just being typical George, capitalising on the rare moment that Jo could be in the wrong, but she didn't take it well.

"Well I'm terribly sorry, George, but when I see people hurt or in pain, I think the best thing to do is look after them," she snapped. "Luckily, we came across someone who has the capability to do that instantly, so I apologise that I spoke up and had people healed before she could get a few points of data for her research, but I think the people who were healed would agree with me."

"Jo, I'm joking" George tried.

"Well, it's not funny, George. I did what I thought was right and if she had a problem with that, she could have stopped them easily." She huffed and George knew that was the end of the conversation. Aaron and Anthony grimaced awkwardly whereas Shinji was just smiling, clearly in his own world.

We walked on in silence for a while. This town really did have everything it needed for such a small and secluded place. We passed a pet shop, a toy shop, a couple of bookshops and an art supplies shop which had paintings hung in the window. Shinji stopped for a moment looking at them.

"They're fantastic, aren't they?" He said. "Aaron, is this the sort of painting you did?"

"Meh," he shrugged with an air of nonchalance. "Not my style."

"What do you mean, they're beautiful. Look at that." Shinji said pointing at a painting of a roaring waterfall crashing down a large cliffside, white foamy surf cascaded as it fell. "You can actually see the water glisten. It's majestic, beautiful. How would they even do that?"

In reply, Aaron stomped on the floor and a rough chunk of ice rose from his feet. This ice cracked and jolted as it took the shape of the large cliffside in the painting. His hands darted hither and thither altering little bits here and there making it look natural. Then holding his hands upside down, his fingers spread out wide and slightly curled as if holding a large bowl, a stream of water fell. The structure he created was a perfect replica of the painting, but the water fluently crashed and roared to scale.

"Well, that's fantastic but hardly fair." Shinji said, with a smile that showed his perfect teeth which to me was more impressive than the painting and replica. "They can't compare with that now, can they?"

The replica instantly melted in to a puddle and faded in to steam leaving no trace that there was anything there at all. "Aye, it's really good work, detailed and all, but just not my thing." A few moments of silent contemplation later, we continued on our way.

We were upon our first house now. There was another small group of people in the distance about to enter another. One of them raised their hands in what I imagine was a sign of solidarity before entering. We followed suit and entered ours. The house itself was beautiful, it was clearly made quite a long time ago but that only added character. The living room was small but cosy, with a fireplace in the middle of the wall. A large rug lay in front of a couch which faced a large boxed telly.

"These villagers must have evacuated this place in the nineties." George said looking at the TV.

"I don't think so." Shinji said lifting a newspaper up with a frown. "Look," he said handing it out. Lana walked up and took the paper from his hands. "The date," Shinji indicated.

"This paper," she said. "I sell it, it is national, this one is recent." She held the paper out for us.

My stomach squirmed for a moment in confusion. The village was abandoned, though – my thoughts began to blur as I tried to make sense of the incongruity. Then the thought came to me as if I already knew the reason. "M's staff must come in to the houses when they have time off, looks like they're worked hard so it must be nice to have some peace and quiet for a bit. A break from that dilapidated motel. She did say the rooms weren't homely. One of them probably left it here." I said completely satisfied. The others studied the paper for a while, then nodded their agreement whereas Jo scowled before shaking her head and looking round alone.

There was not much in the house to take. We picked up a few pillows, tins of food (just in case) and Anthony managed to find an old handheld games console in one of the drawers upstairs. He begged George to help him look for a charger, who instantly dropped what he was doing to do so.

After twenty minutes or so of further searching, Jo had decided we had salvaged all comforts this house had to offer and said it was best to move on. The next house proved to be much of the same, as did the third. In the fourth house, George came storming down the stairs as loud as thunder screaming at the top of his lungs. I froze in panic whilst Jo grabbed hold of a knife in the kitchen and Lana was holding a broom up as if it were a shotgun.

"Jackpot!" George shouted when he was on the same level as us, his hands were hidden behind his back. "We hit the jackpot!" He shouted again. He showed us what he was hiding, holding it above his head as if it were a trophy. "*Monopoly!*" He announced triumphantly.

"Jesus, George. You scared the hell out of us!" Jo shouted, then began to laugh. I relaxed now that I knew there was no danger and now that Jo was finished with being moody. "Lana, what were you going to do with that?" She asked with a grin. Lana looked down at the broom and brushed the air.

"Clean him," she quipped and began to laugh as well. It was nice to see that – even if the joke was weak.

George began to apologise and talk about how there was a few pieces missing but we could make do when I carried on looking round the house. On the mantelpiece, there was a family picture. My stomach sank as I thought about the couple Jo and I wrapped up in the carpet when we were leaving our town. I walked up to this picture and studied it. There was a woman with long blonde hair, two children that looked like twins except for one of them being blonde and the other having jet black hair. The father in the picture had hair as black as his daughter and bright blue eyes - my heart began to race as my vision blurred. My stomach twisted as if my consciousness was trying to escape my body. "I know him from somewhere." I mumbled breaking George's extolling.

"What did you say, mate?" He asked. But, my stomach began to tighten. My throat constricted and I couldn't form the words again. I started to sway.

"Kurt?" Jo's voice sounded heavy with concern but it was distant and reverberated in my head as if it was an echo in a cavern. "Are you okay?"

I looked at the photo again. I had met this man – I knew it. A surge of panic took hold of me, as if I had somehow revealed one of my darkest secrets, but the sensation quickly began to dissipate. The more my eyes focused on him, the less familiar he seemed. It felt like the memory had been cleaned from the annals of my mind. It wasn't long before the photo seemed to not make sense; the sensation nauseated me, I felt myself fainting. The last thing I heard was Shinji's gasp.

*

When I came to there was an echo of Silver Hair shouting at me to pay attention whilst the blackness and bright speckled memories formed a backdrop behind her. It was faint and felt as if I was trying to recall a long-lost memory, though as my brain began to work at full capacity (or at least what I would call full capacity) I knew it had only just happened. For a moment, a face flitted by my mind's eye, a man with black hair and blue eyes. I felt nauseous again so I forced it out of my mind.

"He's waking up. Jo, George, he's waking up." Aaron's voice called out, the rhythmic Irish twang summoned the rest of my friends.

"Kurt? Kurt, are you okay?" Jo said as she scooped her hand behind my neck, propping it up as if I was a newborn.

"Follow my hand." Another voice said. It was light and soft, there was a meekness to it but I followed the instructions regardless. A pale hand was shoved in front of my face, I followed it left then right, up then down, and finally two diagonal crosses before she spoke again. "He seems fine. Is there any food in here?"

"I'll check the fridge, but I doubt-" Shinji started but was cut off.

"I've got a butty in my pocket" George said.

"A what?!" Shinji laughed. "A butty?" He mimicked George's voice quite accurately.

"A sandwich, whatever. I picked it up just in case Anthony was hungry later, when M's staff came out with the tray of food." The sandwich was given to the owner of the pale hand. Jo lifted me up to sitting position.

"Eat this," said the new girl. I took a bite of it. Cheese and ham. As I chewed it I looked at the girl. Her skin was incredibly pale, porcelain almost and her silky black hair – which was both bushy and tamed - made it seem whiter still in contrast. I recognised her from the bus.

"Who are you?" I asked probably sounding ruder than I intended. Her pale face blushed bright red as she avoided my eye contact.

"Um, sorry. My name is Marie. I was walking past the house and I heard your friends shouting," she sounded apologetic for helping. "My mum and dad were nurses. I'm not really sure what I was doing but I just wanted to help."

75

"Oh." I took another bite of the ham 'n' cheese. "Thank you." I said through my stuffed mouth. I chewed for a moment as people watched me with concerned looks. "What happened?"

"You just dropped, mate." George said. "I was shouting about *Monopoly* and you just took a wobbler."

"You're probably overtired." Marie squeaked.

"You have been through a lot in fairness." Jo added.

"Yeah, but fainting again?" I asked, feeling embarrassed.

"Not like that's new to you, Kurt." George chimed in.

"Well, you're fine now at least." Shinji smiled at me.

"I tried to use my power but it didn't work." Anthony piped up and Lana smiled at him. "Shinji said it must be for," he tried hard to remember something, "abrasions and things," he finished, proudly.

"Thanks, Anthony. I really appreciate it." I said and he beamed at me.

I stood up shaking off the sense of disorientation. We sat round for a while with Jo asking if I was okay so many times, it felt as if she wanted me to tell her I wasn't. When the excitement of my episode was over, people bombarded Marie with questions which she answered meekly, clearly not enjoying the attention.

We each told her what we could do, George staying quiet throughout. Marie did not question his silence. Aaron and I showcased ours quickly and Marie in turn showed hers. She held her hands in front of her. Wisps of smoke began to wreathe around them before travelling the length of her arms. The smoke was constantly shifting, here and there it unfurled and trailed off in to nothingness. She then pushed her hand forward and as if a horse let loose from the starting pen, a thick stream billowed forward. It hit the wall, curling in on itself.

"That's fantastic!" Shinji beamed. "That was incredible."

The smoke instantly vanished. "It's nothing. It's not really useful for anything." She replied, gingerly.

"Are you joking?" George said. It was the first time he seemed excited about these abilities. "You can obscure vision making a smokescreen, you can choke people, uh, choke- asphyx- what's that word?"

"Asphyxiation." Jo offered. "Well, asphyxiate."

"Yeah, you can asphyxiate people if you need to. You can send smoke signals! Uh-"

"Ah, the most common form of communication." Shinji mocked.

"Well, can't even send texts anymore can we?" George's rebuttal came and Shinji opened his mouth before closing it and defeatedly nodded in agreement. "Better start getting ready for a comeback on all that primitive crap." Marie looked genuinely shocked that someone was saying nice things about her. She stood there awkwardly, clearly not knowing how to react. "Anyone have a sundial?"

"There is nothing else here." Lana said. She was direct but there was no rudeness in her voice. "We should move on to the next place." Everyone grabbed their current haul. George smiling at his *Monopoly* once more.

"Do you mind if-" Marie said, her voice was louder than it had been hitherto now. When we looked at her, she blushed again but continued. "Do you mind if I come with you all? I came here alone and I was wandering around more than searching. I would just feel a little bit - I mean, if I could come with you..." She trailed off.

"Of course you can," Jo decided, "I've spent the last three years with these two boys, it'd be nice to have more girls around. Plus, you saved Kurt's life. He owes you." She winked and Marie blushed before giggling.

With Marie now a part of our little group now, we searched a few more houses. I was feeling completely fine with the fresh air, though my legs were still a little wobbly. A few we entered were already quite bare, the furniture was out of place and pictures hung askew on the wall. They had clearly been raided by the other people that M brought along with us. We mostly picked up pillows, books, blankets and even some cacti. We had so many things now, that instead of people holding their individual haul, I created a large ball of telekinesis behind me and they used that as an invisible mule.

We walked through the town our little motley crew followed by these floating objects. The town really was beautiful. Aaron asked if we could rest somewhere for a while and George grunted his agreement. We sat in one of the gardens that overlooked the endless forest. There was a bench there that looked as if it had been carved by hand; it was rugged and uneven, but comfortable all the same. We talked about all manner of irrelevant things as we watched the clouds slowly travel across the sky. We did not talk about the destruction and death happening miles away; lightyears away. This was idyllic and too peaceful a moment to sully.

A silence fell on us. Jo was chewing on her lips for a while which meant she had something to say but was waiting for the last possible moment, when she had thought of every counter-argument before she set the topic up. After a while, she nodded meaning she was prepared and asked her question. "Why do you think she wants us to avoid the forest?" She asked.

"I dunno," I admitted. "But she was serious when she said it. For our own safety, obviously." There was a sudden cold breeze that sent a chill up my spine and brought with it a change of mood. I began to feel uncomfortable sitting here. It felt as if the forest was living and listening to our words. I eyed the ocean of trees suspiciously then shuddered the paranoia away.

"Shall we carry on looking?" I suggested, trying to sound nonchalant and the rest agreed. We quickly walked back towards the more densely populated areas. Here, we saw a group of people standing around - in front of them stood the muscular boy from the bus. Next to him was the weedy kid with the greasy hair. They looked like a comedy act standing next to each other, extreme opposites.

We approached them, each person standing there was holding a lumpy pillowcase over their shoulders like a bunch of ragtag Santa impersonators who didn't quite follow the whole red and white theme. "Hello." Jo chirped.

"One sec, babe," the muscular boy called out, holding his hand up to silence her. "We've covered most of the-" He carried on talking and in my head I counted down. *Three. Two. One.*

"*Babe?*" Jo mimicked, cutting him off again. *There it is.* "Sorry, for a second there. I thought you just called me '*babe*'?" The muscular boy stopped for a moment. The weedy boy pinched the bridge of his nose, lifting his glasses, shook his head and sighed. He looked warily at his larger friend.

"You've got a thing about cutting people off, haven't you?" He said. "Cut off the woman who saved our lives mid-speech, now here cutting me off."

"I was saying hello. Plus, I was making sure the injured people were treated." Jo said stubbornly. "Pretty sure the people who were healed would have been thankful." Jo looked at the crowd that the boy was addressing moments before "Were any of you healed?" She asked. There was an uncomfortable murmur of yes's and no's. One boy held up his hand. It was the first boy who was healed - the boy who hugged Anthony and Aaron.

"They fixed my neck. I was grateful." He admitted. The muscular boy scowled and Jo looked smug.

"See!" She said. "So, before you try causing arguments for no sake, I'd suggest thinking twice."

"Whoa, whoa, whoa. Someone has an attitude problem, don't they?" The boy laughed, indicating Jo as if she were part of some prestidigitation for the onlookers. "What's your name, babe?"

"I swear, if you call me babe one more time…" Jo threatened and the boy looked at me.

"Sorry, is 'babe' this twig's name for you?" He looked me up and down with pity, the way most people do. I casually glanced away as if I somehow didn't hear it. "Is she your babe?" He asked.

I felt a hot flush wash over me. The crowd was staring at me. The muscular boy and the greasy kid were looking at me. Aaron, Shinji, Lana, George, Anthony and Marie were watching me. I couldn't look away any longer. I had to reply, I had to say something, but I can't handle this sort of pressure. "Why would I call her babe, does she look like a talking pig?" Instantly, I regretted it.

"For Christ's sake, Kurt." Jo groaned as the boy burst in to laughter. There were a few titters from the crowd, and one boy, a plump bald boy with bug eyes and giant teeth laughed obsequiously almost as loud as the muscular boy.

"Are you serious?" He asked me, then to the greasy haired lad. "Did you hear what he just said?" He laughed pointing in my direction.

I felt my face reddening, blood rushing to my face. I had to redeem myself now or this is how people would remember me. "Don't you know it's rude to point?"

"Kurt, shut up!" Jo scolded me. She seemed more annoyed with me than him. Not sure how that worked out, but I clearly was destroying her image. "You're not talking to him, you're talking to me." She said to him, attempting damage control.

"Actually, I was talking to these and you came over interrupting as you please." He said, smiling at her.

"I was just say-"

"What's your name?" He interrupted. Jo's eyebrows were almost reaching orbit. "Not nice when people interrupt is it... babe?"

"Jo!" She snapped. "My name is Jo! What's your name?"

"Buzz." He said simply. "This is my mate, Blake." Blake didn't say hello but instead continued to gaze in our direction, bored of our presence.

"And why are you all together?" Jo asked ignoring Blake.

"Well, rather than scamper around like, well, you lot, we decided it'd be better to just work as one and get as much as possible. Makes sense, doesn't it?"

"*We* decided?" Jo said. "Doesn't look like you all decided when you're standing in front of them giving orders. Looks to me like you're trying to take charge. One of *those* people." She said rolling her eyes. A few people in the crowd shifted uncomfortably. Clearly, Jo was right.

"Well, it's worked so far and I haven't heard any complaints." He said, smugly.

"Probably because everyone is too scared to cause any more trouble. We've all been through enough. You shouldn't be coming here and telling people what to do." Jo said.

"Says the one who just told me what to do?" Buzz smirked.

"I said 'you shouldn't', not 'don't'." Jo's retort, simple but effective.

"Yeah!" I said backing Jo up. "Shouldn't and don't are different words."

"Oh my god, Kurt," Jo spat at me, "If you open your mouth one more time I'll rip your tongue out." Then she looked to Buzz. He smiled again.

"I like your attitude," he said with a wink. "Let's make sure we're assigned to the same dorm."

"I'd genuinely rather stick a fork in my eye," Jo replied. "Or yours…"

"Suit yourself. Think we're done now, babe. On your way." Buzz said and fluttered his hand at Jo indicating that he was finished with her.

Jo's face epitomised fury. She raised up her hand. Both Shinji and Lana shouted "No!" and grabbed it to stop her. Even I was shocked, Jo was never the sort of person to get worked up easily or resort to violence, but when she came across genuinely awful characters, she sometimes couldn't help herself. When Buzz saw what she was doing, he whimpered walking backward and tripped over Blake's foot. Blake panicked and tried to help him up, only succeeding in pulling himself to the floor. The chubby boy with the bulbous eyes waddled over to help them both up.

"You're crazy!" Buzz shouted.

"I didn't even do anything. I held my hand out." Jo laughed. "There we go," she said to the crowd. "That's who you're taking orders from, a coward." Buzz was wiping the dirt off his clothes. "See you back at the motel, *babe*. Let's go." As we began to walk, a few people began to peel away from the crowd heading toward the direction of the town hall.

There was a strange clicking sound. In front of us, two pairs of phantom feet appeared from nowhere, then the legs joined them. It was as if they were being scanned in to existence from bottom to top. After about five seconds, Blake and Buzz stood before us.

"His ability," Buzz said nodding at Blake. "Like teleportation." Then he held his hand out. "Mine," his hand began to shake violently, there was a humming sound coming from the sheer speed. He moved it closer to Jo who didn't recoil, even an inch. "If this touched you, it could literally rip through you."

"Try it and watch as George here makes you bleed from every orifice." Jo warned, holding her hand to George. "*Every* orifice." She repeated, menacingly. George broadened his shoulders and held his hands out.

80

Blake grabbed on to Buzz's shoulders and pulled him back. Then, in reverse as to how the appeared, they disappeared. Just as they vanished, the bug-eyed boy reached us. "What, where did they-?" He huffed and puffed. "Never mind, I see them. You guys better watch yourself." He tried to threaten. Jo's eyes narrowed and she smiled. The boy didn't expect that as a reaction, he withdrew - his shoulders raised and his chin sunk in to his chest removing any trace of a neck. "He- he shattered a door just by touching it." He said with less hostility. Jo stepped slightly forward and the boy instantly turned, waddling back to where Blake and Buzz had rematerialised.

Jo smiled back then looked to me as if she was about to kill me. "I swear, Kurt," she smacked me on the arm, "I have no idea," she smacked my other arm, "why you feel the need," she pushed my stomach, "to talk at all sometimes." She finished, staring at me for a moment then with a swift motion as quick as a spider catching a fly, she began to twist my nipple.

I yelled out and the rest of the group laughed at me. "That really was a poor display of verbal fencing, Kurt." Shinji agreed with Jo as I was rubbing the area my nipple once was.

"Let's go home." Aaron suggested. Everyone else agreed. The day was done. We headed toward the apex of the Town Hall which stood proudly above the bustle of smaller buildings – my nipples longing for peace from the smarting.

Chapter 9

The opening that separated the run-down motel from the Town Hall and school was cast in darkness. I looked at the stars above, brazen and unobscured by light pollution - I enjoyed the peacefulness of them, how, from here, they shimmered in silence; decorating the night sky. Then, as if being punished for a moment of peace, my mind snapped and the perspective changed. I thought about Silver Hair and her bizarre realm, all those windows in to others' minds, all the pain she could see. I shivered and tried to not think of neither stars nor Silver Hair.

M was waiting there, she had taken to sitting down. She looked a little worn out, more so than she had earlier, which of course, is understandable. A few of her staff members were dotted around the opening standing as still as sentinels. Two at either side of the motel door.

There were a few other people from the bus. Some were sitting around talking, some looking through their haul and some were just laying down as if the day had truly taken the life out of them. M smiled as we approached. Her eyes seemed to scan each one of us before finding our haul floating behind us. There was a flash of excitement in her eyes.

"Welcome back, Kurt." She said when I smiled at her. "Hello Shinji, Aaron." Her eyes stared at Jo for a moment. "Hm...?"

"Jo." Jo told her abruptly.

"Ah, yes. I suppose I must remember that for the next time you speak out of line." M smirked. I tensed and caught George's eye. We both waited for Jo to argue back, but again, it didn't come. I relaxed. Jo had never been so apprehensive in her life. It really was unnerving. "How are you feeling, Kurt? I see you had a little trouble out there." Her voice changed, there was genuine concern in it. I felt a flutter in my heart; not affection but appreciation.

"Wha- oh- yeah, I fainted - wait, how did you know?" I asked.

The smile that spread across her face was filled with warmth. "Kurt, I contacted and monitored you when you were over a hundred miles away. I kept an eye on everyone who was out in the village to ensure safety." Jo quietly scoffed with agitation. M's eyes found hers and lost all maternal traces but when she realised that was the extent of Jo's disobedience, she started back on me. "I sent two of my staff members in your direction to collect you, until this lady came in." Marie shrunk from her gaze.

"I didn't really do anything. My mum and dad were nurses so I thought I could help but, I uh, I'm not sure if I did, um…" Marie lost her words and trailed off.

"Ah but you made the effort to help. Once I felt Kurt waking up, I recalled my staff. I must say, Marie, that truly was a selfless deed." Then back to me. "So, you *are* feeling fine now? I could feel no discomfort when monitoring you, but of course, reading is different from feeling."

"Oh, yeah. I just - I'm not really sure what happened. I just sort of felt, dizzy - I guess - all of a sudden and then I just felt blurry. I can't really explain it. Sorry." The little girl appeared from behind her, she was wearing the same vacant expression on her face, but she was scribbling furiously on the clipboard M was holding earlier.

"He was looking at some photograph," George chimed in and M stared at me expectantly. "I found *Monopoly*, then Kurt was holding a photograph and then he fainted."

"Oh?" M said waiting for me to confirm. It was difficult to do so because I had genuinely forgotten about the photograph by now. Trying to recall it was as difficult as me finishing a hundred metre sprint: almost impossible.

"Uh, I vaguely remember holding it but I can't for the life of me remember the picture itself - as in, what it was or who was in it or… anything." I admitted.

"Fascinating," M said with the hint of a smile on her face. The little girl scribbled hastily on the notepad again. "Not to worry, should you feel faint again, we will have you looked at but it seems to have just been an overload. Well, you must feel hungry. The small selection of food you had earlier could not have sustained you so much that you cannot eat again, or am I incorrect?" There was a muttering of agreement with her words. Jo didn't reply, she wasn't making eye contact with M. M probably noticed and probably didn't care. "You remember eating the food before you left, Kurt?"

"Uh… Yeah?" I thought there was some sort of trick to the question, but I remembered it fine. "I tried to thank the staff member, but he didn't even say 'you're welcome' or anything."

"Yes. That sounds about right," she simply replied. "Well, we have real food downstairs waiting for you. I must notify you now however, that once down there you will not be able to come back out until tomorrow, so feel free to lounge about until sunset, or until the remaining subjects get back, as a few of the others have chosen to do." M gestured her arm out indicating those around us but nobody said they wanted to wait. "Wonderful. Ah, here is the last party we were waiting on. How very convenient; it is as if everyone began to head back just when I needed them to. I like it when things come together," the two staff members waiting at the motel doors sprung in to action and opened them. "Feel free to wait inside the main hall where it is warm. I will be in shortly."

We turned around to see Buzz, Blake and a few others approaching so we made our way in to the motel's main hall. They couldn't have many visitors staying over which would explain the lack of general maintenance. Regardless of whether the village was abandoned or not, the pictures hanging on the walls were dusty, which was fair enough, but some of them had cracked frames or the canvas itself was torn. The carpet was shredded and burned in places, whereas spiders had decided to take up permanent residency, or so it seemed from the cobwebs hanging *everywhere*. My body involuntarily shuddered as the scene in Jo's rooms flashed in to my head. All those legs, crawling over my parents.

My parents... *Were they okay? What if-* A sudden mental capriciousness stole over me, marring my ability to form coherent thoughts. It settled only when Jo spoke.

"I don't like her," she stated whilst everyone else was taking in the dilapidated hall. "She's rude. She's abrupt. She's self-righteous."

"You just don't like her because she's blunt with you." George said.

"Are you taking her side?!" Jo was incredulous. "You don't think she's rude? Seriously?"

"Well, I dunno. She seems a bit cold like, but, she doesn't seem *rude,* I don't think." Uh-oh, wrong thing to say to Jo.

"Right. Well, let's think about this. She holds some weird petty vendetta against me because I talked whilst she was talking, then pretends she's forgotten my name?"

"She didn't say their names either." Shinji pointed out, indicating George, Anthony and Lana.

"Yeah, but she didn't pretend she forgot them though, did she? I mean what is she, like, say, sixty-"

"She's nowhere near sixty! Maybe forty at most." George said over Jo.

"Oh my god, George. She's just behind that door, if you want to ask for her hand in marriage, I can walk you. I'd happily give you away."

"I don't think he'd be her type." Shinji said with a sly smile.

"Why?!" George asked, seemingly genuinely offended.

"I just mean she doesn't seem..." Shinji tried to say but Jo cut him off.

"I was being sarcastic. Maybe not sixty, but fortyish or whatever and she's acting like a six-year-old, no offence, Anthony. Speaking of kids, who is that little girl that follows behind her and why is she so quiet all the time?"

"Jo, calm down." I tried. "We're just tired and hungry. Let's get some food and have a nap, okay?"

"No, Kurt. You know she was being rude you're just too scared to say anything, like you always have been." That genuinely took me off guard. Jo was rarely this vicious, I mean, I know that's not very vicious but Jo would rarely say sly things like that for the sake of it, so it was vicious in comparison. "Also, did she say she was waiting on 'subjects' and then when that idiot Buzz came she was all 'oh and here they are'? Why would she call them subjects? Does she think-"

Jo was cut off by the doors swinging open. The two staff members stepped in keeping them open. M walked in, followed by the small girl, Buzz, Blake, the bug-eyed boy, the remainder of the group that stayed with him earlier as well as the people who were lounging outside.

She stood in silence for a moment and closed her eyes, took a deep breath then smiled. Quickly her staff piled in. The two staff members at the door entered and closed the door behind them. As one, they began to work their way around the walls. They pulled down thick shutters - which seemed to appear from nowhere - over the windows. After a while the room was devoid of any natural light.

The weak lamps were flickering away. The staff members had now stopped behind M in a line, quiet and unmoving. There was a moment of silence in which I questioned M's sanity. Then the room itself began to shake. Motes of dust fell from the roof. A few people coughed. The spider webs tore and fell away to tatters. The pictures on the wall began to rumble, it was a miracle that they managed to stay up. There were a few gasps and yells when suddenly, the walls were lost from sight as four heavy steel barricades rose from the floor. There was a deafening clanging as they reached the height of the roof and locked in to place.

"Calm down," M called out calmly. I was panicking too, but her voice was like an untouched tropical island amid a torrential storm. Instantly I knew I was safe. As there were no more yells or cries of fear, I gathered that the feeling was mutual amongst the others.

The transformation was complete. We were now in a large steel box. Any hint of the foyer we were standing in moments ago had disappeared except for the worn-out carpet we were standing on. The flickering orange glow of the lamps was replaced by harsh, bright fluorescent-white clinical lights.

Everyone squinted as they shone on us. George was holding Anthony whose head was buried in his shoulders, whispering in to his ear. The room shook once more and then it began to descend.

"You are now about to enter the true reason this institute was constructed," M announced, ignoring everyone's uneasiness. "Below here is my laboratory. It is one of the largest in the country and was initially built to accommodate a plethora of research subjects." She smiled. "I say 'initially' because once my research began to bound ahead of all others - deemed most groundbreaking - it demanded more resources and a larger force. The other teams were either relocated to other facilities or integrated in to my research, made to follow my orders.

"The town which you have just looted was evacuated a long time ago. The inhabitants were given the option to stay, or to be in receipt of a lump sum that most would have to work a lifetime to save. We told them this place would be used as accommodation for military infantry. Needless to say, the majority left. Those who denied the offer to relocate did not last long; the town - empty of their friends - lost its charm. They were still given the option of the compensatory sum to start their lives elsewhere.

"I am aware this sounds horrid, as if we uprooted their lives and believe me I asked for the lab to be constructed in a different location," she sighed. "I did not want to have to deal with civilians interrupting any research, I wanted a remote location, but there was already a whole town here as the perfect alibi. I was soon convinced, I could work unhindered. The town consisted mostly of twelve different families who moved out to the same areas. We did not split anyone up. We also gave them the right to visit whenever they wished which is why so many of them left their belongings... but it seems they won't be needing them any longer."

The elevator was still rumbling away as we descended. Though it was moving at a snail's pace, it felt like we were so far underground that we would be coming out at the other side of the world at any moment now. We continued to listen to M's story.

"May I add to my justification, our research and the research of the other teams that were situated here prior to their removal has forwarded medical science in a way never before achieved, never mind conceived. It was privately funded by: billionaires, philanthropists, mavericks, eccentrics and their cohorts - those who wanted personal access to any products we created. As we gained traction, the government started to fund us which meant the tried and tested procedures were shared with facilities all around.

"In fact, my research has not only helped map the functions of the brain in more detail than previously thought possible, but the research has also opened gates to treatments that hitherto now were impossible. We have saved countless lives here and we conduct our experiments in the most humane manner possible. We are efficient and in the interest of modesty, because of myself and my *partner,*" she spat that word out as if it left a bad taste in her mouth, there was clearly hostility behind it and even though I had no idea who this partner was, even *I* felt like I disliked them. "We were on the forefront of evolutionary research!" She exclaimed.

I scanned the crowd and locked eyes with the first one that Anthony and Aaron healed just after we had got off the bus. He smiled and nodded in my direction. I smiled back and tried to mimic his nod, though it came across more like a twitch. A look of confusion spread across his face before he nodded again, the meaning behind this one was not as clear as the last. I was relieved when he turned away from me and back to M.

"Which is why we required the privacy. The experiments were never unsafe or particularly dangerous but to get the best results possible we could not afford the slightest chance of interruption." The large elevator stopped suddenly with a jolt, a thud and a loud clanging. It shook violently for a couple of seconds which nearly knocked me off my feet, but M was not phased at all. She stood still with perfect balance. The big iron doors opened revealing a corridor so bright and harshly lit that even the vainest collection of people would dare not be seen in it. There was a slight tingling in my cornea as all moisture was burned from them.

"This is Sub-Level One," M explained as she stepped out with the little girl. Her staff waited at the back of the elevator as we followed her out. "I shall not bore you with the details of construction and the intended use of each floor as it is irrelevant. This is where the accommodation is located as well as food hall. That is all you need to know.

"There should be no reason for any of you to go to any of the other levels, except maybe for level Sub-Level Two which is where the medical facilities are located. We have everything we need here except for natural sunlight - that is the only downside of working in this specific laboratory or so I have been told – I was never phased. Everything else is state-of-the-art and in working order."

As she walked down the corridors, her confident footsteps echoed whereas all of us huddled in the group behind her were nervously shuffling our feet. I looked behind to see her staff walking in three rows side by side. M stopped as she got to a large set of white windowless double doors.

"This is the food hall. If you need to leave this lab, please present one of my staff with a written note requesting a time. *Do not ask them a direct question.* They will bring any note directly to me and if I grant you the request, they will come right back to you. Paper and pens have been provided in the dorms," she continued, "I cannot emphasise the fact enough that this is for your own safety and any request would only be denied under dire circumstances, but I must take measures to ensure your wellbeing which I cannot do without keeping tabs." She really did care for our safety, I felt as if my soul itself was being hugged. "Now," she said with a fresh tone, "any questions?"

"Can I try calling my mum?" The bug-eyed boy who was with Buzz and Blake earlier asked furtively. M looked at him as if she didn't understand the question, as if this was not something she expected but she regained composure. The boy's hands were once again fumbling and caressing one another as if he was washing them under a tap. Buzz looked at him as if he had just asked the most embarrassing question possible. I on the other felt the same anxiety I felt earlier - when I thought of my parents - flitting to the forefront of my mind, demanding and wraithlike. My throat grew dry and my eyes started to tear up.

"I understand you must be worried, Geoff," M said softly and Jo tutted petulantly at the use of his name, "as I understand everyone else must be worried. I will not lie to you, communication at the moment is extremely limited. I have delegated the task of finding more people to bring in to the safety of this sanctuary to certain staff members; this is their priority as it is helpful in a symbiotic way - one of these members have been ordered to focus primarily on your families. They will work around the clock to make contact, but until then there is not much more I can do." I still felt unsure.

M grimaced. "I cannot locate a specific mind, my ability does not work that way. You cannot give me a name or description and I connect to a directory; my ability, like yours, has limits. I can only scan until I find an open mind, a welcoming personality - I can always go back to these minds like I did with many of you, but that is as concise as I can get," she sighed.

"One of my major goals right now is to remove these limitations; if my research proves fruitful, as I am sure it will, I will be able to do more. Until then, safety of those here is crucial. We must be thankful for that much." She paused for a moment, her eyebrows furrowed. "You must trust me. Every one of you." She knew what she was doing, she had done so much for us already. Of course she was working to bring our families here. "I will update you all tomorrow on the situation outside of these walls, but for now you should eat, decorate your dorms and rest.

"Oh, and Jo, I would like to correct one minor misconception you deem important... I am forty-three." Jo looked taken aback and M had managed to achieve the impossible - she made Jo blush. Without an invitation for more questions, M looked at her staff behind us and smiled. Instantly they broke formation. Two of them walked around us and opened the doors ahead, some shot off in different directions and some, with M, swiftly retreated back to the huge lift.

The young girl's blank and emotionless eyes locked on to mine for a moment. I stared back, paralysed in place. For a fraction of a second I thought she was about to say something. Her eyes widened ever so slightly and her eyebrows twitched before her face went back to the blank canvas it had been since I saw her. She turned and followed M.

We walked in to the food hall. It was large, white, characterless and just as clinical as the corridors. Tables were set out equidistant across the whole hall. A few people were already sitting here eating, all wearing black shirts and jogging pants, some with black jackets. I noticed a few of them from the bus. There were two empty tables next to each other which Jo beelined for.

"Let's join these so we can all sit together," she said business-like. Without even thinking, I gently placed our haul on the floor up against the wall. Then I held my hand out letting my ability wrap around each of the chairs, pulling them out of the way. Aaron gasped and watched me with wide eyes. My telekinesis enveloped the two tables and I pushed them together before realigning the chairs.

"That was so exciting!" Aaron said. I didn't even think about doing it. To me it was as natural as just walking over and manually moving the chairs, like an extension of what I would usually do, I didn't do it to show-off or be lazy, I just wanted to sit down. I always want to sit down.

We ate and listened as Jo began to whinge about every aspect of M. From her ability to her shoes. Not one stone was left unturned when Jo had decided she disliked someone. I just wished it wasn't M she chose, why could she not just stick to Buzz? She went on and on without the need of anyone else talking back to her. At one moment, I tried to hush her when a member of staff walked past which, of course, only made Jo raise her voice. I sighed in resignation.

She worked herself in to a huff, only finishing her rant having psychoanalysed M, drawing her own conclusions about how her childhood must have been, as well as foreseeing her possible future. When people realised she was done with her diatribe, they began their own conversations. Shinji began to tell us anecdotes from his life, each delivered with the wit of a professional comedian and story-teller. I spent half of the time staring at his hair rather than listening to his stories. Aaron then spoke about life in Ireland, his family and how much he prefers cityscapes to landscapes. George argued this but Aaron claimed that if George grew up surrounded by so much green, he wouldn't appreciate the 'beauty of nature' when it means there is literally *nothing* to do.

Even Lana chimed in talking about her brother. I noticed Lana was reticent at best but when she did speak, it was always something poignant or interesting. I hoped one day someone would speak about me with the love she had for her brother. She couldn't help but smile when she talked about all the things he would get up to before he fell ill. Her voice cracked every so often, each time it did, I felt an empathic jolt of pain in my heart. I just wanted to hug her but I feared it would be inappropriate.

George asked Marie some questions but it seemed she had withdrew back in to her shell and didn't feel comfortable answering in detail. It was clear she was not being rude and Jo subtly stopped George's questions by telling people about her own life.

When Jo finished, I started to tell them all about my life before moving for University, not that there was much to tell, when I was interrupted. The first boy Aaron and Anthony healed - the boy I had the awkward nod exchange with - walked up and took a seat as comfortably as if he had been sitting with us the whole time and was simply returning from a toilet break.

"What's up?" He asked.

"We're good and you?" Jo said with a hint of suspicion. She looked over to where Buzz, Blake and Geoff were sitting with a few others who were clad in black. They seemed to be absorbed in a story Buzz was telling.

"I'm good. I'm good," he said with a slow nod. "I just wanted to come and say thank you for healing me. I wanted to say it before but you were arguing with Buzz and then we were in the lift and I wasn't going to cut boss lady off after she spoke to you the way she did."

"Rude, you mean?" Jo asked, skillfully planting her seeds.

"Yeah," he agreed and Jo beamed taking her victory. She smiled in George's direction. George rolled his eyes and turned his focus back to the boy. "Besides she scares me. I'm really thankful for her help and stuff but she's odd, isn't she?" He looked around, then leaned in lowering his voice. "I was speaking to Steph before - one of the other people from the bus. She said they stopped searching the village early and came back to the opening –

apparently, mid-conversation, M mumbled something about a picture, held her hand up and told Steph to 'stop her incessant prattle.'" Jo held her hands up as if that was evidence enough that M was not to be liked. "She said that M closed her eyes as if she just had a migraine or something - even though she was fine through their conversation - she stumbled and nearly fainted. Steph tried to pull her up but one of the weird staff people literally threw her to the floor and helped M up themselves. I'm not about that kind of life.

"She's clearly someone important, but I'm definitely not going to get on the wrong side of her." This information seemed to please Jo to no end. His words, in her mind, had proved all her doubts to be one hundred percent true. "But yeah, thank you!" He said. Then as if he had just remembered it, "my name's Dorian, by the way. Not sure if I said it before." Each of us at the table told him our names in turn and Dorian's face scrunched up as he tried to submit them to memory.

"So... What was it like walking round with him?" Jo asked with a nod toward Buzz, hoping for a second victory.

Dorian groaned. "Horrible. He kept ordering people about. Not cool at all. Telling us how we should raid a home as if every single one of them would have an army waiting for us. One of the girls there didn't listen to him and he *flipped* out saying that his Dad was in the army and that he knows what he's talking about. Seriously no chill."

"I thought so." Jo couldn't stifle her smug smile, happy that her judge of character once again was agreed upon by Dorian. "I could tell."

"Besides, that little guy, Blake? He's like his shadow. He'd do whatever Buzz said as soon as he said it. I think they've known each other for a while - at least before all of this happened anyway. That fat guy as well, Geoff, he's such a suck up. 'Good idea, Buzz!' 'Great plan, Buzz!' But then again, his power is to literally smell like dead farts."

"Looks like I may be quite lucky then," George said, then paused for a moment. "What can you do?"

"Uh, I can't show you down here 'cause I need earth but I can make it do what I want. I can move it and stuff. It's so cool but 'cause there's nothing down here I'm useless really. Well, not useless but I can- oh my god!" Dorian gasped suddenly. I jumped in my chair with the unexpected change. "You guys have *Monopoly*?!" He shouted with glee, his eyes on our haul. George preened. "Can we play? Not now, obviously, but," he looked over at Buzz's table. "Can I come to your dorm and play later? Buzz has already decided I should stay next to them because he likes what I can do but I'll be honest, that's the last place I want to sleep. Would you mind? I'll be the banker if you don't have enough pieces. I just love *Monopoly*."

Now it was George's turn to beam and Jo's turn to roll her eyes. George and Dorian went in to a lengthy conversation about *Monopoly* and its superiority compared to other board games. This somehow shifted in to a conversation about games in general which soon segued in to the complexities of old, obscure movies and the reasons they shouldn't be remade. Jo seemed almost relieved when one of M's staff came to collect us.

"Dorian?" Buzz called over. His group was standing with another staff member, a few of them still getting their things together. He tapped Blake and with a quick nod of his head indicated toward us. Blake placed his hand on Buzz's shoulder. The two of them began to deconstruct from the other side of the room, collapsing in on themselves from head to foot. They reappeared right in front of us. Buzz was staring at Dorian. "Where're you going?"

"They found *Monopoly*! I want to have a game," he said simply. Buzz gave us a dirty look, then shook his head.

"But you said you'd stay with us?" Buzz replied.

"No. You said I'll stay with you, I didn't say anything."

"So, what? Even though you came with us all day you're going to leave us at the last second to be with these?" He said. I caught eye contact with Blake for a moment as he sighed, he instantly broke it and began to examine the floor.

"What are you talking about? Look around you," Buzz did. "Everyone here is scared. Including you." Buzz scoffed. "Not one of us have an idea of what's going on except for boss lady. Not one person knows what to do. Why does me sleeping in a different dorm matter so much? We're safe and we're all here together." Buzz stared at Jo but replied to Dorian.

"Just because…" he managed, weakly. Blake was still looking at the same spot on the floor.

Jo snorted. "Fantastic argument. Really well thought out. Come on." Jo turned around and the rest of us began to follow. Buzz grabbed Dorian's shoulder and spun him round. At this, Jo held her hands out in Buzz's direction, Aaron had conjured two balls of water which floated and rippled ominously above his shoulders.

Geoff, from the other side of the room waddled over, his face bright red. He stood on the other side of Buzz who was staring, unblinkingly in to the centre of Jo's splayed palm. Shinji slapped Jo's hands down and shook his head at Aaron. The water dissipated instantly.

"Make your choice," Buzz said. "These psychopaths, or us."

"Buzz, you're really underestimating how much I love *Monopoly*." Dorian replied which made George and Marie titter. Buzz's face grew almost as red as Geoff's.

"So, it's decided. See you tomorrow, *babe*." Jo emphasised the last word cheerfully with a wink displaying her shameless capacity of utter pettiness, then under her breath, "Kurt, don't say a word."

We left the food hall leaving Buzz, Blake and Geoff standing in the door. The staff member led us down a maze of corridors. One after the other, each one was identical to the last. I was impressed that he didn't get lost. The doors looked the same, the walls and floors were absolutely spotless. I was convinced that once or twice we had travelled down the same corridor. We finally stopped after entering through a large, heavy door that opened in to another corridor with a dead end. The staff member left without so much of a bye.

"Well, here we are. Home sweet home." George said looking around at the characterless white walls, the shiny floor reflecting the bright white lights. "It's nice, innit?"

"Let's just get set up and sleep," Jo said.

The hallway itself was quite long. It had thirteen doors, not including the one we just entered from which, I noticed, had a buzzer and speaker next to it. Most of the doors contained bedrooms, but the two at the end of the hallway had a bathroom/shower in one and a utility/washing room in the other. The door just to the left of the entrance opened in to a kitchen-lounge hybrid. The room was divided in two by a counter which had chairs all the way round it. The kitchen side contained everything you could want in a kitchen except for a dishwasher whereas the carpeted lounge area had only two couches, a lamp and a bookshelf. It was not the homeliest of rooms, but I supposed it would serve its purpose for any scientist living here for a month or two.

The rest of the doors opened in to rooms. Each was an exact copy of the last; carpeted with the most hideous brown and containing a single bed. There was a small wardrobe and a fitted desk for study and research above which was a small shelf. In fact, the rooms were not dissimilar to student accommodation in a sense. They all contained what was needed and nothing else.

For the next thirty minutes, we began to personalise our rooms. I managed to convince the others I should have a *Rubik's cube* which Marie said she found, but would never use it because it frustrated her more than challenged her. There were more books than anyone could ever need. From classics to modern and even a few Shakespeare plays.

I tried moving the bed around but the dimensions of the room were so awkward that it didn't really fit anywhere else; I didn't mind though, it is much easier to try and move a room round when you can literally not lift a muscle yet pick up the heaviest object.

When I placed the bed back where it was, I sat on the edge of it with my legs crossed and my head resting in my hands. I was exhausted - I had more exercise in the past two days than my entire life combined. Everything that had happened since I woke up with my ability played through my head again but this time I felt numb to it. Now that M had us safe and I didn't have to take responsibility for the safety of my friends, a giant weight had lifted off my shoulder.

I was pondering on whether to shower when I heard a strange noise. I looked around the room, my eyes darting from one point to another like a wild animal, wondering what it could be when I realised it wasn't coming from my room, it was next door. A sniffling. That couldn't be right, it was Jo's room. Jo doesn't sniffle.

I hesitated for a moment before I stood up and walked out to see Shinji and Aaron going through the diminished pile. They both picked up a plant plot with a fake flower in at the same time, then began to insist the other should have it.

"Honestly, I just thought it was nice but it would look better in your room." Shinji implored but it didn't work.

"How can it look better in my room when they're all the same?" Aaron asked. They both noticed me at the same time and smiled before going back to their argument of niceties. I slipped in to Jo's room. She spun round looking alarmed and then relaxed when she realised it was me.

"You can still knock," she said but I knew it was typical Jo being defensive and brave. Poor girl.

"I'm sorry, I just heard... Are you okay?" I asked.

"Considering everything, yeah, I'm okay," she replied. So strong.

"Jo, you don't need to hide it you know?" I said with empathy.

"Kurt, what're you talking about?" I could hear confusion in her voice.

"Okay..." I continued, softly. "I heard you sniffling, Jo. It's okay."

"I don't sniffle."

I decided to be blunt, as Jo would have been. "I heard you crying, Jo. Are you sure you're okay?"

"I wasn't crying?"

"It's okay, you know?"

"I know, but I wasn't crying." I looked in to her eyes and realised all the tell-tale signs of crying were absent. No red eyes, no marks from rubbing the tears away.

"I was just saying," I began. "If you wanted to," a knot began to form in my throat. "*If* you needed to cry, I would understand." My voice was beginning to crack.

Jo's eyebrows shifted ever so slightly. "Come here, Kurt," she said, holding her hands out.

I hurried over to her and she hugged me as *I* began to sob. "Honestly, Jo," I forced out between heavy breaths. "I really wouldn't judge at all." Jo held me, rocking me ever so slightly. Every so often she would come out with a gentle 'shh' or 'I know, I know'.

Her door opened again and I pushed her away with more force than I intended. She yelped in fright and I began to busy myself with her shelf, particularly focusing on one of the screws. When Jo regained her composure, she called out. "Jesus, why do you and Kurt think it's okay to not knock anymore?"

"Wha- oh, sorry." George's voice sounded vaguely apologetic.

I started to twist the screw with my fingers even though it didn't budge an inch. "Oh, hey George." I said trying to sound as casual as possible. "Howztricks, buddy?" *Too casual.*

"Have you been crying, mate?" He asked, probably deduced from my voice and new slang.

"No," I lied.

"Yes," Jo said at the exact same time. "There's no shame in it, Kurt. We've been through a lot."

"Anthony's asleep. He started crying as soon as we sat down. He was saying he's missing his parents, his house, his friends and that he was excited to go back to school and, ugh, I feel really bad for him, but don't really know what to say?" He sighed thoughtfully. "I checked the kitchen, by the way. There's food there for us. Shall we go make supper and play *Monopoly* to distract us?" That sounded like the best idea there ever could have been.

We knocked on everyone else's door. I noticed Lana's eyes, too, were red raw but at the mention a cup of tea before bed she smiled. We left Anthony asleep and the rest of us sat in the kitchen. The atmosphere in the room was equally tense and relaxed. Each and every one of us had a lot on our minds, but it was clear to see that we would look out for one another. Regardless of my inability to speak to people easily, I often believe I have a good judge of character. For all I knew, I could be wrong but it seemed like Lana, Shinji, Aaron, Dorian and Marie were just as friendly as Jo and George - only time would tell, but when things got better and we left this little lab, I promised myself there and then that I would try and stay in touch with them.

There was not much conversation until George made tea and toast for everyone and Dorian eagerly began to set up *Monopoly*. As George said, there were not enough pieces. Aaron told us to hold on before we start, then sat on the kitchen counter, his hands moving here and there, his fingers working away at incredible speed. When he came back to the board which now was set in the middle of the carpet, he revealed an ice-dog and ice-car which as far as I could tell, were perfect replicas of the actual ones. Shinji, George, Dorian, Jo and Marie began to play. I wanted to be the banker, because I enjoyed taking part but some of the games were just too stressful. Lana watched as an overseer to stop anyone from cheating.

Amazingly, as a group we began having fun. Of course, we had to get the rules straightened out because no two people have the same concept of how *Monopoly* should be played. We were laughing, joking and mocking one another. We were safe from the horror out there and were thankful for it.

Dorian's self-professed love for the aforementioned board game was an understatement. He was incredibly competitive but not in an obnoxious way. Every time someone would roll the dice, he would throw his arms out as if at any moment someone would try and tamper with the outcome, he would watch intently as they moved around the board making sure they travelled the correct number of spaces and even when they didn't land on one of his properties, he would hold the game up and check each one of his cards.

Whenever he landed on someone else's property, Dorian would offer them a free pass next time they landed on his in the hopes of not having to pay. He tried to form bonds, tried to cut ridiculous deals and almost cried when he was sent to jail claiming that the way he threw the dice wasn't right and he should be given another roll first. I didn't dare admit that I was telekinetically tampering with his rolls just so see his reaction.

Before long, we decided to put *Monopoly* on pause. I pondered the possibility of someone, somewhere in the world since the creation of this game, managing to complete it in one sitting and decided it was probably unheard of. We sat up in to the early hours of the morning talking to one another as if we had all known each other for years.

It wasn't long before Aaron fell asleep with his head resting on Shinji's lap. Shinji, for his part, didn't seem to care at all that this person he had only met today was using a part of his body as a pillow and my stomach fluttered with appreciation for the open attitudes of these people.

Marie convinced Lana to let her plait her hair. Lana did not really put up a fight, but sat there talking to Shinji about Poland, and, the whole time, she was smiling - especially when she was speaking about her brother. Shinji listened intently and would often chime in with a "that sounds wonderful." Again, I felt my stomach flutter with jolts of sentimentality.

I soon found myself leaning on Jo's shoulder whilst she was further questioning Dorian on how Buzz treated people. Dorian, it seemed was giving her all the answers she wanted because Jo was only getting more enthusiastic about how right she was... which of course she knew already, regardless of Dorian's reassurance. I fought to stay awake, but with the gentle hum of different conversations and the atmosphere now void of any tension or awkwardness, I allowed the feeling of complete contention to lull me. My last thought before I was away was how lucky I was that M found me when she did and I dared not think of the outcome if she did not.

Chapter 10

As quickly as I felt the real world slipping away, I felt *her* world forming around me, taking shape. It was as if she had been waiting for me. The kitchen and my friends were soon lost to the black realm and its only resident.

"Hello, Kurt," she said in a tone that indicated familiarity. "How have you been?"

I looked at her suspiciously. "I've been okay, actually," I said tentatively. "I think I'm safe for now at least."

"Oh, that's great news," she smiled and I couldn't quite decipher if there was sarcasm there. We floated there, staring in to each other's eyes for a while. "I've been well, too." She finally said.

"Oh, sorry," I blustered. "How have you been? What have you been up to?"

"Not much, surprisingly." She said softly, I could hear the sarcasm in that one. "I've been waiting on you actually." She saw the look of surprise in my face and smirked. "I have something to show you."

"Are those closed windows open now?" I asked, but she made a noise that was a mix of a grunt and a sigh, grabbed me by the neck and pulled me with her. We traversed the great expanse for a while until she stopped in front of a window. "Watch this."

The window displayed a vast green field as a small patch. Whosoever this vision belonged to was flying incredibly high. After a few moments, the vision snapped to her leg which was spurting with blood. A hand smacked over the wound, then the second joined it. It began to blur as tears obscured it. I could see the vast field grow larger as this person hurtled to the ground – unable to concentrate on flying. As she got closer, there was a small group of black dots which turned out to be a group of people who were each holding crude weapons.

There was a moment were the vision paused as the owner managed to stop herself crashing in to the floor, in to death. The group of people seemed to be howling with laughter as they crowded around her. One woman holding a gun was grinning and another patted her on the back. They tried to grab whoever the vision belonged to, but the person tried to fight. Then, the woman holding the gun turned it round and with a great force smashed it to the eyes. After that, the vision went black before replaying.

"Oh my god." I gasped. I could feel tears already trying to form. "What happened to her?"

Silver Hair frowned at me. "Awful, isn't it? But I think you need a closer look." She grabbed the back of my head and forcefully shoved it in to the window before I could even think of protesting.

I was suddenly inside the person's mind. The vision replayed over again, but this time I could *hear* the world around me. The wind whipping past the ears, the scream as she was shot. Her panicked and desperate sobs as she tried to staunch the blood flow. It was a different language, but it was clear she was praying as she hurtled to what she must have thought would be her death, the jeering of the black dots getting clearer the closer she got. The sheer effort exerted to activate her power and stop the impact. The congratulating of the shooter. The begging to, I imagine, be left alone. The thud of the gun that knocked this poor soul unconscious. Then I was ejected from the window.

I was crying this time. "Is she... Is she dead?"

"No, not dead." Silver Hair said in a bored voice. "My guess is she's unconscious and she's just replaying the last moment of consciousness in her mind. I've not seen this happen until now."

"So," I gulped. "So, how can you be sure she's not dead?"

"Look around you, child," she snapped. "You may not have noticed but the number of windows around have decreased massively." There were still billions scattered around, but now she mentioned it, they did look diminished in number. "They cease to exist here when they die," her face grew dark and she said gravely. "I've seen it happen. The last moments in countless people's lives."

"But..." I was lost for words. "Why did they shoot that girl?"

"I can't be sure. I have only witnessed the same as you." Silver Hair said rolling her eyes. "But, from other visions, Kurt, I think I may have the answer. There is a common theme. It seems not everyone out there has been awoken." George's face shifted in my mind's eye. "Human nature consists of pettiness and spite more than you can know. I've seen, from the minds of the gifted, plenty of cases like this. Those without abilities capturing, brutalising and killing those with."

"But," I squeaked, "we have to do something! We have to help her."

At this, she beamed. "Exactly." She took hold of me again and we began to soar through the void until we reached her destination: the two blocked windows. "This is exactly why we need to free my daughter and this second window, whether it be her child or not. They must be in danger – both windows have been blocked this whole time. Unfortunately, you are my only means of their rescue." She grabbed my shoulder and spun me round until we were face to face. "It may only be a matter of time before they are lost, like so many others. Do right by me." Then she shoved at my chest.

*

With more effort than anyone should be expected to exert when waking up, I forced myself out of bed. I was still in the clothes I was wearing the day before. I could feel them clinging to my body with sweat which is when I noticed just how dehydrated I felt. I walked out of the room to get a glass of water, when in the hallway I saw Aaron and Shinji sitting at the end of the corridor.

"Hello." I croaked.

"You do not *not* look great in the mornings." Shinji notified me and Aaron cackled.

"Yeah," I said trying to tame my hair with my hand. "I'm not a morning guy. What are you both doing in the hallway?"

"Waiting for a shower. Lana's in there, but she's taking forever!" Shinji mimed banging on the door. "No, I'm joking, she just got in."

"Do you always wake up this late?" Aaron asked me.

"What time is it?"

"I don't actually know," he admitted, "but you're the last one awake anyway. George and Jo are in the kitchen. Oh, there's a note- oh, and clothes."

"One sentence at a time, Aaron." Shinji remarked.

"Want your shower early, do you?" Aaron said with mock anger and from his hands shot tiny jets of water. They soaked Shinji from head to toe. Shinji stood up instantly holding his shirt out trying to rinse the water.

"I can't believe you actually- I'm soaked. I can't believe you just did that me." He said with a half-laugh, half-shout.

"Once sentence at a time, Shinji." Aaron replied and Shinji burst in to laughter. Aaron held his hands out absorbing the moisture leaving Shinji completely dry once more.

I walked into the kitchen and was hit with a powerful whiff of food. I could smell sausages, bacon, eggs and an underlying smell of tea and toast.

"G'afternoon, sunshine." George called out from one of the couches. He was sitting next to Anthony who waved at me with a smile before looking at my hair. His face went blank. Once again, I pushed my hair down. "Want something to eat?" George asked and I only nodded.

I sat myself next to Jo who had an empty plate in front of her, Marie was on the other side of the counter speaking to Dorian. As I sat, Marie poured me a glass of orange juice and Dorian decided he should tell me just how delicious George's cooking is and persisted even when I told him I had been eating it for the past three years.

"Good sleep?" Jo asked when Dorian had finished telling me he had never had a pepper-to-scrambled-egg ratio quite as wonderful as this one.

"It was alright, but I can't remember getting to my room. Who brought me there?" I asked.

Jo nodded toward Dorian and then George. "These two."

"You *were* having a bit of a mare though, mate." George said. "Kept mumbling about being shot." In my mind's eye, I saw the blood spurting out of the leg and hurtling to the green patch of field below.

"Yeah, uh…" I was about to tell them about Silver Hair but I stopped myself. If I tell them, they'd either think I was disturbed or try and make a big thing out of it. Frankly, I was too tired. "Must have been everything that's happened taking its toll me or whatever. Active imagination." Jo scrutinised me for a second, I stared back trying my hardest to conceal my thoughts, as if she was the telepath. Her eyes narrowed. She could always sense reticence, even when people didn't mean to be. "This is delicious, George." I said quickly making sure I closed the time-window for her to speak to me.

"Thank you, kindly," he chirped, oddly jolly.

"Oh," Marie squeaked and bent over picking something up from one of the chairs. "These are yours." In her hands was a pile of folded black clothes. I appreciated how neat they were before I unfolded them to look: a black shirt, a black jumper, a black jacket, black exercise pants and black pumps. There was a little tag on each item with calligraphic '𝒦urt' on it.

"Ugh." Is all I could reply. Loose clothing usually meant exercise and I was not ready for this.

"There was a big pile of them when I came in this morning." Marie said.

"Each one of them tagged with our name," Jo added, "and sizes which I think is a bit weird."

"I mean, Kurt can make things float with his mind, so knowing our clothes size isn't that weird. Actually, it's quite ordinary in comparison." George said.

"Oh, I swear…" Jo growled through gritted teeth pointing a fork in his direction ominously.

"I'm just saying." George said with his hands up in the air.

"It came with a note." Dorian said. He looked to the left, then to the right before checking his pockets. "Uh... Ah." He lifted his plate up and underneath was a crumpled piece of paper with splashes of red and brown sauce, a squashed bean sat at the top. "Here it is." He picked the bean off and handed it over. It had the same handwriting as the tags. I skimmed over it quickly before reading it again.

Tenants of Dormitory #3

I hope you slept well. Please change in to the exercise uniforms provided. There will be one for each of you; at the end of the day you will place these in the laundry room. New sets will be distributed when necessary.

When you are ready, please buzz the button at the end of your corridor and someone will come along to collect you.

You will be brought outside for testing.

Sincerely,

M.

"Testing?" I asked. Jo sipped her coffee and nodded at me. The look she gave me had some smug meaning to it but I ignored it.

"Prob'ly," Dorian said with a mouthful of toast - seemingly his stomach was as bottomless as George's. "Something to do with our abilities." He finished. Jo opened her mouth, I could feel the mordacity about to pour, but she stopped herself. We smirked at one another. Dorian was the one who agreed M was odd and she obviously knew it was best not to jeopardise that alliance.

Lana entered wearing her black exercise clothes, her hair was still wet. "So baggy," she said before she threw herself next to Anthony. Anthony looked up at her clearly not sure how to react. Lana looked back at him, stretched her exercise pants out and said, "why does that lady think I'm so fat, Anthony?" Anthony gave a hearty chuckle. "That Shinji is so sweet," she continued, completely changing the conversation.

I really liked Lana already, though I could never be sure how to approach her. She was either talkative and sweet, or on the verge of tears. It seemed a shower, some food and clean clothes (regardless of how baggy) did wonders for her mood.

"I come out the shower to see both boys fighting and laughing to get in before the other, then Shinji says he will be a gentleman and walk me to my room," she held her hand in the air. "He takes my hand like this and walks me down past your door and your door and your door then opens my door for me." She preened. "I'm his princess, he told me."

"I don't think so." I heard Jo say under her breath. It wasn't like Jo to be jealous, but as long as she weren't causing anything I didn't take her on.

"Then he says to Aaron who is looking out the door, 'Do you want to come and see Princess Lana back to her room?' and Aaron says 'No,' really quickly, like that 'No!' and slams the door. Shinji runs down the hall saying chiva- something is dead."

"Chivalry?" Jo offered.

"Yes!" Lana squeaked. She began to laugh as if this was the funniest thing that had ever happened in her whole life.

Jo watched her for a moment and smiled before turning back to us sitting around the counter. "Obviously it has something to do with what we can do now, why else would she need to test us?" It took me a second to realise she was responding to Dorian's earlier deduction.

"I won't be needed then." George joked, but in true Jo and Kurt fashion, we locked eyes sensing the bitterness.

We sat in the kitchen at our ease, taking our time to get ready. Aaron came in completely dry, he looked at Lana and absorbed the moisture from her hair leaving it dry. Not long after, Shinji came in which led to Marie leaving to take her shower. Whilst waiting on Marie we began to clean the counter and wash the dishes.

"Wait," I grimaced when my fingers touched a left-over splurge of tomato ketchup. I let my mind wrap around all the dishes and levitated them in a clump together above the sink. "Aaron?" I said. When he saw what I was doing he beamed. He held his hands in front of him, his palms tracing a circle which left a trail of water. Once he had finished, he waved through the disc of water. Then he pushed forward and the disc gained depth, becoming a large globe.

The globe travelled above the sink where the dishes hovered. I began to rotate the dishes in my ability, as Aaron began to vibrate the water with his. As the sauce, crumbs and leftover food was cleaned from them and floated aimlessly in the globe of water, Shinji cheered as if we had just won a gold medal. George threw his hands together as if a miracle had just been performed. "That is literally *the best* thing that has come from all of this."

Marie came back in after the kitchen was clean and I went to get my shower - feeling the pressure of them all waiting on me, even though we were given no timeframe - I rushed.

I quickly dried in my room and changed in to the clothes that M provided. Justifying Lana's mood, they *were* really comfortable. When I got back in the kitchen and everyone was ready, we decided it was time to leave. I pressed the little buzzer next to the main door and we waited there for a couple of minutes before we heard footsteps from the other side, followed by the door unlocking. One of M's staff members stood there, her face, just like the others, blank and lacking personality.

We followed her down the network of white corridors and stopped only when we arrived at the large elevator. Once inside, the steel barricades rose and the lift began to judder and reverberate as it ascended. When it shuddered to a halt, the barricades receded back in to the walls and were hidden from sight. We found ourselves back in the rickety old hall. I looked around, even though I was aware this place was a facade, I could see no hint of the gigantic lab beneath.

The front doors were open and we could see people outside. The staff member walked up to the reception counter and returned with a clipboards and pens. On the clipboard was a questionnaire.

"What's this for?" Jo asked but the staff member ignored her. She resigned and we began to fill them out. Jo's tuts grew progressively louder at each question.

After filling in the forms we handed them back to the staff member who collected them and headed for the open doors. We followed her out. Again, on either side of the door were another two staff members. Upon the one with our forms leaving, another walked up to the door, took the sheets from her and retreated. None of the staff spoke to each other, not a word, not even a slight facial expression betrayed a hint of what they were doing or feeling.

As soon as we walked outside, the woman who brought us here retreated back in to the main hall. The two staff members on either side of the entrance closed the doors. There was a faint rumbling inside as the lift was obviously going back to M's laboratory.

The sun burned my eyes as I began to look around, I threw my hand to my forehead, shading myself. Like yesterday, there were people waiting around in groups, people talking to one another. It seemed a small group had taken a ball from somewhere and were running around throwing it at each other. As the ball hit one of the girls, she yelped and her body transformed into an exact replica of the ball. Both bounced on the ground for a while before she reverted, howling with laughter.

"Have these people forgotten that just yesterday so many people died?" Jo said, ever the bearer of fun.

"They're just unwinding, Jo." George replied. "Try it."

"I just think people aren't really taking in to account what's going on."

"Well, we don't even know what's going on yet, do we? Let's just wait and see what we're supposed to do." George said. Jo tutted and George's rebuttal came in the form of tutting back louder.

We found a patch of ground that was unoccupied and, well, occupied it. We sat in a circle and began to mock Dorian for his competitive nature in *Monopoly*. The conversation drifted as fluently as a stream, bifurcating in to sub-topics and sub-conversations before rejoining the main flow.

"Oh," Shinji called out stopping the conversation. "You haven't showed us what you can do yet, Dorian."

"Oh right, yeah, right. Okay." He placed his hands on the ground in front of him and began to tap the dry soil below him. Dust rose and the mud shifted ever so slightly from his patting "Can you see it moving?" He said looking up at us. Each one of us were staring intently at the area he was patting. We nodded. "There you go." He said and sat back smiling at us all. We sat silently, not quite sure of what to say. I felt Jo's hand clamp on my elbow as she tried not to laugh. "I'm joking!"

He held his hands in front of him, palms pointed up toward the sky. Below him, the soil began to crunch as it became compact. Then a chunk ripped itself from the floor and hovered in front of him. His hands clawed and the chunk of soil began to take the form of a large ball.

"That's fantastic!" Shinji exclaimed.

"Wait! Rotate it. Slowly!" Aaron called out right after. His hands, once again, began to work away in the air making those intricate movements that made it look like he was conducting an orchestra. Water flowed from his hands like a web, taking form around the orb. He purposely left certain patches of the soil dry but kept telling Dorian to rotate it. Soon, an almost perfect, albeit discoloured, replica of Earth, was hovering in front of us.

"Keep it there." Marie said. She held a fist in front of her and the other one above it. She opened each in three rapid movements as she moved her arm. There were three small clouds of smoke in front of her. With a hand above, she commanded the smoke to part and form around the orb. "Clouds."

Out of nowhere, Lana produced thousands of light particles which formed a larger sphere which she positioned slightly above the miniature planet. "And the sun," she beamed.

We watched as this beautiful replica clung in the air rotating slowly. Aaron's dexterity shining once again; the water seemed to have a mind of its own, complete with waves and ripples. The clouds moved separately of the planet, lazily drifting and the faux-Sun shone on one side of the planet creating light and dark hemispheres. I held my hands up, and let my ability wrap around the planet. "I know you can't see it, but I'm gravity." I said. Jo groaned in disappointment not quite sure if I was making a joke or not, but decided to show her dissatisfaction regardless.

The planet exploded. I fell back in fright, the sun dissolved in to the thousands of bright particles which fell to the floor and bounced like beads. The smoke rose and faded, whereas the sphere of soil just fell to the floor in bits; Aaron's water moistening the area.

"Kurt." Jo scalded.

"That wasn't m-" I began to defend myself but another voice cut in.

"Earthquake." Buzz said from behind me. He was throwing and catching a rock in his hand. Blake and Geoff flanked him. "It happens."

"Oh, I do *not* have the energy to deal with you right now. Do us both a favour and go away," Jo said, "and Kurt, don't say a word."

"Isn't she cute when she's angry, boys?" Buzz said and nudged Blake, who smiled awkwardly whereas Geoff sneered. "I like a fiery Latina."

"Did you *seriously* just say that?" Jo snapped. "Let's deconstruct the ignorance, shall we? First of all, I'm not being 'fiery', I'm trying to understand why your brain works in such a way that you feel you have to come over and speak to us. If you want to apologise, then do it. If you're here to annoy us, don't bother. If you're bored, read a book - there is no valid reason for you to be here, is there?" Geoff's eyes widened as Jo began to walk toward them. Buzz just stood there, his smile grew. "Secondly, I'm not Latina; I'm of Greek descent. You were already high up on my list of irrelevant nonentities, which is a better list to belong to than my list of outright racists because on the former, I won't want to kill you where you stand. At least when you're irrelevant, I won't come for you."

"Greek, Latina," he said, holding his hands out like scales weighing the two, "what's the-"

"No!" Jo shouted holding a finger out. "Don't you dare. Don't you even *think* about finishing that. Honestly, Buzz, we don't know how long we're going to be here for, but I swear on my life - I swear *on my life* that if you say the word 'difference' at any point today, I will seriously make your time here feel like an eternity! Whaddya say to that?" Buzz's smile had faded.

"He really isn't racist," Blake said, which caused Buzz to push him, almost knocking him over, before the trio sulked away.

As Jo sat down, Marie beamed at her and began praising her for not only standing up for herself, but the way she handled it. "I wish I could stand up for myself like that."

"Well, nothing's stopping you but for as long as we're here, I'll take care of that." Jo winked and Marie beamed again.

After the excitement of that little episode faded we began talking again. Conversation was flowing as easily as before, as if the interruption had not happened, until suddenly we noticed that everyone else had grown quiet and were watching something. We turned to look in the same direction as the rest and saw M come around the corner with a small army of staff behind her and another group of people like us, who walked straight in to the motel, seemingly happy but avoiding eye contact with any of the groups sitting around the opening.

The staff on either side of the door flung it open allowing the group in. The one who took our questionnaires ran up to M, handing them to her. She flicked through them, glancing at each page then nodded slightly. At that, the little girl who followed her around held up a plastic wallet, one of the members of staff behind her came to the forefront, collected the questionnaires whilst another took the wallet. The questionnaires were swiftly placed in the wallet and handed to another staff member.

Two more came out of the motel with a small briefcase, the team behind her sprung in to action; stamping, sorting and stapling paper together. It was ridiculously smooth, like an efficient well-oiled machine – each cog performing its function. The whole time, M stood in front smiling. When finished, a group of five staff members ran in our direction and began ushering us toward her as M called out, "Dorm Three." We stopped in front of her. "Well, I see no reason to tarry," she said tersely as she turned to leave. We nervously followed, the eyes of everyone else on us. As we left the opening, the din of conversation returned.

*

We walked in silence behind M and the small girl whilst her staff followed in formation behind us. She led us through the deserted town, past a few stores, an antiques store which, in the window displayed a frayed box of *Scrabble*. Hardly an antique. Dorian noticed it at the same time I did, he nudged George and nodded his head in that direction. George grinned. *Great.*

We walked slightly out of town where a solitary shack stood on the outskirts of the forest. This structure was crooked appearing to be made by hand with wood and hay, thrown together last minute by one of the three little pigs.

M and the little girl entered and the staff waited outside. Inside, it was incredibly quaint, but I suppose cute and cosy in a medieval kind of way. There was a tattered old rug laying on the floor which was dotted with little brown and orange stains. A boxed TV that must have dated back to the Aztec civilisation sat in the corner with an antennae jutting out the top and a pile of VHS tapes next to it.

"How are you finding everything so far?" M said in a flat tone. We all nodded slowly and tentatively. "Wonderful. Wonderful. Your living facilities are satisfactory, I presume?" We nodded again, all out of time like big-headed ornaments placed on a dashboard. "Fantastic. Is there any questions?"

"I-" Jo started, but when M and the rest of us looked at her waiting for the question to come out, Jo's eyes widened and she blushed. "I'm so sorry. I forgot what I was going to say." Jo seemed flustered, confused.

"Yes, sometimes that can happen to people of a certain IQ." M's eyes travelled down Jo's body quickly before travelling back up to reach her eyes. "It has never happened to me of course, but I suppose that carries its own connotations." M said and I had to contain myself to stop from laughing in support of her sass. Jo's eyebrows furrowed, her eyes narrowed but she bit her lip. It seemed she was finally learning to keep her mouth closed. "I do not want you to worry about these tests, it is nothing drastic and if at any point you feel uncomfortable, tell me. I will understand." The small girl behind M silently shifted her weight and M turned round quickly. The girl corrected her posture without a word slipping from M's lips.

"We are all in this together," M continued and a certain tune that I am rather embarrassed to know began to play in my head. Remembering she was a mindreader, I tried my hardest to think of another song, *any* other song but her eyes already flickered to me before continuing. "I will be taking you out one by one," she glanced at George, "well, most of you. We will discuss your ability, what you have learned so far and we will do some 'experiments' as it were, to see how they can be applied.

"The previous dorms were very co-operative and already a few have learned something about their new abilities hitherto now they were not privy to. The aim here is to help both of us. As a scientist, I cannot help but want to understand more about this change and there is nothing better when the experiments carried out can be symbiotically beneficial. Imagine being the first person to be cured of a terminal illness because you agree to work with the relevant people. Think of it as thus: you will learn how to master your gift and I will understand the nature of said gifts, whilst seeing them in praxis.

"As I have to get through all subjects at the facility, I fear we cannot linger to chat, as fun as it is. Dorian, follow me please." Dorian looked petrified at his name being called out with no warning. He swallowed his fear then began to follow her out.

"Can we watch TV?" George blurted out just before they left.

"The entire town has no electricity." M said on her way out.

"Your lab has." George answered back and I elbowed him in his ribs.

M spun around to address him. "My lab runs off its own source of energy that cannot be corrupted from the outside. There is a plethora of generators and back-up generators all with the intention of keeping specimens frozen, rooms warm, lights working and computers running. It is not linked to the power grid for the rest of this town, boy, because during the creation of the lab, we knew it was imperative that we remain self-sufficient as we understand that science cannot pause.

"However, during the creation of this facility, we did not consider the importance of an insolent child who speaks out of term and his need to watch an old television set on the edge of a forest in a tree surgeon's... shack. I wonder how they kept their jobs after this clear flaw in planning." Then she spun round, sass once again on point. Dorian shrugged at George as if to show a clear distinction between M and himself before following her out.

The old wooden door creaked and from the little square window, we watched M, Dorian and most of her staff walk towards the trees before they were lost from sight. A few of M's staff stayed outside the building. Jo grunted and George swore under his breath.

"She really isn't a big fan of us, is she?" George said. Jo reiterated what he said in a not so PC way.

"She just doesn't like silliness, does she? Like, she's just direct," I defended M.

"Says her favourite 'subject'," Jo spat at me, using her hands to air-quote the last word.

"How can I be her favourite subject? I just know my place," I scoffed, but was secretly elated.

"I like her," Shinji cut in before Jo's reply. "She has a job and she's doing it-"

"So did Hitler," Jo mumbled stubbornly.

Shinji ignored her, "even when everything else went to hell. I respect that. Can you imagine the immense pressure she must be under?" The conversation revolved solely around M and her attitude. It was mostly led by Jo struggling to find something nice to say, George backing her up (now that

109

he had been in the line of fire) and Shinji saying he understands their point of view, but he doesn't think she's a bad person, just a blunt professional. When Dorian came back, he was smiling. M called Jo's name. She stood up with a strop and followed her silently. They left without another word.

Dorian began to tell us of the testing. He said it was mostly talking, but when it came to the actual abilities she was clearly knowledgeable. "And look at this!" He lifted his hands, pointing out the window, "she said something about controlling earth, and one of her staff members had a tub of sand. It felt the way soil does in my mind, but lighter. She was banging on about the world and natural layers and how I should be able to control more than just soil and I did. I lifted the sand up. Then she got a bottle and look, just watch." We watched in the direction his hand was pointing and the window itself began to ripple slightly. "Isn't that amazing? She's incredible! She said something about glass being made out of sand and I thought she was joking but I think she was telling the truth 'cause I can kinda feel glass when I *really* focus and she said if I keep practicing and if her theory about my ability is true I may even be able to control *metal*!" Dorian finally allowed breath to enter his body.

"See," Shinji said. "She can help us as long as we let her."

"In fairness," George said. "That is a little bit brilliant." If Jo was here, there would have been some rebuttal to that, but in her absence George was free to appreciate Dorian's progress.

Jo came back not long after and Marie was taken away. Jo was telling us how she refused to use her abilities on M's staff even though they stood there blank and willing. Then she said how M told her they don't need to be at each other's throat as long as they respect each other and promised M she was going to try... but I knew this was probably not going to happen, if Jo didn't like you, there was a good chance you will never redeem yourself, whether you were aware or not. In the end, Jo used her ability. She was about to explain what she had learned when M came back with Marie. It was my turn.

Once again, I found myself walking behind M and the little girl whilst her staff followed behind me. I watched as the girl walked beside her and tried to think back to if I'd ever heard her actually talk. I don't think I had. Maybe M only speaks to her in her mind and she can reply or something? Did she even have an ability? She looked around the same age as Anthony, but they acted *so* different from one another. Then again, Anthony was comfortable around us, or at least as comfortable as you can be in two days whereas this little girl had no idea who we were just as we had no idea who she is.

"She is my daughter." M said.

"What?" My bum clenched so tightly that it could have been used to crush diamonds.

"Megan, she is my daughter," M answered. "I heard what you were thinking."

"Oh, sorry, I didn't mean to. I just wondered, uh, yeah..." My inability to speak to teachers, my boss, general authoritative figures had transferred to M.

"Not at all. I nurture an inquisitive mind."

"Does the Dad live close by?" I asked, appreciating her openness.

To my surprise, she actually chuckled. "Oh, Kurt..." I waited for the rest of her sentence but nothing came.

"Why doesn't she speak much?" I asked.

"Megan was born mute," she stated. No pity, just simply factual. "She is a special little girl and as soon as she could walk and use her hands, she has been my most faithful assistant. You see, Kurt, that is why I see these abilities as gifts, regardless of all the terrible things they have wrought in such a small timeframe... Megan and I were always in sync, but now I can actually *hear* thoughts, my daughter and I can converse freely, regardless of her inability to form words."

My heart bled for her. M, the fiercely intelligent scientist who was behind the rescue of about a hundred people, the woman who used her time to understand this change in order to help, was simply, human. A mother. She could have retreated in to her lab where food is vast, safety and shelter is provided, but no, here she was helping. She was a philanthropist and that is the thing Jo was struggling to see.

"Correct," M said. I blushed as she stepped out in to a section of the forest in which the trees were cut down and the woodland floor was level. "Do you know why I contacted you instead of your friends, Kurt?"

"I don't." I admitted.

"It is because you have a great mind. You have not had much handed to you in life so you often take things at face value. Your mind, to me, even at distance, was like an open door - a window left wide open inviting me in. Your thoughts flow freely, you are not self-righteous or entitled. I knew that as soon as I would speak to you, you would listen. You will follow orders without feeling like a drone." Her staff began to whizz around the open space. They were setting cones, colourful balls and ropes out. All of them working again, as if each were important mechanisms in a complex machine. Passing a sack from one to another, helping each other set everything up without a word. It was almost graceful.

111

"I find it easier to hear the thoughts of those gifted. Your thoughts were welcoming, easy to read. I did not have to *try* to hear you or to contact you. Think of it like this: your mind is similar to a good book, the sentences are constructed coherently and the narrative is easy to follow.

"Your friend Jo, though gifted is very close-minded in her thought process and therefore it is more difficult to wean sense from her. I can read her mind if I focus on her, but she does not make it easy. That does not mean she is intelligently superior to me, if anything, it means she is not susceptible to fresh ideas or change. If her thoughts were likened to a book, think one with words that are blurred or reading with little light. They are there, waiting for you, but you must exert unnecessary effort.

"George, on the other hand, the boy without a gift is different. His thoughts - sticking with the book analogy - can be likened to something along the lines of, hmmm," she paused for a moment. "Think of a children's book with just images, or a piece of foreign literature with a poor translation. Almost unreadable in its simplicity. It is often nonsensical, incoherent - sometimes difficult to understand what he means. Again, I am not commenting on the intelligence of your friend, but rather the state in which I find his thoughts. This is not exclusive to George's mind, all my staff are the same. Not one of these people working for me here have abilities, their minds are similar to George's. There is a haze, I can contact but find it difficult to read."

"Do you think though," I began to ask the question without even realising I had thought of it, "that George may have an ability? Maybe something passive, or, that he may develop one or something?"

"No, Kurt," she said simply, "I cannot say for sure whether those who have not been gifted can develop abilities down the line as too little time has passed to support any evidence, but I can say with absolute certainty that your friend, George, is normal."

I thought this over for a moment as M's daughter handed her a sheet from the clipboard she was holding. *Well, that was that.* George did not have an ability. Nothing. He was, as M said, normal. I then thought about Jo and how she and M had been since we arrived here. "I know Jo can come across as rude and believe me, you're not the first person she's acted like this to, but I think it's things like trying to read her mind that really gets her annoyed."

"Sometimes, Kurt, it cannot be helped." She replied.

"What, you can't help using your ability?" In a flash, she snatched the clipboard from her daughter's hand (her daughter didn't seem surprised by this at all) and launched it at my face. My ability acted before my hands, it grasped the clipboard in mid-air inches from my head. "What the hell?"

"Did you actively pluck that out of the air?" She asked and I admitted that I didn't. "Then my point stands, sometimes I cannot help but hear thoughts. I am new to all of this, too. You must keep that in mind. Though I have a plan, it does not mean I am a master of my ability. In fact, I have found a limit to my ability already. Something happened on the day of the change which almost killed me. Of course I do not need to go in to detail about this as it is irrelevant to your stay here, but in the fashion of a true scientist, I have attempted that feat once more since which yielded similar, but not identical, results."

"What was it?" I asked.

"As I said, it is irrelevant to your stay but something I will try to uncover on my own. Until then, I have the rest of you to study," she turned around. Her staff continued to set up around her as Megan silently followed in tow. When everything was set up, the testing began.

At first M was asking me to levitate the little colourful balls that her staff placed earlier. She held a red one in her hand and asked if I could catch it before it hit the floor. As soon as she let go, it was already in my mind, suspended in mid-air. I could feel the ball was squishy, like one used for juggling. M beamed as she stared at it. She held up another letting it go, which again I grabbed in the air. Then another, then another, then another. She asked me to try it without using my hands. According to her it was unnecessary, but most people used them as a visual aid to help focus their abilities.

"Wonderful," she smiled. "Now, Kurt. Tell me, are you focusing on each individual ball or all at once as if they were a collective?" I let my mind feel the balls and wondered if she could feel what I did were she to enter my mind. "I cannot." She replied. It was difficult to comprehend the fact that my thoughts weren't silent. "Focus on testing, Kurt, I have much better things to do than compile notes of your thoughts. No offence intended."

I explained, "I can feel them all in my mind, but it's not like I'm holding each one individually if you get me?"

"Of course I *get* you," she called over. "Describe the sensation the way I likened your thoughts to books."

I gave it a try. "Um… I don't know how to explain this using books."

"You don't have to use books." She laughed and I couldn't help laughing too. "Just relate it to something natural, universally understandable."

113

"Oh, I get you. Okay, the way I'm holding these is like, a net, but like one made of skin because I can feel- no- I know! Think of a kangaroo's pouch, they can feel their- uh, Joey, in there, but they're not actively carrying it?" As soon as I finished talking, I felt a hot flush of embarrassment.

"Kurt, when I said universally understandable why did your thought process lead you immediately to marsupials?" She asked with an eyebrow raised.

"I honestly have no idea." I grimaced.

"The peculiar thing is, I do indeed understand. Okay, can you focus on them individually?" She asked and I tried to. It was doable, but more difficult than holding them as if they were in my *pouch*.

"I can do it, but it's not as easy. Like, trying to do long-division in your head?"

"That was a better comparison. Okay, try and operate the balls individually and move them about in opposite directions." She insisted. As I tried, I could feel my thought straining. It was like trying to pat your head and rub your tummy, or draw a figure eight in the air with your finger and trying to do it the opposite way with your foot. A lot of the balls went in the same direction, but two or three went in different directions.

"I see. I see," she said. "Fascinating. Thank you." Her daughter began to scribbling away. "Okay, now hold all these balls together, in your… mental pouch." I brought them all together, so they were floating in a clump once more. "Wonderful. Now with this ball," M held up a yellow one, "please try and separate the two entities. Keep the red balls in the pouch, but try and focus on this yellow ball as a separate item."

She let go of the yellow ball. I plucked that as I kept the cluster of red balls afloat. "Okay, this is like literally holding a bag in one hand and the other ball by itself in the other." The daughter scribbled once more. M continued to hold more balls up, all yellow, before letting them go and watching as I caught them. She would nod, and make noises of approval and bite her lip as Megan scribbled away. This continued on until in front of me were separate clusters of red, orange, yellow, green, blue and purple balls.

"Does it tire you physically to hold all of these? She asked.

"Not really, it's difficult when I try and focus on them individually or move them separately like before, like I said with the whole long division thing." I noticed I now felt completely comfortable speaking to her. No awkwardness and I felt incredibly proud of myself. "But holding them here like this, just equidistant isn't challenging. Either way though, it isn't *physically* tiring."

"So, there is no physical effect on you when using your abilities at all?" She asked.

I mentally scanned my body. "Not that I know of. Not so far anyway."

"And how old are you?" She queried.

"Twenty-two, just out of Uni." I wasn't sure why I mentioned Uni, but I'm rarely sure about anything.

"Okay. Who is the oldest in your dorm?"

"Lana… I think, but she can't be much older. How come?" I asked.

"I have a feeling that using abilities can affect people differently. My findings thus far have shown that each case has its own rules, but there are similarities at the same time. Evidence shows, however, that there is a correlation with how over-exertion occurs and the age of the individual. Most of the people here are between the ages of ten and thirty. Those older than thirty, like myself, can use our abilities as aptly as you can use yours, but it seems some are physically affected by them.

"Kurt, something I need to look in to is if using our gifts affects us in any negative way and if so, what causes it. When we do that, we can attempt to nullify the negative effects and reach our true potential. Like I said, I was forced to use my ability in a way that was so mentally taxing, and it almost killed me. We *need* to understand. I will figure it out.

"What is strange, is that some people cannot fully control their abilities and I need to understand if it is the nature of the ability itself, or the mental state of the person controlling it." My mind flashed back to the fiery girl clutching the charred object to her chest. "In other words, I want to see if the car crash is caused by a malfunction in the vehicle, or the ineptitude of the driver."

"What car crash?" I asked, pushing the footage out of my mind.

"It was a metaphor, Kurt," she sighed. "I have an idea of how that can be," she gave the wryest of smiles, "*tested*."

This was all a bit much for me. I followed what she said, but I'm not a scientist. It wasn't for me to think of the answers - it was obvious I was just part of M's experiment so *she* could find the answer.

"Tell me, Kurt." She said as she walked through the cluster of balls toward me. I could feel the outline of her body as she passed through them. "When you fainted yesterday, what do you think induced it?"

My mind went fuzzy as I tried to remember. "I can vaguely remember there was something that made me feel weird? Something that caused it?" I shuddered suddenly and she raised an eyebrow. "I felt scared, or like I was trying to catch smoke - there was just a gap in my mind that I couldn't bridge." She nodded slowly. "I wasn't using my ability, though."

"The information is still vital... and you cannot remember at all the reason your mind was thrown in to this state?" I tried my hardest to picture the moments before I fainted, but it was no good. It was vague. Too ambiguous. I shook my head.

"Prior to your ability, were you prone to fainting?" I shook my head again. I had fainted a few times in my life, but wouldn't consider myself exactly 'prone' to it. "Fascinating, I cannot read your thoughts when you are trying to think of this moment. It is as if whatever caused it has been plucked from your mind just like you plucked those balls out of the air." She studied my face for a moment. "I asked Marie what happened. She claimed when she arrived to help, there was a *photograph* beside you."

There *was* a photograph, but of what? My mind began to grow foggy once more. I began to feel sick. It felt as if my brain was growing heavy and clouded. I almost stumbled off balance and all the colourful clusters of balls fell to the floor.

M threw her arms around me, catching me. "You are not fainting this time." One of her staff members ran over with a paper bag. "Sour confectionary, eat some." I grabbed a handful and scoffed them up, gratefully. The sugar was very welcome. M watched me intently with a triumphant smile, her daughter was scribbling so furiously on the clipboard that I was astonished it didn't catch fire from the friction. After that, she just asked me to try and make shapes with the rope and to try to navigate objects of varying weight in and out of the cones her staff placed. I did what she asked, but it was clear she was being careful not to push me out of my comfort zone anymore.

"Thank you." She said finally. "You have been wonderful to work with and I am certain that my contacting you was the best thing I did that day, Kurt. You have a wonderful mind and so far, have helped me more than the others. I thank you, sincerely." I blushed and bowed my head slightly.

She handed me the rest of the sweets and I began to eat away at them as we walked back out of the forest to the shack. Before we entered, M stopped me and said, quietly. "I *will* remove any limitations these powers present us." I nodded and smiled before she opened the door and walked inside. When I sat down, M asked Anthony to follow him. Anthony grabbed George's hand and was half way through asking George to come along before he stopped mid-sentence and walked to M.

116

When they left, Jo asked how long M and I were kissing for. Apparently, we were gone a lot longer than they were, but it felt as if I was there for around ten minutes. We were talking as M came and took the rest of us, one by one, in to the forest to test us, of course, leaving George to sit in the shack the whole time.

When we were done, we walked back to the opening where everyone else was still sitting patiently. The fourth dorm were taken away, then the fifth, then the sixth. It was starting to get dark now and though there was no sun, the wind was carrying warm and gentle breezes.

By the time the last dorm were taken away, the courtyard was aglow with a range of abilities. It warmed me deeply to think that every one of them was due to being rescued by M. Lana had conjured thousands of her little light above us which swirled around one another like dust motes in a vortex; there was a large purple fire in the centre of another group who sat so close to it that it could not have been giving off heat. There were glimmering orbs, and pulsating shapes, twinkling body parts and a constant hum of conversation. It was beautiful.

It turned out that in our group only Dorian had learned something new about his ability in terms of actually using it, but Shinji and Jo had more of a theoretical understanding of how theirs worked. Jo's ability apparently had a different effect depending on who she used it on. When she finally agreed to terrify the staff, M focused on *their* minds to see what was happening to them. Each one would envision something horrific, grotesque, demonic, supernatural and terrible, all in different forms. M explained to Jo that her ability drew on their fears which within itself could open a whole new field of research.

The sky above was now a blanket of blackness, but the multicoloured abilities below danced, swayed and shifted around the area and across the buildings creating an aurora borealis of our own. Groups were mingling, a few people came over to say hello to us but it was flitting and brief at most. Every so often, someone would use their ability which would either explode, or screech making everyone jump before they laughed with relief.

Finally, M came with the last dorm. They looked tired as anything, but M and her staff seemed as awake as ever. We were led back to the lab and she offered supper which we declined as George said he would make us something. "Gotta be useful for something, haven't I?" He joked and I gave him a fake laugh as my stomach clenched awkwardly.

Once we were back in our dorm, we threw our clothes in the laundry room and put on plain pale-blue pyjamas that were provided for us, tagged with our name. George made toast with a chocolate spread, hot chocolate and porridge for us to eat. We tried to continue the game of *Monopoly* but no one could go a few seconds without yawning. I tried to stifle a particularly potent yawn and my lower lip trembled as my eyes began to water.

"I may go to bed." I said. "Lana can take over as the banker?" I looked over for her approval not realising she was already asleep on the couch. We decided to call it a night, Jo said she will wake Lana up and walk her to bed. After saying our goodnights, I went to my room and for the first time since I was a teenager, I was actually excited to sleep.

Chapter 11

The dark void surrounded me. The twinkling stars of memories blazed all around in the distance. Silver Hair smiled when she saw me; there was a subtle menace behind that smile which made me shudder.

"Hello, Kurt," she sang, her voice light and pleasant. "I've been busy since you were last here." I stared back, nodding slightly, not exactly sure what she could be busy doing, but decided asking was not going to be exactly beneficial. "How have you been?" She asked, floating lazily toward me as if a delicate tide was pulling her ashore.

"Yeah, I've been- uh- can't complain." Is all I could say.

"Good. Good," she grinned. "I'm glad. I couldn't help but notice the two windows remain unchanged." She was right in front of me now. Smiling. My stomach began to squirm like snakes and centipedes were wriggling about. "Well," she sighed, "I'm sorry I must do this." Then, like I was a helpless insect, she grabbed me. I tried to fight against her, but this was her world and her rules. My ability was ineffectual, her arms gripped me tight. "Don't struggle, it's just a lesson."

I floated backward, no way of stopping, and like that, the void was gone and instead I was staring at a large piece of machinery. Within the mind of someone else - my vision, my hearing, dictated by them and their surroundings. The person I was witnessing looked around, they were in a dark, dusty room. There were red danger signs and yellow warning signs plastered over the walls and on the machine itself.

"It's a generator," I heard Silver Hair's voice explain. "This man is tasked with supplying electricity for a small facility."

The man's eyes looked towards the door and he sighed longingly but there was no visible lock on it. He sighed and looked back at the generator. He rubbed his hands together, sparks of static electricity spouted from them, then, around his arms in which the hairs stood on end, electricity wreathed and crackled. He placed his hands on the generator, and squinted his eyes as the dark room began to flash a bright white-blue. The generator roared and sprung in to motion. It began to rumble and shake. The man removed one of his hands, wiped his forehead then put it back on.

"Taxing work, wouldn't you say?" Silver Hair asked. "I have watched this man for a while, he has three breaks a day and five hours of sleep. If he stops without permission, he is beaten, brutally." The machine roared on, the man's hand remaining in place, his veins large and bulging.

"Why doesn't he just run away?" I asked. My stomach sinking low.

"This facility is situated deep in the ocean. They retreated there for safety in solitude. Even if he could swim the distance to land, one accidental use of his ability could spell instant death for him."

"So, what? He's just trapped here?" The hum of the generator was beginning to give me a headache. "He has to do this day in, day out?"

"It's not all bad," She chirped. "He has earplugs."

I felt a jolt and I was pulled out of his mind. "Is that happening now? Like, that other girl, the one that was shot at, you said she was unconscious."

"He's conscious, yes. Happening right now as we speak. Lonely, taxing and trapped. With very little company, scarce food, few comforts." When she spoke, she didn't seem interested. She seemed bored if anything.

"But… That's horrible!" I knew it sounded childish as soon as I said it. Of course it was horrible, it was terrible, horrific, inhumane! "We need to do something."

"I whole-heartedly agree," she nodded before lunging at me again, constricting me. I acquiesced this time and allowed her to take me. "I'm sorry, Kurt," she said before throwing me in to another window.

There was something wrong with this vision. I couldn't quite discern what it was, but something was off. I could see the torso and legs of the woman I was witnessing, laying on a hill which overlooked a forest. The grass leading up to the forest was a bright and vivid green, whilst the forest was a dark, rich green. It was beautiful. The woman was humming a jaunty little tune to herself.

She stood up and began to walk toward the bosky vista. "Just wait," Silver Hair teased. As the woman approached the trees, her eyes settled on a squirrel about twenty feet away. I noticed it was eerily quiet - there *was* noise, but it was altered. The squirrel was staring right back at her. She waved in its direction, but the squirrel did not move. She began to approach it which is when I noticed the critter's every body movement was impossibly decelerated.

By the time the woman had reached the squirrel, it hadn't even managed to fully turn its head. She reached down, her hand outstretched and stroked it gently. She sighed then, a long-drawn out sigh. She lay down next to it - closer to the creature than any human should be able to manage with wildlife. She was so close, she could see individual strands of its fur, its whiskers, it's dark eyes wide with fear. As she looked up at the trees above, there was a bird, its wings were spread wide, but it appeared to be frozen in the air; the leaves and branches of the trees were just as still.

"Why is everything so still? So slow?" I asked Silver Hair.

"They're not. If you or I were to be here, the trees would be swaying with the wind, the squirrel would have escaped us, the birds above would be chirping and fluttering away." She didn't say anything for a while as the woman looked all around at the silent forest. "This woman sees everything like this since that day. Her ability, I suppose can be described as: super speed."

"But why doesn't she just stop it?" I shuddered.

"She can't. It's passive, this is how she sees and hears things. I have seen her round people. They speak so incredibly slowly, move at an infuriatingly reduced pace that they may as well not exist."

"So, this is it for her? She won't be able to speak to anyone again?" I tried to swallow the lump that had formed in my throat.

"She writes notes, which often deteriorate with the speed, or catch fire which luckily, she is quick enough to put out. She gets by, and can get anything she wishes because others simply cannot stop her. But yes," she sighed, "this is her life."

Once again, I was yanked out of the vision and my eyes readjusted to the void. "I can't believe she's lived like that since the change."

"A day for us must feel like a year, or maybe even longer for her. She is ageing at the same rate as the rest of us, so as long as she lives, she will have to endure these circumstances." Her voice was dry and colourless. "One more."

"Please," I begged. "I don't want to see anymore." I felt weak, my eyes blurred but I blinked the wetness away before tears trickled down. That poor man, that poor woman. I really was so lucky.

"Unfortunately, Kurt, you do not have a say in this." This time she reached her hand out and I grabbed it willingly knowing there was no point in fighting it. She would show me what she wanted until he decided I was done.

"Why are you showing me these?" I asked, but she was silent. She pulled me until finally we were in front of another window.

"Now, Kurt," she whispered with melancholy. "This one is the most difficult to witness."

"Why, what-" I didn't finish the sentence, I was pushed in the window.

There was a voice of a child, begging. "Please," it screamed through its sobs. I couldn't tell which gender the child was because the voice that came out was barely human - it was hollow and anguished. Like a trapped animal. "Please!"

Another voice replied. "Only a little while longer," It called over the crying. "You're doing great."

"I don't," a roar of agony, "want to-" a sob, "want to do great!" The child looked up at its arms. I could see through the tears that they were fettered in place with shackles, it pulled and pulled at them, but the grip was too tight, the chains too thick, too strong. There was no way they could be broken. Not by a child.

"Hush, hush, hush." The voice soothed, as if this was simply a crying baby that needed to be rocked. "Not much longer now. Don't fight, you know what happens when you make this more difficult." The child wailed before giving up. Its head dropped to its chest, then it closed its eyes for a while. The screaming continued, positive reinforcement from the voice kept coming ensuring the child there would not be much longer, that they were helping their cause, ensuring their safety.

The child opened its eyes and looked, furtively, at its legs. There was a weedy female, with large glasses and ragged hair sitting cross-legged in front of them. The woman's fingers were sharp and serrated like a steak knife; bone coloured and crude. The woman looked up at the child who, from my perspective, shook its head, silently pleading her to stop. She looked back down ignoring it, then pointed her talons at the child's thigh, stroked the skin delicately before thrusting the hideously deformed finger deep in to the flesh. Blood squirted out, accompanied by piercing screams of sheer terror.

"Good, you hit the vein first try this time." The man's voice praised the woman. She smiled, took her finger out and then swiped at the other thigh. When serrated bone met flesh, the woman began to pull and push her arm, sawing through the child's leg, flesh fell off in chunks, the child screaming and squealing for release, the woman crazed and feral, the man's voice congratulating her and child in turn. "That's enough." He said when there was a soft, wet thud.

The child looked down, its whole body shaking as if it was experiencing a seizure. A severed leg lay on the floor, its ankle still shackled, blood still pouring from the top of it. It looked unreal, as if it was some prop, too bloody, too gory to be real. The line of sight moved to the remainder of its limb, more blood fell from it like a waterfall, gushing past the ripped tissue and reddened cartilage. Flesh hung from the leg, like frayed ribbons. Then, after a few seconds, the skin started to ripple and I watched in amazement as the limb began to regrow. The skin reproduced, the bone reformed. Within a minute, the child had its leg back, hanging above the one on the floor.

The woman was sitting in front of the child still, inspecting her bloodied hand. The man ran up next to her, his face was a dark purple, the features shifting constantly; eyes, nose and mouth, moving around as if they had decided they were bored of remaining stationary. "Hold the leg still," he ordered and the woman grabbed the child's new leg, pinning it to the wall with the palm of her hand. The man unlocked the shackle from the severed leg, placed it around the regenerated one and locked it. He handed the detached limb to the feral woman. "Throw that in with the rest, send Ayleen down for target practice and tell Stephen that the females here are proving much more apt then his males."

The woman grinned and nodded before scuttling away. The man stood up, his hand reaching below the child's chin and lifting it up so they were face-to-ace. The child's vision was still blurry, unfocused. "I am so proud of you." The man whispered softly, his mouth careering from one ear to the other, his eyes on separate ends of his face. I would have laughed at the Picassoesque aesthetic if the scene I had just witnessed had not made me so violently sick to the core. "Just one more for the day and then you can rest. I promise." He grinned and turned away.

I was yanked out once more. Silver Hair's face was sober and morose. "Immortality. Cell regeneration. That child cannot be killed. At least, not easily." I couldn't even speak. Words would not form in my head, never mind escape my mouth. "If it doesn't comply, it is tortured." Silver Hair must have noticed a shift in my face because she answered exactly what I thought. "Yes, worse than that. If the child makes it difficult for them to test their powers, it is thrown in to a tank of water and locked in, a state of constant drowning; a plastic bag thrown over its head, enduring asphyxiation for hours at a time; thrown in to a blazing furnace, the flames licking at its flesh before engulfing it completely." She floated still, bobbing up and down slowly. "These abilities, they are terrific and terrible at the same time. Some control them, some controlled by them. I am trapped in my ability, but thankfully, not experiencing something on that level. You *must* prioritise freeing my trapped windows. They may be suffering like those you just witnessed. If you can somehow do that, I can speak to Melanie and she can try to free these poor souls."

"I can't," I whispered, truly knowing that I was out of my depth. This was bigger than me. "I don't know how to. I'm safe. I can't help these people from where I am."

"You have to find a way," she insisted as I began to tremble. "Kurt, if someone you loved was trapped like one of these. What would stop you from rescuing them?"

Those scenes she showed me replayed in my head, but instead of the man and the generator, it was George. Instead of the woman, condemned to a tedious, lonely life, it was Jo. Instead of the child, it was Anthony - the two had similar abilities to an extent, after all. If he was kidnapped for his ability, I would do anything to free him. "Nothing." I admitted.

"Please then, understand. My daughter and whoever the smaller window belongs to may be suffering along these lines, maybe worse. If you just listen to me. I am certain I can contact my daughter, then we can save the others."

"I- I-" I was lost for words, my body shaking violently.

"You *have* to try harder before you disappear," she said and then pushed me hard in the chest.

*

I was in my bed, drenched in sweat. I sat up and before I could stop myself I vomited. I was traumatised - but nothing to the extent of those poor people. *That poor child.* If Silver Hair could save them by me finding this Melanie then I had to try. But what could I do from here? I was in the middle of nowhere. I was safe, that much was true, but was the reason I didn't want to leave down to the fact that I didn't know where to start or because I was too scared to jeopardise that safety?

My thought pattern was interrupted by the smell of my own vomit which made me hurl again. I quickly wrapped my sheets up, trying to shake off the images replaying in my head. I threw them in the washing machine, picked up another set of pyjamas and jumped in the shower, after which, I felt slightly better but there was no way I could go back to sleep.

I changed and was about to go to the kitchen to get some water when I heard a mumbling coming from one of the rooms. I froze for a moment before I tiptoed down to investigate. It was coming from Shinji's room. I placed my ear against the door.

"It's not that big of a deal, though. Is it?" Aaron was saying. "Do you really think they'd care?"

"Not really," Shinji's voice replied. "But it's not something you want to go shouting about is it. Imagine you could do what you can before the change. If you were the only one, would you go around telling people?"

"No," Aaron groaned. "But that isn't relevant because in the context we're not the only ones."

"I know, but I just don't want to go telling people when they don't need to know. That's all." I had no idea what they were talking about and I felt incredibly guilty for eavesdropping, but I was so happy for normality, so happy to hear two of my friends having a conversation about something else - no matter how mundane or interesting it was, I needed to be a part of it. I needed company. A distraction. So I rapped lightly on the door. I heard the two boys gasp inside the room, there was a fumbling around and hushed whispers before the door opened slightly and Shinji popped his head round.

"Hey," I said a tad too nonchalantly. "How're you guys? Uh- You? How're you and only you?" I added hastily, trying to cover my eavesdropping tracks.

"I'm well." Shinji replied and brushed his fingers through his hair. The resulting effect made it look even better than it did a moment ago. "What are you doing up so early?"

"Bad dream," I opted for the half-truth. "I needed to get water and thought I heard talking."

"Yeah. I was, um… Aaron's here." He opened the door more to show Aaron sitting on Shinji's bed with the blanket wrapped around him like a cocoon. "Just talking about things and stuff. Aren't we, Aaron?"

"Yeah," Aaron quickly called out. "Things and stuff."

"Ah… Things and stuff. Sounds interesting. Shall I leave you both to it?" I asked feeling unwelcome, but willing him to decline and invite me in.

"What? Leave us to what? No. Of course not." Shinji laughed and Aaron rolled his eyes.

"Sorry, Kurt," Shinji added. "You made us jump when you knocked, that's all. Come on in." Shinji opened the door fully. I followed him over to the bed and he pushed Aaron aside, slipped a pillow from underneath him and threw it at me. "The floor or the bed, your choice."

I wrapped my ability around the pillow and placed it against the wall behind me as I sat down. The three of us began to talk and talk. They asked me what my dream was about and I used my powers of digression to avoid having to tell them. They in turn were talking about the possibility that abilities were limited, that we can only use them so many times. Shinji had theories of where it came from which all stemmed from the ideas of evolution, like the mutants in *X-Men*, whereas Aaron was convinced it was some form of polluted water or radiation.

I wasn't really present during their conversation, but I tried my utmost to focus on giving it the main stage in my brain letting everything else flutter away. The things I witnessed were so atrocious, so inhumane that a part of me could try and tell myself they couldn't be real. Similar to when I thought of the deplorable conditions of the death camps - it seemed too evil to be real; like some sick fiction, so disgusting in its nature that it simply couldn't exist.

Luckily, the conversation droned on with no pause and I was able to let their voices keep me anchored. Time trickled ceaselessly and before long, the others were awake and tottering about outside.

George had already started breakfast by the time Dorian came out of the shower, dressed again in the exercise clothes that M had provided. Her note this time told us to be ready by noon and to be prepared to take in a lot of information.

We showered in turn, George woke up Anthony and Jo woke up Lana. Everyone showered, ate, got dressed and when we were all ready, we continued the ongoing game of *Monopoly* for about thirty minutes. I was actually managing to smile and laugh. There was a buzzing outside just as George landed on Dorian's Mayfair with a hotel.

"Oh well, let's go," George said, throwing his hands in the air.

"No, wait. Pay me first, then we go." Dorian yelled.

"I don't think M would like to be kept waiting, mate." George said standing up.

"Fine, but everyone saw this, yeah? Yeah? We all saw this, yeah?" Dorian said and he went around each one of us nodding until we agreed. "When we get back, you give me the money you owe me."

"Fair is fair," George smirked, "now come on, M really needs me."

We were escorted down the maze of corridors, just like the day before, only this time we entered the food hall straight away. The room was nearly full, there were rows of chairs in the space where all the tables usually were. The group of us sat together, Anthony sitting on George's lap. More people piled through the door behind us. I spun round in my chair to see who it was. A few people who I hadn't seen before now walked in first, then Buzz, Blake and Geoff. Buzz winked over in my direction and I froze for a moment until I heard Jo groan. He was winking at her. That made more sense.

The separate dorms were talking enthusiastically between themselves. When the last dorm came in and all the seats were taken, M followed shortly after. Her presence killed the throng of conversation.

"I have a lot of information for you. If you have any questions," she looked directly at Jo, "you hold them until after I have finished. Understood?" No one stirred, bar an almost inaudible exhale from Jo.

"Firstly, let me say how grateful I am for your cooperation during the field test yesterday. The results were fantastically informative and the mysterious nature of these abilities is starting to unfold before me, or rather, prove my theories." M waited for a moment. As if this was a signal, her staff sprung in to action and began to fit a large whiteboard on the wall behind her.

"Let me explain. Prior to this change, it may come as a surprise to learn that these powers were still very much existent and prevalent in everyday life. The problem is, not many people knew it. Abilities would usually manifest in the form of incredible feats of strength, miraculous stories or wild levels of intelligence. Individuals whose minds could scale to these heights believed themselves to be regular people: artists, musicians, scientists, mathematicians, leaders of countries, theorists, cleaners, carpenters, technicians, actors the list goes on. These abilities do not discriminate."

The lights in the room switched off and an image of a brain was projected on to the whiteboard. I turned to see M's staff working a projector that was not there when we entered. "I will try to keep this simple. The human mind is the most complex structure in the world. It controls each one of our bodies and though it is formidably resilient, it is incredibly malleable and susceptible. Most people I have studied have no interest in challenging themselves," she paused, letting people take in what she just said. "For instance, you are all capable of learning a second language, yet only a small fraction in this room speak more than one - fewer still, fluently.

"That is because you have not experienced an environment where it is necessary. If I was to drop you off in the middle of a foreign country, at first you would be at a loss but before long, your brain will automatically, through osmosis as it were, begin to connect the dots. Without actively making the effort, in a years' time, you would comfortably speak the language - you may not be a master, but you could get by. Do you all follow?" Silence. "I know for a fact you all speak English, so please respond. Do you follow?" A murmuring of 'yes' was her reply.

"Wonderful, keep this in mind when I am talking about your abilities. Before now, your brain had no reason to bring these abilities in to the forefront. Even if it was necessary, many people will refuse to believe the impossible and hinder themselves. However, very few will not." She smiled. "I am certain you will have heard the story of a woman lifting a car off her child in danger? This woman managed to haul an impossibly heavy object in order to save her child. This was explained with adrenaline surging through the body, but when I interviewed this woman and she agreed to let us scan her brain, we noticed something." She pointed toward a section at the top of the brain. "Her parietal lobe was functioning at a level more advanced than anything we had ever seen before."

There was a click behind us and the image on the board changed, showing just the specific section of the brain she was talking about. "The parietal lobe is responsible for: movement, orientation, recognition, responding to stimulus, etcetera. You see, when this woman's child was in danger, she did not think of the impossible, she had a task to carry out. This acted as a catalyst and her brain was catapulted into action. She was the first actual case of mental growth manifesting in to physical powers I had ever seen and that is when I knew exactly what we had to look for.

"Since studying this specimen, we began collating brain scans from hospitals all over the world. When we found a specific lobe performing at a level greater than generally considered *normal* we studied it, spoke to that person and tested them. It is rare, but a few revealed abilities that often even they were unaware of. The results were even better when the subject was given performance enhancing drugs, but this could also inhibit the ability," She paused. "Unfortunately, when the stimulus wears off, they believe it was a momentary thing, an impossibility, a miracle that they cannot command at will - some would outright refuse they witnessed anything at all.

"Spontaneous combustion, mysterious disappearances, unexplained deaths and even a certain mental illnesses - such as schizophrenia, dissociative disorder, hearing voices or even simple traits such as narcissism - can all be linked to the development of these abilities and the lack of comprehension, capability or control. The abilities manifest and can destroy the person slowly, or even instantly kill them.

"Through my research and with the help of my mutinous *partner*," M almost growled the last word through gritted teeth, "we discovered that the nature of the abilities are linked to different parts of the brain. This was mostly a theoretical, educated guess which was linked to very questionable or vague evidence but now, finally, I can confirm it. Soon, you will all be subjected to brain scans in order to provide me with material that I have needed to compile for so long." At this, there was unified uncomfortable shifting in our seats. A few people had the audacity to mumble quietly.

"Calm yourselves," M placated. It was not an order, it was a suggestion and one I felt happy to follow. "You will not be under any danger, it will be as simple as the field test yesterday. We have seen the flowers, but I must now study the seed. Understanding these abilities could be the key to the survival and growth of humanity.

"I feel I must put in to perspective what is truly happening out there. The world has changed drastically. The government is no more, authority is now a relative term and enforced by those with the power to do so. There is no

England, America, Spain, France, Russia or Germany. There is no 'unified people' anymore and this is only three days since the change. Though our minds have advanced, our reasoning has reverted to medieval times. The only reason people are sticking together out there is because they believe there is survival in numbers, but there is no trust or order." She paused and stated gravely, "the sheep of yesterday are the wolves of today." Another click, back to the brain.

"Whilst you are here, trust me when I say you are safe from this neo-primitive zeitgeist. Most groups are disorganised, scared and without a plan. They are staying wherever they feel is safe and will remain there until the food runs out or they are forced to move on. It is textbook survival.

"However, there is a common enemy," she paused and glanced over the horror-stricken faces in the room. "Someone else who had access to the exact same information I did, someone who has already displayed incredible control over her abilities and that is because she understood how it worked. That is the aforementioned *partner,* the woman who used to work as my equal. A while back, we discovered something. There was a boy, a sick boy. His brain scans were sent over to us. He was not from this country and was receiving subpar treatment, which is all his family could afford. So, he went for years without showing up on our radar.

"When he was brought to our attention, it was like finding the holy grail of research. This boy, every section of his brain was functioning at a level higher than anything we had seen before. You must understand this seemed impossible." There was another click showing a simple bar chart. Most of the bars were around the same level whereas one rocketed above the others. "Look at this woman's chart. That bar is the parietal lobe as I mentioned before." She explained pointing at the tallest bar. "Now put this chart side by side with the sick boy, and you will see…"

Another click. Two bar charts were placed next to one another. The woman's tallest bar was dwarfed by this boy's. In comparison, her most impressive bar, the one depicting the parietal lobe, was a bungalow whereas each of his were the Empire State Building.

"Magnificent," M smiled and glanced in our direction with the hint of a smile before turning back to the board. "Even now it gives me chills. You see, this boy, though not intelligent, had such a versatile mind that we *had* to study him. He was dying, and spent most of his time bedbound at home. We could not interfere lest it contaminate the results." There was a whimper a few seats over, but I couldn't take my eyes off the board. I was completely in awe of this boy's potential. M was speaking fast, excitedly and it was infectious. My heart was beating rapidly. "I believe due to his physical inactivity, his mind had the time to grow. This coupled with his constant seizures which forced his body to fight, to strive, helped him reach his true potential."

"Kurt..." Jo whispered and nudged me. I ignored her.

"The worse his condition grew," M continued, "the more his brain function increased. My partner began to grow more concerned for the boys' health rather than the possibility that *we* could possibly use the data we had collated as we always intended." She grunted. "She wanted us to fund his healthcare, we had the money and it meant we could study him for a prolonged amount of time, but she did not have the foresight that I did. Prolonging the life of this wonderful individual could undo the work his brain had done, it could revert his high-functioning prowess and thus unravel our research, take it back a few incredibly vital steps."

"Kurt!" Jo nudged me again and I slapped her hand away.

"She would not listen to reason - the boy could not be saved. There is *no* surefire cure for cancer, it could destroy everything we had waited so long for, everything we had worked toward and it may not save his life after all. One casualty - whose death was already impending - would be a sacrifice to infinitely improve the human condition. He was the key to everything and we were too close." She was shaking with anger now, I could feel it, her desperation. "She stormed out, turning her back on our research - on me - and I feared she was going to interfere with the patient. Not long after, the change happened and I knew it was due to the patient, the sick boy... The Catalyst."

Another click. Projected on the board now was a pale, gaunt and sunken face. My eyes widened when I saw him. I *knew* him from somewhere. I had seen him somewhere. He was- he was- A scream. Everyone jumped in panic. My ability pushed a sphere around me and those caught in the radius were momentarily suspended in mid-air. As soon as I saw the room begin to fill with thousands of tiny lights, I dropped to the floor and pulled whoever I could down with me.

When I managed to look up, Lana was the only one left standing. All around her, light particles were shooting out at startling speeds. A vortex of those tiny bright motes was whizzing around her. I could see her clawing at her face as another raw shriek was ripped from her lips. Others were shouting in panic and fear all around but I couldn't discern any words.

I was frozen in panic, my mind was screaming at me to get up, calm her, comfort her, but failed to instill within me the wherewithal to do so. That boy on the screen. The one M called The Catalyst. *It was her brother!* The boy who was taken by the Treeboy on the day of the change. The boy Lana had been responsible for. *He* was the key to all of this? M had known about this boy before we even knew Lana's name!

Lana pushed her hands out and a wave of her power gushed forth, smashing into the wall and bouncing off. As Lana dropped to her knees, the particles grew brighter still and actually began to burn. There was screams of pain all around the room, mine adding to them. It felt like thousands of burning needles were being injected all over my body, biting at every inch. It didn't make sense; Lana's lights hadn't burning properties to them before so what was happening?

M was standing in front of her daughter. She covered her eyes from the lights, but she didn't seem worried. If anything, she seemed intrigued. To the left of me Shinji jumped up. His arm was thrown up in front of his eyes, but the rest of his face that I could see was scrunched up in pain. His other hand outstretched and was edging toward Lana who did not realise. Shinji howled as his arm pushed through the chaotic-yet-beautiful vortex, but as soon as he made contact with Lana, all the lights in the hall fell to the floor and began to bounce about wildly before they dissipated.

Though Lana had stopped screaming, there was still yelling and whimpering all around from the others. Anthony had already began to conjure his water, he was hugging in to George and all the singed marks on them began to fade. Aaron jumped up and ran to Shinji, who was now holding the unconscious Lana in his hands, one of which was burned a bright red.

"Anthony!" Aaron shouted. Anthony looked horrified, but he conjured a large glob of water and Aaron commanded it with his ability. He washed Shinji and Lana, then Anthony and Aaron began to send the water all around the room to heal the rest of us. The panic and screams of pain died down, but the whimpering and fear was still prevalent.

M was looking over at her daughter who was, even now, hastily writing on the clipboard. Her staff ran over to Shinji and yanked Lana from his arms. Jo jumped up to grab hold of Lana, refusing to let them take her. "Let go of her, you insolent child," M demanded. "This is exactly why we need to study these abilities. They are a part of us, we *must* know how to control them before they control us."

"I'm not letting them take her!" Jo shouted back. "Not for your stupid tests. I'm taking Lana and we're going to find her brother."

"And how do you propose we do that, you silly girl?" M's rejoinder was flat and impatient. One of the staff members grappled Jo who squirmed, managed to break free of his grip and threw her hand in his face. My heart sank as I realised she was using her ability. But, he didn't react. Instead, M screamed. She pushed her daughter aside for a second, before falling to the floor. Then as quickly as she started screaming, she stopped and the staff member Jo initially tried to terrify began to yell in fear. He kept asking for his wife, screaming for his wife. M was bordering on rabid with fury. "I will not have insubordination within my walls. I brought you here so you could *survive*. Do you have a death wish?" There was no reply from Jo. "We will acquire her brother when we are equipped with the knowledge and offensive ability to do so."

"You can't." I said then slapped my hand to my mouth. I didn't mean to talk out of place.

"And why is that, Kurt?" She asked. I looked around the room, everyone was silent, all their eyes focused on M and me.

"On the day of the change when I went to help Lana," my voice was weak. "There was someone else there. Some woman with shadow powers. She had a group with her - I think they were convicts – they took him. The Shadow Lady is way too powerful."

"All that says to me Kurt is you lack the vision," she judged. "Not only am I aware that The Catalyst's sister resides within my walls, but I have known for a long time that my ex-partner obtained him."

"Your…?" I couldn't even finish the sentence.

M's lip curled. "Your 'Shadow Lady' is the woman who once combined her intellect with mine to achieve incredible feats – a woman who I stupidly accepted as my partner. She spent years by my side researching with me, a brilliant mind in her own right, but foolish. Now, that same woman has the most important individual in the world and the freedom to act as she wishes."

"But… How? Why?" I mumbled, this was too much. I was struggling to keep up.

"I tried to contact The Catalyst that day, but he was barely conscious. I attempted to contact your friend Lana, but her mind was too erratic. I sent you to save both before they were taken, but we were unsuccessful. Now, I am trying to discover where they are residing. When we find the location, we find The Catalyst." M took a step forward. "But now is not the time to discuss such things. I can explain in detail tomorrow if I have time. But for now, everyone, go back to their dorms." Most people rose instantly and rushed out of the door where some of M's staff were standing, their faces were showing no signs of panic. They were clearly over the commotion.

132

"What about Lana?" Jo asked. She was not being stubborn, I could tell when Jo is stubborn. No. This time she was genuinely worried. I shook my head slowly and M smiled at me. Jo looked in my direction and I continued to shake my head. She sighed looking at Lana. "I'll stay. I'm sorry, I just - I really feel bad for her. How long will she be away from us?"

"As long as it takes and I accept your apology. Now please, all of you go back to your rooms." M then turned her attention on Lana. Most people had left the room by now. Aaron was holding out Shinji's arms and studying it for any burns. Anthony was in George's arms, his face buried in George's neck whilst Marie and Dorian were standing behind Jo. "And Jo, it seems collecting your friend's sick brother is mutually beneficial for us, so you can rest assured that we *will* focus on that task, which is more than you could have done were you to leave, but please keep in mind," she looked directly in to Jo's eyes, "that will be the last time you challenge me or attack my staff. Now get some rest."

With that M closed the distance between us, she looked at Lana's limp frame and then, without a word, the staff carried her out. Jo did not try and stop them this time. When they disappeared out the door, the only people left in the hall was our dorm, of course, minus Lana, and the staff member who initially brought us here.

"Poor Lana." Shinji bemoaned when we were back in our dorm. His voice had broken the spell of silence we were under and alleviated the tension that clung heavily, fog-like. Shinji had not only been silent until we got back, but completely despondent. Aaron had tried to cheer him up with a rose made from brilliant blue ice, but Shinji only shook his head to show he wasn't in the mood. After Shinji spoke up, Aaron seemed shocked he was still capable of speech. "I hope no one is angry with me for putting her to sleep, it was for her safety as much as for everyone else's."

Everyone agreed with Shinji and his body sunk in to relaxation. No one was annoyed with him- I hadn't even thought to be angry at him for doing what he did. I just kept thinking about Lana, what she was going through, how scared she must have been when she saw her brother's face; my heart was breaking for her. She had had it worst since all of this started.

Anthony helped George cook small bits and bobs, but no one was very hungry. More hours of further silence passed before it was time for bed. We solemnly said our goodnights. I lay there for hours trying to get to sleep, but I just couldn't switch off; Lana, M, Silver Hair, Patrick – The Catalyst and the terribly powerful Shadow Lady that turned out to be - of all people - M's ex-partner. It was too much, I got out of bed and walked down the hall. I knocked on Shinji's door and waited for him to open.

Aaron opened the door but Shinji's leant his head out of the bed to look round Aaron. "Can," I asked, fidgeting awkwardly, "can you put me to sleep?" He frowned. "Please, Shinji?" He gave a doleful groan, then smiled.

"Go to your bed and get comfortable, I'll be there in a few." I walked back and waited for about three minutes before I heard Shinji's door open and close outside in the corridor. He knocked on my door and I called for him to come in. "You ready?" He asked, sounding sullen as he kneeled at the side of my bed. "I'm sorry if doesn't feel great. Are you certain you want this?" I nodded. He gently placed his hand on my cheek.

"Good night," his voice echoed around the walls of my brain, as if from miles away - as if from a different universe. It was a sweet, warming and soothing feeling and then finally, my anxiety disappeared and I was dead to the world.

Chapter 12

When I felt lucid, I half expected Silver Hair to be there waiting for me but she wasn't. She was nowhere to be seen. I was in my room, in the pyjamas provided. The last thing I could remember is Shinji saying goodnight and it felt like that was seconds ago. It was as if I had blinked and had skipped a few hours of life.

I felt rested, but also a little out of sync. I put it down to the side effects of Shinji's ability. My body was technically resting, so I would have got the benefits of rest but at the same time I didn't feel like I had slept. If Silver Hair didn't visit there must have been some mental block Shinji's power induced that stops any cognitive brain function. I couldn't decide if I enjoyed this sensation or not.

I stood and decided to shower. As the hot jets of water doused my body, I couldn't help but think about Lana. The image of her clawing at her face amidst the vortex of light was etched in my brain. Unfortunately, Shinji's ability couldn't find a way to block that. I waited for M that whole day.

The next day was much of the same. I asked Shinji to send me to sleep, I woke up before the others – no visit from Silver Hair - I got ready, waited and nothing. We sat around doing our own thing, still succumbing to an air of uneasiness, a tension that soaked us through, which we tried to dismiss but was clinging on to every one of us. George cooked, we ate. Night time. Sleep.

This went on for a week with still no sign of what was happening with Lana or M. During that week, more staff members entered bringing fresh food, laundry, supplies and everything else we needed but news. For the second week of nothing, we were allowed outside for two hours a day. None of the other dorms were around so George said it was probably down to either: they thought we needed privacy, or, they were doing it one dorm at a time, a rota, to stay on top of things. Either way, I started to have my doubts about what was going on and whether staying was a good idea or not.

By the end of the second week, we were getting used to Lana's absence. I mused on this. On the one hand, I had actually only been with Lana for a few days so it felt stupid being so bothered by what had happened, but on the other hand, without her here, we felt incomplete as a unit. I couldn't really claim she was the core of the group or anything, because, well no one was. We had only just met each other, but considering the circumstances we had been through a lot together. I came to the (probably arrogant) conclusion that because we saved her, looked after her until now and she had no other family here beside Patrick, we felt responsible for her safety.

I tried to bring this up with Jo but she was despondent. It wasn't right. Jo was never reticent when it came to her opinion, or especially when it came to me expressing my feelings, but she just told me we could talk about it later. In fact, when I brought Lana up with her, Jo had been quite short with me in general. When I walked in to her room, it would be one word answers and rushing me out. She wasn't being rude, but she wasn't being her usual self. I missed the bossiness.

After George had made us supper one day and Dorian, feeling restless, begged us to play *Monopoly* once more, Marie finally brought Lana up to the group. "Guys?" Marie asked as Jo had the dice in her hand and was lazily about to roll them. "Do you think Lana is okay?" As soon as her name was brought up, my heart sank. From the looks of everyone else in the room, it seemed to be a mutual sensation.

"I hope so." Shinji said. "I still feel guilty about the whole thing."

"We've talked about this." Aaron mumbled but Shinji just gave him the slightest side-eye as a reply.

"I don't think we should be talking about Lana. M wouldn't appreciate it." Jo stated.

"What?!" George and I gasped in disbelief.

"Clearly, she wasn't in the right state of mind. She isn't having a great time as it is and doesn't need us sitting here talking about her." This was not Jo – that is not how she worked.

"I didn't mean to make anyone uncomfortable." Marie began.

"Let's just drop it." Jo cut in. Marie shrunk in to herself.

"Jo, are you okay?" I asked tentatively.

"Yes, let's just play the stupid game. Look, I rolled a six." She grabbed her piece and began to move it. I grabbed her hand and Jo looked at me in a way she never had before. She looked angry, not Jo-angry but actually angry as if she was going to hit me. Then her eyes widened. She looked at me as if seeing me properly for the first time in a while. She slapped her hand to her mouth. "I'm so sorry. I don't know what came over me." She said.

"Are you okay?" I repeated. "I didn't realise she meant that much to you."

"No, no. It's not that," she said, then quickly added, "well, yeah, I do care for her, but it's not that. I just felt really, I don't know, scared talking about her?" She shook her head. "I don't know what came over me, I just felt like it would make things worse for her, or harder on us... I don't know. I'm sorry."

"Jo," George said. "With all due respect... You've *never* been scared to talk about anything since day one." I laughed nervously. Everyone else watched us silently. Jo stared at George for a moment with a look of confusion, then her face softened, she sighed and began to laugh too. *And breathe.*

"I know!" Jo said. Then she began to laugh harder as if the relief had freed her, elated her mood. "I know! I have no idea why I was so scared to talk about it." She began to wipe tears of laughter away from her eyes.

"Coping mechanism?" Shinji offered.

"I don't think so. I think I was just worried and didn't want to voice it. I'm so sorry, I feel like I've been carrying a weight around with me. I'm sorry if I've been a bit horrid in general. I'm sorry. Marie, sorry for cutting you off. I wasn't thinking."

"It's okay," Marie squeaked, but there was a relaxed smile on her face.

"No. No it isn't." Jo said and grabbed Marie's hand. "Look, when I put Lana to bed the other week, the night before, well, that day. I sat with her for a while. Did you know she had literally no one else here? All her family is back in Poland. She said she feels silly, but that she feels like she finally has friends to confide in. I mean, she didn't say it in those words exactly but that was the gist of it.

"She really opened up and I was thinking 'There we go. Breakthrough moment. She's learning to trust us properly.' Then the next day *that* happened. That's why I got so angry with M, but- I shouldn't be taking that out on the rest of you." Jo held her hands up. "I'm going to say it: I am," she held her hands higher, "Kurt and George can confirm how big of a deal this is," a pause, "I am sorry. I was in the wrong." George and I gasped dramatically for effect and the rest of the group began to laugh along.

The conversation after that focused on Lana and how M is probably getting her back on her feet as we speak. Maybe Lana requested a bit of time away because she wasn't feeling emotionally stable right now. I would understand that, I felt emotionally unstable before every menial exam, or even getting undressed in front of people, so I couldn't imagine the intensity of what she was feeling.

We decided next time we saw M, we would bring Lana up and ask if we could visit her. If not, to at least bring her something from us. George said he would make her a cake and we began to get excited thinking about the day Lana would come back and we could welcome her with open arms. I daren't tell the rest of them about the doubt niggling away at my mind, but I didn't have to. We were happy once more and what happened to Lana was no longer the elephant in the room.

Now the tension was gone, the night went on and we were laughing and joking. Anthony had become my banking prodigy which after a while kindled Dorian's suspicion. Even though it was just a case of me getting the money ready and passing it to Anthony to pass to the relevant player, Dorian accused George and me of working in cahoots. During Dorian's fourth counting of George's money to check for any discrepancies, Jo admitted that she had landed on his property and because he wasn't paying attention, he missed it.

Dorian argued she had to pay and she parried saying that he had to be vigilant. Dorian's reaction to this was pulling a strop and demanding to do something else because *Monopoly* is a "stupid game anyway". We sat there for a while before Anthony came up with an ingenious idea. Seemingly more comfortable with the group he jumped off George's lap and asked Marie to create two lines of smoke going "one way," and another two "criss-crossing." The resulting effect was a small grid. He then took Aaron by the hand, pulled him to the centre of the room and said, "middle one, cross." Aaron stared at Anthony for a second as if he was speaking a different language before George jumped up.

"Noughts and crosses!" He yelled. "Yes, Anthony!" George hoisted Anthony off the ground and squashed him so hard his eyes all but bulged out, resembling Geoff's. We played that for a while, Dorian refused to play with anyone but Anthony with whom he managed to beat a few times. It was nice to just sit back without the tension and not only watch Aaron and Marie work their abilities but to do it for something so relaxed.

When the yawning and stretching began, George whipped up supper and we decided to call it a night. I went to bed feeling smitten and content. Jo came to my room with me and we spent about half an hour talking about Lana. Jo admitted it was for the best as M could monitor her condition and said it was the best chance of getting her brother back if Patrick really was in the hands of her research partner, the Shadow Lady.

There was a knock on the door and George entered. We made room for him on the bed and the three of us sat there for hours talking about everything. George even apologised for being moody when it turned out he didn't have a power and said he was just being stupid - he had us with him and that is all he needed. Jo mocked him first, then hugged him after.

We discussed what M could be doing and why she hadn't tried to contact us to update us on Lana, or even follow out any more tests. George reckoned she was in and out of the lab trying to get more intel, whereas Jo was hoping she was trying to get in touch with the Shadow Lady in order to make amends, even if just to reunite brother and sister. I had doubts that was true, but again, I kept them to myself.

Truth be told, I *had* wondered why M hadn't been in touch with us. I spent the first week waiting for her to summon me, but that wasn't important right now. I was in the room with my two best friends, I could feel myself getting tired and for the first time since Lana's breakdown, I didn't feel the need to go and ask Shinji to help. In fact, sleep came so smoothly and swiftly that I didn't even realise until Silver Hair was waiting for me.

*

"And *where* have you been?" She yelled with a look of equal parts fury and relief.

"What do you mean?!" I squeaked defensively.

"I have not been able to contact you for *weeks*." She grunted. "The windows flickered! The block was removed for a fraction of a second. I was terrified, I thought they were going to die."

"What did you see?" I asked with genuine shock and intrigue.

"Nothing! It happened too quickly. I've been waiting to speak to you since, but you haven't been here." She ran her hands roughly through her silken hair. "I thought I had lost the last chance of saving them. Of speaking to my daughter. What is happening out there? Where have you been?"

"Oh. Oh!" Then I realised! When under the effects of Shinji's sleep, I truly *was* gone from the world. "My friend, Shinji, he has an ability that can help put me to sleep. I didn't realise he was blocking you out. I'm so sorry," and I was, "I've just been through a lot and I needed, uh, assistance to sleep."

"You weren't *asleep*. When you sleep, you come here. You were comatose. Don't let your friend shut you off," she ordered, the way she did it reminded me of someone, "it isn't natural."

"I mean," I thought about whether to finish the sentence. "I wouldn't really call this natural either."

"What isn't natural is the fact that there is a woman and possibly an innocent child clinging on to edge of a cliff with their little fingers and you are the only one that can help them up, yet you refuse to act on it. Where is your sense of responsibility, Kurt?"

It seemed the fact I knew I could now escape her if I wanted had bolstered my querulousness. "I don't mean to be rude, but, how old are you? You look, say, twenty-five? Why call me a child?"

"Looks can be deceiving. For instance, when I first saw you I thought I could rely on you."

"When you first saw me, I was confused and terrified!"

"Precisely. A *coward* needs to put the extra work in to impress someone!" She roared.

"I'm not a coward," I cried back, but there was an abrupt change in surroundings and the void vanished. I sensed a movement beside my bed and I froze. A voice.

"I assure you, Kurt, I have no reason to believe you are a coward." No. No. No. No. *No*! I pulled the blankets up to my chest covering my torso. I let my mind spill out in the room and I switched on the light. Standing, beside my bed, fully clothed… M was staring back at me.

Chapter 13

"Bad dream?" M queried as a smug smirk spread across her face.

"You could say that." I croaked, as I tried to tame my wild bed hair, my voice still not awake.

"I'm sorry to wake you, but I have just got back from a trip and have no time to waste."

"A what? A trip? Whilst all this is happening? Where did you go?" I asked. My eyes were melting in my sockets from the light. I kept blinking furiously. One of my hands was still trying to tame my hair and I rubbed my eyes with the other. M raised an eyebrow.

"To visit the pyramids." She said. "I have always wanted to see them."

"Oh. Yeah, me too." I admitted, gingerly. "I heard they-"

"That was sarcasm. I did not go to see the pyramids. It was not a trip for leisure. I had business to attend to," her tone was not appreciated. "After your friends' episode, I had to act fast. I contacted some of the groups forming out there, convinced them to work for me in return for supplies. I learned the location of my ex-partner and sent an emissary to her stronghold."

"Stronghold?" Strange choice of words considering that was feudal time structures.

"It is not a strange choice of words, Kurt." Once again, I forgot she could read my thoughts. I resigned myself to the fact that I would probably never remember my mind is private around her. "She has chosen an already strong structure and fortified it beyond measure. The emissary I sent is the first time I have tried to contact her on civil terms since she stormed out."

"What did you say? What did you tell the emissary to say?" I asked. Then a sudden fear struck me as if I was stepping out of line. "Sorry, I'm just curious."

"Inquisitive minds should *never* be sorry." She paused. The fear dissipated. "I gave him a letter."

"Like you do with your staff?" I asked.

"Similar, but no. This is one of the people working for me on the outside, they had abilities like us."

Had? I thought, but M did not answer that thought, so instead I said, "Ah. Makes sense. What did the letter say?"

M studied my face before she began. "I told her the truth. I gave her a chance. I told her The Catalyst's sister is within my walls and the she needs him back." She stood up. "Get dressed."

I froze for a moment at the sudden order, then instantly obeyed. My hand was still on my hair but I used the other to lift the duvet up to cocoon me. I used the elbow of the hand on my hair to clamp the blanket in to my chest whilst I bent over looking for my blue pyjamas. I couldn't even remember taking them off to sleep. That's probably when Jo and George left.

"What are you doing?" M asked. I looked up at her, bent over with the blanket cocooned around me. Her eyes scanned my body, an eyebrow raised.

"I'm trying to get dressed but, uh, I get self-conscious when people see my body."

"I can turn around if that would make you feel more comfortable," she offered with a tone of boredom.

"Please," I squeaked. M rolled her eyes at me then turned to face the door. That's when I noticed Megan was in the room too. I hadn't even seen her a moment ago, but she was standing right beside M. As quiet as a statue. Both of them were looking away.

"Jesus, I didn't see her there. Your daughter." I said.

"Fantastic," was the only reply. I shed the duvet and could see my blue pants were trapped within. I hopped into them and fell over. My ability caught me, but in the process my arm flailed out and I knocked the small clock off the bedside cabinet. "How you manage to be so clumsy whilst you have telekinesis is well and truly beyond my comprehension."

"No, my ability caught me. My arm knocked the clock off trying to break my fall. I still have reflexes, even if my telekinesis is faster." I said in my defence. I checked under the duvet looking for my pyjama shirt but it wasn't there.

"Another example of your ability passively protecting you. Is that not absolutely wonderful? It is still new to you, an addition to who you are and already it is ensuring your safety. Truly magnificent." She said.

"You know when I first got the power, like, on the first day? Do you know what I thought?" I asked as I checked under the bed. There it was. I grabbed it and began to struggle in order to put it on.

"I am not too sure. I was trying to speak to a lot of people that day telepathically. Maybe I know what you thought, maybe I do not." She said.

"No, I don't mean 'did you read my mind?' I mean- it doesn't matter. Basically, I remember thinking... If I can move stuff with my mind. If I could literally do everything with barely moving, would I get fat?"

M made a strange noise. I stopped moving for a moment. My arm was sticking out the neck hole. It was a strange noise to come from M. She was chuckling! When I finally had my shirt on she was already back facing my way shaking her head. "That is the first time I have truly laughed in weeks." I grinned at her. Then her face lost all signs of warmth. "Tell me, Kurt. Does it usually take you this long to get ready?" I nodded apologetically. "You have no reason to feel nervous around me, Kurt. None whatsoever." She smiled and as if it was as simple as a switch, my nerves and anxiety dissipated. In fact, I felt incredibly comfortable. "Follow me."

We were silent until we left my dorm corridor. I followed behind M and Megan as they made their way down the identical white corridors. At the end of every corridor, two of her staff members were positioned.

We walked in silence for another while, from one corridor to the next, to the next. For all I knew, we could have been walking in a square, travelling the same halls again and again. We passed more staff members. Our footsteps echoed around loudly. I searched for a topic of conversation, my mind flitting through vacuous this and insubstantial that before I remembered M had sent someone to the Shadow Lady. "Oh, you didn't tell me exactly what happened with the emissary."

"Simply, Kurt, it has been proven that she is as stubborn as ever, but now without having to worry about legal constraints set by the judicial system, she has grown ruthless. I will tell you the truth, I never thought she was capable. The Catalyst is an extraordinary boy. I briefly explained the science behind him, but he is much more than the key who unlocked these abilities. He has the power to increase potential, too."

"How do you mean?" It was surreal to consider the local shopkeepers sick brother had caused all this.

"Have you ever heard of the Giant Sequoia, Kurt?" She asked

My brain grasped for forgotten knowledge. "Is it a dinosaur?"

"It is a tree, Kurt. The largest tree in the world. As we speak, even with your advanced brain functions, you are still the seed of a Sequoia. Think of that as your current level of potential." She paused for a moment. "The Catalyst, even in his sick state has the ability to make that seed bloom in to the fully-grown tree. Instantly." I was confused, why was control of nature so worrisome? "It is a metaphor, Kurt. Did you not study English?" M said, her tone piqued. We were at the lift now. Two guards opened it up and the three of us entered. "He has the potential to transform an ember into a blaze. A gentle breeze into a hurricane. A lazy capillary wave in to a tsunami. If he focuses his ability on you, Kurt, your power will increase to that equal of a deity for that period of time; akin to a god. I believe my ex-partner is trying to harness this power, Kurt. She wants to use that sick boy for her own gain. She has the chance to rule this new world. It is only a matter of time before she succeeds and then we will be the first to face her wrath. There is no doubting that. With me gone, she will be unmatched."

It was momentarily difficult to breathe. My throat began to constrict. "But if she has him there, why hasn't she already?" My voice cracked as I spoke.

"It will not be through lack of trying, I assure you. As I said, that boy is close to death. It now makes sense to me why she wanted to keep him alive, she must have been conducting her own research alongside our joint research. As a team, we were trying to unlock the latent abilities in the human mind, but she," M shook her head, "she focused on her own advancement. She needed to keep him alive and as soon as the world changed, she took her chance." The lift doors opened. It looked as if we were on the exact same floor as the one we just left. M walked out and once again, I followed behind her. On this floor, there was no staff. The corridors were empty. "I can only imagine the terrible experiments she will be conducting on that boy. I tell you, Kurt. Death would have been a mercy to him. He is probably chained to a bed, forced to stay alive through her medication but not truly living.

"We have carried out experiments on test subjects before, of course, they gave permission. We study their blood, we map their thought processes and subject them to field tests not dissimilar to what you experienced. The Catalyst is a guinea pig for her and she will not quit until she can somehow use his power on tap, whether he is alive or dead when she achieves it will not matter to her. I always suspected, but now it has been proven." M opened a door. As soon as I entered, a blast of freezing cold air chilled my bones in place. I could see my breath fogging in the air.

"Why is it so cold?" I asked. In the room, there was a chunky computer, a large adjustable single bed. On the wall was a whiteboard and the desk even had a TV. Surely this temperature was not good for electronics.

"This is the medical wing, Kurt. The rooms are incredibly versatile in order to offer perfect hospitality for anyone who finds themselves here. Each room is equipped with state-of-the-art equipment. If we have someone with a burning fever in one room, we want to make them comfortable by making the room cold. If someone's sickness gives them shivers, we heat it up for their comfort."

"That's incredible," I said in wonder.

"No, Kurt. It is air-conditioning and central heating," she said flatly. I hugged my arms around my chest to keep myself warm. "As I was saying, I always suspected my ex-partner had something different about the way she processed information, the way she saw the world, but it was not relevant to the research or relationship so I never questioned it. But I finally have proof. She is a sociopath." M walked over to a bed. "I have always said there is more than one way to reach a conclusion. Whilst my emissary was carrying my message to where my ex-partner currently resides, I was doing some recon of my own. I was trying to figure out a failsafe in case Plan A - which was reuniting with my partner - did not work. By the time I finished my task, my emissary was returned to me." M's face changed as she gripped the blanket on the bed. "I hope you're not squeamish." She ripped the blanket off revealing what was underneath.

I stumbled backward until I crashed into the desk on which sat the TV. On the bed was a body, or what was left of one. It was barely recognisable. Most of it was covered in purple or yellow bruises. The mottled flesh that wasn't bruised was covered with dried blood. My eyes travelled up and down the corpse. Fingers and toes were missing, the severed parts were still open, blood had coagulated and was glistening in the bright light. Boils and welts were ubiquitous, similar to the orb woman who was killed by the Treeboy all that time ago – making me think it was probably him ordered to do this. His eyes were open, but obviously lifeless. Dark purple circles framed them. His mouth uncontrollably agape and I saw only a few teeth remained in his gums. I felt bile rise and I was about to scream, or cry, or break down. Then, moments later, I was instilled with an alien but welcome acceptance. "What happened to him?" I whispered.

"Do you really feel the need to ask stupid questions, Kurt? You are not dumb, please stop acting so. This is the world out there, like I told you. I unknowingly sent this poor man to his death. The letter I sent simply called for a truce. It said we could work together once more, that she has The Catalyst and I have his sister who will do anything to see him and if she had an ounce of humanity left in her, she would reunite the two. If she can find it in herself to just come to her senses, we can work together to bring peace to the world. *This* is what she sent back. This was her doing." M's voice was more of a growl now. "Her message is very clear."

"I can't believe anyone would do such a thing." I whimpered.

"Yes, you *can* because you are looking at the evidence." M slapped the side of the bed as she said this. I jumped at the sound. "Kurt, my ex-partner has evolved from a selfish scientist secretly working for her own gain, to a psychopath that has let her ability rule her. You have witnessed her immense control already and you know we cannot let her continue. If she manages to harness The Catalyst's ability, anyone who opposes her will meet the same fate as this abomination."

"What can we do?" I asked, then something more urgent entered my mind. "Wait, if she knows we have The Catal- Patrick's sister, what's stopping her from coming here and taking her. If she had Lana, she could use her to control Patrick. She could torture Lana until he does what she wants."

M stared at me for a moment and *smiled*. "You are now starting to understand, Kurt. That is exactly something that would cross her mind, and I imagine she would try... but she will not succeed."

I shuddered. I wasn't sure if it was due to the temperature or the mutilated body. "W- Why?"

"When I tested you, I mentioned I did something on the day of the change, unaware I was capable of such a thing. Do you remember?" I thought for a moment, then nodded. "I *ripped* the memory from her mind."

"What?" I asked completely shocked and in awe at the same time. "How?"

"I am not entirely certain. As I disclosed, I attempted to do something similar on a lesser mind and almost fainted. It seemed like such a simple thing at the time," M paused for a moment, took a deep breath and continued. "Before connecting with you, I contacted her and I am ashamed to say I was begging her to come back to the lab. She refused, but in her mind as I had just mentioned it, I could see the structure sitting there as if it was an ornament on a shelf. I was furious with her inability to cooperate and so I *grabbed* the memory and plucked it from her."

"But if you can do that, then why didn't you take the knowledge of Patrick from her mind? Wouldn't that have made things a lot easier for you? You could have stopped her getting him before any of this happened." I said stupidly, as if she could turn back time and simply fix things.

"That is true. If I removed all the information we had gathered about The Catalyst from her mind, then I could have cut the problem at the root. Unfortunately, things rarely work the way you need them to. She was not thinking of The Catalyst at the time, Kurt. That knowledge was not accessible like the laboratory was - it was out of sight. I cannot delve in to thoughts, but only what is currently on display. The process itself overwhelmed me and severed the link between us.

"I am unsure of why it took such a toll on me - the extraction of this memory. That is why I want to study the limitations our abilities may present us. Perhaps it was the distance in which I attempted it. Perhaps the anger fuelled me; if I was of a calmer disposition it is possible I would be unable to conjure the presence of mind to bolster my ability and manage such a feat." She sighed, wistfully. "I would usually test myself ruthlessly until I have the results I require. However, I am tentative to do so, but not of concern for my health. No, the apprehension resides in a deeper form.

"When the link severed, Kurt, I found myself unconscious." She winced slightly. "Allow me to correct myself. I was conscious, but it was as if my mind was transported to a dreamlike reality. My first thought was afterlife, but I quickly banished that silliness from my mind. I have never believed in an afterlife and that was not the time to start. I noticed there was a presence in this second reality, I could feel it - I could sense it somewhere deep in the distance. It was familiar, yet alien. Hated, yet loved. It was *approaching* me. I feared it and so I focused on composing myself. The world had just changed and I had work to do. I had no business resting in a coma-like state. So, as if it was a simple choice, I woke up." Her sheer will fascinated me – I could barely force myself awake after a nap.

"I was still weak from the exertion, but instantly began to search the area where The Catalyst was currently residing. That area was, of course, where you lived. As I have already explained to you, your mind is very open, very welcoming - in my exhausted state, it was like a warm inn amid a bleak, cold terrain. I latched on to your mind, desperate to find someone who could help me, but you were asleep. Strangely, I found myself back in that bizarre second reality, so I detached myself and managed to actively block my mind from it – as simple as closing a door." She paused. "I regained energy, waited until you were awake and contacted you again."

She began explaining her plan, how she was trying to get in touch with as many people as possible from where she was whilst simultaneously trying to arrange transport to save them. Knowing that she would have to travel from the safety of her laboratory in order to help people, in order to help her research. Whilst Jo, George and I were panicking, M had already planned this. She was incredible. She really was a saint. "You saved so many people. You helped me save Jo in her room, and Lana from probable death." I mumbled and M nodded.

"I did," she agreed humbly. "But my ulterior motive was to get The Catalyst before she did. I dared not enter her mind again, I could already barely support myself as it was," she closed her eyes for a few seconds, then continued. "I was concerned for your safety of course, but at the same time, I was using you. You were a contingency; a means to get to the conclusion by taking a different path. I contacted others as well, the rest of the people here in fact. I wanted to save them, but it was also for my own gain." M shook her head, looked at Megan for a moment, then back to me. "Kurt, bringing you all here, does that make me a bad person?"

I didn't even have to think. "No," I said quickly. "Regardless of whether you brought us here for testing, or to use us, or whatever else you had in mind, it doesn't matter. You saved me, you saved George and Jo. You saved Anthony, Aaron, Shinji, Lana, Marie and Dorian. All my friends, the ones I had before and since the change, they are alive because of you. Just like everyone else here. So no, I don't think you're a bad person at all."

M's eyes seemed to flash. She smiled then lifted the blanket back over the lacerated abomination which somehow escaped my mind, and headed for the door. "Thank you, Kurt. So, you trust me?"

"Absolutely." I said and when the word came out, I knew it was true. "I owe you my life, which I suppose on the whole isn't worth that much, but I do." I paused. "I meant my life isn't worth much, not you saving it."

M tapped her head. "I know what you meant. Both - intended and accidental meanings - are untrue." Then she took my hand. My body responded to her touch in a way that I had never felt before. I felt like crying, like I owed her everything, like I would do anything for her. "Kurt, I am trying all I can but I feel like we must act soon. Trepidation and inactivity is tantamount to surrender. We need to take The Catalyst."

"But how?" I asked. She opened the door, leaving the room with the corpse and walked further into the lower level corridors.

"It is simple," she stated as her footsteps echoed down the corridor. "We go to her stronghold and pluck him from her."

She opened another door. A giant whiteboard spread the length and width of one of the walls in this room. On it, there were pictures of people and locations, some had giant red crosses over them whereas others had question marks. Strings led from one picture to another, writing scrawled all over. Three of the faces had large blue circles around them.

"Using the contacts I have made since the change, I believe we can mount a rebellion with enough force to take her. Even with The Catalyst under her control." M stated, staring at the board.

"But," I said, "how do you know you can trust them? The people out there?"

She simply tapped her head, "I know." She smiled, "every day I learn something new. I fear we are running out of time, but I have collated more information than anyone else could possibly manage under these conditions. I understand so much about these abilities, but there is still more to learn. With my knowledge and leadership, I believe we really do stand a chance. Anyone who opposes us or attempts to betray us will be mowed down without a second thought." Her face was stern and somber, "you understand that is necessary, do you not?"

"I do." And I did. This was more important than just a few lives. Whether they were innocent or not, if they were to ruin M's plans or even simply give our location away then that would spell the end for any resistance against this Shadow Lady. It would only be a matter of time before she could control Patrick's ability and then we were all as good as dead.

"*Exactly*, Kurt. As good as dead is right." M patted me on the shoulder and I preened, ecstatic that we were on the same wavelength. "Extreme circumstances call for extreme measures and there is no room for mistakes or complacency. We have waited too long already, I fear."

"Let's go then." I said, eager to get up, defend M, her research, this lab, my friends - ready to reunite Lana with Patrick. M beamed at me.

"I appreciate your enthusiasm, Kurt, but if we rush in right now we risk an unprepared assault. They have managed to ally themselves with other groups; all of who have banded together in a desperate attempt to rekindle some form of government – there is an opposing force forming, so they will be expecting an attack. Also, she knows I have her location and she will be ready. She may have an ambush prepared. Even if we successfully entered her walls, and managed to find her, she would kill The Catalyst outright. She will do anything in her power to stop us getting him."

"Then how can we do it?" I felt my blood boiling. My hatred for this woman I had never met, the woman who abused M's trust, the woman who kidnapped Patrick from his sister, the woman who had caused so much of Lana's pain. "How can we save Patrick and stop her? How can we *kill* her?" Adrenaline rushed through my body.

"There are others with abilities like Patrick. Not the same, but work in a similar way. I like to think of these as 'symbiotic abilities'," M tapped the three faces framed in blue circles on the board. "These are three such people. Alone, their abilities are nothing, but against others, they are incredibly powerful. These are the people I have been keeping tabs on and they are pivotal to taking The Catalyst from *her*."

As if a fervour took over her, she began to talk quickly, excitedly. "Abdul Mujeeb Kazami. I call him *The Leech*. His ability, Kurt, is whatever is used against him. If I were to try reading his mind I would fail to gather any information, but rather galvanise his ability. He would effectively *borrow* mine, but he can only use it once. That is it. He steals a power and has one chance to use said power before he loses it again. He is currently residing in a strict ceasefire zone, known out there as a 'sanctuary'. It is forbidden to use abilities in those walls against someone else. Before you think this is prudent - a peaceful alternative to this change - keep in mind those who do use their abilities against someone else, even accidentally are sentenced to death. Lana would have fell under that violation."

She pointed at another picture, a young girl around the same age as her daughter. "Charlotte Yu. I call her *The Mute*. Her ability suppresses that of another. If you were to be soaring through the sky and she was to focus on you, you would fall - hurtle toward the ground with no chance of stopping.

"If The Catalyst was to focus on her, Kurt, she could potentially silence the whole world, rendering all abilities void… but if she focuses on him, she would cancel his power giving us the momentary pause we need. My partner would not think of this, I am certain." M pointed to a crude image of a gun and a lightning bolt. "Unfortunately, someone else has figured out her useful ability and has taken her. Her parents were murdered and she is being kept deep in military barracks – one of many encampments under the jurisdiction of a cluster of groups adhering to primitive politics - by a terrible man who can command electricity. Trapped and detained because of what she can do."

M then moved to the final picture. This one had a large woman with beautiful straight teeth, dark skin and mesmerising eyes. "Chiamka Tinibu," M smiled. "*The Jinx*. Her ability is to make yours backfire. If I try to read her mind, I will give her a pathway in to mine. If you try to fly, you will be pulled to the ground. If your friend Shinji attempts to knock her out, he will find himself unconscious." I felt dizzy from all the information, trying to imagine how those abilities could help and the complications they could cause. "If she focuses on The Catalyst whilst he is increasing someone's ability, then she will reverse the effect, again, voiding it, or weakening them." Her hand then indicated a large square with several vertical lines through it. "She is the leader of a small group - a branch of a larger movement attempting to reform the government. They have taken over a prison, but are not hostile unless forced to be." She paused for a moment.

"Seeing Lana's ability morph during her breakdown proved my theory that emotions can affect the abilities potency. If Patrick was to experience something on a similar scale, the repercussions could be catastrophic. That, in fact, is when I knew I could not wait around. That is what I have been working toward day in, day out. As I have told you, there is more than one way to reach a conclusion. On this wall, we have three options to take away the threat The Catalyst poses and capture my ex-partner." M turned away from me completely, looking at the wall. One of her arms rested on the other as her hand stroked her chin. "We just need *one* of these people. She will have no contingency plan for something like this."

"I want to help. I really want to help. I'll do anything to get Patrick back to Lana and anything to help you. I really meant it when I said I owe you my life."

"I know you meant it, Kurt. That is why I can trust you with this information." She reached her hand out and placed it on my shoulder. I felt honoured. Humbled. Privileged. "There is a way."

"Name it." This was the most eager I had ever been. For the first time in my life, I could do something. I could truly help someone. I could make a difference. "Honestly, anything."

M turned and looked at me in the eye. "I wish we had more time, Kurt. But, unfortunately, we do not. Soon, everyone in this facility will undergo further testing. I will study who is capable, who is in control and who can be utilised. After these tests, Kurt, I will know who I can depend on." She looked at the board, her brain probably already conducting strategies and counter-strategies. "Those who are will be sent out, in teams, to collect The Leech, The Mute and The Jinx," M smiled. "Once we have those three, we make our way to her and we take The Catalyst. Once we have those three, she will be stopped and we can work on a peaceful future. Once we have those three, we will lead the future."

I smiled at her. I was terrified, but at the same time the fear was fuelling me. "I'm ready whenever."

"I know. I must make a few arrangements, but I am hoping to start the testing by the end of the month. Thank you for your time, Kurt."

I was utterly reinvigorated as we made our way back through the medical wing, my mind full of wander. Then, a sight drained my mood instantly. I felt hollow. Next to a door, in a little slat was her name: **Stawski, Lana**.

"Is that... *our* Lana?" I asked. M nodded. "Is she in there?"

She stopped and turned. "What did I say about stupid questions, Kurt? Yes, she is in there and her condition is stable." I was about to ask if I could go in. "She does nothing but wallow in grief and has requested no visitors. Not yet." I tried to interject but she cut me off. "None. We will not tell her about the plan to retrieve her brother for the minute chance there is a hitch in its execution. Also, you will not tell your friends. Not yet." She tapped her temple again. "I will know, Kurt."

"Of course. I understand. Of course I won't say anything. But she *is* okay?" I asked.

"She is healthy, physically. Mentally, she is not. But she will come around, I assure you." As soon as M said that, I knew Lana would be fine. I knew she would recover swiftly. It was M. She hadn't failed any of us yet.

For a moment, I had a strange thought. An overwhelming feeling. I hadn't realised before, but it felt like, well, like I *loved* M. Not in love with her, but, loved her for what she had done. Saving my life for one.

I stuttered before I could form the sentence. "Thank you for looking after her. She really means a lot to us, even though we haven't known her long."

We were silent as we ascended to the accommodation level of the lab and walked through the corridors. I smiled the whole way. When we were back in front of my dorm, M rummaged in her pockets and handed me two small glass balls each about the size of a golf ball. "What are these?" I asked, rubbing them against each other.

"Dragon eggs." She said and I gawped, before staring back down. "Are you familiar with glass, Kurt?" I nodded. "And spheres?" I nodded. "Then you should clearly deduce they are glass spheres."

"Oh, right. Of course." Then I hesitated for a moment, before deciding I should ask. "But why did you give them to me?"

"They are for your friend, Dorian. Most of you can use your abilities down here, you are using them in everyday life. Dorian, down here, has nothing. However, as he does have the ability to control earth, sand, rock, etcetera, he will be able manipulate glass, maybe even metals. If he applies himself he should be able to manipulate those balls," she noticed the confusion in my face. "You remember when you said that your trying to do too much at once was like trying to figure out long division in your head?" I nodded. "This is his long division, if he can master manipulation of glass, then his command over everything else will seem as simple as colouring by numbers. Leave them on the kitchen counter with this," she handed me a tag with Dorian's name. "Do not tell your friends anything that I have told you, regardless of how much you want to. Information will be disclosed to all those relevant soon enough, but they are not ready yet."

"I won't. I promise." I admitted.

"I know. Goodnight, Kurt," she said and then they both began to walk away as I ran in to the kitchen, placed the glass balls on the counter with Dorian's name tag next to them, then ran to my room feeling *giddy*. It felt like years before sleep managed to take precedence over all the new information that was rushing through my head. The last thought I had was of me standing on a castle spire - the Shadow Lady's body crumpled far below, defeated - holding The Catalyst in my arms...

Chapter 14

In my sleep, she was waiting for me. Of course she was waiting for me. She was like I was in my teenage years: needy, dependent on someone else and had nothing better to do... in fact, that's still me. I was about to talk, but she held a hand up to silence me. "I'm sorry I got so angry last time, Kurt," she said meekly, "but please understand how incredibly frustrating this all is for me."

"No worries." I said.

"No, let me explain. I have been here for a long time, long before you hit puberty never mind gaining your ability." I smirked when she said puberty but she pinched the bridge of her nose and continued talking. "Time is different here and I cannot sleep to pass it, I am always awake and always aware. I have gone without friends, family and company. In fact," she took a deep breath, and said with a defeated, resigned acceptance, "my friends are more than likely dead now."

Her eyes began to glisten as a single tear formed. "You have never felt loneliness like this - with no escape, no hope of an end. When I first fell ill, I would often dream of this place... when my condition worsened, I would see more of this place than my hospital room. It wasn't long before this was the only world I knew. For a while, I hoped. I thought there would be a chance I would wake back up in the room, with the nurses busying themselves around me, or a doctor or visitor - I didn't even mind if I was out for years, as long as I got to see my loved ones again. But it wasn't to be.

"This was my life now. I thought it was all within my mind - which I suppose it is to some extent - and I willed for those out there to pull the plug, to end it all for me. My daughter hated me for how I treated her, some part of me hoped her fury and bitterness toward me would win over and she would command they cut off life support. But she never did, whether she asked them to keep me alive or not, I do not know. All I knew is that I was alone."

"I know it must-"

"Let me finish." She said. I thought she had. She began to drift leisurely whilst talking. My body followed behind her, effortlessly floating through endless space and millions of specked gateways to the mind. "It was nothing but tedium and mundanity for too long. Then after all that time, I felt something else. A disturbance to the natural stillness of it. Imagine a ripple in a pond alerting even the smallest creature within that something has changed. I sensed the anomaly and I rushed toward it, as fast as I could. I was fearful to hope, but I couldn't stop myself. It was what I had longed for all this time, and, as I got closer, even though she was different, I sensed my daughter. I knew it was her. But when I got there... I found you."

"I'm sorry." I murmured.

She shook her head and wafted her hand as if to eradicate the apology. "No need. It was not your fault. Even though I was upset that my daughter was not here, I was still hopeful and thrilled to see *someone*. In the midst of that confusion - the emotions alone were enough to overwhelm me - but then came the introduction of millions of new windows.

"After you left, I searched for her window erratically. I found that when I focused, I was drawn to a direction. I followed that pull until I came across the two blocked windows. The fact that I was drawn to them, the fact they felt familiar was enough to convince me one of them belonged to her," she sighed. "But why were they blocked? I couldn't find a plausible reason. Out of all the new windows that arrived, none of them were blocked. After seeing all the horrific scenes going on out there, it dawned on me soon enough that they must have been trapped somehow."

She was silent for a while as we drifted onward. Soon enough, we arrived at the two windows; the larger still completely blocked, whilst the other remained hazed over – impossible to see within, but clear enough to see that there *was* vision. "As we've discussed, I decided the second window must be a child - regardless of Melanie's life choices – a grandchild. *My* grandchild." She smiled at that. "But my daughter and my grandchild were trapped. The only connection I had was you. You, Kurt. A boy who found himself here – I still can't accept it as coincidence." Her bright blue eyes were wide.

"And I was too selfish to understand you had family; you had parents and loved ones out there." I didn't have the heart to tell her my parents *were* my loved ones, plus Jo and George. "And I selfishly pushed and pushed you to help *me* out. So, I wanted to apologise profusely for my abhorrent behavior. If I've learned anything from residing within here, it is that I should apologise before it's too late." Her voice faltered and she forced a sad smile.

Her sincerity had moved me almost to tears. I had cried so much since the change that I tried to hold them back - I imagined she saw them glisten anyway, because a smile full of genuine thanks spread across her lips. "Then let *me* apologise." I started. "I know how much this means to you. I do, I can hear how desperate you are. But I don't know what I can do. I'm so far from my home. We've been transported to some high-tech underground laboratory. Did you know that?" She shook her head. "Yeah, I barely get to go outside. So, you've been asking me to save these people with no way of knowing who they are and even if I did, I have no idea where to start. And I can't just pop out for a few minutes to find a trapped woman or kid."

"Kurt," she said quietly, holding her hand up. "I won't put pressure on you. I will try to stop that, but, you really are the only one who can get these for me."

"Well," I said, resigned but appreciative of her approach. "I will try. I will be more vigilant, but there's not much I can do from where I currently am and that's me being honest."

*

When I woke up, I could hear shouting in the corridor. I jumped up and the contents of my room rose with me. There was a hushing noise almost as loud as the initial shout, then giggles followed. Confused, I rose from my bed and stretched my body, I gently placed the floating objects back down before making my way over to the door.

Dorian was kneeling in front of a long winding white-blue structure. My eyes followed the structure which wound and spread the length of the hallway, it split in the middle and rejoined. It was a brilliant slide made of pure ice. Aaron, Shinji and Jo were at the other end of the corridor. Marie in the middle. She had made large smoke rings at three separate sections, equidistant.

"Sorry, did we wake you?" Dorian asked, his big brown eyes looking up at me. The kitchen door swung open, revealing George who was followed by a waft of bacon. He handed me a sandwich and I grabbed it eagerly.

"What're you all doing?" I croaked, taking in the ice slide.

"M left me these," Dorian said holding up the two balls I left on the counter for him. "So, we decided to make a slide."

"Of course you did," I said smiling. "Surely, she wants you to use those balls to try and learn how to control your ability more, don't you think? What if you break them, or what if she comes in and sees you messing about with them?" I asked.

George rolled his eyes. Dorian stood upright. "Wannago?" He said holding the balls out.

"Yeah, alright." I stuffed the rest of the sandwich in my mouth, hovered the plate over to Dorian for him to hold and took the glass balls out of his hand, running up to where Aaron, Shinji and Jo stood.

The game was essentially a race, letting the two balls rush down the lanes. Aaron changed the track slightly each new round, and I managed to stay on for six consecutive races... before they realised I was using my ability to tamper with the outcome.

Then I was exempt from playing. During my games ban, I wondered about Patrick and how his power would increase our abilities. M basically said we would be akin to a deity, that he could turn a gentle breeze in to a hurricane so it had to be something immense. I was only a seed and I could be a Giant Seq, uh, *what did she call it*? It sounded like a dinosaur. A Giant Seq... a big tree. But how would it affect someone like Jo's ability who relied on other people's minds? What about Shinji? It was easier to imagine what would happen to Aaron, Dorian and Marie but it was still a lot to take in. I suppose it wasn't for me to think about - that was M's job and she was much better at it than I was.

These three people that M's plan surrounded, surely there would be rules and limitations to what they could do. I couldn't remember their real names but: The Leech, The Mute and The Jinx is what M called them. So these three could use their abilities to interfere with The Catalyst? If it was *that* important, surely M would get them herself. Then again, she is a busy woman and I guess indispensable. A thought struck me. She probably has a lot more going on that she hasn't told me about - other means to get to the conclusion as she put it. It was nice to know she trusted me with this much though. She said she would tell the others - but when? Of course, after the tests. What tests could prove we were capable of bringing these people home? How would she discern who would be useful? Especially when their powers could effectively make ours useless.

"Kurt?!" Jo shouted as she was clicking her fingers. I looked at her blankly. "Are you with us?"

"Sorry, yeah. I was just thinking." I said.

"Oooh, careful." George quipped.

"Bloo, blareful," I shot back before I was told my games ban had ended.

*

Just under two weeks had passed since M spoke to me on the medical floor. Not much happened, we were left to our own devices again, devoid of contact and like last time, our only visits from anyone outside was her robotic staff bringing food, clothes and supplies. Considering M said we had to act fast and there was not much time to waste, I thought we would already have began the new testing. It was all I could do to not tell my friends about what M had told me, but as she said, she knew she could trust me and I owed her that much, even if I didn't like keeping secrets from them, especially Jo and George.

Aaron and Shinji had stopped talking for a couple of days, Aaron refused to be in the kitchen with Shinji who in turn would only roll his eyes when Aaron entered ensuring he made a dramatic show of grabbing something to eat, slamming cupboards and stomping around before storming out, saying goodbye to everyone except Shinji. Jo and I tried to ask Shinji what had happened, but he simply shook his head.

I offered to write to M for Aaron, thinking he may like some time outside. "I'm not the one who needs help getting *out*; that's Shinji!" He snapped before slamming the door. I told Jo about this and she nodded with understanding before reprimanding me for being nosy.

One day, when Aaron came into the kitchen, grabbed a glass and filled it with his own power, dropping two spherical balls of ice in before storming out, Shinji followed him. I asked Jo if she thought I should go out to check on them but she shouted, "no!" It was fine though, the two must have argued until they resolved it because after about an hour they came back exhausted but happy.

*

Silver Hair had stopped being so forceful with urging me to free her daughter and the child which I was eternally grateful for. Instead, when I entered her world in my sleep, she would show me the thoughts of others all around the world. It seemed the situation out there was, like M said, massively different. Most of the windows we visited were people either living alone, in small packs or tense communities. Each residing in some warehouse, cave or forest away from others, using their abilities to defend themselves, forage and survive.

It was like watching different character's perspectives of the same apocalypse show. The sheer versatility these abilities gave the population was astounding. People traversed the world as if anywhere was accessible. Flyers, teleporters, climbers, speedsters. Obstacles were overcome with ease – those who did not have agile powers would find other ways to overcome obstructions to their path; cars melted, walls crumbled or simply passed through, whole trees uprooted and shifted like toothpicks. It was phenomenal to watch, yet absolutely terrifying.

*

Dorian, after claiming he was 'definitely giving up this time' (for the fifth time), had now managed to levitate the glass balls. He was nowhere near comfortable yet, but he could now make them hover from one side of the room to the other slowly and awkwardly.

157

"When I can control them properly, we'll play the slide race again." Dorian said with a cheeky smile.

"You're obviously going to do what Kurt was doing." George said dryly.

"No. No, I won't!" Dorian argued vehemently.

"Then why not play it now?" Jo asked.

"No, not yet." Dorian begged and everyone burst in to laughter.

*

Four weeks had passed since the meeting with M. The only time we left our dorm, I thought it was for the tests. However, it turned out M had finally got around to doing the CAT scans. She wasn't there to conduct the examination herself, but we were given concise orders as well as a list of rules to follow. The scan was incredibly tedious, I was just left there with my thoughts and nothing more, which was often uncomfortable for me. I began to daydream about scaling castle walls and liberating Patrick from the Shadow Lady. M would cheer with happiness and Lana would finally want to see us again. The scan ended and I was excited to see what would come from it - how my brain had developed from the change. I realised, strangely, just after I got out that I was missing M.

*

I had stopped counting the weeks since I was woken by M. There had been too many with very little happening that time seemed to muddle in to a thick, slurry stew. The effect of her urgency had fizzled away leaving me with no goal to work toward, only enjoyment and peace. I found I had thought less and less about The Leech, The Mute, The Jinx and even, to my shame... rescuing Patrick.

I woke up one morning with a headache. I had somehow managed to catch a cold even though I had been around these people for a while. Jo came to check up on me and said it was probably due to lack of fresh air, or possibly something George didn't cook properly and not a cold after all.

"Whatever it is, it's unpleasant!" I sniffled, not quite pronouncing my consonants. She brought orange juice and toast but I couldn't stomach it. George came in and then not long after Marie followed. She felt my forehead as Jo and George stood watching her like worried parents. "Honestly, I'm fine." I croaked with unquestionable valour. The built-up phlegm in my throat, mouth and nose betrayed my statement.

"I don't think you are," Marie replied mimicking my voice. "I think you just need to rest. Let's see how you are tomorrow, if you don't improve, we will force M to come down to get you." I nodded. "Do you feel nauseous?"

"Only when I tried to eat the toast." I said. "But Jo puts way too much butter on, so it may have been that," I whispered. When Jo was about to argue, I added, "please, let me sleep." She did so, but not before shooting an evil glare at me.

The hours after they left passed as slowly as a snail's marathon. As the hours trawled by, I started to feel worse. I couldn't sleep, but I wasn't fully awake either.

In my state of twilight lucidity, I kept having thoughts about the Shadow Lady. I pictured her on a large shadow podium similar to the day I saw her in person, before I knew who she was. Hanging behind her in shadow nooses were The Leech, The Mute and The Jinx. She had a necklace on, the talisman of which was Patrick's shrunken head. I was squirming and sweating, wriggling painfully out of the duvet like a snake shedding its skin. I wished I was fully asleep so Silver Hair could keep me busy.

My wish was soon granted. "Hello," I heard her say, "how are you?" She was above a window depicting lightning strikes and rain clouds.

"Sick," I said piteously, but when the words came out, I realised I didn't feel sick here. "Well, out there I'm sick. Been stuck in bed all day." She rolled her eyes. "I was actually hoping to come here, I kept day dreaming, or 'day nightmaring', uh, 'daymaring', whatever, because I couldn't sleep and wanted you to keep me busy."

"Sick for a day and need an escape. Imagine what Melanie and my grandchild are-" she began.

I rolled my eyes. "Please, not today." I said holding my hand up. She opened her mouth for a moment before closing it and nodding.

"What happened in the daydreams?" She asked.

I was about to tell her I can't say, but why not? She had no true sway out there, M didn't know who she was and she didn't know who M was. "Have you ever heard of The Leech, The Mute or The Jinx?" I asked. She looked at me with a raised eyebrow, her head shook slightly. "Never mind. They're people with special powers but, wait, can you find people here? People from out there?"

"Yes, just a moment. Let me just locate the directory," she said. I smiled from ear to ear before I noted that she was joking. "You know it doesn't work like that, Kurt. The only reason I can find you so easily is because I can *feel* when you arrive. Everything else is sort of a flux, it changes and shifts constantly." She rubbed the nape of her neck. "Most of it anyway."

"Ah, fair enough." I thought she could maybe try finding one of those three so I could have more of an understanding of how their powers work. M said that The Jinx oversaw her own little group whilst The Leech was in some safe zone, but The Mute, the youngest one. What was her name again? Where was she? I wondered what her life would be like if Silver Hair could show me it. The poor girl was only a child, her family killed and she was kidnapped because they knew about her... about her... *Oh my god*. She was kidnapped and trapped because they knew about her power! I began to shake. "I know where she is. I know where she is." I roared, my voice cracked.

"Who? You know where who is?" Silver gasped. "Melanie?!"

"No! I don't know, maybe! But the trapped child for sure – the smaller window. It's a girl. It has to be her. She's the Mute. It makes sense!" It all began to fall in to place in my head. "Oh my god. It's so simple. A young girl. She was kidnapped for her power! She's been held against her will because of what she can do - *trapped in her power* like you said. It's got to be here." I was speaking too fast. Silver Hair seemed to be excited by my enthusiasm but skeptical about my explanation. "Her ability is to stop other people's abilities. Think about it, you try and get in her window but you can't? This is your power and she's passively blocking it. Wake me up. Please!"

"Who is it? Where is she? Can you get to her?" She gasped excitedly.

"I can't remember her name. We should be going to get her soon. She's been imprisoned somewhere because she can block the power of the person who started all of this, it's a long story. I need to tell M. Can you just wake me up?!" My speech rattled like a machine gun.

"I can," she nodded. "Are you sure this is the child from the blocked window? The one linked to my daughter?"

"I don't know, do I? I reckon so. It fits too well." I yelled. There was no one else it could be. It made sense, such an important little girl, it was all too coincidental to be irrelevant. "Oh my god. You said she might give in at any time. If she was to die and M finds out I knew something about her, she'll be so mad. I need to tell M now! Wake me up! Wake me up now so I can finally do what you've been pressuring me to do."

"I hope you're right," she said and pushed in to my chest.

I woke up in my bed coughing gutturally. I tried to stand up but I couldn't. My legs were too weak from the sickness and lack of food. I had to get out though. I had to tell M that we needed to go after The Mute *now*! That poor girl had been tortured for her ability this whole time and here we are taking our time. Now I knew who it was, even if I didn't know her personally, I couldn't just put it out of my mind. Not until I told M what I knew! I had to do this for that poor girl. I had to do this for M!

One girl! Rescuing her would make Silver Hair happy, would please M to no end, would be a counter to The Catalyst and would allow Lana and Patrick to be reunited! One girl is all we needed to finally turn the tide of the change from bad to good, or at least neutral!

I stood up using my telekinesis to stabilise myself. My brain was in agony, but I soldiered on. I walked over to the door and used my mind to open it. In the hallway, I managed to make it to the dorm entrance. I pressed the buzzer in as quick a succession as I could manage but there was no answer. I heard the kitchen door open behind me. "Kurt?" Jo's voice. "Kurt?! George, get here." There was thudding noise as the rest of them began to run to the corridor to see what was going on.

"What's up, mate?" George now. They were right behind me, but with concentrating on staying conscious and The Mute taking up my mind, I couldn't pay any attention to them. I buzzed and buzzed.

"Is he okay?" Anthony asked, rife with panic.

"Yeah, buddy. Don't worry." George again. I felt his hand on my shoulders, pulling me away. "Come on mate, let's go back to b- whah." I couldn't tell George to get off verbally but my ability threw him backwards down the corridor. I heard footsteps going to retrieve him as gasps filled the hall. Anthony began to cry. The noise pierced my ears. They all started shouting suggestions but I needed to focus. If only they would just shut up. I needed to think of a way to get out and tell M.

"I need to get out," I said. "The trapped girl. It's The Mute!" I mumbled.

"What are you talking about, Kurt?" Concern flooded Jo's voice.

"He's delirious," Marie groaned. "Get him some water. Aaron - wait, we haven't tried it yet. Anthony?" I felt his healing water spread across my body, but it didn't take the migraine or sickness away.

"No. I need to see M." I could picture her in my mind. If only I could reach her as easily as she could reach me.

"We don't even know if she's here, Kurt!" Jo said. She touched my shoulder for a moment, I could tell it was her touch but she quickly removed it. "He's not listening. Marie, what can we do?"

"I don't know! My parents were the nurses, I just picked up little bits here and there!" Marie was starting to panic now. *If they could only shut up so I could think of a way to open the door.*

"Shinji, do you want to put him asleep?" Aaron asked.

"No! Not while he's sick. I don't know what it might do." Shinji replied, his voice echoed in my head. I grunted and the corridor was filled with renewed gasps.

"Well, we need to do something. He's sleepwalking, or-" Aaron was shouting, but stopped when I held my hand up for silence. My eyes were shut tight wincing from the pain. *Fight it, Kurt.* I told myself. *M must know.*

"Aaron," I said under my breath. "Aaron. Get here." Instantly, he was beside me, holding my hand. I could feel him trembling.

"What's up? What do you need?" He mumbled anxiously.

"Freeze the door." I told him.

"Why?" His voice was high now.

I let go of myself and almost crumpled to the floor. "Jesus. Just. Freeze. The. Door." I felt arms catch me as I fell, Aaron yelped as I used my mind to pick him up and pushed him toward the door. His body tried to fight me but I held him rigid, only letting his arms free. "Freeze. It." I forced out through gritted teeth. *M needed to know.*

"Kurt, stop it! You're scaring Anthony!" Jo begged.

"Will you just shut up for once?" I snapped back. "Aaron, do it now!"

"Okay. Okay!" Aaron submitted. My face clenched in pain. I could hear the cracking and crunching of the ice as he began to freeze the door.

"Dorian," I barked. "Break it." He didn't argue. There was a thud as his foot hit the ice-door.

"This isn't a good idea," Marie warned, meekly.

"I'm not arguing with him," Dorian shouted as he kicked the door open again. "Not while he's like this." If I could muster the energy I would stand up and kiss him right now. The only one here with sense. That's all I needed: complicity. *Thud. Thud. Thud. Crack. Thud. Thud. Crack.* Each impact echoed and bounced off the walls of my skull. Rattling my brain. The pain was making me feel worse, my stomach was heaving, wanting so much to hurl its contents up, but I was determined. *M must know! Thud. Thud. Crack. Crunch. Boom!* The door was down. Open. I could leave!

My friends followed behind me keeping a safe distance, the effulgence of the corridors burned my corneas. Jo and George called my name in sharp whispers but they daren't touch me. If they did I would throw them back down the hall, whether I wanted to or not. M needed to know The Mute could give in and die at any time. *M must know.* She trusted me. If the Mute dies, that's one less chance of stopping the Shadow Lady. One less chance of reuniting Lana and Patrick. One less chance of gaining M's approval; her love. All I wanted was her love.

I turned corner after corner not exactly sure where I was going. There were usually guards here, why was it empty now? I thought too soon, it seemed. As I turned another corner, there were two of them standing at the other end. They did not react. They didn't seem at all bothered at the fact there was a floating boy followed by a group of people. As I got closer, the faces became clearer. A man and a woman.

"I need to talk to M." I urged whilst trying to get the woman's attention. She did not respond. She stood there without even moving. I grunted then turned to the man. "I need to speak to your boss." No! *No, no, no, no, no!*

It was him. I knew him. That face. My thoughts began to blur in my head. Those blue eyes. That black hair.

I *know* him. I began to shudder as disorientation stole over me. He was in a photograph somewhere. That was important for some reason, but my thoughts wouldn't connect. Then for a moment, it all became clear. The realisation overwhelmed me.

My head collided with the floor as consciousness drained. It didn't make sense. This man - his picture was in the house we looted, but M said this town was evacuated. What was left of my cognitive thought had escaped. Thousands of miles away, my friends were crying my name. The world turned black.

Chapter 15

Consciousness budded and wilted many times. When it managed to permanently take root, I became aware that my body was torridly dry. My tongue so coarse and lips so pruned that I felt even Aaron would struggle correcting the problem. I scraped my tongue across my lips and it felt like flint on tinder. I shuddered. The effort of opening my eyes was barely more than I could manage. When I finally did, I shut them again instantly. It was bright. Too bright.

"Hello?" My voice was weak and croaky. "Where am I?" There was no reply. I lay there groggily waiting to fully wake up. Mentally preparing myself as I did so many mornings before uni or work, coaching myself on the positives of sitting up and getting out of bed.

I vaguely remembered pushing George, knocking him backward but I couldn't remember why. Memories began to flit through my mind. I was sick. That's right, I was pretty much in bed the whole day. Then... I fell asleep and... *The Mute*! As soon as she entered my mind, the whole day flooded back. Silver Hair, the trapped child is The Mute. I was looking for M. She needed to know! Did I faint? No! I saw something. *Him!* Who? An image of a face floated in my mind; the features were corrupt, incomplete but there was something. I didn't just faint- well I did, but not due to the sickness.

My face scrunched up in pain as I tried to remember. I knew him. Those blue eyes. That black hair. A face in a frame. A framed photograph. That was important, but why? There was no reason for it to be. It felt like the more I thought about it - the closer I got to figuring it out - the worse I felt. I pushed it out of my mind. Laying still for a further ten minutes or so before I finally mustered the strength to sit up. When I did so, I felt a sensation of snagging and suction all over my body. *Pop. Pop. Pop.*

That's when I realised I was in the hospital wing. Wires were attached to my body, all over as if I was a puppet. I was about to dramatically rip them all off my body as you see the actors do in movies, but fretting the financial repercussions of such an act I let loose a pulse of telekinesis which gently plucked them from my bare skin.

I looked around the room. Everything reflected the harsh lights. I checked the clipboard at the bottom of my bed. There was information, dosages and updates that I didn't understand. I found it very strange how my body could require something to stay healthy, yet my brain did not know what it was.

When attempting to leave the bed, my legs almost gave way. *How long have I been here?* I tried to contact M, picturing my mind like a beacon for her telepathy, but it was no good. Surely there should be a button or a buzzer somewhere in the room? Where was the little thumb-clicker that calls for help? I searched half-heartedly before giving up. I needed a drink more than anything else. I looked around finding no source of water.

I left my medical room and began to walk down the shining corridor. Something felt strange. Considering I was underground, my body felt strangely sensitive to a cold breeze. I was suddenly paralysed in fear... I was naked. I ran back to the room, my feet slapping the floor. There was no sort of hospital garb around so I pulled the plastic sheeting off the bed and draped it over my shoulder like a toga. It wasn't flattering, but it would do the job.

I left once more in search for any form of hydration; a confused animal separated from his pack trying to find the watering hole... in the medical wing of a highly advanced research facility where everything is provided for us. I pondered on that for a moment as I travelled down the corridors. Why was I in the medical wing if I fainted? Last time, I woke up to Marie. Why wouldn't she just wake me back up again. *'Thank you, your Kurt is fully restored. We hope to see you again.'* As simple as that.

The ghost of a thought flitted by my mind's eye again in the form of a photograph, I felt my stomach lurch again. *What was this photograph?* Whenever faced with a problem or an obstacle in life, I prided myself on my effortless ability to ignore it. Whatever this thing was that decided to haunt me, it was irrelevant and unimportant.

Wait! My heart rate began to increase. The Medical Wing?! I couldn't help but feel excited. My mind forgetting the thirst and the stupid photograph. Lana was here! I couldn't remember what room number she was, but seeing as I was stranded here, I decided I may as well go check up on her. M would understand - Lana is my friend. Also, as soon as I told M about The Mute, she would appreciate my loyalty regardless and forgive my misbehaviour.

I started to power walk down the corridors. I cursed my inability to grasp simple directions. These corridors - though all the doors were labelled - were just as confusing as the level above. Did the scientists require a map to get around these halls? I sure would, never mind multiple floors. I walked on, checking the doors. Some of them had slats with names on, but they were either locked or windowless. I tried to ignore the names, there was only one I was looking for. **D-17, D-18, D-19, D-20, D-21, D-22, D-23, D-24, D-25.** Corner. **E-1, E-2, E-3,** Etc, etc.

I somehow managed to travel from corridor **E**, to **F**, to **H** (no sign of **G** anywhere), somehow back to **D**, then to **F** again, and finally I stumbled across the slat I was looking for. **J-20: Stawski, Lana.** I paused staring at it. I was happy I found it but incredulous at the fact I had managed to find **J** without passing **I**. I looked around, then deciding now is a good a time as any, I tried to push the door open. Locked as well. I tried again a little harder but it didn't budge. I shook the door in frustration - it opened. It was a pull door. All the other doors would have been the same and I didn't even think to check. I blushed in spite of myself as I slipped inside.

I paused when I saw her. I half imagined her sitting up, reading a book, to smile when I walked in and rush to embrace me, but she did not. She lay there on the bed, a network of plastic tubes attached to her body as they were mine. From the door I could see her chest rise and fall with her deep breaths. With each inhale, sporadic motes of light rose and clung around her like fairy lights framing a sleeping princess, only to drop to the bed and disappear when she exhaled.

I felt my eyes watering. I approached and stood above her, letting my brain process the image. She looked so peaceful. No tears, no brave face, no worries. A deep sleep. "Lana." I whispered. No reaction. The beeping of a machine nearby, identical to the one in my room droned on. "Lana?" I tried again, a little louder this time. Still no sign of recognition. One of the plastic tubes resting on her chest bifurcated and trailed in to her nostrils. Poor girl. "Lana?" I said louder still and I nudged her gently. At my touch, her beautiful specks of light spewed forth and bounced off my hand before disappearing. No burning this time. I froze in horror. A large pink scar spread the length of her inner arm. I traced it delicately, there was a gentle whimper from her unconscious mouth. I had never seen *that* before.

I checked the clipboard at the bottom of her bed. It seemed she was on a strong dosage of *Propofol* at six hour intervals. I nodded as if I agreed with M's dosage before popping the clipboard back in, actually gleaning little information on her current state. She just lay there. Still. Unmoving.

I walked back over to Lana and brushed her hair back. "When you're better again," I said to her pitiable form, "we're going to get Patrick back. I promise."

Frustration and a feeling of futility infused within me giving birth to a half-sigh, half-groan. Something in the room seemed off. Not quite right. I shook the feeling away. Next to the beeping computer was a small book. I hovered it toward myself and used my hands to pluck it out of the air. A notebook? Her diary? *I can't read her diary.*

Then suddenly, out of nowhere the diary *fell upward* off the bed in to my hands, open on the first page. Who can say whether my ability did that or not (I can. It did). What else could I do but read? At first glance, her handwriting looked familiar. No, this wasn't Lana's handwriting... In fact, I had never seen hers unless the giant 'HELP' counted. Then whose was this? Why was it familiar?

My mouth dropped open. This wasn't Lana's diary, this was M's status report! Hand to heart, I tried to put the book down but I couldn't tear my eyes away. We had spent so long with no proper information on her condition that my respect for M was swept to the back of my mind as if trying to convince myself it wasn't an invasion of her work.

Patient:	*#29*
Name:	*Lana Stawksi*
Age:	*27*
Ability:	*Conjuration and manipulation of photon particles*
Properties:	*Brighter than most other sources of light; not a source of energy. Cannot be used to charge solar products. Usually no dangerous effect, but when subjected to stressful situations, exhibits thermal properties. A result of emotions, or lack of necessity when calm? [Ref: Rsrch module 107 - Hidden Natures] Further experimentation req.*
Caution Req?:	*Moderate - mostly neutral. Emotionally unstable. Prone to breakdowns. Easily controlled. Responds well to sedatives*
T.ment:	*Propofol [6 hr intvls - no long-term effects, impossible to interfere with ability]*
Notes:	*Related to The Catalyst [Sibling] Exhibits no superior prowess in tandem with his. Inconclusive, but useful.*

M was not kidding when she said we were her subjects as well as her responsibility. Why did she not mention any of this when talking to me about Lana's progress? My brain began to work overtime. "Rsrch module 107" was obviously linked to some report or other, that was clear enough, but "Patient #29"? There were twenty-eight patients prior to Lana? That couldn't be right. Plus, what the hell is *Propofol*? It hit me then, the unsettling feeling that something wasn't right... her room was as clean as my hospital room. Almost untouched, but Lana... She had been here for-

The door opened behind me, M stood framed. "Sit down," she ordered. Her voice did not betray how she was feeling, but I obeyed her words without question. It was as if each word was all I could think about until I sat on the desk, legs together, hands on my lap. "What are you doing here, Kurt?"

167

I tried to speak, but words would not come. "I- I-" Nope. I wanted to apologise, to tell her that I woke up in the medical room by myself. That I needed a drink and I tried to contact her.

"I see," M entered the room fully and let the door close behind her.

"I'm sorry. I- I just wanted to see if Lana was okay whilst I was here. Please don't hate me. P- Please, I just- I've been worried. We've all been worried. I just wanted to check. I'm sorry. I'm really sorry." I could feel tears streaming down my face, I weren't sure if it was due to fear or they just wanted to escape as well. "M, honestly," my nose began to run, I sniffled pulling the contents of it back in. "I woke up and when I realised I was in the medical wing, I tried to buzz. I didn't think about looking for Lana until I was outside my door."

She raised an eyebrow slightly. "But you still actively searched?"

"Yeah. But not to disobey you," I whimpered. "Honestly, I just wanted to check on her. I didn't want to annoy you. I never want to annoy you."

"So, to combat doing so not only do you wander the halls of one of my wings with no supervision - after causing damage to your dormitory entrance, I might add - you also intentionally looked for a patient, regardless of your connection to her? Not only do you do this whilst being fully aware it is not permitted, but you proceed to read *my* personal notes?"

"I…"

"In regards to her medication, I deign to remind you of your limited knowledge in the field of medicine and advise you to never question my judgement in what your friend requires. However, to quell your simplistic paranoia, it is a strong sedative that keeps her in this relaxed state whilst not addling her brain." I didn't understand why she needed to be kept asleep, though. Surely, she would be more useful awake. "Yes, Kurt. That is what I requested but she is still so overcome with grief she begged for an increased dosage to negate her having to *feel*." She took a deep breath. "I refused at first, but then she took matters in to her own hands, resorting to drastic measures in an attempt to stop the pain she was feeling," M indicated her arm. The scar. "So, I went against my better judgement for Ms. Stawski's wellbeing, even though there is a risk it would mar any results."

I began to cry for poor Lana, she didn't deserve any of this. And M, she had been nothing but gracious and helpful and I come in here disrespecting her authority and good-natured heart. I dropped to the floor and overcome with grief of my own, I began to hug M's legs. She stood for a moment before she spoke again.

"Enough. Get up." As if her words had induced a state of catharsis, I calmed down. My body shuddering and reeling, but my emotions, thankfully, sated. "Your miscreant friend, Joanne, would have done something along these lines; snooping through areas that are out of bounds in order to allow her paranoid brain free reign in finding something out of the ordinary, but not you. You trust me. I *know* that is true, so why did you doubt me just now?"

"It's not that I doubted you. It was just a lot of information-"

"Because you were doing something wrong, your mind automatically makes stories to justify your actions. Do not question my research, my medical knowledge or wander freely around these halls again, Kurt. If you wish to explore without prohibition, you may leave this facility."

I nodded at her. I felt incredibly weak and powerless. M's eyes looked me up and down. I held the hospital toga closer to me and she shook her head. In a swift motion, she held her status report down and as if appearing from nowhere, her daughter was there reaching for it. She reminded me of a shadow, always present but rarely noticed. M smiled at me when I thought this. I tried to smile back, but instead, I shuddered again.

M busied herself around Lana's bed for a while. She checked the wires, typed a few commands in to the computer next to her and scribbled something on the clipboard before rounding on me. "So, tell me, Kurt. What was it exactly that possessed you to destroy my door?"

"Your door? Oh! The dorm. Oh!" Excitement replaced the fear. Maybe this was my chance of redemption. "I was looking for you. I buzzed and buzzed in the dorm, but no one came. I tried to get your attention from my mind but I couldn't. I was really sick and wasn't thinking properly."

"Yes, the sickness must be what led to your collapse last week. Have you been eating well?"

"Yeah, I think it may- Last week?!" I gasped. "I've been out a week?! Are you serious?"

"No, Kurt. I thought now, in the face of your brazen disrespect for me, I should attempt to dabble in trivial insincerities." She was back at the computer now.

"Sorry. Yeah, of course. I just didn't realise I was out for that long, is all." I thought about my friends. They must be worried sick. "Is everyone else okay?"

"Believe it or not, they have managed." She left the room. I wanted to squeeze Lana's hand goodbye, but I didn't dare. I followed M and her daughter, my mind was still racing over Lana and I couldn't get the image of the scar out of my mind. After being the rock that kept her brother anchored, after being his constant, the reason for him to never give up - she had reached a point where *she* wanted to.

Bewildered, I only counted turning two corners until we were at my room. M held the door open and I entered before her. "On the bed." She ordered.

I hopped on the bed and slumped over. M was annoyed and disappointed in me. It felt like I had obliterated the trust of all my favourite authoritative figures. The teachers I respected, the barista at my favourite coffee shop who would often give me the drink for free when my card didn't work, my parents. I wanted to cry but it wouldn't help, I wanted to apologise but it wouldn't matter.

"Do you miss your parents, Kurt?" M said whilst scrolling through some complicated colour-coded graph on the computer which peaked and dropped. Hair rose on my skin when it dawned on me that this graph represented my health, those peaks and drops were something to do with me.

"Uh... of course I do, but," I thought for a moment. In my time here, I actually hadn't really allowed myself to dwell on my parents. Every so often I would think about them, but it would fall out of my mind. I had no idea if they were alive and if so, how they were coping through all of this, but even now, thinking about them briefly, it felt as if they were detached from my emotions. I hoped they were okay, but it wasn't my duty to ensure they were. M was smiling at me. I needed to answer and honesty was the best policy, especially with a mind reader. "To tell you the truth, I haven't really thought about them much. Is that bad?"

M shook her head slowly. "The change you have gone through is drastic. It would be natural to worry about your parents but you are independent, you moved to a new city and took *that* change in your stride. If you still depended on them, maybe you would be sick with worry. Perhaps the reason you have not worried about their safety too much is because you would crumble if you did. It shows you are strong."

I smiled and nodded then wondered if she missed her parents. She studied me for a moment. "I did not know my father. My mother was a disappointment. She had the potential to be so much more. She was weak. Worse, she was ignorant. I cannot abide ignorance so I turned my back on her." M said this matter-of-factly, as simple as deciding what to eat for lunch.

My throat tightened. *Change the subject. Change the subject, Kurt.* "Is everything okay with me?"

"When you were unconscious, I could not read your mind. Your thoughts were blocked off and I was unsure when you would recover." She opened a drawer and pulled out a sheet of paper. "Look here, Kurt," she handed it to me and I studied it for a moment. A bar chart, similar to the one she showed us with the woman and The Catalyst.

"Is this my brain?" I asked finding it bizarre my mind could be displayed so simply.

She rolled her eyes. "You see, your ability is linked to your frontal lobe." I nodded. The bar that corresponded with that lobe towered above the rest. "I managed to stabilise brain activity by keeping each lobe stimulated. I succeeded, of course. If not, I fear you may have been left brain damaged."

"You've saved me twice now." I allowed, eternally grateful.

"Let us not try for a third," she replied as her daughter pulled up a small chair for her to sit on. "So, now I am up to date with your health, do tell me what happened."

Okay. Now was my time to win her back over. "Well, I fainted or collapsed or whatever it was when I saw one of your staff. My mind went all fuzzy again like it did that day we were collecting things from the village." M scribbled on the board. She was looking at me, but she wasn't at the same time. She was reading my mind as I was telling her what happened. "But the reason I was looking for someone in the first place is because I needed to tell you something." She shifted in her chair, an eyebrow raised. I had her attention. I knew something she didn't. I could help her. "The Mute. The Mute is in danger."

I thought about Silver Hair. How long she had tried to warn me that her daughter and potentially a child were trapped. That I had to act fast but instead procrastinated; all that time I could have brought The Mute to M's attention. How it was all connected, Silver Hair's face clear in my mind. M's mouth dropped open. "When you said we don't have much time, you were right. We should go for The Mute first because *she* is trapped in her ability, somehow, I don't know the ins and outs of it."

M stood up. The clipboard dropped. She was shaking! She mouthed 'No.' but words did not come out. "Yes!" I said. "Look, since this change I've been having these weird dreams. It's like when I go to sleep I'm transported to, a-uh -"

"How could I not see this?" M mumbled to herself, but I was barely able to register it.

"- a different world of some sort. There's some girl there, I'm not really sure what her power is but she can, like, *see* people's minds. It must be a bit like yours." The colour from M's face had drained. "She's been looking for her daughter, Melanie, even though she's only young herself I think - but who am I to judge - I don't really know what the right age is anymore.

171

Anyway, she said the only way to get to her daughter is through me. I reckon if we can get The Mute, we could reunite her with this Melanie and at the same time use The Mute to get Patrick back!"

She was frozen. A living statue in front of me. Like her staff. "This is impossible…" She muttered.

"I know it sounds impossible - it's a bit awkward to explain but basically she says people's minds are like windows – she actually thought her daughter was in her weird little world at one point and tried to approach her. Do you know if family members have a link or a bond with one another's power at all? Have you researched in to that? You should," her eyes were wider than I had ever seen, she looked confused for the first time ever, "because she found these two windows, right? But they were blocked and she reckons they belong to her family. Said she can sense it or something."

"How has she hidden this from me?" Her voice was almost inaudible now.

"She said the windows are blocked because they're trapped." I preened as I had worked this out alone. "It makes sense. The Mute is trapped- Ow!"

M slapped me hard across the face. I flinched too late and held my hand to my cheek. She slapped me again. "How *dare* you!" She roared. "How dare you, you ignorant child!" She held her hand out and my body sat down. It felt like she was forcing me to do it, but at the same time, it felt as if it was what I wanted to do. I was crying again. "I protect you. I save you from the chaos out there and you, *you* deem it fit to go contacting people! Do you understand the risk you are putting yourself, your friends, *me* and my work at?

"Do you not think? Is that brain so incapable that you lack the prowess to allow simple thought processes to occur? You have been conferring with an outsider every night? Not just any outsider, my- oh no."

I was trembling, terrified. "No, she's not like the rest of us, she's only awake in her little void place," I was rubbing my face where she had slapped me, "and, it wasn't every night, when Shinji put me to sleep she couldn't get to me. Honestly, I haven't compromised any-"

"Shut your mouth," she snapped and I slapped myself in the face. I had no idea why I did it, but I was saving her the effort. "You have jeopardised more than your pathetic life is worth. Think of her. Think of this woman as clearly as you can."

I did. I thought of everything about her, the things she had told me, the way she speaks, the way she floats around in her void. Then it felt as if my brain was burning. M began to tremble and for the first time, I heard her daughter make a noise. She screamed in agony. M slapped her daughter

172

across the face. "Pay attention!" She shouted at her, then turned back to me. M was shaking, or my brain was shaking; vibrating in my head. It was too difficult to discern. My vision was blurring, the image of Silver Hair in my head began to fade. I tried to focus, I tried to keep the image clear for M, I had to. That is what M required of me and I must obey - but it was fading faster as if there was a mental eraser, rubbing the memory away. M held her hand out, the image was almost unrecognisable, just like the image of that photograph. *What is happening to me?* I began to scream in pain - focusing as much as I could handle on the image, trying to keep it sharp. M dropped to the floor and the burning sensation dissipated.

"It is not working," she groaned, exhausted, "too weak. Too taxing." Her eyes were unfocused.

At this, Megan held her hands to each side of her head and began to scream once more. "Help! Help me!" There was no tone to her voice, it was a peeling screech. As if she was being throttled! "I'm lost! Mummy, stop-" The sound made me reel. She was *mute*! She couldn't talk. M said so. I already felt dizzy, as if I was about to throw up and faint once more. I couldn't. I didn't have time to faint. M needed help, I needed to get her up off the floor. The room was spinning, things didn't make sense.

"No." M screamed, composing herself and instantly her daughter was silent once more. I teetered and tumbled, grabbing anything I could to support myself. It felt as if my brain was re-constructing itself, a network of neural pathways were completely rerouted, re-wired, as if my usual thoughts were whispers trapped in a tornado - irrelevant and lost. My ability was uncontrollably spilling out of me, trashing the room.

Then, for a second - a fraction of a second - everything was peaceful. M and I were looking directly in to one another's eyes, panting heavily. The screaming, whirring panic in my head was stilled. M maintained eye contact, her face contorted in to that of pure fury.

My mind centred on Silver Hair but now, instead of the image fading away, it was stronger but altered. She looked older, much older. I could see her young aesthetic in tandem with her aged appearance. Her frail, old, wrinkled and pasty face before me. *Gaunt, pathetic, weak. A quitter. A liability.*

All I felt for her was pure hatred. I despised her. Everything about her. How she treated me, how she controlled me, how she threatened me. How she refused to accept my girlfriend. *What girlfriend, Kurt?* How she raised me. *She didn't raise you, Kurt!* How she tried to undermine my work. *What?*

How she gave up on me, the way she gave up on her health! *When*? I preferred it when she was comatose.

M and I screamed at the same time. The door burst open behind her and her staff stormed in. They ran around M, like a wave passing a rock that jutted out of the ocean. They picked me up, I was too disorientated to fight. They slammed me against the wall and pinned me there, their arms pushing at me, almost crushing me.

"You!" M said and the staff members spoke with her. Her daughter was back to the usual emotionless automaton state. "You will never contact her again." My face was damp with tears. Her arms spread wide, the staff pulled at my sides like a human torture rack. "Will you?" I conceded and begged – I knew I never would. Then I was dropped to the floor where I wept.

After a while the room was calm once more, the only sound was my crying. When I managed to look up, the staff had left. I hadn't heard them go. M was sitting in a chair and her daughter stood next to her. M's eyes were red raw and a pang of guilt struck my heart, resonating through my body like a gong. She looked in my direction. "Tell me, Kurt." She spoke quietly and slowly "Did you ever tell her where we were? Did you ever reveal my identity?"

"I didn't. I told her I was in a facility, but I never said anything about you, or exactly where we were. I don't even know where this place is." I tried to think if I had ever mentioned anything of significance, but I couldn't think of a moment. "I really am sorry." She nodded. "Do you know her?"

Her eyes narrowed at me. I looked away instantly. "I used to." She stood upright. "You say when your friend Shinji puts you to sleep, she cannot reach you?"

"Yeah." I squeaked.

She studied me for a moment, then bid me follow her as she left the room. "The final test is tomorrow, now you are recovered, I expect you to participate. You will not tell your friends about what happened down here. You will not speak of Lana. You will not tell them about the dangerous woman in your dreams," I felt a surge of hatred when M mentioned her, "will you, Kurt?"

I wouldn't. Even if I wanted to. I owed my life to M. I truly did. I would do anything to make her happy. I was not keeping secrets from my friends, I was respecting the only person trying to save people out there. The lift doors closed behind us and began to ascend. I felt exhausted, physically and emotionally. I felt like crying, but I was too tired. I wanted to shake this day off. I wanted to rest for whatever tomorrow held. "Perhaps you need

174

something to prove I am your only hope - something to show you that she will stop at nothing to reach her goal. I hope it doesn't come to that, Kurt."

The lift jolted and the heavy doors opened before us. We were back on Sub-Level One, not that I could tell the difference. The two of us- no, the three of us - her daughter was there, I almost forgot somehow... Her daughter. Why did she scream? *No*! If my questions would not help further M's goal, I would not ask them. The three of us walked in silence. She had the door to our corridor repaired.

She opened the door and motioned for me to enter first. I did. She smiled wryly and I felt anguished, yet devoted. Within seconds, the kitchen door swung open. Jo beamed when she saw me. "Kurt!" She called out then ran to hug me. I hugged back with what little strength I had. "We've been so worried." The rest of my dorm ran out from the kitchen – Dorian had *Monopoly* money in his hand - but as soon as they saw M they stopped. Jo held me at arm's length and there were tears in her eyes. She hugged me close again.

"Shinji," M said paying no attention to Jo.

"Huh? Me? I mean, yes?" Shinji said, clearly confused.

"I require your gift," M told him.

"Of course. Anything you need," he offered obediently.

"You do not let Kurt sleep naturally. You utilise your ability to ensure he is switched off. Through the previous tests I can confirm that there are no lasting side effects from your ability, so you will do this and you will not hesitate." Shinji looked from M to me. I smiled and he nodded in reply. "If you see Kurt is getting tired, you take him to his room and you put him to sleep. If Kurt is sick and does not leave the room, you put him to sleep. If Kurt so much tries to stifle a yawn, you put him to sleep. Am I understood?" Shinji nodded. "If he does fall asleep naturally, wake him then use your power."

"Why?" Jo asked.

"It is what I need." I replied before M had to. She should not have to deal with Jo's blatant disrespect.

"Precisely," M added, "I suggest you get some rest. Tomorrow will be the final test before I make my decision on delegation." She turned to leave, opening the door and then stopped. "Kurt, consider your priorities." I made a noise in agreement. I knew were my priorities lay, in the form of the woman that saved my life. "Shinji, what I have asked of you is not a request, it is an order."

"Of course." Shinji replied nervously and M left without another word, though it felt as if her presence still lingered.

"Kurt, are you okay?" Jo asked before I was subject to a fusillade of further questions.

"Yes!" I snapped. I was furious, the anger so intense that it didn't even feel like my own. "Just for once, can you all shut up? I've just got back and I need to sleep."

"Kurt…" Jo grabbed my hand and I snatched it back, not exactly sure what had possessed me.

"Mate, there's no need to be like that." George looked taken aback and disappointed by my behaviour. "We've just been worried about you. You never get sick like that, then out of nowhere you're gone for a week. We're just happy to see you, so stop with the attitude, alright?"

"Like your opinion matters," for a fleeting second, I felt like I wanted to hit him. I wanted to hurt him. "You don't even count as a person anymore." I regretted it as soon as I said it. I didn't even mean it, it wasn't what I thought, not actively anyway. It was autocued, picking out an insecurity he had and using it to hurt him. Ready, aim, *fire*! The words didn't even belong to me.

He was about to argue, but instead simply shook his head and shrunk away in to the kitchen with Anthony. Jo gave me a concerned look before following him. Dorian followed after, then Aaron. I wanted to run in and say sorry, but it would be pointless. I would sleep and apologise tomorrow.

Only Shinji and Marie were left. Marie spoke first. "He's been really worried about you. That was such a horrid thing to say." *I know*. I knew it was a cheap shot. I didn't mean it. It wasn't what I thought. I was drowning in guilt but I just had to sleep the damn day off.

"Please just… just come and make me sleep." I sighed, defeated. Shinji put his arm around my shoulder and guided me to bed.

"Ready." I said when I was completely comfortable. As Shinji lent down beside me, it dawned on me why Lana would beg for a higher dosage of her sedatives. Betraying M and belittling George had only just happened but it was already too much for me to handle. I just wanted to sleep to not have to feel. Shinji's hands were on my head now. If I was in Lana's position, I would want exactly that, to not have to feel. I began to blink slowly as Shinji's power drained my consciousness.

Chapter 16

I woke up to Jo switching the lights on and pulling the blankets off me. "Come on. Wake up." Her voice was too loud, too chirpy. At this hour, it mocked everything I stood for. I reached for the blanket but she snatched it further away and threw it to the floor. I covered my eyes and dragged the blanket from the floor with my mind. "No you don't, Kurt. Get up." She gripped my torso and with more strength than a freight train, she pulled. I fell on the floor.

"I mean for once, Jo, can you not just gently wake me up?"

"I could and I have done before. You'll say you're awake and you'll be out in ten minutes, then I'll come back in and you'll be asleep, then I'll wake you up and you'll get moody and we'll bicker, then you'll wake up properly and we'll forget about it. We don't have time to sit around, we need to be up within an hour for the final test." She made a strange noise. "Well, our final, your first."

"Fine. Give me five minutes and I'll be up." I said. I jumped up as I was doused with ice-cold water; the blanket and my pillow rose in to the air with shock. "What the hell are you doing, Jo?"

"Helping you shower, now you've started, you can finish. Get up." She smiled sickeningly in my face then walked to the door holding it open. "I've got a towel and your tagged clothes waiting in the shower for you, everyone else is ready and eating. Your turn now, come on."

As the shower rained on me, I couldn't help but be thankful for Shinji's ability blocking Silver Hair. It was infuriating to think that she had been using me, that she knew M this whole time and was trying to make me her little servant in the real world.

I dried and got ready before walking to the kitchen. I put on my best 'I-am-so-terribly-sorry-for-my-actions-however-may-I-ask-for-your-forgiveness?' face which was pretty much puppy-dog eyes, looking down to the right and a slight pout of the lips. I took a breath and walked in. Breakfast smelled amazing.

"Morning all." I said to the kitchen as one. I was impressed with the softness of my voice, it added to the evidence of my guilt. Shinji smiled and said good morning whereas Aaron, Dorian and Marie gave me a weak smile in reply. George and Anthony ignored me completely. I was used to being ignored (and often) but never by George.

"Glad to see you're awake bright and early." Jo smirked. I was about to make a snide remark but it would juxtapose my apologetic state.

"It smells amazing in here." I announced, obsequiously. "Your cooking always smells spot on, George." He ignored me. I sat at the counter; the room was silent and tense. "So, what were the tests like?" I asked. Nobody replied for a while. As soon as I picked up a plate, George scraped the leftover morsels in the bin. I wiped the surface of the plate with my shirt as if that was my intention all along.

"Intense," Jo finally said, "a lot of pressure on us all."

"Not all of us," George corrected her, "the boy who doesn't count had to sit here and wait."

"Why?" I asked. He didn't reply. Dorian was whirring the glass balls around the air, they would often change shape, clearly a result of the previous two tests. "You've come a long way with that, Dorian."

"Yeah. M knows what she's doing," Dorian's reply was polite, but curt.

"Yeah... cool." I took a deep breath and slowly exhaled. "Uh, George? Can I have a word quickly?"

"Nah, wouldn't wanna inconvenience my superiors, Kurt. Soz."

"Don't be like that. I didn't mean it. I was just tired and had been through a lot. I saw Lan- uh- lots of things and M was saying I could have been brain damaged. I was just cranky. I'm sorry." It was a weak apology and not how I expected it to come out, but there it was.

"Well, bit of truth in everything isn't there?" He said stubbornly. "Sorry. Isn't there, *Master*?"

"No, I don't think that. You know I'm not like that, George. I'm too self-conscious to have a superiority complex."

"Yet. There you are." He indicated to me ostentatiously with an open arm.

"George, please. I don't want t-"

"Kurt, leave it. I need to get ready for the test," he barked.

"What? You said you weren't allowed t-"

"Well, she's asked me to for this one, hasn't she? Needs someone who doesn't count as a person it seems."

"What. Why would she need you?" I wanted to bang my head on the desk. "That came out wrong. I just mean has she said why she wants you to join?"

"Nope," drier than the Sahara, "must have ran out of staff to use as fodder, needs another person to stand there for target practice."

The image of the child who regenerated limbs flashed back in my head. I suppressed the shudder. "Don't be silly, George. She must think you're useful! You're sporty and look after yourself, maybe-"

"Just drop it, Kurt," he grunted, his anger flaring. I did. He clearly wasn't ready to talk. He left the room, Anthony and Dorian following him out.

"Just give him a while, Kurt. It was crappy of you, but he'll get over it. It's not that big of a deal." Jo soothed.

Now George had left, Aaron, Shinji, Jo and Marie were more comfortable talking to me. I was telling them about being unconscious and waking up not realising how long it had been when the hall buzzer went off outside.

"Ah, there we are. Once more unto the breach," Jo said, then called out to the corridor, "everyone ready?"

When we left, George tagged behind with Dorian and Anthony, Jo kept popping between the two of us. I still felt guilty, but I didn't want to have to worry about George *and* whatever the test would bring so instead, I just spent my time trying to quell my nerves.

We followed a staff member to the lift. When inside, Buzz, Geoff and Blake were in there with the rest of their dorm and another staff member. Blake avoided our eye contact, Geoff was nervously fumbling with his hands. But Buzz, he was staring right at us.

"Y'know," Buzz called out over the churning and clanging of the lift. "When we get to the top, you can just wait for the door to open - you don't need to break it. Okay, lapdog?" Geoff giggled and a few of the others in the lift tittered. How did he even know about that? Why did he call me a lapdog?

"Y'know," Jo replied mimicking his tone. "You could try an insult that isn't subpar at best for once."

"And how can I be a lapdog, do my ears look floppy?" I added.

Buzz laughed. "Oh, come on, darlin'. You must be sick of trying to stand up for that."

"You must be sick of standing in general. Let me help," Jo said, clearly not in the humour for this and quick as a flash she kicked behind one of his kneecaps. The leg buckled and gave way and he crumpled to the floor. Now it was my dorm's turn to laugh.

We walked separately from the other dorms. The sun was beating down and the sky was almost cloudless. At least it was a nice day for my first test. Having been trapped inside for so long, the fresh air filled my lungs with pleasure as well as oxygen.

As we left the more densely built area of the town and the forest was clearly in view, I could see the rest of the people waiting on the outskirts. There was at least a hundred people there, it seemed like there were more than the last time we were all out here together but that could only be a good thing. Amid all these people clad in black, stood M's staff. Perfectly equidistant from one another. Like markers, rather than humans.

People were testing out their powers. Vapours clung to the air in all colours imaginable, looking like a retired old rainbow that just couldn't stay up any longer. The air itself rippled here and there. All manners of energy were flying from one to another; chatoyant beams, whirring discs, pulsating spirals, glistening orbs of all different sizes buzzed and shot in front of our eyes.

I could see, just on the edge of the forest, people racing. One boy was running on all fours as fast as a cheetah, he was way ahead of the rest and his face was full of joy until a girl, who was travelling just as fast caught up and matched his speed. The boy looked at her and his joy turned to determination, but the girl didn't seem to be tiring out - instead of legs, there was a small dark whirlwind.

Shinji grabbed hold of my arm and yanked me to safety. I heard a whizzing noise fly past my ear. Moments later, someone appeared in front of me. "Sorry! She was aiming for me, don't worry - it doesn't hurt." Then they were gone in a puff of smoke before I could tell them not to worry about it. I was in awe. It was like the first day when I left my house, everyone trying out their abilities, but now people seemed to be in complete control - no fear, no violence. We continued to approach the rest until our staff member stopped still at a certain point and would not move after that.

Within half an hour, M arrived with her silent cortège and addressed everyone there. "Thank you for arriving here promptly. Your cooperation, as always, is greatly appreciated." The crowd was completely silent. Not a stray coloured vapour in sight. "Welcome to the final test you will be taking with me. After today, things are going to change."

M began to speak at length about The Catalyst, The Leech, The Mute and The Jinx. She did not go in to the same detail as she did with me, but she said enough to clue them up. Every so often, there was a gasp or mutter of disbelief from my friends, mostly when M spoke about the malevolence of her ex-partner and the lengths she will go to in order to use Patrick's ability, regardless of him being alive or dead. My friends didn't know I was aware of this information, so when they looked at me wide-eyed and pale, I employed my best acting skills to appear as if this was brand new to me too. Luckily, they were too busy listening to question my abysmal acting.

"You will be working together as a dorm whilst simultaneously competing with the other dorms. I want to see you work together, make split-second decisions and prove to me I can entrust you with these tasks." She smiled and the whole crowd tensed, seemingly eager to please her. I felt it. I would do whatever I could in the test to be given the responsibility. "The test is simple. Each dorm has a flag, your objective is to attain as many flags as possible. To do this, you take them from the others. The restrictions are as follows, though the first should be self-explanatory: you may harm, but you cannot kill." There was an uncomfortable shifting in unison from the crowd. "The flags must always remain visible. If your flag is taken from you and you do not get it back quickly; you are disqualified.

"There will be a signal to start. After five hours are up, you will be given a signal to stop. When this happens, you can no longer fight, or use your abilities. The test is over and any action that happens after that will not be counted. The winners will be tasked with the more important objectives - they will also be rewarded beyond their imagination.

"You will follow your assigned member of staff in to the forest. I will be watching from their eyes. No abilities are to be used until the signal sounds. I have seen fantastic work and incredible improvement over the previous tests, this is your chance to put together everything you have learned." I shuffled awkwardly. "I am very excited to see what comes from today."

She began to walk away from the forest. The staff in formation behind her spread out, they took off their backpacks and handed them over to the staff members that brought the dorms here. "Repay my kindness by doing your best. Good luck." She called out to everyone. As she walked past our group, she smiled at George and said, "enjoy," then continued on her way.

When she was almost out of sight, the staff member assigned to our dorm sprung in to action. They knelt, opened the bags pulling out a bright, silky piece of fabric attached to a thin pole. The staff member made a sudden jolting motion with it and the pole extended.

"Is that the flag?" Dorian asked, then realising there would be no answer, he turned to ask us. "Is that the flag?"

"Clearly it's the flag." George replied red-faced, his voice suppressing rage.

The staff member then pulled out a small canister with a speaker-horn attached to it. Dorian tutted at that too. A green box was pulled out and handed to Jo. First aid.

Jo grinned. "Won't be needing this will we, Ant?" He smiled back, but lacked her confidence.

The bag was then zipped back up, thrown over the staff members' shoulder and they began to walk in to the forest. I looked up and down the outskirts - everyone else's staff member had begun walking at the same time.

There were a few nervous looks between people, but most were just looking ahead.

As soon as we stepped into the forest, we could see another group in the distance between the trees, but after walking a little further the trees grew thicker and they were lost from sight. It was still bright in the forest, but not *as* bright now the canopy above filtered the sunlight. I noticed the forest was absent of birdsong but abundant in thick humidity. Only the sound of our footsteps snapping twigs and crunching old, dead leaves could be heard.

Soon, the thick trees gave way to a clearing. The staff member walked slowly to the middle and then jabbed the flag in to the soft muddy ground. Dorian held his hands up, palms facing the ground, while the two glass balls hovered on either side of him. His eyes focused on the flag.

The Earth began to shift and rise until the staff member snatched the flag from the mud and used it as a switch to smack Dorian's hands with. He yelped, pulled his arm back and a clump of hard, compact soil surrounded his fist. He was about to punch the staff member, before I stopped him.

"We need to wait for the signal, remember?" I secretly hoped M would have seen me obeying her. She had smiled at me earlier, that was a start. If I could just keep proving myself to her, everything would be fine again.

"If he hits me again, I swear..." Dorian threatened and the clump of soil dropped to the ground.

It was silent in the forest. Only the swish of the leaves above swaying in the breeze could be heard. The eerie silence only fuelled my excitement *and* my anxiety. Suddenly, our staff member lifted the canister and pressed it; a deafening honking sounded from the horn. He stopped and the sound of the other horns in the distance died away straight after. I tried to note where they were all coming from to give us an indication of their locations, but it was too quick.

Dorian instantly domed the flag. "Wait," I said. "The flag has to be visible at all times." Dorian nodded and then crafted a misshapen doorway and two sad excuses for makeshift windows. "Perfect."

The test had begun.

*

For a while, no one moved but Dorian who was ensuring the dome was secure. The rest of us stared from one to another. "Come on," Dorian urged, though I had no idea what he wanted me to do. There was a glint in his eyes. Ah, this was a game. A competition. Dorian was in his element. "Right, Kurt, you should fly up to the top of the trees, you can be look out." He wasn't taking in to account that my eyesight wasn't the greatest. "Shinji and Jo, you two stand ready, as soon as someone comes along use your power on them."

"It should be Shinji," Jo insisted. "If I do it – and I'm just throwing this out there – surely someone screaming by us would just be detrimental to the whole 'keeping the flag' thing."

Shinji started to reason. "But keep in mind I'll need to be closer to put them asleep than you need to be for your ability. In the second test we found that distance affects my ability's potency, if I'm too far away I may only manage to make them yawn." I stifled a yawn as he said the word. Then he looked at Dorian, apparently accepting he would have the final say. "But I guess I could hide in this wonderful little structure you so deftly crafted, then put someone to sleep if they come too close?"

"Yeah, good idea. Okay, Shinji, you make sure if anyone comes close to the flag, you put them to sleep straight away, okay?" Dorian stressed, speaking fast and loud. Shinji smirked at Dorian's sincerity. This was a matter of utmost importance to him. "Okay?"

"You mean, exactly like I just said?" Shinji replied. Dorian held a finger to his lips to shush Shinji. "Yes, Captain." Shinji whispered.

"Okay, okay. Um, Jo, you're the back up. If something happens to Shinji, you use your ability, okay?"

"Excuse me, Captain. What, exactly, is going to happen to me?" Shinji feigned fear.

"We don't know what's waiting for us out there, Shinj. Anything could happen." Dorian clearly missed the sarcasm.

"Jesus Christ, mate. This isn't World War Three." George leant against the structure containing the flag causing a mini dirt avalanche. "It's a game of capture the flag, nothing major."

"I'm not going to lose to all these people, especially since I was supposed to be in Buzz's dorm at the start." Dorian's eyes widened for a second as a thought struck him. "Just think, I could have been competing *against* you all." He whistled wistfully. "Count yourselves lucky. Right, Aaron, if it looks like we're going to be overwhelmed, you freeze the floor - that'll slow them down," Dorian stopped, held his hand up, opened his mouth, then scratched his head before nodding, agreeing with himself.

"Wait." Aaron said. "Why don't we just see what happens? If someone comes for us, we can just use our initiative to stop them? There's no point in planning when we have literally zero idea what they can all do out there. There could be someone that can turn invisible listening to us right now."

Dorian looked around as if to find the invisible intruder "You're right," he whispered. "We need fortification." He sized the opening around us, then held out his arms.

The ground started to shake, there was a rumbling noise as the earth itself began to rise. Dorian erected four crude walls of soil on either side of us. They were thick enough, but nowhere near stable. Dry soil toppled from over, hitting the ground below. M was right, this complete control over the raw element must have derived from his practice with the glass balls.

However, his fortification was shortlived as George pointed out that giant muddy walls would be a tad conspicuous in the middle of a forest and would attract more unwanted visitors than it would deter. Dorian took George's point seriously and hastily arranged a democratic vote. His idea was *trumped* as we voted against the wall - like any smart person would.

Dorian began to pace up and down. George and Anthony took shelter with the flag inside the dome while the rest of us stayed outside. George argued that the dome was pretty much unnecessary as well, but Dorian refused to let that go just in case there was another individual with telekinesis or something similar. Every time someone tried to start a conversation, Dorian would flap his hands to shut us up.

"Okay, I have an idea," he called out with his finger held in the air. "How long has it been now? One hour? Two hours?"

"About half an hour," Marie told him. She was right, it hadn't been long at all. We heard no sign of anyone nearby, no distant explosions or whir of energy to alert us of imminent danger.

"Okay, no one move for a second." No-one was. Dorian pointed both his hands at the floor which, as if being polite, began to gently vibrate and part for him. Within a few seconds, there was a large hole in the ground. "Damn, if only Lana was here. I could use her light." His brazen mention of Lana caught me offguard. The scar on her arm flashed through my mind and I felt sick. I shook it out of my head. M was looking after her, she was going to be fine. In fact, this test was to help us get Patrick back. Lana will wake up very soon with her brother waiting for her. I felt fuzzy imagining it

Dorian was now fully underground. "What's he doing?" I asked the group. No one knew. "Okay, as long as we're all on the same page." George laughed from inside the dome and I smiled at him through the shabby window hole trying to capitalise on the opportunity, then as if remembering he was annoyed with me he turned away.

After a few minutes, Dorian re-emerged from the hole, stood next to Marie and manipulated the soil until it the hole sealed and gave no sign it had ever been tampered with. "Now we have a trap for if anyone comes to take it. Watch." Dorian looked around, then grabbed Marie's hands and pushed her. She stumbled backward standing on the patch of land he had just covered.

"Ow. Dorian!" She moaned. A few coils of smoke unfurled from her hands as she rubbed her shoulder where he pushed her. "That hurt. *Argh.*" The ground beneath her gave way and she fell in to a deep trench below. Dorian beamed at her, helped her out then covered the area with soil once more.

"Okay, that's clever enough, but was it necessary to push me in to it? Could you not have just told us?" She asked.

"I had to make sure it worked. You can't be too careful." Dorian replied, still grinning.

"Then you jump on it to show us." Marie complained holding her arm. There were a few scratches on her arm, only one drawing a little bit of blood. Dorian apologised but told her it was her first war wound. Anthony tottered out of the dome, held her arm and his faint water healed the scrapes. She hugged him in thanks and ruffled his hair which he fixed, but smiled.

Dorian showed us how to recognise where the earth was hollow. There was the smallest anomaly in the way the soil rested; you would only notice it if you knew what you were looking for, a slight raised line which traced the entire trap. "So just make sure you avoid that if people come. Okay?"

"I'm not being funny," George called out from the dome, "but if we just wait here, how are we going to actually get another flag? Isn't that the point? Shouldn't we split up or something?"

"No. We have to stay together." Dorian urged.

"Yeah, but then we just have one flag? We can't win with one flag?" George was speaking to Dorian the way he spoke to me when we used to play games together in his room. Explaining his tactics as if they were the only obvious choice. "I'm not sure why M wanted me to come along, but I can hazard a guess that it wasn't to sit in a mud hut."

"Ugh. Okay. All in favour of splitting up?" Dorian asked. We discussed it for a moment before holding our hands up. "Okay, then let's say Kurt, because he can fly. Jo, because her power will be more useful out there, and uh, Aaron or Marie?"

"I'll stay here with you, Shinji, George and Anthony," Aaron said quickly.

"Okay, us five and you three. Wait, that's not fair, it should be even." Then Dorian began to argue with himself. "But I suppose three people would mean travelling light. But then if they slip-up, we're three down and can't do anything." This went on for about thirty seconds or so before he rested on a decision. "Okay, let's give it a trial. It's been about two hours now, right?"

"Probably just over one," Marie corrected.

"Okay, let's say you have one hour before you come back to us, yeah? If you're not back within an hour, we will assume something major has gone wrong."

"Okay," Jo agreed, "then what will you do?"

Dorian opened his mouth then closed it again. "I don't know. We'll think of something." Then with a revitalised spirit he urged us on our way. "C'mon. Go, go, go! Time is short."

"You heard the Captain." Shinji said pushing us away until we were out of the clearing - careful to step over Dorian's trap - he was giving us mock military orders and telling us that if we disobeyed Captain Dorian, we would never live it down. "Good luck, soldiers." Shinji saluted our farewell.

"I think *you're* going to need the luck," Marie grimaced looking over at Dorian who was now standing in front of Aaron, positioning his arms. Aaron was staring at him as if he was crazy, but Dorian persisted and began to show Aaron how to disarm people, though I doubt Dorian knew exactly how to do it.

Shinji rolled his eyes. "I better go save Aaron," he then walked back over to them only to be hauled into the demonstration. Marie giggled as we turned to walk in the forest.

Contrary to his intentions, now we were without Dorian's insistent orders, we actually began to take the test quite seriously. We travelled as quietly as possible, nervous and excited. Nothing happened for about five minutes until I heard a mumbling. I froze both of them for a moment. "Sorry, that was me," I whispered when I felt their hearts beating in panic. *"Listen."* There was definitely someone close by.

I signalled for them to wait and hide. They did so as I hovered toward a tree and began to rise, using my hands on the large trunk to steady myself. I was about halfway up before a thick branch jutted out. I pulled myself across, weightlessly, using it like a rope in the water.

A small group of people sat below an umbrella of low-hanging leaves from another tree. I could clearly see their flag, but it was encased by a buzzing light blue barrier. I extended my physical thought to sweep the area gently, ensuring I did not move anything. As my thought caressed the barrier, I felt slightly numb. It was as if it didn't exist at all. There was no way I could pluck the flag and flee. I continued my scan and could only feel six of them – it was either a small dorm or they'd sent others out to collect flags like we had. Six against three... but we had the element of surprise. I retreated to Jo and Marie whose heads were poking out the side of a tree like two bizarre squirrels. We considered different approaches, mutedly arguing, agreeing and disagreeing until finally, we decided on one.

Jo and Marie took position next to one another. Marie's smoke was already starting to form. I flew back up to the branch that overlooked them. I could feel the excitement driving me. If this failed, I could always fly down, grab them and speed off. I took a deep breath and allowed my ability to spill over the group. Though the barrier was void in my mind, the people were not.

Once I was certain I could secure them, I gave the nod. Marie nodded back and I closed my eyes, focusing. I clamped their bodies tightly – they screamed and yelped in unison. Instantly, their bodies were struggling against my hold, six arms trying to punch out, six legs kicking wildly. It was beginning to cause a strain, when I felt the light haze of Marie's smoke fill my area of effect.

The flailing intensified and it felt as if sections of my brain were being pounded. Before long, one of them stopped their fight – the smoke having knocked them unconscious. This was the person who created the barrier, because as they fell limp, the void-space caused by the barrier disappeared and the flag poked out. I snatched it greedily, letting the group drop.

"I've got it," I shouted, opening my eyes. As I looked down, I could see the cloud of smoke which had limbs poking in and out of it like a cartoon fight. Without my hold to keep them there, someone escaped from it but ran right in to Jo's open hands. They tried to retreat, but it was too late. They fell to the ground screaming. I cheered for her as I reached out to grab the flag with my hand.

Suddenly, another figure shot out of the smoke. However, this one did not run to Jo. It swiftly scampered up the tree I had been resting on. It ascended the large trunk by spiraling around it as deftly as a monkey. It was less than a second before it was on level with me, it sat on its haunches then preceded to spring off the trunk and collide with me.

I tried to fly up, but it was too quick. I screamed in pain as its unnecessarily sharp nails clamped my leg, ripping through my exercise clothes and flesh alike. With its other hand, it reached for the flag. I heard Marie scream below. It was my turn to flail my leg. I did so as I pulsed a wave of thought and the creature clinging to me peeled off. I drifted away from the trunk and watched as it fell, but it managed to grab the branch of another tree, darted up that one lighting fast and pounced off it toward me. I

187

threw my hand up and grabbed its body, deflecting it until its trajectory changed.

Its hand clawed in to a different tree trunk, giving it purchase that I could not loosen. It spun with its legs until it was out of sight. I could feel my ankle stinging from where it grasped. This went on for a while, the creature darting from trunk to trunk, swinging from branches and lunging at me; only for me to deflect it, or strafe and narrowly avoid it. Words from a wise being entered my head: '*A warrior's greatest weapon, is patience.*' I paused, having focused on its erratic movements and tried to anticipate the next attack. There was a scuttling sound – I threw my hand out in that direction, creating a large sheet of thought. It collided with it and instead of deflecting, I clenched my fist and the creature's body followed suit, balling up. It was trying to swipe at me, but I was in control of its movements. It looked gruesomely feral, rabidly foaming at the mouth, the eyes were yellow and there was more hair on its face than any human had a right to have.

I looked below, clutching the flag to my chest. The smoke had dissipated, but two people lay flat whilst another two were in front of Jo whimpering, one girl sat there on her knees with her hands up and the last, of course, was still trying to break out of my mental shell. I gently touched the ground and began to walk in their direction. Jo beamed when she saw the flag in my hand. "Well done."

"Thanks," I grinned, breathing heavily, "and you two." Marie clapped excitedly, clearly proud of herself. She then shifted her torso to look at the person floating behind me as it growled and cursed. "This thing took a bit of my leg from me." I said, lifting my ankle up to show them the bleeding.

"That's your first war wound," Marie mocked, mimicking Dorian's voice.

The girl on her knees looked at my leg then tutted. "You're the dorm with the little green lad, aren't you?" She said in a northern accent. I recognised it; it wasn't too far from my hometown. I nodded at her, feeling strangely sad. "Ah, you'll be fine then. Can't he fix that kind've stuff up?"

"Should be able to," Jo answered for me. "And don't worry, your friends'll be fine in a while. It's just a case of waiting for it to wear off." She then looked at me. "M showed me how to control the potency – to an extent."

The girl stood up then and looked at her friend floating behind me. "Jesus Christ," she gasped, "you're the first person to have calmed Bethany down in weeks." *Bethany?* The terrifying beast-human that attacked me was a *Bethany?* I smirked. "That's worth a flag within itself," she said, holding her hand out to shake mine.

"Thanks," I laughed, "definitely wasn't easy." I held my hand out. Just before we shook, Marie shouted to wait and slapped my hand down. The girls had adopted a golden hue and she curled it in to a fist, her face suddenly contorted with rage. With my other hand, I pushed with more force than I intended and she shot violently backward screaming. I saw her shoulder slam in to a treetrunk which exploded with a shower of golden sparks as she continued to hurtle backward. "Cheap tactics." I shouted after her and Marie giggled nervously with a 'phew'.

I gave the flag to Jo and she agreed to terrify Bethany lest we are ravaged as we tried to escape. The yellow eyes narrowed with anger, before the pupils dilated and she began to howl and jerk. I gently placed her down and the three of us looked at one another and ran off, roaring with laughter and adrenaline.

We continued to explore the forest, feeling mighty confident in our ability having taken down a group twice our size. We boasted about our plan working, knowing that Dorian would be annoyed he couldn't share the glory. After a while, we heard a deep rumbling sound as if the heart of the forest was thundering nearby. We approached the noise to scout the area until we came across an incredible structure.

Giant black walls towered above us, reaching half the size of the old trees around it. We gawped at it, having been instantly humbled. The surface of the wall flashed with static electricity. Atop the side facing us, there was a crude wooden platform jutting out on which a guy sat with his legs dangling over. He seemed bored of being the lookout because it appeared he was talking to himself. Jo, Marie and I looked at one another, silently letting our eyes convey how we felt. Marie shook her head and mouthed we should leave. Jo nodded in agreement but I stubbornly held my hand up halting them.

I looked around until I found some dead wood on the floor. I grabbed it, then began to hover it toward the structure. Jo and Marie were whispering for me to stop, but I was intrigued. I launched the wood as a projectile at the wall. The flashing white quality of the wall sprung in to action, converging on the area the wood hit; there was a zapping sound as the wood stuck to the wall before shooting off in a different direction leaving a trail of white smoke. The boy talking to himself shouted, jumped off the platform and disappeared before reappearing by the dead wood. A nearby section of the wall opened and a group of eight people came storming out, accompanied by shimmering body parts and strange orbs.

"Yeah, okay," I whispered. "I reckon it'd be unfair to get two flags anyway." I joked and we fled as quickly as possible, constantly glancing over our shoulders and giggling excitedly. Surely if M saw that, she would know that being smart enough to count your losses was a good quality.

We decided it was best to return and check in before Dorian had a panic attack. Marie led the way, seemingly comfortable navigating the forest. Then after a while she stopped dead in her tracks and gasped.

Ahead, we could see our clearing, but, it was transformed. Marie ran ahead then stumbled backward. "No, no, no..." She mumbled, weakly. Anxiety possessed me. I ran to see what was going on, Jo was right behind me. The murky forest setting we left earlier now looked like a microcosm of a vast eternal winter. Pure ice white stalagmites of varying sizes had been erected from the floor, powdered snow covered the entire clearing. The trees encircling the area, including the one we were looking from had formed blue icicles which clung to their branches. There was no sign of the natural green or brown whatsoever, however, there were patches of red liquid sprayed and stained in to the powdered snow.

The small crude mud hut that Dorian created at the start of the test also had now acquired a shell of thick ice. With a crunch, I stood out on the white floor. "Guys?" I called out. Marie and Jo followed behind me.

"Kurt? Is that you?" George's muffled voice answered from the hut. I could tell instantly he was truly scared.

"Yeah. Do you guys still have the flag?" I replied. The side of the hut opened wide, Aaron, Anthony, Dorian and Shinji were inside. They were calling us over, their faces stricken with fear. "What? What's happened?"

"Get here. Now!" Shinji shouted. There was no hint of friendliness in his voice. We rushed over. As soon as we were close enough they grabbed us and pulled us inside. Once in there, I could hear they were panting. Aaron instantly closed the gap we entered through with his ice, casting the hut in a beautiful pale blue before Dorian resealed the earthen layer of the dome thereby reinforcing it. We were now in the pitch-black.

"We need to keep the flag-" I started. We had to keep the flag visible, M's direct orders. We would be disqualified or even anger M if we didn't play by the rules she had set out.

"Shut up," Shinji shot, uncharacteristically direct. His breathing was still heavy, yet hollow. There was a sniffling noise.

"Anthony, are you crying?" Jo asked but before he could answer she asked another question. "What's happening?"

"Keep your voice down," Aaron ordered. "There's people out there."

190

"Yeah, that's the whole point of the test." I said, failing to grasp why they were so scared. They knew what this task entailed.

"We can fight now we're all here." Marie added confidently. "We did really well when-"

"No!" Shinji snapped. "People who weren't here at the start of the test. Not part of us. People who have never been in M's lab. Outsiders."

"They're trying to kill us - kill me." George chipped in.

"What?" Jo, Marie and I gasped in unison.

"They all ran in before, completely surrounding us." I could clearly hear that George had been crying. His voice was hollow. "Aaron was the first to notice, they weren't dressed like the rest of us."

"I panicked," Aaron agreed. "As soon as I saw they were outsiders, I just shot ice everywhere. I don't even know what I did. It just happened."

"An instant cold snap," George agreed.

"You were brave," Shinji added. "He made sure we were all inside. I saw one of them hit by his ice. They literally slammed into one of the columns as it came spouting out the floor. It hit him just in his jaw and blood spouted all around." His voice faltered. "That's when I realised something was wrong. They didn't call time out. They didn't ask to stop. They were furious. They roared at us."

"When everyone was inside, I covered it with thick ice, then Dorian finished it off." Aaron again now. "We could hear scratching from the outside, they were attacking the hut but then they just stopped out of the blue."

"But they were shouting at us." George added. "They were shouting that if *these* don't let them kill the one without powers, then they'll kill all of us. They wanted to kill *me*."

"Why? How would they even know you don't have powers? Where are they now?" Jo asked. There was a noise outside. We all became motionless with fear.

"Get out now!" A voice demanded. A male voice. A voice I vaguely recognised. "We'll give you ten seconds before we crush that shell with you in it. We'll kill you one by one. We'll rip your limbs off... or you can give us George and we'll be gone."

"How do you know his name? Why do you want him?" Jo called out. The response was mimicked alongside jeering and laughter.

"We want him because he doesn't have a place here anymore. He's on our eradication list." The same voice. Where did I know him from?! My brain wasn't blurring this time with the inability to pinpoint the memory like it did with the photograph, I just couldn't think. "Homo Sapiens killed the Neanderthals; survival of the fittest. History repeats itself. Most of his kind are dead now. It's been a long time coming."

He continued to talk, but Jo began whispering to us, almost inaudibly. "When I say, shoot the ice and the soil as hard as you can in every direction."

"They're planning an attack," a girl's voice screeched. "They are planning an attack. Get to cover."

Jo swore, then shouted. "Now!" There was a crunching sound as the ice and mud exploded outward. The sunlight that managed to filter through the canopy above showed the attackers all around us.

Him! He stood there, a smile spread across his face. "Hello, pal," he mocked. Treeboy stood feet away, behind him thousands of vines wiggled, heaved, flowed and undulated. The vines worked round him and shot toward my friends and me. I threw my hands to the side, creating my own dome of telekinesis. The vines hit it ineffectively and he laughed. My friends and I huddled in to one another. A crystal ice belt formed around us followed by clumps of earth which began orbiting us. Finally, Marie's smoke hovered ominously above. Our abilities joint protection against theirs.

"It's him." I whispered to them.

"They're talking again!" The girl yelled in a shrill voice. I turned to see her. She was there on the day they kidnapped Patrick. The small girl. From the still green forest behind Treeboy, the rest came. The boy with the long leather coat and the goatee, the boy with the giant fists, the particularly average looking boy and the pale green girl with sharp teeth who looked uncomfortably like a snake.

"Wonderful to see you," the snake girl said. "It's been a while," she smiled; her teeth looked sharper than they did back then, almost ending in a needlepoint. She licked her tongue across them, surprisingly, it wasn't forked, but it was so lacerated that it barely resembled the pinkish muscle that the rest of us have. She slithered up to Treeboy and rested her chin on his shoulder. He grinned but never took his eyes off me.

"These are the people that kidnapped Lana's brother on the day of the change. The one's who attacked her for no reason." I told my friends. "What do you want?!"

"Oh, boy," the small girl mocked. "We want your friend *dead*. The useless one."

The average looking boy stepped forward. "Now, which one is he?" He asked as his hands began to glow orange with little flecks of black whizzing around it. He threw his arm out with a fist in front of him and the orange glow around his hand shot off and hit the ground by us. I gasped and lifted my leg up, still focusing on the telekinetic dome around us. The boy laughed and repeated the process. I couldn't move the embers with my ability. They just sat there in the snow which I noticed was rapidly melting around the embers.

"We're not saying which one it is." Shinji called out.

"We'll just murder every one of you to be certain," Goatee spat. He unsheathed a blade from a leather case attached to his belt. He slowly raised its point toward us - I held my arms out reinforcing the mental dome, but he turned the knife on himself like last time. He lifted the sleeve of his coat up; bright pink scars wound around his flesh like rivers. He placed the point of the knife on his flesh and pressed hard with a smile. Pointing his arm down he pierced the skin and slowly drew the blade down the length of his forearm, his smile growing more menacing as he did so. "Gravity helps the blood leave quicker," he explained. He pushed down on his veins with his thumb and slid his hand down. Even more blood gushed out.

When his arm was redder with blood than any arm had the right to be, the liquid began to bubble before it lifted off his skin and separated into small red bracelets that rotated around the forearm he had just sliced. "You caught me right on the chin with the ice there," he said. "Thank you." The red stains from the ice rose in to small globules and floated over to him.

"Wait," the boy with the large fists said. His eyes were out of focus for a moment as if the scene was irrelevant, but then he snapped back in to focus. "It's the muscly white guy. He's the one with no powers. Kill him!" He ran toward us, his fists out in front of him as if they were a plough.

"Now!" Treeboy shouted. Ordinary boy nodded and began to roar, the orange embers below started to brighten, but Dorian threw his hands out and the earth below us rose out of the ice and curved over in a tidal wave covering the glowing heat. There was a succession of loud pops as soil below exploded everywhere; drifts of the powder snow erupted like geysers.

"Split up. Protect George." I shouted. I stopped Bigfists in his tracks, and threw him as far back as I could. He grunted as his back crashed in to a tree.

Treeboy lifted his arms up, two sharp stakes protruded through his skin and he shot them in my direction. I threw a wall of thought in front of me, but I need not have bothered. Aaron had created a thin sheet of ice. I could see the dark objects hit the ice which crunched on impact, but stopped them. "Thanks," I shouted, but Aaron was already away.

Halloween orange embers began to fill the clearing causing explosions to boom everywhere, adding to the cacophony of shouting. An ember landed right behind Anthony and George then began to rapidly glow brighter. As I couldn't move it, I locked my mind on them and threw them out the way. George yelled in fear when he was thrown, but it was all I could do. The cinder exploded and more snow shot in to the air before it began to delicately drop as if it had all the time in the world to settle.

The small girl began to scream. Her hands were clamped to her ears. *She was their weakest link. Always take care of the additions before tackling the boss.* I ran over in her direction holding my hand out to snag her and slam her into the nearest tree but something wrapped round my legs. The Treeboy's vines?! I fell face first into the ground. I felt and heard my nose crunch. Blood began to pour from it. My eyes were blurry but I looked down as I tried to free myself from the snare, but no, it was not Treeboy. Even in my blurred vision I could see I was tangled by red ropes. The blood from my nose began to trickle *away* from my face. The boy with the goatee, kicked me over. My legs were free now.

I felt a strange cold wash over my face, as if my head had been dunked underwater. Anthony's ability! The pain in my nose faded away. I held my hand in front of me, as the boy began to lash at me with his blood-whips. A simple dome protected me and gave me the moment's respite as I blinked the tears from my eyes. I then pushed and the mental dome shot up, knocking Goatee backward. With force he smacked in to one of the stalagmites Aaron had conjured earlier with a grunt, before falling to the hard ground which gave way beneath him to Dorian's hidden tunnels. Marie ran above the area he had just fell and began to pour thick smoke in to it. Goatee began to cough as oxygen was purged by thick, heavy smoke that billowed with the sheer volume. I ignored the desperate gulps for air from within.

Marie spun around, smoke now wreathing her body making her look more ghostly than human. She ran over to Ordinaryboy, who saw her a little too late. Instead of using her ability, she caught him with a fist – an arc of smoke trailed the trajectory. Two bits of smoulder shot on either side of her as the boy started to panic, but she punched him again and he fell backward. The fury in Marie's face is something I could never forget. When the boy was on the ground, she booted him in the jaw with full force. He screamed as the jaw crunched slightly out of shape and she commanded the smoke that surrounded her body to enter his mouth. He began to shake and struggle to get away, before he lost the fight.

I stood up to continue toward the small girl, but something collided with me, winding me. I was coughing, trying to get up but there was a flurry of sharp claws scratching at me and holding me down. Snake girl was on me, I couldn't escape. Anthony's healing water was covering me again, fusing the slices as she made them. She grunted and looked away. "Kill the little boy first, he's keeping them alive." I took that chance to send a pulse out, but as it pushed her away, she gripped my hands tighter and I was pulled up with her.

She scratched at me but I blocked it with my arm. She lashed her other hand out at me and I blocked this advance with my mind. "I know how you work, *Kurt*. I know you can't do it all at once," she hissed with effort as she pushed in with both arms trying to impale my temples with her claws and it was all I could do to not let her. She was right, if I stopped concentrating on stopping her arms to try and send her flying, it may be the last thing I do. How can she know that - how my power worked? *Now is not the time, Kurt!* All she needed was three inches or so to end my life. "You're getting weaker," She taunted with glee, flecks of phlegm dropping on me. Her sharp serrated teeth threateningly close.

Two hands chopped each side of her neck. She winced in pain and let go of me. The hands that hit her then rested on her temples. Her eyes widened with fear, her mouth opened wide showing her mangled tongue frantically jolting as she let out a harrowing scream. Jo was standing behind her. "Come on!" I nodded my thanks, my body was soaked with what I hoped was only sweat.

"Where's George?" I shouted to no one. I could no longer see him or Anthony... and for a moment, I didn't care. For a moment, I wondered why I was making such an effort for him. Treeboy had a point when he said George was part of the old race. Wouldn't I be rid of a burden if he died? For a moment, I *wanted* him dead. That madness was quickly ousted. *They are not my thoughts*! I was just scared.

"Behind there," Dorian shouted. Hard earth in the shape of a seashell was in the middle of the clearing. Bigfists was back in the battle, he was holding either a small tree trunk or a gigantic branch which had more length and girth than a lamp post, but was handled deftly. I noticed on the ground just over to the side, lay Shinji. He wasn't moving.

Bigfists had also noticed Shinji on the ground. He held the weapon above him and was about to bring it down to Shinji's head when a new stalagmite of ice shot from the floor meeting the wood. Someone roared. I looked in the direction and saw Aaron. His black hair was now completely frosted over, his arms white with ice. Bigfists looked up at Aaron and smiled at the challenge.

He repositioned himself, holding the large wooden pole over his shoulder. When Aaron was within range, Bigfists tried to swing at him. Aaron threw one arm to the side and a large shield in the shape of a giant snowflake formed, floating just inches away from him. Aaron continued to walk as the wood hit the shield. There was a thud and a crack on impact, the ice splintered but Aaron was untouched. As Bigfists realised he had little time, he dropped the oversized weapon. He punched his paws together in a sign to fight which generated a small shockwave, but that was his mistake.

Aaron had taken the opportunity when he saw it. He threw his frosted arms in front of him and ice began to form around the huge hands. He struggled to pull them apart, and maybe he would have achieved it, if the rest of his arm was not already covered in ice. As Aaron got closer, he left a trail of water vapour behind him. The boy with the large fists began to shake his head, begging for mercy shouting "She made us. She made us!" His teeth were chattering. The ice had spread over his entire body now, leaving only his head free. "She told us to kill-" his speech stopped suddenly, his eyes unfocused as his head lolled backward, unconscious. The ice encasing him fell backward and hit the floor with a thump. Aaron gave one last glance at him to make sure he was out before turning his back on him.

He bent down to Shinji feeling his chest, then began to cry and hug into him. I felt sick. I turned to see Treeboy standing next to Goatee who had clearly managed to get out of Dorian's pit filled with Marie's smoke. The two of them were sending red and green ropes in the direction of the earthen seashell, but Dorian was now on the other side with George and Anthony. Whenever a piece of his shield chipped off, or chinked revealing those behind, he would instantly reinforce it, refusing the attackers a chance. I had never seen Dorian look so focused – the glass balls darted behind him.

"Stop stalling you cowards," Treeboy shouted to his people. "He *has* to die. You heard what she said to us. 'Failure is not an option.' If we do, you know she'll punish us." Then to us. "Give him up so the rest of you don't have to die!" Vines jutted out from the snow beneath him, as if nature itself was on his side, wrapping around his legs steadying him, rooting him in place once more. Just behind him, another mass of vines was wriggling away, like a pit of angry snakes. My heart skipped a beat when I saw Jo's face in the midst of them. Her eyes were closed, she was not fighting. *No.*

I roared, I grabbing Treeboy with my ability. "Help," I shouted. I held him and all his vines in place. I was furious. He shouted something inaudible and Goatee turned. The rope that was lashing at Dorian's seashell of earth still trying to find a way in recoiled and hovered above his head awaiting his command. It shuddered with anticipation as it was about to shoot at me, but a screen of smoke formed between us and I jumped to the side.

196

"I think Shinji's dead," Marie's voice came from behind me. The smoke travelled toward Goatee. I kept Treeboy tight in my ability. It did not take much focus. My anger had increased my ability's potency. It was easy to keep him steady. I could feel every single vine trying to break free, his muscles desperately fighting, his heart hammering in his chest. His quick, hollow, panicked breathing.

The smoke began to whip and whirl around Goatee before a chunk of ice shot past me. It hit Goatee in the solar plexus. He doubled over in pain. Two separate streams of ice formed from the floor and shot upward, crashing in to Goatee's head at such a force he was knocked unconscious. Aaron was not holding back now. The small girl screamed when she realised they were losing. They had no chance. A wave of water surged toward her and she turned tail, running off in to the forest.

"Aaron," Marie cried. "Is Shinji- is he?"

"No," Aaron's reply was weak. He ran over to her. "He's breathing, but he needs help. We need M!"

Goatee lay on the floor, his legs jittering unconsciously. Ordinaryboy had been taken care of. Snake Girl was still crying, holding in to her dangerously skinny body. Bigfists still almost fully entombed in Aaron's ice. Small Girl had fled. Only Treeboy was conscious, held rigid in my anger.

"It's just you left now," I screamed. "Your friends can't fight." The smoke began to fade away. The dome protecting Dorian, Anthony and George slowly crumbled. "You're going to tell us *where* The Catalyst is or I will rip you in two." I shouted.

As soon as Dorian saw Jo was in the vines, he ran over to them and began to yank at them in an attempt to free her. Anthony was already conjuring water and Aaron was sending it around each of us to heal. The Treeboy was still struggling. I pulled downward on his legs and upward on his torso. I could feel his body stretch slightly. He screamed in agony as his rough, coarse flesh rippled while he tried to disperse. "Where is Patrick?" I shouted.

"I don't know!" His reply came through gritted teeth.

"How did you know George had no ability?" I shouted, realising my eyes were stinging with tears which were a manifestation of my pure fury.

"I just knew," he replied. I pulled further still, tearing another scream from his lips. "We were told by *her*," he cried.

"How did she know? How is she getting information on us?" Then I froze in fear. "How does she know we're here?" Shadow Lady must know the location again. He was silent. I pulled again, there were slight jolts in my thought which I knew were his bones popping out of place. Dislocating all

197

over his body. Every outlet of pain I heard only made me happier. I could feel his struggle, the fury I felt had given me incredible presence of mind. It was just a case of employing it.

I used my ability to focus on his right leg, while keeping the rest of him still. I tried to crush it, he screeched in pain. *It wasn't enough.* I started to twist the leg, I felt it resisting as the socket had pivoted as far as it could, but that didn't stop me. I continued until I felt the socket itself completely shatter. The howl that came from his lips was glorious. I hungered for more. There were voices all around now, but my vision was tunnelled by my anger. I folded the leg upward, forward against his thigh until it was a right angle. There was no more resistance from it now. It was completely broken, a mere appendage - an attachment. Yet, it was connected. *It wasn't enough.* Treeboy had stopped screaming now, but he was conscious, in shock. The voices all around me increased, shouting, but I refused to let them deter me. I twisted the leg, I spun it around as if it were the stem of an apple. I spun and spun and spun until I felt the flesh tear. I felt the cartilage breaking apart, the stringy veins still whole. I twisted further, creating a spiral strand of tissue, sinew and muscle until, with a scream, I ripped his right leg clean off. I felt his body fall limp as he fainted.

But his heart. It was still beating. *It still wasn't enough.* He deserved *death*.

"Release him," a voice called behind me. Her voice. *M was here!* I turned and looked her in the eyes. Determined to refuse. I hadn't noticed it, but the entire clearing had been filled with my ability. My friends, the enemies, were all floating helplessly. Only M and her staff who stood just out of the clearing were on the floor. "Now, Kurt!" She ordered. Whether I wanted to disobey or not, in that moment, I couldn't. It was as if her words were a trigger, forcing me to do what she wanted - it seemed that even at my worst, I respected her enough to pay heed to her orders. Everything dropped to the ground.

M's staff members were all over the scene in seconds, picking people up, checking vital signs. "Go back to the lab, Kurt." She ordered. I stood up ready to obey without question, before stopping and walking back to her.

"This is the boy who took Patrick! He just tried to kill George." I walked up to M, her eyebrows raised in surprise. She gave George a quizzical glance. "He knew George didn't have powers. He knew George was vulnerable." M's eyes narrowed at me now. "He works for your ex-partner. She has more information than you thought; she is more dangerous than you're aware. We don't have time. I want to leave for one of the three people we need tomorrow."

M nodded. "I think we have you to blame for that, Kurt. Your constant connection with that woman in your sleep has finally allowed them to find our location. We will discuss that tomorrow. Now leave, I will take care of these." M seemed displeased. Aaron ran back over to Shinji, his body was now frostless. Marie followed and the two held him up. Just out of the clearing, behind the trees, I could see more people from the lab looking aghast and shocked, frozen in place. They had come with M.

"Blake," M called out. "Please transport Dorm Three back to the lab, leave the injured here - my staff will see to them." The staff tried to take Shinji from Aaron, but he argued until Marie hugged him. Shinji was carried away. I began to cry as they picked Jo up too. Where was the staff member through all of this? In fact, I hadn't seen any since the test started. "You handled yourself incredibly well, Kurt. More than any test could prove," she paused, "and, you managed to keep George alive through such an onslaught. That proves you can protect people. I can rely on you for what is to come. I am very proud of you, Kurt."

Fleetingly, I felt happy at her words but it was quickly sobered by the scene before me. I cared more for George's life than for M's affection. M was staring at me as if she had never seen me before. I didn't care if she was reading my mind. She pursed her lips. Blake was upon us now. He looked gingerly back at the crowd, Buzz was staring nonplussed. He looked just as horrified as everyone else.

"This is much worse than I expected," M said. Treeboy was in a slump on the floor. His leg was still spurting blood. "Anthony," she called. He yelped in shock. "Heal his leg." *What*?! How could she even think that? *Let him bleed out. Let him die.* Leave him here for nature to reclaim him - he could control it, he had used it against us and now he was defeated. Let him rot! I grabbed Anthony but Marie snatched my hand back and gave him a gentle nudge forward. Anthony stood over Treeboy, he was shaking violently. Terrified. The water spouted from him and poured on to Treeboy's stump of a leg. The brown-green skin began to fuse together, but to my delight, the limb did not regrow. I was about to argue with M again, but she held a hand up silencing me. "*Kurt*, leave! I will take care of this. Everyone head back to the lab. The test is over." She was clearly furious, regardless of how she was hiding it. Why? We had one of the enemies in our hands. Plenty when the rest came to. "Now!"

Aaron, Dorian, Marie, George, Anthony and I looked at Blake who tried to smile at us. I nodded, not returning the smile. He held his arms out for everyone to touch, just before I gripped it I looked at M. "Make sure you interrogate him. Do everything you can to get the information we need. Please." It was an order and a plea at the same time; M's face betrayed no emotion. I grabbed Blake's hand and the clearing disappeared before me - the rustling of the leaves, the whimpering of the Snake Girl, the quiet smattering of conversation from the other dorms - revealing the motel facade of M's lab.

I hugged George and apologised for everything. He hugged me back as tightly as possible telling me not to worry, that it was fine and thanked me for saving him. I dropped to my knees from exhaustion and began to cry. Aaron joined me. If George had died today, I don't know how I could have lived with myself.

"They're going to be okay," Aaron managed through tears, "Shinji and Jo. They were breathing, they're going to be grand."

"I know. I know," I replied wiping my tears away with my black shirt. I felt my stomach burning with hatred. Shadow Lady was a coward. Targeting George as he couldn't fight back. It was a cheap shot. It would serve no purpose to her overall goal. It didn't even make tactical sense. But I understood what M meant now; she had to be stopped. No questions asked.

Then we sat in silence waiting on everyone from the lab to catch up. Tomorrow I decided I will beg M to send me out in order to find either The Mute, The Leech or The Jinx. I will bring them back and we will storm Shadow Lady's base of operations. By the week's end, we will have Patrick back. By the week's end Lana will be happy. By the week's end, Jo and Shinji will never be in danger from the likes of Treeboy again. George will be safe. Shadow Lady had caused enough indirect damage to my friends and I refused to sit round for the next attack.

I shuddered in spite of myself. M was responsible for punishing Treeboy and his gang. I could only imagine how she would deal with him. If I hadn't wanted him dead - all of them dead - I would have almost felt sorry for what he would soon have to endure.

Chapter 17

Without Shinji present to put me to sleep, I found myself in Silver Hair's void. Upon my arrival, I was frozen in place. I could see the silver sparkle in the distance grow bigger as it approached at speed.

"Kurt! You're back!" She almost collided with me as she had done the first time. She hugged in to me. "I'm so glad you're safe."

"You!" I pushed her away viciously, recoiling from her touch.

"Kurt?" She gasped, clearly shocked.

"This whole time. *You* have been working for her!" I roared. "You lied to me. You caused this."

"No! Kurt, we had it wrong," she insisted. Had it wrong? *We* had it wrong? The audacity.

"I thought you needed my help. I thought you wanted to find your daughter?" I shouted. "The Mute was in danger and I tried to help her... only for you to betray me!"

"No, you misunderstand. I saw my daughter. She's the one that has y-"

"Shut up!" I was trying to hold her with my power, but it didn't work here. I was at her mercy, anger bubbled. "Because I trusted you, my friend was almost killed!" She held her hand to her mouth. "Because of you, Shinji and Jo have been injured!"

"No, it's not what you think." She sounded sincere, but I was wise to it. I would not be manipulated.

"Yes, it is!" I snapped. "You are going to rue the day you asked for my help. I am going to slaughter the Shadow Lady. I am going to rip her in two. I will crush her bones with my ability and tear her apart. That is *your* doing. You are going to be stuck here forever! I swear. Lonely, until your body rots away out there. Like you deserve!"

"Kurt, listen to yourself!" She shouted. I tried to shout back, but words failed me. "You have it wrong!" A flush of red coloured her pale skin. She really was beautiful. Even in her anger. Yet, the old woman version of her I saw when I was in the medical wing flashed before me and I was confused. Disgusted. Was the image here another deception? Was the old woman what she truly looked like and she was taking this form in an attempt to get her own way? Another blatant lie I willingly swallowed. "My daughter is the dangerous one out there. I saw you! In the real world. I saw you speaking to her; she had you pinned to the wall in a small room.

"She lost control of her hold. For a moment, Kurt, the smaller window opened. The child I have been asking you to free this whole time. She was never trapped – neither of them were. Her mind has been blocked *by* my daughter, Melanie! When she lost her concentration, the block disappeared and I could see everything – she was screaming for some release. You have been under Melanie's care this whole time. That must be why you're linked!"

My voice was back. "M *saved* my friend's life. She saved us! *You* jeopardised that safety, that harmony! I'm not stupid. Don't try to manipulate me anymore. It won't work."

"I am not the one trying to manipulate you," she was tearing up but I wouldn't let her confuse me. It was a pathetic attempt. I wanted to strike her. I witnessed Shadow Lady's people trying to murder George – nothing Silver Hair said could trick me now. "I have been worried about you!"

"Shut up! I'd slaughter you right now if you were here in person. Mark my words, every one of your people will *die*."

She stopped still, dejected. "You're wrong. I hope you see before it's too late."

*

I woke up. Once again, the objects in my room were afloat. They rotated and swayed in my manifested thought. I shook my head and let them fall; they crashed to the floor but it didn't matter. Nothing mattered but the death of Shadow Lady. I knew where my mind was - I knew my goal. No one would mar that. I owed M.

I walked to the kitchen. There were voices in there. I rushed in hoping Shinji and Jo would be sitting there, laughing with breakfast ready. They were not. George, Aaron, Anthony and Marie sat around the counter. They looked up expectantly as I walked in, then half-smiled, half-frowned when they realised it was me alone.

"Any news?" I asked.

"Not since M was here earlier." George said, his tone devoid of optimism.

Yesterday, we waited outside for a while after Blake teleported us. When the rest arrived, we were brought downstairs, M was not with them. We waited for a while in our dorm. We barely spoke. I just kept hugging into George. He seemed unfocused, staring in to space. Every so often there would be a heaving breath, but when I looked, he was not crying. Aaron on the other hand was not faring too well. Apparently, Shinji was at the receiving end of the spores that Treeboy shoots out. Shinji turned into them, screamed and scratched furiously at his face before fainting. The image of the boils on the child and orb woman, as well as the mutilated corpse, were summoned from my memory and made my skin prickle. *Poor Shinji.* "But he was breathing, that's a good sign, right? M will be able to fix anything that went wrong, won't she?" He asked, then said more to himself, "he was still breathing!" We all nodded and agreed hoping he was right, but said nothing else.

No one had saw what happened to Jo, but Dorian said she managed a splutter when he was tearing the vines away from her body which was hope enough. I just needed some good news to cling on to. We sat in the kitchen, exhausted. I tried to fight sleep, but I was losing the battle. Then, after about three hours since we were back in our dorm, M entered which scared the lethargy away.

"Your friends will be fine," was the first thing she said. She knew what we wanted to hear. She stared at Aaron. "Shinji inhaled toxic spores, but luckily we have tested with the toxin that intruder can produce in previous experiments, prior to the change – it is remarkably common. There may be some aesthetic damage," Aaron's eyes watered. The only conjuration of water he could not fully control. "But, he will be healthy."

She rounded on George. "You are *very* lucky to be alive," she stated. "I questioned that boy when he regained consciousness using methods that some may not feel are orthodox. That group were sent here with the intention of killing you. They believe people who did not acquire an ability in the change do not deserve a place amongst their superiors." Her eyes switched to me. "They are truly brainwashed, whether by an ability or by her dangerous charismatic persuasiveness, I am unsure, but they are devoted to her. *Zealots.* They believe this change is a gift, a restart to the world and those without abilities have no way to serve their leader." She scoffed. "She always was narcissistic but this is a whole new level."

"What about Jo?" I asked. If she was going to waste our time talking about the Shadow Lady, I wanted to hear only how we would bring about her demise. If that was not the topic at hand, I wanted to ensure Jo was fine.

M rolled her eyes. "Simple concussion. She sustained a heavy blow to the head. No permanent damage, but were she left untreated, she may have suffered some brain damage. I believe the case is similar to what happened with you, Kurt, when you were unconscious. The rest of her brain gave up, but her ability, functioning at a higher level was enough to keep her safe." I felt guilty for cutting M off. Once again, she saved a life. "On the contrary, Kurt. *He* saved her life," she indicated Dorian. His face the epitome of confusion. "The vines she was bound in, they were cutting off her oxygen. If constricted much longer, that is where the brain damage would have occurred. Both Shinji and Jo are now in the hospital wing. Their conditions stable."

"And the others?" I asked, slowly. Carefully. "The intruders?"

"They too, are in the hospital wing." M stared in to my eyes. Marie gasped, Aaron stood up and Dorian shook his head.

"They're what?" I slammed the table with both of my hands. A ripple of telekinesis inadvertently flowed across forcing a few cups left on the counter to topple over.

"Sit down, Kurt!" She insisted. Each of them are sedated, bound and monitored. They will not be able to escape their shackles and the research of their powers is as invaluable as the information on our enemies.

"They can break out and finish the job. They can get Lana too while they're down there. Do you want to kill all of my friends?" I snarled. I hovered a knife to my throat and lifted my chin up. "Why don't we just do it for them?"

"Kurt, behave yourself. I will not abide your dramatics right now. Do you think I would risk their lives?" She asked. I thought for a moment, if it meant the advent of new research then it may be possible. M glared at me and I cowered. "They are safe. As for you, get some rest. I will be sending you four out tomorrow." Then her eyes rested on George and narrowed ever so slightly before she turned and left.

I left the room not long after her focusing on the fact that if tomorrow was a step in the direction of defeating the Shadow Lady, then I will get all the rest I needed. I didn't even think about Silver Hair until I saw her in my sleep.

Now it *was* tomorrow and we were all back in the kitchen again. Their eyes were red raw. If they had slept at all, it wasn't enough. George went to wake Anthony up after a while and began making breakfast for us. "You'll have to eat something before you go. At least let me do that; I'm the reason all this happened." We disagreed with the latter part of the sentence but agreed to the former.

I spent about an hour or two on a piece of toast before the buzzer in the hall went off. Aaron, Dorian, Marie and I ran to get ready. We had expected some form of notice. George waited in the corridor with Anthony as we busied ourselves around him.

George hugged the other three, and the other three hugged Anthony. I was last in queue, I gave Anthony a quick hug and he squeezed extra tight. Then I stood up at full length to face George. His eyes were watering, but he blinked the tears away. "Kurt, mate. Please, please, *please* look after yourself."

"I will," I promised.

He squeezed my arm tight. "No, Kurt. At any sign of danger, you run away, all of you, you bail. I can tell you're angry, mate, I've never seen you this determined before, you're like a different person - but your life is more important than her death. We almost lost Jo last night, that's not how it works. We're a package deal, remember? Everyone used to say that. We come as a three. 'Buy one and get the other two free.' You need to come back safely tonight so if Jo is back up and running," he tried to blink the tears away again, but it was useless, they were streaming now, "*when* she's back to her arrogant, headstrong self," he paused forcing a smile, but his lips were quivering. "You can help me deal with it. She's too strong for me and you know it. If there's one thing you come back for, it's to help my deal with her. Yeah?" I nodded. My eyes were stinging from trying to hold my tears back, but I failed. There was a stream pouring from each eye. He hugged me tight sniffling in a way George had never sniffled before. As if his body had just discovered this way of dealing with emotions. He held me at arm's length and pulled me tight again. Just like Jo had.

"I know. Honestly, just remember, this isn't a fight we're going to. We're just going to see if someone will help us when the fight comes." I insisted. George nodded but I doubt my words were of any comfort. He hugged me again.

"I love you, Kurt. You and Jo are the two most important people in my life." We hugged again.

"I promise I'll be careful. I'll see you tonight." I tried to smile. George rubbed his tears away with his black sleeves, then nodded.

"Argh, I hate feeling useless. Go on then. Go get the person you need. It's the least you can do after making us lose all those flats." That felt like years ago, now. A lifetime ago. That was something the old Kurt had to deal with. I laughed in spite of the circumstances. "And mate, if anyone crosses you, do what you did to that green guy. Rip them apart. Better them than you." He wiped his eyes again and smiled. He pulled me in once more, kissed me on the forehead and patted my shoulder. When I turned, I could see Marie had been watching us talk. She had teared up, her lower lip was involuntarily curled outward.

We left the corridor and I heard George's sobs renew. He must have felt so powerless, in all senses. He didn't have to worry, I was swimming in motivation - there was no way I was going to fail today. No matter where M sent me. We were led to the food hall. It was empty of furniture. Groups of people were standing, separated in to dorms. On our arrival, Buzz ran up to us. "Is everything okay?" He asked. I stared at him. "I'm really sorry. Is, er, is Jo okay?" I nodded. "And what about the other guy? The Oriental guy?"

"Japanese." Marie barked.

"Sorry, I didn't mean anything by that. Is he okay?" Buzz asked. He seemed genuinely concerned so I nodded and he sighed with relief.

M walked in and a group followed behind her consisting of her staff and some of the other dorms. M pushed through with her daughter. They stood at the front of the room, waiting for attention.

"Silence," she ordered and all noise ceased. "In light of recent events, it seems we cannot dawdle any longer," she paused. "I have seen what many of you can do over the previous tests and I know what you are capable of. As I know you will agree, I have done so much for you – I believe, quid pro quo, it is time that you show your gratitude."

One of the staff members walked to M and handed to her personal files. M's daughter was standing next to her. I studied her for a moment thinking about Silver Hair's words, I felt doubt. Could that truly be her granddaughter? No, of course not. They looked barely alike. I cannot let her trick me now, not when we were finally about to initiate M's plan. M should not be doubted.

"Dorm One," M called as she looked at the files in her hand. There was a shifting from a group over toward the front of the room. "You are to be in charge of perimeter patrol. You will spend every day, every hour walking the outskirts of this town, ensuring there is no chance of a second invasion. You have the most agile abilities, capable of quick escapes and swift scouting. Should you see anything, you will not fight - your objective is to alert. We will devise a rota to ensure you have sufficient rest whilst still allowing the patrol to remain continuously maintained.

"Dorm Two," a murmur from another group, someone held their hand up but another grabbed it and pulled it back down. "Your abilities are more suited for defensive purposes. You will position yourselves outside this lab, on the upper-levels. Use your strength and shielding powers to slow down any attackers. If Dorm One do their job correctly, you will be notified of any incoming attack, but should something go wrong, I expect constant vigilance.

"Dorm Three, originally one of my choices for an integral acquisition mission," M started. It took me a second to realise this was us, "but, as you are two members down, I feel we cannot risk sending you out."

"No!" I interrupted. Instantly I regretted it, but I was not giving up the opportunity. "M, please. Don't take this away from me. I want to be the one who helps bring your ex-partner to justice like you said. Please, send us out.

The four of us are competent, we're adept with our abilities. You know we can handle it. The four of us are, as of now, the only people here who have actually taken on a proper fight." M was smiling. I was winning her over. "We kept George alive - we work as a team. Jo and Shinji may be out, but we can do this. I promise. I have trusted you this whole time, so please, this time, trust in me. Trust in my friends. Trust our ability to do this."

M looked back at her notes for a second, then nodded. "I suppose it is possible." My mind longed for her to say yes, I willed it. "Okay. I am tasking you the acquisition mission with minimum risk. You will leave immediately and will be transported to the prison where Chiamka Tinibu - The Jinx - currently resides. I refuse to contact her personally lest she compromises my ability.

"You will explain to her that we must have her here, it is of utmost importance. She is a woman of reason, the prison is a sanctuary in her eyes and no harm should befall you as long as you do not give cause to bring it on yourselves. That being said, should she refuse to cooperate, you may do whatever is within your power to bring her here. Keep in mind, she has the ability to reverse yours - *think* before you act." She looked up at us.

"They *cannot* know the exact location of this facility. You are on your own when you leave this town," he smiled directly at me, "good luck. Do not let me down." One of her staff broke from the ranks and walked in our direction. We followed her out. People watched us as we walked, some sympathetic, some avoiding eye contact, most - and this affected me more than anything else - seemed to be scared of us.

"Dorm Four," M continued. "Your dorm as a whole boast the wilier abilities, I am trusting you with the liberation of Charlotte Yu - The Mute - from her captors," we heard her say before we left and the door closed behind us.

So, it came to this. Dorian, Marie, Aaron and myself were responsible for bringing one of these three back. The four of us. I know it would have made more sense to have a bigger dorm do this, but now, I was absolutely focused. I could do this. We could do this. M knew we could do it. Even though we did have fewer people and this was a low risk acquisition task, she trusted us. This was one of the most vital missions that could help us kill Shadow Lady.

"We will do this," I said as the lift ascended. "For Jo, Shinji and Lana."

"And everyone else out there who has suffered," Marie nodded. Dorian gulped, Aaron's gaze never left the floor.

*

It felt like years since we were last on this bus. It was somehow comforting being on it again. I thought it was probably down to getting out of the lab, no waiting around to hear about Shinji and Jo, the way we had to with Lana; something to keep my mind busy. Alternatively, it could be because the last time I was on here was the day I met these people who were now my friends. I felt hollow without the presence of George and Jo, but needs must and all that. I sat next to Aaron and Dorian sat next to Marie. We were silent for most of the journey. The staff member did not get on the bus.

Miles and hours were lost as we travelled. The bus droned on and on, gliding over smooth roads, bumping over rough land, fields and hills, turning sharp without caution. We were thrown into each other, but it didn't bother me. I sat and waited patiently. My body could not decide whether to tense up completely or relax, it shifted between the two states. After being on the bus for so long with no entertainment, I found my mind on Shinji and Jo in the hospital wing. The Treeboy and his gang were on the same floor. M had managed to keep Lana sedated for her own good, was it possible to keep those guys under sedation too? Were Jo and Shinji truly safe? No. That wasn't my concern.

The black ooze covered the bus from the start of the journey but left most of the windows unobscured. I had absolutely no idea where we were. We could have been at the top or bottom of the country by now and I would have no inkling.

"Think we'll be fine?" Dorian asked, his voice implied he had been mulling the question over in his head before finally having to ask us.

"I know we will be," I lied. Not that I didn't think we would be - it was just something I couldn't promise. No one could. Not even M.

After what seemed like a lifetime, the bus stopped. I was absolutely thrilled. The sun was shining brightly, I covered my eyes using my hand as a visor. I nudged Aaron whose eyes flickered as he stirred. "Wha'?" He murmured.

"Wake up. We're here, I think," I whispered. He opened his eyes and stared at me for a moment as if he did not recognise me.

"Shinji?" He croaked, hopefully.

"It's Kurt." I corrected to his clear disappointment.

"Oh," he rubbed his eyes and sat up. "I thought you- never mind, I must have been dreaming." I was envious, I wished I had friends waiting for me in my dreams rather than the traitorous Silvery Haired girl. My face scrunched involuntary with anger at the thought of her. My jaw clenching. Teeth grinding. The long journey was worth it alone to get back at her.

The door of the bus hissed open. The four of us stood, stretching - our muscles sighing with relief - and slowly began to file down the aisle. As we stepped off, I took in the surroundings. In front of us was a large field. Most of the grass was yellow or dying. Rubbish was strewn across the desolate span. It stretched out as far as I could see.

I turned back toward the direction of the bus, but it was no longer there. I could see a slight anomaly rippling in the air. If I was even a few feet away, I would not have noticed a thing. I could still hear the low rumbling of the engine, reaching my hand out I felt the hot metal still there.

I then focused on the edifying walls we could see through the bus. They were taller than a two-storey house and probably almost as thick. Barbed wire sat aggressively on top. I shuddered at the sight, it had a stark resemblance to Snake Girl's teeth. The walls were built out of dull grey concrete - most of it was smooth, but here and there were chunks and holes battered in to them; the stone crumbled, but still, the walls stood proud. In the middle of these walls was the pièce de résistance, a large, moody wrought iron gate. The spiked prongs at the top also had barbed wire wreathed around them, dedicated to keeping anyone out. Unfortunately, 'anyone' included us.

The four of us looked at each other. "Looks welcoming," Dorian said. Nobody laughed. "Well, shall we?" He added and began to walk to the gate.

"Wait!" I called out, grabbing his elbow and pulling him back. "I know M said this was a sanctuary, but we can't be too careful. Shall we scout first? Just to make sure nothing seems suspect." Aaron and Marie nodded their agreement. "Okay, you two wait here. If you see anything, either send up a giant water globe or smoke pillar or whatever, just give us a signal. I'll fly to recce from above, Dorian, do you think you can burrow beneath?" He nodded.

"Ready when you are," he said. I gave him the thumbs up. "Okay, let's do this." He dipped his hands in to his pockets and the two glass spheres floated above him. Then his hands were focused on the floor. It began to rumble and part beneath him. I gently tapped off the floor and began to rise slowly, using my hands to carefully guide me up the wall like I had with the tree. As soon as my face reached the top, I almost died out of pure, undiluted terror.

There was the face of a giant - a titan - staring right back at me. I froze in panic. It was a man; his skin a caramel brown and the beard that covered it had strands of hair as thick as cables. He smiled revealing teeth that must have been the size of vehicles. If he weren't the size of Godzilla, the smile would have been almost goofy. "Hello," his voice boomed. In my fear, I tried to escape reflexively shooting up, but instead I was snatched to the ground like a sling shot. I slammed hard in to the dry soil and saw a pillar of earth erupt from the ground next to me throwing Dorian into the sky. He screamed as he was flung upward in to the air - before I could react, the giant's hand slowly reached over the wall and caught him delicately, like a child with a dandelion seed.

My whole disposition was infected with sheer panic. I tried to fly to save Dorian from the giant's hand, but again, instead of soaring upward, I was slammed into the ground. "Dorian!" Aaron shouted, he threw his hand forward and a jet of strong water blasted him backward. He yelped in fright as he went. I was completely disorientated; the wind had been knocked out of me. I attempted to fly again, but only succeeded once again in crushing myself in to the solid dry mud.

"People here," the giant called out, the volume of his voice rebounded in my head, vibrating my skull. I began wiping the dust off my clothes. I dared not try and use my flight again.

There was a whooshing noise above us. On top of the iron gate, a slender girl was floating. "Opening the gate," she hailed. She held both her arms outwards and as she stretched them wider, the gate began to rumble. With a reverberating clanging, something shifted on the other side, followed by wrenching and screeching noises as the gates began to open. "If you attack us, we will treat you as hostiles. You do not want us to treat you as hostiles."

From the gates poured a small army of men and women. They had guns and batons and were dressed in protective gear which was clearly meant for prison guards. Every one of the guns pointed at Aaron, Marie and myself. Even though the world had changed and there was much worse that could be pointed at us, instinct took over and I was horrified. I wondered if I could stop bullets with my telekinesis, but I would rather not put it to the test.

We stood there, not allowing even a single muscle to move. Dorian's muffled shouting could be heard from the other side of the walls. Out of the gate, another figure. She was dressed in a beautiful blue speckled Kanga. She walked slowly toward us, as if taking a leisurely jaunt down to the seaside. Smiling to herself, completely at ease.

"Put those things down, you damned fools," she ordered in a distinct Nigerian accent. She laughed and waved her hand. As one, all the guns were turned away from us. "Now, children. I *should* apologise for using my ability on you just now, but I won't. I cannot be too careful in these times as I'm sure you understand." We nodded. I understood. She looked different in person. She exuded a jovial warmth. It was *The Jinx*. She stood before me. "Now get in here before you draw any unsavoury folk." She said looking up and down the large open savannah-like field ahead. "Not that it would matter," she chuckled heartily to herself.

The armed guards parted and let us walk through. I looked at them and my stomach began to squirm, there was something not right about them. They stared back, they watched us; their eyes were distrusting. That's what was wrong! They were showing their thoughts. Either they were not as trained as M's staff, or they had no reason to hide their feelings. I actually missed the ignorance of the guards that I had grown accustomed to. At least I didn't think they were menacing, but these guards, showing their own emotions, having their own thoughts - all it took was one of them to wilfully disobey The Jinx and we were dead.

We were escorted through the gates. The giant placed Dorian down, who in turn held both his fists up ready to punch. The giant guffawed as he started to shrink, the sound of mirth transforming from almost deafening to a more agreeable volume. Within seconds, he was an acceptable height, a height that didn't break my neck to stare him in the face. "I'm sorry, I had to catch you. You were going to fall on to the wire."

Dorian ran back over to us. I mouthed 'are you okay?' and he nodded. There were people dotted all around the yard inside. Most looked in our direction half interested, but it seemed that to some, the advent of new people did not deserve even so much of a glance sideways. The prison stood just as tall and crude as the walls that surrounded it; there were barred windows carved in to the walls. It lacked personality and character, not exactly an aesthetic that you could put on the cover of a holiday brochure. I shuddered. The Jinx followed my gaze then turned back, nodding with a smile.

"Never seen so many people wanting to stay in prison before, have you?" She howled at her own joke as she looked around at everyone else obviously expecting them to share the laughter. Most did. I smiled awkwardly back, staring straight at her. "Then again, never has a prison been so safe." I had to be confident. She clicked her fingers. "Chermaine," any sign of laughter had dissipated instantly. A petite girl with a large afro came bounding over. She looked at The Jinx with adoration and at us with distrust, "what do we have here?" The Jinx asked her.

Chermaine pursed her lips then wiggled them around as if tasting a particularly sweet treat. Then her finger pointed directly at Dorian. "Earth, you control earth, uh, soil." There was no hint of a question. She knew. "Wait, and sand? Glass?" Dorian looked terrified but nodded. "Maybe metal if you practice." Dorian began to shake his head, he was about to disagree as he hadn't managed that yet, but was cut off.

The Jinx snapped her fingers at Dorian. "Silly boy, don't be stupid. Chermaine here is quite the connoisseur, she hasn't been wrong to this day. If she says something and you think she's wrong, you simply don't know yet. You will see in time, baby. You will in time." Dorian nodded again submissively. "Trust me. She has not made an error yet." Chermaine then sleuthed the rest of our abilities, much to The Jinx's pleasure.

"Apologies for the invasion of privacy, but it is something we must all go through here," she stated, as she studied all four of us. "Besides, I tend to appreciate knowing what I am dealing with before I reverse it. Makes things much less messy." I nodded my understanding before looking around the rest of the people in the yard again. A whole new breadth of abilities were on show here. Watching them all, using their abilities harmlessly, playfully - that is what I wanted. I noticed The Jinx was watching me, so I snapped my focus back. This was official business - I was not here to goggle at new abilities, I was here to bring The Jinx back to M.

"So, my babies," The Jinx said as she studied us from head to toe. Her smile faded - there was something she didn't like - a momentary look of hostility. She tutted and made a sudden movement. I almost fell backward with anticipation. "Would you like a bite to eat?"

"What?" I was shocked. That was not what I was expecting.

"Look at you, you scrawny things. Are you not eating well? I think you need a bit of nourishing to keep you happy." She whispered something to the girl beside her. The girl replied loudly in a different language but The Jinx held her hand up suddenly and the girl flinched, kissed her teeth then laughed. "Never too old to get a backhand from her mother." Her daughter hovered toward the soulless prison, one toe leaving a line in the sand.

"Thank you, but, we don't need food." I said. No one else was speaking. Marie was eyeing up the others. "We're on an important mission."

One of the guards tittered to himself. "That won't stop her feeding you, son." He called out and The Jinx nodded in agreement.

"An important mission, is it?" She chewed that in her mouth for a moment, then clicked her tongue. "Humour me, child. What is this mission and why is it so important?"

"We- uh-" I looked to the side. Aaron nodded at me. "We have been sent from our, uh, leader, I suppose, M, to bring The Jinx back to the lab." I tried to muster all the authority I could, but I was aware it was not enough. "Meaning you."

She raised her eyebrow then held her forefinger to her chest. "The Jinx?" I nodded. In a swift hand motion, she slapped her thigh and howled with

212

laughter again. I nervously joined in. "I have been called many things since my mother gave me Chiamka, but never have I been 'The Jinx'." She paused for a moment before her laughter renewed.

I watched her as she howled freely. She was a curvy woman, beautiful in all aspects - the picture of maternity. Even though she was laughing in spite of me, the purity behind it made me smile too. I was genuinely laughing now. "And why should I leave here?" She asked happily. "Abandon my friends, my family, my community to come with you? These people rely on me for safety, you know?"

"We, uh, M can use you," I tried, but her smirk spread wider still. She was enjoying this. "What I mean is, uh, have you heard of the Shadow Lady?"

"The Jinx. The Shadow Lady. Dear child, do you not use names where you come from?"

"Uh, yeah, sorry... It's just," it dawned on me then, I never actually knew the Shadow Lady's name, "I don't know it."

Her daughter returned with a small basket containing stew and bread. I shook my head, politely refusing it. "Now don't you stand there and refuse to eat my stew," The Jinx said, surprisingly stern. "I have a deal with outsiders. I work hard to keep food coming to my home and when someone is brought inside they eat! In these walls, children, you are my responsibility and God can strike me down if you leave here saying Chiamka," she smiled in spite of herself, "or The Jinx if you prefer - did not feed you." I shrugged, took some bread and dunked it. It tasted incredible. "Never did someone turn down my food. Even my worst enemy would forgive a grudge if he or she could get her hand on Chiamka's stew." The daughter holding the basket rolled her eyes.

After that, the atmosphere calmed somewhat. It was strange how relaxed I felt, especially under the circumstances. M's lab was a place of science and research - a facility to improve the future, but I felt better here, at an institute of incarceration.

"So, tell me about this Shadow Lady of yours," The Jinx said as if she was asking for a fairytale.

"Here?" I asked, aghast.

She nodded, with a raised eyebrow. "I don't see why not. We have good company, sunshine, fresh air. I tell you, babies, let's enjoy the milder season while we can – we don't know what the winter will bring now."

"Okay," I shrugged and began to tell her about the Shadow Lady and The Catalyst. Aaron and Marie would nod and interject with anything I missed out, whilst Dorian continued to eat the stew and the bread. I told her about M, what she had done for us, all the lives she had saved - how she was researching this phenomenon even prior to the change and had used her knowledge and research since then to try and fight for order. I told her, after a while, about the girl with the Silver Hair but in all honesty, I barely understood it myself.

A thin girl standing next to The Jinx stared at me the whole time I was speaking. She did not blink, nor give any expression. She just stared and listened. I felt uncomfortable saying this in front of so many people, but it also came as a relief. As many people that could hear about Shadow Lady's plans, the better.

When I began to tell her about her power of reversing abilities and how it can be used to stop The Catalyst, she stopped smiling. To compensate, I told her there were others, The Leech and The Mute. A crowd had gathered fit to burst, now. They listened to me talk about the tests, about Treeboy working with the Shadow Lady and how they had tried to kill George. How they would stop at nothing to kill anyone else and that it was of utmost importance that she came back with us right away. When I finished, she took a deep breath, nodded slowly, then she looked at the thin expressionless girl.

"Did you get all that, Tiana?" She asked her. The thin girl, Tiana, nodded suddenly and quickly as if coming out of a trance. The Jinx smiled.

"Yes. Every word," she said quickly.

"This girl's mind is amazing. Can fit everything in there and recount it with no fault. A mnemonist they call her, each of our bases have one," The Jinx said and the girl smiled. She stared for a moment, her eyes flickered about in her head as if listening for something before she nodded slightly. "Seems we have a problem here." There was a change to her tone. She did not seem as friendly. "This Treeboy of yours," she mused, "we have heard tell of him before but not how you put it." She shook her head. "This Shadow Lady as you call her also sounds very familiar someone we work with. We call her Eloise and she leads another Reformist base." I felt hollow. Had I walked right in to the snake pit? Had Shadow Lady already made deals with these people? What was a Reformist base?

The Jinx looked up at the sun. "The problem is, my babies. We are safe here. My abilities deny anyone attacking us. I have kept my daughters safe. Even if an army of people did try to take this place from us, that will only provide me the ammunition to destroy them." She held her hand out to the daughter that brought us the food. Then she indicated behind her, the crowd parted and I could see a young girl around four-years-old playing with a boy of about the same age in the midst of a rippling white halo. "There are plenty of facilities like this out there, controlled by small groups like ourselves - we

214

have a peace treaty." She held her finger up, interrupting herself. "Most of us, that is. No need for death if we can live in harmony as the Lord intended. Eloise is one of the people trying to transform that from a treaty to a law, so your story of her secrecy worries me. It doesn't quite fit."

She grabbed the basket from her daughter and handed it to the normal-sized giant. "Soreena, bring this back, we're almost finished here." He made to leave, but she grabbed his arm. They shared a silent look, before he nodded and left.

"However, I must admit I am curious," she looked in the direction of the sun again before looking back at me. "Eloise, the *'villain'*, has been very generous to us." She continued. That was bad. If Eloise *was* The Shadow Lady, then her being friends with The Jinx was extremely detrimental to M's overall plan. "Very generous indeed. She doesn't sound like the dictator you think she is."

There was no room for failure. "Look, she's dangerous. She's evil. She's trying to procure The Catalyst's ability to use for her own selfishness. If Eloise *is* the Shadow Lady, she is *using* you. You're falling for it. If she is successful, she'll destroy everything you have here. Your ability won't be able to stop her. Not with The Catalyst behind her. Don't let her outsmart you."

One of her guards muttered. "Sure you've got that the right way, kid?"

"I tell you what," The Jinx ignored the guard, "I respect you coming here and you seem like a nice bunch." She paused for a moment, looking down at the floor. She smiled so wide at her shoes that I briefly questioned her sanity. "I will not make a decision just yet as Eloise has not mentioned any Catalyst which also strikes me as odd. Maybe there is an innocent reason behind it, maybe not. I will confer with the other leaders and find out one way or another. I always do."

She placed her hand on my shoulder. "I am sorry to disappoint child, but I will not be coming back with you. I do not know your leader and I do not trust those that I do not know. If Eloise is a snake, at least I can keep her where I can see her. Unlike your M." She squeezed my shoulder tight for a moment then pulled her hand away. There was a snagging on my shirt after her hand left and I was about to scratch my neck.

"Careful," she spoke with urgency to my shoulder, then smiled at me. "There is no death in my compound, not even for insects." She reached her forefinger and thumb then plucked. As much as I hated insects, I tried to look but couldn't see anything. "There we are. Fly away, sweetling," she sang as she held her hand above her head. "That's how we solve things here, peacefully and more importantly face to face.

"Tell your leader I will consider her request, if she comes here herself. If she wishes to use my ability, then she must earn my trust. That is the *only* way I will believe she truly needs my assistance. I will work with Tiana here to listen to your story again and again and we will speak to Eloise and the other Reformist leaders before we act." I was about to argue but she held her finger up to silence me. "My friends here," she indicated her daughter and the armed guards, "will escort you back outside."

I turned, feeling confused and defeated. I walked with Aaron, Marie and Dorian for a few steps before stopping. *I can't walk away now.* We had travelled so long to get here. This was about finally ending the Shadow Lady. This was about M's plan to stop a dictator before she ascended to power. This was about Lana. This was about George's right to stay alive. This was about Shinji and Jo. "No!" I yelled turning back to her. She cocked her head with intrigue. "You have to come. I'll- I'll force you if you don't."

She chortled. "I'm afraid you don't have a choice, baby." I felt the rage bubbling back up inside me. I held my hand out. All around her, every single person did the same. Objects appeared, orbs hovered, energy swirled and spiralled; flames crackled in a ring around us. A chorus of eerie sounds filled the yard. The Jinx didn't even flinch. She just smiled showing a row of perfect teeth. "Don't be a *fool*, child."

Marie lowered my arm. "She'll think about it. We've done all we can."

"But," I said helplessly, "it's dangerous out there."

"Baby, it was always dangerous," she sighed," only now people don't need to hide it."

Why didn't she understand the severity of all this? "This is bigger than you could imagine."

She chuckled. "Sometimes," her eyes scanned my face and shoulders. "Sometimes, it's the smaller things that we need to worry about." She winked and the sound of the heavy gate opening behind, stirred a sense of helplessness. As we left, The Jinx and everyone around her burst in to hysterics.

M's fury would be boundless.

Chapter 18

The bus home was treacherous. First of all, I told The Jinx everything M had told me. Secondly, if all these leaders have their treaties and M was not a part of this, she was in an unfavourable position.

As the vehicle rumbled and groaned down the roads that were hidden by the black substance, my stomach churned. I refused to let myself fall asleep. I would not allow Silver Hair to exacerbate matters. M would be furious enough that I saw her again yesterday, never mind failing to bring The Jinx home.

It was strange though, something about leaving M's lab made me feel good; restored in a sense. Like a haze had been lifted, but not entirely. I couldn't quite understand what it was, my mind felt clearer, I felt more like myself than I had since the day of the change, even without Jo and George by my side.

Though, the bug that The Jinx took off my shoulder must have bitten me before she let it free because I kept feeling an irritating itching sensation. I would scratch, which would sate it for a while but it would reoccur a little later on.

The journey back was just as long as it was here technically, but it felt much longer with the weight of failure dragging me down. My heartbeat increased to a rapid fire when the bus began to slow down. M would already know we failed, our minds would be open for her and she would know that we did not have The Jinx. A plethora of scenarios went through my head, all bad. I felt like crying. When the bus stopped, I stayed in my seat for a few seconds just trying to catch my breath. Marie, Aaron and Dorian stood up almost instantly - ready to leave.

The ooze rolled down and the windows were transparent once more. I could see the town hall illuminated white by the moon. It was dark and cloudless outside. I was terrified when I turned to see M already waiting for us. Dorm One must have notified them because Dorm Two were standing with her. She dismissed them when she saw it was just us. I felt more scared returning to M than I did arriving at the prison - surely that wasn't right. I took my time getting off the bus, allowing the others to go before me. Maybe they would get the brunt of M's disappointment.

Her staff spread the width of the front of the building. M stood in the middle. I noticed her daughter wasn't there. Maybe she was expecting an attack of some sort and wanted her daughter to be kept safe? Maybe she - *stop thinking, Kurt, she can hear you.*

I gingerly scuttled behind my friends until we were feet away. "You failed," she spat. I felt like breaking down there and then. "You requested this personally, you asked me to send you when I thought it was not fitting and you *failed*?"

We stood there like children being scolded by their parents. The woman who had done so much for us finally trusted us with one thing to repay her kindness yet here we were, failures. "I'm really sorry, it's just, she was too -"

"Keep your mouth shut," she snapped. My mouth felt as if it was locked; there was nothing I could say, no words would form, even if I tried. Her words affected me physically. I shuddered as if her order itself was shaking me. "I cannot even begin to put in to words how disappointed I am. It seems through all my hard work keeping you alive through this change, you still fail to respect me or the severity of the situation we are in." She waited for an answer but I couldn't even form a single vowel. "*Speak!*"

"No, you don't understand." The words burst out as if they were always there, waiting for me to just say it. What was stopping me?

"Then make me!" She said with vitriol.

I looked between my friends hoping they would start, but they didn't. "Okay," I began to think of everything that happened in the compound. How what was supposed to be an epic mission of heroism fizzled in to a chat and a bit of food.

"Well?" M said.

"I was thinking it. Sorry, I thought you'd read my mind," I apologised. It was what she did, why wouldn't she just do it now? To see if I would tell the truth? It was usually easier for her to get information, unfiltered by my vocabulary. "I - uh- well, her power... It makes ours - we're less than useless," I said. "The fact that we have abilities puts us at a greater disadvantage."

"She said she'd think about it if you speak to her. Our powers make us weaker to her," Marie explained. "You'd be better off sending your staff to get her, at least they are immune to her ability."

"You *dare* tell me what I am better off doing whilst you stand before me as failures?" M's breath grew heavy. Her face grew redder. I started to feel weak at the knees when her staff behind her looked just as angry.

"M, honestly, I'd like to go back. If we can get more people, maybe we can overpower them, but..." I shook my head slowly and wiped a tear from my eye. "There really was nothing we could do. They have a lot there; a lot

218

more than you can imagine. They are protected and The Jinx - her power really is what you said." M scoffed at me, as if I dared think she may have been wrong. "If I tried to do anything, if any of us tried to do anything, we would have just attacked ourselves. We need to go try a different approach."

She stared in to my eyes for what felt like an eternity, then she smiled. That smile was wrong. It didn't sit right in the context. Something was awry. "No," she said barely louder than a whisper, "you just didn't have the motivation you needed, but I *assure* you, Kurt. When you see your friends, you will regret not doing more."

My legs went weak, I felt my ability flush outward around me. It tugged at the collar of my black shirt. "What do y- What's that supposed to mean?" I asked. Suddenly, nothing else mattered. Only Jo, Shinji and Lana.

"Get some sleep. If Dorm Four and Dorm Eleven are as disappointing as you, I am afraid we will have to take drastic measures." She ignored my panic.

No. I can't just put it out of my head. "Are my friends okay?" I asked, defying her.

"Get. Some. Sleep." Each word fit for a religion in its own right, the meaning sunk in and I realised that the most important thing, more than my failure, more than my friends, more than anything… was sleep. I was powerless. Unable to disobey. The word 'sleep' drifted around my head, it took centre stage. I barely even paid attention to my friends who seemed to be thinking the same thing.

Some of the staff members were with us as the lift descended. *Sleep.* The doors opened and for a moment, I wanted to slam the staff into the wall and go down another level. To get Jo, Shinji and Lana. To kill Treeboy and everyone else who tried to attack George, but no… I wanted sleep more!

We were at our corridor now. When the dorm door opened, George came sprinting out the kitchen, Anthony following behind. He hugged us all. I hugged him back but it was just going through the motions. M said I should sleep, not to see him. George stood with Anthony, both perplexed at the fact we were outright ignoring their questions. I had to sleep before anything else. I was not tired, but I had to sleep. That was my goal. That was the one thing I had wanted in my entire life. To sleep. I needed to sleep. I lay in bed, wide awake, waiting for sleep. Sleep. *Sleep.*

*

I was not sure if I actually had slept or not. There was no visit from Silver Hair, but I certainly was not fully conscious for a while. It was as if I just sat trapped in stasis for a while, thinking about the concept of sleep and wishing for it. But something disturbed the process, a noise, a consistent, obnoxious wailing. No... A siren. An alarm. That's what the sound was. It broke me out of my stupor. Outside in the corridor, outside the hall, the entire lab was victim to the klaxons.

I jumped out of bed in fright. Everything in my room fell out of place. My bed itself was floating this time. The sirens blurred on. I stormed in to the corridor. Marie, Dorian, Aaron, George and Anthony were there too. They seemed just as startled as I was.

"What is that?!" I shouted above the alarm.

"I think it might be an alarm, mate," George shouted back covering his ears. Anthony was hugging in to him, George's arms held him close.

"But what the hell is it going off for?" I screamed.

"Do you think Shinji is okay?" Aaron said. I could barely hear his voice. Water rippled from his hands in time with the sirens. "You don't think that..." He scrunched his face up and shouted louder. "You don't think those people escaped from the medical wing, do you?"

I couldn't hear my inner voice, my thoughts were drowned out. It was clouding my head. No, M said they were safely constrained. I looked around the hall and saw a miniature horn just at the top corner of the corridor, above where the buzzer was. The sound was coming from there. I held both my hands to my ears so I could block noise out and focus more. I let my thought wrap round the horn and I ripped it from the wall.

The immediate sound dimmed, but there was still a screeching from outside and all around the rest of the lab. At least now I could hear myself think. "You don't think it's the Shadow Lady, do you?" I asked my friends. When I looked up at them, colour had faded from their face. They were staring behind me as if they had just seen a ghost. They instantly jumped into action. Two whips of water shot round either side of me, followed by two ribbons of smoke. Dorian's glass orbs stayed above his shoulders hovering, each had taken the shape of a spiked mace, vibrating with tension.

I turned and was almost knocked down with surprise. How did he get here?! The giant from the compound! What was his name? Sauron? Sora?

"Sora?" I squeaked. He stood naked in our dorm. Well, naked besides the two shards of ice encasing his hands, pulling his arms out on either side. The ribbon of smoke hovered dangerously close to his nose and mouth, threatening to enter. Why was he in our dorm? *How* was he in our dorm? This was wrong. This was surreal. M would not take kindly to this.

"It's Soreena," he shouted above the sirens outside. He looked at his hands and the smoke in front of him with apprehension, but then his body began to enlarge. I took a few steps back. He was almost too big to fit in the corridor now. He yelled in pain as the ice cracked under the growth and fell to the floor. "Please, I am here to help!" He said before he reverted back to his normal size. "You have been lied to this whole time."

I slammed him in to the wall. "What's going on?!" I shouted. Two globes of water shot to his hands again before freezing.

"I came home with you. To help you," he shouted, "you almost killed me a thousand times hitting your neck."

"What?" He wasn't making sense. Confusion was giving way to anger now. The sirens outside were seriously stressing me out. "How did you get here?"

"My ability. I can enlarge in size easily and revert to my normal height," he smiled for a moment. "The Jinx reversed it. She shrunk me. She put me on your shoulder. We're going to save you!"

"We don't need saving," I shouted. I pulled him away from the wall and slammed him back in to it. The ice around his hand travelled with him. "We needed The Jinx here. Not you. She is one of the three who can stop The Catalyst - Patrick! Why can't she understand that?"

"No, *you* don't understand," he was also getting angry, "Eloise isn't what you think she is. We have worked with her. We have visited her base of operations. We have been trying to find you for a long time. If you don't trust me and she finds out we're here, your friends could be dead by the end of the night."

I paused for a moment. Fully terrified. "Let him go," I ordered Aaron. His brown eyes locked with mine for a moment, a frosted tear adorned his cheek once more. "I am *not* risking any of their lives," I yelled. He nodded.

The ice faded from Soreena's hands and he rubbed them. He took a deep breath and looked at each of us. Then he grew larger again. We all took a step back in unison. He was kneeling, but his head was touching the top of the corridor. His voice began to boom over the sirens. "Okay, listen to every word I say. You are going to be very confused now, but trust me. At least try.

"Chiamka and the rest of the new leaders have been trying to find a way to get to you for a long time. Eloise knew there would be trouble, but there was no way of finding where your leader was. We have tried every form of scouting known to man, we have raided any old government building - those that still stood - in the hopes of finding the location of this laboratory. We almost gave up hope.

"Your leader, Melanie, she was completely off the radar and then you, the four of you stroll in to our compound as simple as that. You don't understand how phenomenal that was. We thought, for sure, it was a trap, there was an ambush but it was simple. So simple. As you stood there talking to us, Chiamka was arranging a plan." I started to get dizzy. Where was M? *What was going on?!* "We have strategies in the prison. Chermaine's ability can link minds.

"As you were telling us about the *danger* we were in, Chermaine had created a network that everyone of us were tapped in to. As you spoke, we were listening - the whole compound - to Chiamka's orders. She was telling us what to do the whole time. That is how I knew when to use my ability, that is how Tiana knew to absorb the information of the story.

"Chiamka truly is a magnificent tactician. She can best even me and I'm renowned. Tiana has all the information we needed locked in her mind. She was the one paying attention to you as you spoke; Chiamka only half doing so. Tiana is an archive in human form. Everything you said, everything we read from you is locked in her mind for everyone to decipher. We could see the lab in your mind, we could see the village, but we did not know the way. This was the lab that was ripped from Eloise's mind - your leader did that in her anger. But you, kid. *You* gave us what we needed.

"That's when Chiamka told me to take the dishes in. She used her power to revert mine. She placed me on your shoulder and I sat there. I was in touch with three of our mindreaders. Poor Chermaine almost died trying to keep the link over that distance, but she would die for Chiamka and thank her for the opportunity to serve her. We all would. No doubt. We owe our lives to her as it is.

"I was their GPS. I was the link from the prison to your lab. I held in to your shirt and I did not lose focus once. I told them every time there was a sudden right, a slow left, a straight path. Tiana, once again was linked to this network - she was retaining the information as I said it. It was as if she was on the bus with us. She heard it from me and now it is in her memory forever," he smiled his big toothy grin. "They will be here soon to help you. They followed behind as quickly as they could. They contacted Eloise. Your freedom is almost at hand."

I stood there completely overwhelmed by everything that we had just been told. How much of it was true? How much of it was a lie? After willingly allowing Silver Hair to control me, I would not make the same mistake again. Pure rage began to bubble in my stomach. How *dare* he lie to us after sending his people to kill George! "You're a liar!" I screamed. I pulled at the gigantic strands of hair on his beard. Aaron crashed a wave into

222

his face and then froze it. Soreena almost screamed in pain but the ice froze his face in place mid agony.

"Aaron, the door. We need to tell M!" I shouted.

"But what if he's tell-" Marie shouted, but I clenched her jaw shut. M was in danger! That was what the sirens were. We were being invaded. *After everything*!

The door was already completely frozen. Aaron had known what to do after last time we broke it. Soreena was back to normal size and was clutching at his face. It was red raw; the ice had ripped parts of his skin off. "You idiots!" He shouted. Dorian and George both booted the door until it shattered. Anthony was crying behind them, his hand held up waiting for George's. "Come on!" I shouted and we began to run.

"Wait!" Soreena yelled behind us. I shuddered at the thought of him sitting on my shoulder the whole time. Why could M not sense his mind when we got back? I felt like puking, or crying, or fainting, or something, but that wouldn't help. M would help. She was the one I needed.

I saw another group of people from a different dorm running toward us. They were clearly confused, but safe. Dorian was shouting for them to help, but they froze for a moment looking past us with abject terror before they took a sharp left. Behind us, there was a thudding sound and the giant was crawling through the corridors after us. He was gaining speed. I screamed involuntarily, but Dorian shot both of the spiky glass balls towards him. I heard a wet ripping sound as one of the balls pierced the film protecting his eye. His scream vibrated the halls. He began swearing in pain. Cursing us for our ignorance in two languages.

"Come on, let's follow them," Aaron cried over the sirens. His arms and hair were blue-white with frost. I did a quick take behind me to see a thick ice wall blocking us from the giant. Aaron ran in the direction of the other dorm. We followed behind him. Anthony was sobbing, but he kept up. George would not let go of him.

"We have to get to Jo!" I shouted. "Where is the lift?"

"This way," Marie replied, her voice heavy with distress. There was a resounding thump from behind us, then a glacial smash as Aaron's ice wall crumbled at the thunderous pounding of Soreena's titanic fists. We ran down the hallway. Now we were closer to the lift, we could hear shouting all around us. Other dorms were running to it too. *Where was M?* "Okay, if we turn left. There!" She was right. The lift was open, almost completely filled with other denizens inside; almost to capacity. They waited for us, motioning us to come closer. The thudding behind increasing in volume and pace. The giant was getting closer.

We sprinted. I was out of breath, my chest stinging with the effort, but I could hear the bounding of Soreena approaching us. He was getting closer. I couldn't stop. Not now.

As one, everyone in the lift screamed. I knew then that Soreena had caught up. That they could see him behind us. "Get back here!" His voice rattled my bones to the marrow and I almost fell with an impending sense of failure, my legs turning to jelly, ignoring my brain's order to keep running. *Keep running. The lift is just there.*

"Close the door," someone was shouting in the lift. It was Buzz! Soreena was crawling closer, I looked back to see an ocean of blood and puss pouring from the open wound in his eye. "It's too late. Close it!" He shouted. There were shouts of agreement and shouts of outrage. I saw Blake, his hand reached out to us. His face a shade of green. I reached back, but we were too far. He tried to break free, but Buzz stopped him. We were so close now but the door began to close in front of us. Sealing our fate. We were stuck at a dead end.

Marie conjured smoke - thicker and blacker than she ever had before. It swirled and spiralled down the hallway. Aaron erected glacial stalagmites between us and Soreena. Dorian's glass orbs were now two impossibly thin, razor thin shards. As he pushed them forward, launching them at Soreena, some of the lights above began to spark and explode as the metal framing obeyed Dorian's command. *Just like M said. Just like the girl at the compound said!* But why would she tell him? Why would she help? It ripped the plaster and tiles from the ceiling, but followed his shards of glass in the smoky, icy hazard.

The coughing we heard was grotesque. A cough amplified is not a pleasant sound, especially when combined with Anthony's sobbing, billowing smoke, sparks of electricity and sirens. There was a crashing sound. Aaron's ice, definitely. Though Soreena could not be seen, his gigantic hand reached from the depths of the smoke, the sharp stalagmites tore the flesh, sheets of which, the size of duvet covers flapped with blood. The clinically white floor was flooded with claret, the hand continued its approach as the giant screamed. "Stop!" We didn't. I held my hands in front of us, creating a forcefield, preparing for the hands to reach us - hopefully I could stop him until we figured out what we could do. Dorian's shards of glass slashed relentlessly at the grasping arm as the metal crudely attempted wrapping itself round it to shackle him. More ice was sent from Aaron, more smoke, yet the hand continued. It was the width of the corridor. It was large enough to squash us whole, massive enough to break every bone in our body with the slightest pressure.

I felt something behind me. Something grabbed my shoulder. I screamed and my telekinesis splurged out. I pinned whoever it was to the wall before turning. *Blake?* "What are you doing?"

"I can't take my whole dorm," he squealed. "But I can take you lot. Hold on."

"Everyone. Hold Blake!" I screamed. My friends turned and held tightly on to him. If they were surprised to see him, it didn't show. My ears began to ring. Cold wind bit at my hot, sweating body, whipping at our clothes. The sirens were in the distance, muffled now. The night sky was above us. Stars decorated the darkness above. For a moment, I thought of Silver Hair. Then M. I needed M!

In front of the Town Hall and small school that faced the motel were others. Not from the lab, people I had not seen. More than I could count. They waited on top of the building, below it. Some clung from the window sills, some effortlessly sticking to the flat smooth stone. Most looked human, but a few were beasts, shadows, morphed and distorted. Some hovered in place, some bobbed up and down, some flying from side to side in the air, few winged, most non-winged.

In the centre of these, something drew my attention. A glittering silver ball was hovering, the shape of someone could be seen silhouetted inside it in the foetal position. Standing in front of that ball was a tall, thin woman. She was dressed all in black; the clothes clung to her body snugly. Her face was pale, her eyes beautifully dangerous. She smiled when I locked eyes with her. *The Shadow Lady.*

"Tiana?" She said, her voice crisp, concise and relaxed. Tiana, the girl from the compound stood next to her and nodded eagerly before pointing at each of us.

"Marie, Dorian, Aaron, Kurt. I believe that boy must be George, their friend, he has no ability. They did not tell us who the younger boy, or that other boy was," Tiana explained, pointing from Anthony to Blake.

I was frozen. How could I escape this? How could we get ourselves away from this? There was a chorus of panicked cries behind us as the rest of the people began to pour out of the lab.

"I believe a thank you is in order," The Shadow Lady said. I stared back at her. More people began to crowd around us now, most of them were silent, some gasped when they saw the sheer amount of people facing us. "I have

225

been trying to locate this lab, my old lab, since the day of this change." My body shuddered. I did not know if it was down to the wind, or the only reaction I was currently capable of. "I should apologise for taking so long, leaving you here with my deranged partner. I can only imagine what she has put you all through."

The crowd behind us began fussing. I turned to see M was walking from the lab with her staff, armed with guns, behind her. We were saved - we may have failed to acquire The Jinx, but we still had the Shadow Lady, in our territory - our land.

"Ah, speak of the devil," The Shadow Lady said, smiling.

"And she doth appear," M finished, then nodded curtly. "Eloise."

"Melanie." The Shadow Lady replied, returning the nod. Melanie... So that's what the M was short for. Wait, Melanie? That's what Silver Hair had said - my train of thought stalled, Shadow Lady continued. "Where is Megan?"

"Away from here," M stated. The group had parted and M was level with us now. Her army of staff, more than I had ever seen together, behind her, staring blankly ahead.

"But," she said shaking her head, "I see you kept the locals as pets? Corrupted them until they were mindless zombies?" The Shadow Lady asked.

"They have served their purpose; there is only so much a genius can do... especially when her partner abandons her." M's voice was tense and disgusted.

"Oh, you blame *me* for this?" Shadow Lady said in mock surprise. Then with sincerity continued, "I see the awakening hasn't changed your narcissism. This isn't my doing, Melanie, this is what you thought you deserved from day one. An army of people to obey your every command. You tried it with the staff even before you gained your ability. Tell me before they escaped you, how many did you kill?" What was she talking about? M didn't kill the staff, they were standing right here, well behaved as always, even in the face of danger.

"Only as many as were necessary," M said dryly. "Let us cut to the chase, Eloise. Where is he?"

"If you tell me where our daughter is, I'll tell you where Patient Zero is," Shadow Lady bargained.

"I have his sister," M said, "he will want to see her."

"I'm aware, your emissary sent the message. Did he not relay what I told him?"

"He did…" M admitted, "more fool him."

"More fool anyone following your orders." Shadow Lady reiterated. Then she looked at us, our little group, my friends and Blake. "May I ask your test subjects a question?"

"I would rather you did not," M said, but there was no intonation to her voice.

"There are many things we would rather the other didn't do, yet, as imperfect as we are, we do them anyway." Shadow Lady replied. "Tell me, Dorian," Dorian gasped in fright, "oh, she's worked you good. Tell me, how often do you think about your parents?" Dorian went to open his mouth, but no sound came out. He closed it again. "Marie? Kurt? Aaron?" She shook her head as none of us answered. "Tell me," she continued, "in a world filled with such horrors, how is it you have not spared the time to think about your family, your brothers, sisters, cousins. Old friends? Grandparents?" Shadow Lady's voice began to grow louder. "Tell me, any of you people standing here before me, when have any of you made an attempt to not even rescue your parents, but simply check if they're alive?"

"M has people working on it for us!" I shouted back. There was a shifting from all those in the town hall as they stared at me. The eyes of hundreds of them.

Shadow Lady shook her head sadly. "You poor thing. Pray tell, Melanie, how much of this brainwashing is due to your general manipulative charisma and how much of it is due to your thought manipulation ability?" Her what? She was a *mind reader*.

"How do you know?" M spat!

"Chiamka Tinibu sends her regards," Shadow Lady smirked. "She was so impressed that you managed to locate her and have intel on her gifts that she sent some of her most valuable talents to help take you down. Chermaine?" She called and the dainty girl with the afro hopped forward. "Nothing can be hidden from us now, Melanie. You've had all these poor children fooled."

"M be careful. Don't read their minds," I urged, "that girl, Chermaine, she can link their minds! They are all tapped in listening to one another! The giant told us how it worked!"

"He's right," Shadow Lady admitted, without even a flicker of panic, "and now everyone here will know exactly what you have done to them. Unless you come with us."

"No!" M grunted and for the first time since I had met her, she seemed scared. "I can block it."

The Shadow Lady groaned impatiently. "I am giving you a chance now, Melanie. For old time's sake. For everything we had together - will you give yourself up?"

"You know me better than that," M spat through gritted teeth.

"Unfortunately, I do. You've lost, Melanie." Her tone was sombre. Then, "Andre, now!" A boy around my age standing a few feet away from the Shadow Lady burst in to action. Two thin silvery glittery discs shot toward M. The ball of the same substance encasing the silhouetted figure behind Shadow Lady rippled slightly, becoming momentarily transparent but a group stood in front of it. Before I could even move to protect M, two of the staff members on either side ran in front of her. The discs collided with their bodies, wrapping round them like a bola, pulling their bodies tight before the silver fizzled away. They fell to the floor, wriggling to get out. "Oh, come now, Melanie. Have you not already put them through enough? You tore them away from their poor families. We knew these people! They welcomed us." The Shadow Lady called out. She sounded impatient now. "Look at yourself. You have lost."

Without a word, the rest of the staff members behind M raised their weapons and began firing at Shadow Lady's people. A plethora of forcefields and barriers were thrown up, blocking the fusillade of bullets from them. A chorus of clangs, pings, hums and cracks sounded from in front of the town hall and faded softly in to the night.

"We both know that you didn't think that would work, Melanie," Shadow Lady called. "But how dare you! How *dare* you. I have come here in the interests of offering some level of impunity. Release these people. Release the villagers. Release the children! You have a chance to retain a modicum of dignity, now prove to me you're not the monster that I see before me. Show these people you deserve amnesty."

"I will give you whatever you want if you give me The Catalyst," M shouted.

"You will never get him!" Shadow Lady gloated. "You have no ante."

"No ante?" M laughed. "I can make your own allies kill you. I will kill anyone to get The Catalyst-" M froze for a moment, her anger replaced with a smile which twisted uncomfortably on her face. "If you do not tell me where The Catalyst, I will *kill* Megan."

Now it was Shadow Lady's turn to show fear. "No," she gasped. "Melanie, you have already hindered Megan's life enough since the awakening. Was it really worth torturing your own flesh and blood to use her telepathy?"

What? M was the telepath...

"She was scared. She didn't understand. I *made* her do what she had to," M replied, seemingly confident she now had the upper hand. "My power worked well with hers. Symbiotic almost; I had a direct link in to her brain - her ability. I didn't *steal* or *hinder* her mind; it was there to use. You would have done the same with any tool in your arsenal."

"A tool? *She's our daughter!*" Shadow Lady emphasised the last three words by using one hand to punch the palm of the other. "If that means anything to you - which I'm beginning to doubt - then I know you would at least keep her alive because losing her would be detrimental to your cause." She sounded like she was trying to convince herself as much as M.

"You *doubt* me? I will do anything - I mean, *anything* to ensure my research can go on unhindered!"

"You're so good at manipulating people that you've managed to fool yourself!" Shadow Lady roared. "Look around you - this is nothing to do with your research. All you want is Patrick to give you the power to control everything. You've always had that incessant need for dominance. You need to let go. You need to let me take control."

"I need only The Catalyst!" M shrieked.

Shadow Lady shook her head. Her face showed incredulity. She shook it off, then, from behind her, an ocean of shadow poured out. It roared in the direction of M. Her staff all around her scrambled to get in front. To Shadow Lady's credit, she was right; they did not seem human in this moment. They threw their bodies forward, encasing M's body entirely. Limbs jutted out of the mass of staff members, some bent in ways that must be incredibly painful, but none of them let out even the slightest of whimpers.

The materialised shadow halted before M and her human shield. Tendrils branched out of it, trying to pull away staff, but as soon as one was thrown away from the ball, another would shift their position ensuring there was no way M could be seen. The Shadow dissipated. "You are beginning to test my patience!" Shadow Lady called to M. The grotesque ball of staff was wriggling, each person trying to protect M. Sacrificing their lives to save hers.

Her muffled voice called out from within the tangle of bodies. "You left me. You left me when I needed you most."

"I left you when it was clear you would not listen to reason," Shadow Lady corrected her, "I walked out on your incredibly stark immorality." She continued, her voice the only thing now filling the distance between us. She was crying now, "our research was supposed to improve the human condition. Sacrificing even one life would be detrimental to our goal. One life is worth the same as any others."

"No. Your interference with his natural decline was going to reverse everything; all of it would have been for nothing. We could have stopped this change before it happened. We could have been the only two people in the world to have control of these abilities. We could have ruled in the name of science! You ran out because you were *weak*! You fled because you were not ready for this new world!"

"Yet, here it is and I am the one who remained level-headed," Shadow Lady insisted sadly, the people standing with her nodded. "The one whose disposition was not mangled by the awakening."

"*Weak!*" M screamed.

"Why do you still keep fighting? The world has already changed – it is too late to attempt what you wanted. I am part of a movement trying to reform the government! Tell me why you won't just come back with us now. Face your punishment - we will not harm you, Melanie. We will keep you safe; keep others safe from you. Tell me why you can't do that!"

"Because I want *him*!" She screeched. I'd never seen her so out of control – not even the time in the medical wing compared to this. "He can give me the power I need. With him, I will have the platform to progress this pathetic planet in the direction I know it needs."

The Shadow Lady laughed. "You know, Melanie. I think that is the most honest thing you've ever said to me in all our years together."

"Let me create the world in my image." M continued. "Hand him over and we will have peace!"

"On your terms," Shadow Lady replied, "the only way that can ever happen is if I am not here to stop you and as you've said, I can be maddeningly stubborn."

"And I can be infuriatingly persistent," M shouted. Her anger began to fuel me, it began to control me. It was infectious; a disease that coursed through my body. I could feel everyone beside me moving too. The entire lab. It was as if our bodies were vessels, waiting for M to tell us what to do. If she wanted us to move our right hand, we would, if she wanted me to use my ability, I would. If she wanted me to kill *anyone* I would. No hesitation. No second guessing. M's decision was total.

At once, a plethora abilities were catapulted to their side. Once more, force fields, shields, barriers and shining bulwarks were thrown up, but now it was more than bullets bombarding them. It was: explosions, energy, smoke, vapours, ice, fire, water, earth, it was tooth, it was nail, it was whole bodies. People ran from our side of the field at those facing us.

Shadow tendrils poured over the blockades and slithered beneath, wrapping themselves around people's legs, constricting their arms to their sides in an attempt to stop them from aiming their powers. She was trying to block people's abilities from reaching the barriers, but there were too many, from all directions. Shadow Lady was strong, but she wasn't that strong.

A part of me wanted to stop. Somewhere deep, deep down knew this wasn't right - knew there was more to the story than we were told. I felt myself lift from the ground, I was flying towards them. One of the others were flying towards me. They had large thin diaphanous wings. I could hear them shouting something, but the only part paying attention to their words was the part of me hidden away. The part that resided in obscurity behind M's control. I grabbed their wings with my ability and I ripped them from their body. They wailed in pain and began to hurtle to the ground.

Below, the beauty in the chaos took my breath away. It looked as if the apocalypse had come. The ground was shaking, brontides of various decibels were sounding constantly, fire erupting all over, vivid colours – contrasted by the night - clashed, explosions of all different sizes and properties were sporadically dancing across the field. The town hall itself began to crumble under the impact of such an onslaught.

I could see a sheet of smoke and knew it was coming from Marie. She was creating a smokescreen that the others from the lab - others we had never spoken to - were shooting through indiscriminately, all working together like the intricate, almost choreographed and designed movements of a machine; with the same unified flow that M's staff usually sported.

I saw something else. Something that made the voice deep inside me scream, the part that wanted to flee and panic uncontrollably. *Treeboy was here.* He was standing by the human shield of M's staff. He was shooting his wooden stakes *towards* Shadow Lady. It didn't make sense. My thoughts began to blur again. Snake Girl was there too, with Bigfists, Goatee and Ordinaryboy. All using their abilities to attack the person that was supposed to be their leader! There was no sign of the girl half my height.

More shadow tendrils spouted from the floor, pulling all those who could fly to the ground like a toad catching a fly. I felt one wrap around my leg and it snapped me down.

A man tried to pick me up, but I punched him in the nose and bit his neck. He screamed and recoiled as he dropped me. Now I had a clear view of him I pushed my hands out sending a strong pulse his way, he shot upward in a trajectory that smashed him in to the wall of the town hall. He fell to the ground, leaving a dent in the building. Rubble toppled down after him.

The suppressed part within began to rage a battle with the part taken over by M. My priorities smashing in to one another. Was Patrick more important than my friends? I shook my head. *Where is Treeboy?!* Had he killed Jo? *Had he killed Shinji and Lana?* I stood up and began backpedalling to where M was still encased. A sparkling beam whizzed right past my eyes, whooping as it did so and hit one of the staff members. Their body tensed up before flopping to the ground. Though M was still fully protected, the shield was beginning to thin.

No, she was more important. I had to protect her. I saw others from the lab, the other subjects - *subjects? Your friends are there, Kurt* - subjects, had had the same idea. We were all one, we were all M's. No, we were all M! We encircled her and continued to fight ensuring our life would be taken before hers.

There was an odd squelching sound that began to drown out the shouts and noises of the abilities around us. It grew louder and more sickening until a gigantic figure towered above us. I thought for a moment it was Soreena, but the body was pitch-black, coal-black, darker than dark in the same way Lana's lights were so bright that they seemed make sunlight itself look diluted; material so black that it made the night sky behind look bright in comparison.

It reached its giant hand down toward us, fitting the human shield and M herself neatly in its grasp. Instantly everyone turned their abilities on the shadow titan's hand, but it was useless. The projectiles that were not deflected by Shadow Lady's tendrils - which wreathed the body of this Vanta-black titan - merely collided with it and rippled with little to no effect.

Still, as I heard M scream from within, I torpedoed toward the hand, deftly weaving in and out of the abilities aiming at it. All rational sense of survival escaping my mind. I was fully ready to die for my research – *M's research, Kurt* – my research! Before I could reach it, a breathtakingly large silver disc clashed with the humungous hand, wrapping around it with the same bola-like effect I saw earlier.

There was a chorus of cheers from in front of the Town Hall. As the disc wrapped fully round the middle of the fist, it shimmered and opened in to a spherical force field - similar to the one that hovered and glittered behind Shadow Lady earlier - covering the shadowy hand. Once complete, the hand itself began to fade leaving just the staff members and M encased in a nightmarish snow globe.

Suddenly, it was as if my mind had snapped back to normal. The voice deep inside of me, my voice, took precedence. The fury I was feeling now was my own, not M's. Without her clouding me, I soared above again looking for Treeboy in the crowd. Most people had stopped what they were doing, each looking just as confused as I felt, but lacking the fury that was surging through me. Shinji, Jo and Lana had to be alive. *There!* He was easy enough to spot. Whilst most of the others from the lab had paused, now released from M's sway, there were a few still hurling their abilities.

Treeboy was one of them. I beelined straight for him, swiftly flying down. He was completely unaware that I was close by. I pulled my leg back and with all the strength I could muster, kicked him hard on the side of the head. As he dropped to the ground, small brown teeth flew out of his mouth from the impact.

He held the point of impact, rubbing the pain away. His arms were thick with vines that heaved. He looked back in my direction and smiled a deep, evil grin. As he took an awkward step forward, I noticed that instead of his right leg, there was a wooden counterpart - no doubt created by him; vines also writhed around that, supporting it and keeping it attached to him.

"Why are you attacking your boss?" I shouted, realising my voice had no tone even though I was filled with rage. It was as if my vocal folds had given up, as if I had reached my voice's limit. It was scratchy and throaty.

"How are you *this* stupid?" He laughed with disbelief.

"Did you attack my friends in the medical wing?" I continued.

"I wasn't in the medical wing, you idiot! You've been played. It's over. That woman is going to die tonight and then no one can stop M." He shot two wooden stakes toward me which I caught and shot back at him. The section of his torso that was about to receive the impact swirled around in a flurry of leaves until the stakes passed through before reforming.

"She- what?!" Though I was still raging, his words knocked my thought process off kilter. "*M?*"

"We're working for the same woman," he grinned, flashing his hideous brown teeth and the gaps. "This whole time. She just didn't need to use her ability for my involvement!" He spat a cloud of spores at me. I fell to the floor.

"Kurt, watch out!" I heard George call from behind me. I dodged the spore cloud by dropping down, but two more timber stakes shot toward me whilst I was on the floor. I encased myself in a ball of thought - I felt the two sharp spikes pierce it, but held them in place until I stood up.

"I've been waiting to kill you since you messed things up for us that day," he said conversationally, then dispersed with a quick shift to the side. He reformed and instantly shot another two stakes which I deflected. "M said we could use you, but I'm sure she can do without now the guise is up."

"You're lying!" I roared.

He smiled. "You wish." Two vines shot out, I grabbed those with my ability entangling them, a spore cloud followed, more vines and two more stakes. It was all I could do to step back from the spore cloud, I deflected the stakes again, redirecting them around my body before halting the new vines.

There was a grunt of pain then a thud from behind me, followed by two screams. I knew their voices. Marie. Anthony. The Treeboy's eyes widened for a moment as he focused on them. He seemed shocked. Then, he began to laugh maniacally.

"No!" Marie gasped.

"The *irony*," Treeboy forced through his laughter. "This is too perfect." I wanted to look round but I was scared he would take the opportunity making it the last thing I did. There was a billowing sound behind me, followed by another scream from Marie and her smoke shot in front of me. Treeboy winked, dispersed and before I could even try and hold the leaves still, before the smoke got to him, he was weaving and drifting away.

I turned to see George standing upright; a stake protruding out of his chest. Blood poured out of the wound, making it look like his chest itself was weeping ruby tears. He stared at me, his face didn't look as if to be in pain, but rather, apologetic. He opened his mouth to say something but instead of words, more blood began to spew forth. I felt hollow. He fell backward, Marie tried to catch him, but his weight was too much. She fell with him. Dorian was quite a distance away, I could hear his voice calling surrender. George lay sprawled on the floor; his leg began to kick and jolt. Then his whole body began to convulse. "No!" I cried. "No. No!"

Anthony ran over to George and with strength I wouldn't think him capable of, flipped George so that he was laying on his back, then proceeded to sit on top of him. His ghostly water began to pour - in volumes that I didn't think were possible - all over George like a waterfall. My whole body relaxed. If they didn't save Anthony that day, George - my other best friend - would be dead.

In that moment, my anger had transcended sense and survival. I was going to kill Shadow Lady. I turned to face the Town Hall. In front of it, lit by abilities of all kinds, I could see her standing over the silver sphere that contained M. Everyone from the lab had stopped fighting. We had lost. We had surrendered. M was somehow rendered incapable in that dome - but it wasn't over. Not yet. Not when my best friend had almost been murdered for the second time.

I stormed toward them. Aaron ran to my side and tried to hold me back but I snatched my hand away and held him in place in my mind. He was trying to reach for me, trying to keep up but I wouldn't allow it. I continued toward her refusing to accept there may be any danger.

When some of Shadow Lady's people saw me approaching, they instantly stood forward creating a human barrier between her and myself. I lifted my hands up to send them flying but she spoke.

"No. Let him through," Shadow Lady said, "she can't use her power; he is no longer controlled by her." They parted and let me through. "Kurt, I am sorry."

I threw my fist out to try and punch her, but a tentacle of shadow appeared and pulled it down to my side. "Why are you trying to kill George?" I said through gritted teeth and a clenched jaw. "Why can't you just let people without abilities live?"

The look she gave me was not what I expected. It was pity. "Curious. Even without her ability, you still cannot see. Kurt, I haven't…"

"Shut your mouth!" I hissed.

"How do you expect me to explain if you don't let me? You are acting like her," she said not unkindly whilst looking at M and the shield of staff members with disgust. "Possibly a lingering side effect to prolonged exposure. Kurt, listen…" She began to speak, but then behind her, I saw him.

A weak fragile boy; his clothes clung to his skeletal body. His skin was sagging in paper thin folds, pasty white, colourless, devoid of complexion, health and happiness. He was laying on a stretcher in the foetal position. The same position I saw silhouetted before in the glittering silvery force field that now encased M.

"Him…" I said.

Shadow Lady looked behind her at the boy. "Yes," she confirmed, "we can only block one person at a time. This ability wrapping Melanie is impervious to anything, inside or outside. She can do you no harm whilst in there, so you don't need to worry. Patrick does not need the shell now she is captured."

"Patrick…" I repeated his name. He was only feet away. His sister just below the ground. This was what I wanted from the start. "The Catalyst," I muttered. He lay still, unmoving. If it weren't for the slow, weak breaths he was taking, I would have thought it was a corpse laying before me. "We've been looking for you," I said to him.

"He can't hear you. He's too weak," Shadow Lady responded. "We couldn't leave him at my base, we had to bring him for his own safety - he is much too valuable. Kurt, you have to listen to me. Melanie has had you all under a trance - no, not a trance - a susceptibility. Since this change, she has used this ability to coerce innocents like yourself in to..." Her voice continued, but I stopped listening.

This whole time. We were kept underground for our own safety. M trusted us with the information. The Leech, The Mute, The Jinx. The aim of those plans - the objective was for The Catalyst. Patrick. The boy who lay feet away from me. M wanted him for his ability, for what he could do. I wanted him for his sister - to reunite them. Shadow Lady may as well have been speaking a different language for all the use it was doing her.

"I know where his sister, Lana, is," I uttered and Shadow Lady stopped her talking.

At that, his weak fragile frame stirred. His body stretched slowly, painfully slowly from its curled-up and secure position. He placed his thin hands on the stretcher and they shook violently as he tried to pull up to a sitting position. The Shadow Lady watched in awe as Patrick looked in my direction.

"Lana?" He managed. His voice barely a whisper, a rasp, a raw croak.

"Yeah. We saved her the day of the change. From the shop. We didn't know who you were - M told us to go and help. To rescue you."

"She didn't want Lana, she wanted Patrick. You were not the only people she sent," Shadow Lady interrupted, but I ignored her. Patrick was staring right into my eyes.

"She's in the lab. M promised we would reunite you both. I can bring you to her now..." I froze. Patrick's arm rose and pointed toward me.

"No, don't!" Shadow Lady begged desperately.

Suddenly, everything was irrelevant. My power was infinite. I could do *anything*.

I heard Shadow Lady gasp next to me. I could feel the gasp, the motions her body went through to create it. I was still staring into Patrick's eyes. He wanted his sister. He trusted me to get her. I turned slightly and with the mere echo of a thought, I cleared the path between the lab and me. Everyone who was in that path was thrown to the side with incredible force. M was right: *Ember to a blaze. A gentle breeze into a hurricane. A capillary wave into a tsunami. Equal to that of a deity.*

I was the Giant Sequoia.

It was overwhelming. I could feel *everything*. Each tree in the surrounding forest, each branch, each leaf. All the houses and shops in the town – the separate materials required to construct them - were in my ability, were at its mercy. Every insect, every blade of grass, every mote of dust - I could feel the shifting currents of the air itself, blowing hither and thither, over and under, swirling and waving with my telekinesis.

I thought for a moment. *Why risk moving Patrick when I could bring the lab to me?* It was simple enough, simpler than simple. It was nothing. My ability focused around the building disguising the lab and I unhinged it, tore it from the ground and sent it hurtling. It then seeped deep below ground, feeling around all the layers of earth, all the pipes, sewage tunnels and connections that ran below. The lab went further down than I thought, but, as if it were a child's toy - a flower that had taken root, I plucked it from the floor. Ripping it away from the earth itself without exerting the slightest effort. The noise was deafening, the sound waves rippling and reverberating in my thought. I could control *them* if I desired.

People scampered away from the lab that was now floating, all the floors, above the ground. The hole that it left was colossal. I could feel the hum of electricity from within the lab as it died; I could feel back-up generators kicking in. I could feel the smooth laminated floors of the corridors. I could feel those within the lab, more than we were told, laying in bed. I could feel Jo, Shinji and Lana. Shinji's face felt altered, but they were alive. The wires connected all over their bodies, the machines that were collating data still running from the generators. I could feel it all. Everything. Everyone.

Though I was infinite, anything and everything; though I could crush Shadow Lady where she stood, crunch every one of her people into fine dust; though no one could stop me right now if they tried… I faltered.

I could feel everyone. Mentally sense their fear manifesting in their bodies, their desperation to escape my hold, their hearts pounding with sheer panic. Everyone's heart – but one.

There was a small lad, crying. Heaving deep, heavy sobs. He was crouching over another boy. An older boy. The smaller of the two, his heart was rapidly beating in his chest. It mocked the older boy's whose was silent.

The older one lay there, motionless.

Motionless, but for the blood trickling out.

Through his still heart was a thick, sharp wooden stake. The heart itself had been punctured.

I could feel the tough rubbery muscle itself had burst, torn. Beyond repair. It was no longer performing its function - no longer beating.

George *was* dead...

My George. My friend since I moved away. A third of our trio. *Buy one, get the other two free.* The boy who treated me like a brother, who accepted my awkward gangly self and appreciated me for me. I loved him; he was family, my player two - and there he was.

Gone...

I lost my balance. I stumbled to the right, and everything - *everything* - shifted with me; the whole town, everyone, every last thing in it from the minuscule to the large. Their cries, their shock, their fear, I stilled. Holding the sound itself. *No. No!*

In my fury I began to rise, wanting to escape. The entire town flew up with me. Without trying, I unweeded every single thing from its foundations - everything I felt before, as if gravity bowed to my will.

Everything was still. I brought his body to mine whilst everyone else was frozen in position - nothing could move an inch, it was like I had paused life itself and only George mattered. Everyone fought to break free, but it was futile and they knew it. People couldn't even talk because I would not give their throat the freedom to form words.

George.

The scream that left my mouth almost tore my throat to shreds. It sounded like thunder inside my own head. The only noise I allowed to travel.

I looked into his face, the mouth and chin stained with blood - the thick liquid frozen in place with my thought. The wooden stake was still in his heart; Anthony's ineffective healing liquid still glistened off his skin. His eyes half closed. He wasn't struggling to break free like the rest. His body was limp and malleable like *Play-Doh*; but I kept him still in front of me. Shaking violently. Dumbfounded.

The rage turned in to sheer refusal. This couldn't be real. It just couldn't. I closed my eyes. I felt dizzy, my head began to spin. It felt as if my surroundings were caught in a vortex, whirring around at impossible speeds. When I opened my eyes again, I realised it wasn't a feeling - my surroundings *were* spinning around. My inability to grasp the situation had manifested in a maelstrom of telekinesis powered by The Catalyst who I instinctively held behind me.

"George!" I whispered, reaching out an unsteady hand to touch his face.

People were trying to scream. I could feel the bile rising in their throats with no escape. My ability began to spread further - it travelled miles in seconds. Brushing the entire landscape in a massive radius, spreading further and further out - everything within it caught in the whirling mass of sorrow.

I began to deconstruct M's lab, to deconstruct all the buildings within my grasp.

Then there was a voice in my head which managed to penetrate my grief. "Patrick," it said, it was not my inner voice. It was not M's voice. "It's Chermaine, from Chiamka's compound." It continued, desperate but calm; her voice juxtaposed life itself. "You have to let him go. I've connected you both. Try. Release him or he may kill Lana!" Lana no longer mattered. *George was dead.*

Nothing mattered.

I felt Patrick's hold loosen. My ability began to reduce in potency. It was no longer infinite.

As my spread receded, the beings and objects caught within were flung from the force. The radius shortened and shortened until it held only George, Patrick and me.

The world grew black. This was not supposed to happen. We only needed Patrick. M promised.

I felt myself dropping to the ground - exhausted. I was no longer under the effects of The Catalyst.

It was all I could do to stop George's body and myself crashing hard into the ground.

I felt someone catch me in their arms. I looked up to see a stranger's face. I was lost to everything. The world went dark. The last thought I had was of George's eyes. Half-open. Half-closed. Glazed over, staring into nothingness.
Dead.

Author's note

Thank you for reading my debut novel. I sincerely hope you enjoyed this story as much as I did writing it. If you wish to find the epilogue to *The Catalyst*, as well as details for its sequel, *The Martyr*, please visit:

www.bradleywalker.co.uk

www.gbpublishing.co.uk

Other GBP Science-Fiction

Warring corporations, dangerous worlds and the darker sides of the human psyche will ultimately change the direction of mercenary Davian Kurcher's life. In his frantic hunt across known space, the balance of power dramatically shifts

WINNER & FINALIST
Indies Book Awards - Horror

DANTE magazine, Juliette Foster: "Fusing horror, psychology and new age religion this novel repels as much as it fascinates... with nuggets of ironic black humour. Surreal reminiscent of Stephen King's *The Shining*."

FINALISTS
Indies Book Awards – Fantasy & SciFi

The Sun ☆☆☆☆:
"a weird, vivid and creepy book, not for the faint hearted. But its originality and top writing make for a great read. "

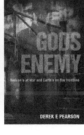

Read2Write: "Texas 1883, a terrifying story that fuses sci-fi with history and theology. Pearson is in electrifying form"